A STOLEN TONGUE

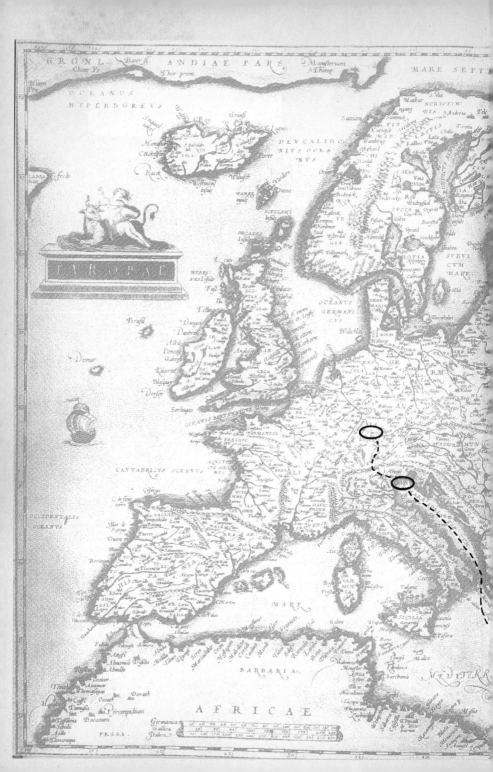

A STOLEN TONGUE

SHERI HOLMAN

ANCHOR BOOKS
DOUBLEDAY
New York London Toronto Sydney Auckland

AN ANCHOR BOOK
PUBLISHED BY DOUBLEDAY
a division of Bantam Doubleday Dell Publishing Group, Inc.
1540 Broadway, New York, New York 10036

ANCHOR BOOKS, DOUBLEDAY, and the portrayal of an anchor are
trademarks of Doubleday, a division of Bantam Doubleday Dell
Publishing Group, Inc.

●

A Stolen Tongue was originally published in
hardcover by the Atlantic Monthly Press in 1997. The Anchor Books edition
is published by arrangement with the Atlantic Monthly Press.

Book design by Laura Hammond Hough

Library of Congress Cataloging-in-Publication Data
Holman, Sheri.
A stolen tongue/Sheri Holman.—1st Anchor Books ed.
p.   cm.
1. Christian pilgrims and pilgrimages—Palestine—Fiction.
2. Catherine, of Alexandria, Saint—Relics—Fiction.   3. Fabri,
Felix, 1441 or 2–1502—Fiction.   4. Middle Ages—Fiction.
5. Detective and mystery stories. gsafd.   6. Historical fiction.
gsafd.   I. Title.
[PS3558.035596S76   1997b]
813'.54—DC21   97-31616
CIP

ISBN 0-385-49124-7
Copyright © 1997 by Sheri Holman
All Rights Reserved
Printed in the United States of America
First Anchor Books Edition: February 1998

1   3   5   7   9   10   8   6   4   2

To Sean
Who I hope will wander with me, always

I
THE SEA

i

The Sides of Ships

We are separated from death by the span of only four fingers, those of us at sea; and from what I can tell, it is that certain knowledge, more than any monster or misfortune, that terrorizes pilgrims on their ships. If you were never unaware, not even for a moment, that a hand's-width of wood alone stood between you and the fathomless waters, wouldn't *you* be inclined to drink a little too much? I ask you, is it fair then to label a man a buffoon and a jackass, as I heard someone call him, for falling, drunk, into the Ocean? Who on board this ship hasn't, out of fear, drunk himself nearly overboard?

I stand beside the winch while the first mate's crew hoists our dead burgher off the harbor floor. Four galley slaves wait on the wharf below, their arms lifted to catch all three hundred pounds of him, their knees flexed in anticipation. They will walk him, dripping, through the ribbon streets of Candia, to the convent I recommended, just outside the city's gate. There they will help dig him a grave and stand solemnly by while I say a mass to speed Burgher Schmidhans's lurching, insensible soul on to Purgatory.

"Oh, goodness. Was he that fat?"

My patron arrives just as the burgher's thunderous Bavarian body rains upon the slaves below. They turn away their faces and reach up blindly to unhook him.

"Bloated," I offer.

Lord Tucher and I knew him only as a fellow German who lodged, as all German pilgrims lodge, at Zu der Fleuten in Venice and who aspired to take this pilgrim ship over Contarini's because we were on it. His berth was next to mine belowdeck, and though he kept me from my bedtime prayers too often with his idle settling of the world's problems, I blame him for one thing only. On nights after the lanterns went out and the waves groaned around us like evil spirits in a nursery, he would draw my attention to the worthless curve of gopherwood, as he called it, that separated us from a watery grave. "For the length of the trip," he wondered out loud, "shouldn't we call *that* Savior?"

"Let's go." My patron touches my back. "Ursus is waiting."

The Mediterranean sun has been kind to Ursus Tucher, my patron's son, bleaching the first dark smudge above his upper lip, buying him a few more months of childhood. He squats at the bottom of the gangplank, watching a naked brown boy repair a crack in the ship's hull. The water is so clear we can see him, three feet under, kicking out his legs like a frog, carefully painting the crack with tar.

"I bet Schmidhans's head made a hole," Ursus tells us. "When he fell."

Ahead of us, the galley slaves count three and bounce the burgher to their shoulders. We follow this giant dripping horseshoe crab as it slowly crawls away from the sea, past wooden doors that bang wide to reveal bolts of tamarind silk and orange-dusted spice barrels, beyond fish stalls where women clad sluttishly in the Mediterranean fashion lean over baskets and buy those creatures that leap highest for their dangling breasts. I look over my shoulder to see the ship's crew raise a black silk flag between Captain Lando's lion banner of Saint Mark and the immense white and red cross ensign of the Holy Sepulchre. I've observed that Lando only pranks up the ship when something is to be gained thereby—when he wants to impress or intimidate a foreign power. At sea, with only an audience of pilgrims, he furls the holy flag of Jerusalem and hides from us the proof of our journey, begrudging even that little comfort a pilgrim might find, contemplating it at sea. Lando must want to advertise the empty space on board our ship. Certainly reverence plays no part in hoisting the black flag; he would have left Schmid-hans to be picked clean by fishes, had not Lord Tucher bribed him with five ducats.

My patron looks down the dirty Greek lane, perplexed. "I don't know what I was expecting." He frowns. "Marble?"

What a discerning patron I've found! I know Abbot Fuchs worried about my traveling so long in the company of secular persons, but Lord Tucher is a grave, reverent man, much concerned with the state of souls, his own and ours. He, more than any other, saw how Schmidhans's drowned body had become like a magnet, luring pilgrims to the ship's side to stare past their reflections into our dead friend's aqueous eyes. He saw his own son, Ursus, walk away from his lessons to stand with the common crowd and wonder at the mythical properties of water: how like slumbering Neptune Schmidhans looked in death, magnified and pale, the wild hairs of his beard stiffening into strands of purling bubbles. Something had to be done, Lord Tucher knew, for Schmidhans's corpse was becoming a distraction.

My patron walks purposefully beside me, his money pouch jingling softly against his chest. He dresses strictly by the pilgrim's handbook, in a white robe with red cross chasuble and a gray felt hat, lovingly stitched with crosses by virgins dedicated to God. He lets his sparse facial hair grow, as all male pilgrims must, and shoulders a leather pilgrim's scrip containing water skin, bread, and hymnal. Lord Tucher is conscious of the town's eyes on him, as head mourner to the horse-shoe crab, and stares piously back at the Greeks, who cross them-selves and shrink into their shops when we pass. Ursus capers around us, peeking in this window, spitting in that. He will be fourteen at summer's end and will straightaway trade his pilgrim's clothes for a page's uniform in the household of the illustrious Count Eberhart of Württemberg. Ursus is young to be on pilgrimage, but his father rashly promised him a knighthood of the Holy Sepulchre to raise his status among the other pages, and the child doggedly holds him to his word.

"Why did you pick this particular church, Friar?" Ursus grumbles. "It's so far from the ship."

"I understand they have a fine wine cellar there," Lord Tucher says.

"The Franciscans, where we are headed," I tell them, "have Saint Katherine of Alexandria's hand."

"Saint Katherine again!" Ursus cries. "You make us stop at every statue of her. You make us kiss every painting!"

"But this will be the first relic we'll venerate on the way to her tomb in Sinai."

Lord Tucher nods. "That will be edifying for us."

Edifying indeed! It will be as if the heavenly cloister opened its gates and she pricked her ear at our arrival. It will be as if she raised her paper-nicked finger from the book in her lap and shyly extended her hand to earth, for me to kiss and press to my cheek. I chafe when our slaves spill Schmidhans across the path leading out of town and we are forced to wait while they pick him clean of pine needles.

"Look, Father, that must be it!"

Ursus speeds ahead, up to the thick daub walls and iron gate surrounding the monastery. Carved herringbone detail work softens the edifice of the church, and a red dome, skirted with flaring tile roofs, gives it the slightly effeminate look of all Eastern buildings. Upon Ursus's persistent yanking of the entry bell, a brown-robed figure comes to the gate.

I introduce myself. "I am Friar Felix Fabri with the Dominican Preaching Brothers in Ulm. We would like to inter this drowned man in your cemetery."

The Franciscan eyes us suspiciously, taking in my black-and-white Dominican robes, our pilgrims' chasubles, the slippery, peat-flecked flesh of corpse Schmidhans. As a rule, the animal- and poverty-loving Franciscans have no great fondness for the more intellectual Dominican order, but at least I'm not decked out in the tall hat and showy chin beard of our common enemy, the Greek Orthodox.

"And, of course, we'll pay for masses," Lord Tucher adds.

The gate swings open.

The Franciscan leads us through the dark church and out under a shady latticed arbor plaited with pea-sized grapes, just flushing purple. This region of Crete is famed for its malvoisie, the sweet boon to pilgrims and reviver of flagging spirits. Would that Schmidhans had not been revived even unto death.

"Plant him over there, then," the Franciscan tells me, stopping in their cypress-lined graveyard. "I'll lay out the things for mass."

Oh, how Katherine inhabits this place! The Franciscan told me her hand is put away in a jewel-encrusted box, locked inside the airless sacristy, and yet I feel her take a seat beside me, here on this stone bench, and watch, as I do, the slaves turn fresh earth. Her white robe falls in tidy folds around her ankles; her wheel, that instrument of torture, rests harmlessly underfoot. We put our heads together, and her blue eyes smile into mine as a fond wife's would, happy to be reunited, even if it is in such a place as this.

"Where's Ursus?"

My bride evaporates at the sound of Lord Tucher's panicked voice.

"Did he go inside?" I sigh. Ursus is forever running off.

"Ursus!" his father calls sharply. "I've told you a hundred times not to leave us."

I push open the unlocked back door of the church and march across the apse. Sunlight slanting through the red-and-gold glass bodies of the Holy Family melts three sacred hearts across the flagstone floor.

"Ursus, are you in here?"

Huddled on a back pew, mottled by the blue bird-light of Saint Francis's lead-paned grackles, my patron's son sits beside a stranger.

"Ursus?" I take a step closer.

"Here, my friar will confirm. Friar Felix," Ursus prompts, "there are no ladies on our ship, are there?"

The stranger rises expectantly, hoping I will contradict my charge. What sort of question is that? Why should this man care that we sail womanless upon the sea, if we consider it our great good fortune? Perhaps because he is a handsome man; tall, dark-haired, richly clad in a black doublet and yellow leather boots, he fancies himself a dandy? And yet his full mouth is drawn into a frown, and his somber eyes promise anything but a flirtation.

"That is correct, son," I say. "All the ladies rode with Contarini."

"You are certain, good Brother Dominican? No women have recently joined your party?" The stranger speaks the perfectly accented Latin of the university or novitiate.

"I can happily answer, Yes, I'm certain we have not a one. Why do you ask?"

"I'm looking for a young woman." He smiles self-consciously. "She ran away several days ago, and I tracked her as far as this monastery. You are Jerusalem pilgrims, yes? You continue on to Sinai?"

"We certainly hope so." I smile, for, without knowing, he has touched upon my deepest desire. "We plan to continue our pilgrimage across the Sinai even to Saint Katherine's Monastery, God willing."

"God's will may not be the only one at work, I'm afraid."

The stranger turns to leave. I follow his eyes to where they light briefly on a misfired glass portrait of Katherine, her bubbled yellow sword flaring like that which bars the gates to Eden.

"I hope you make it." He pushes on the door.

"She is a bad girl, this lady?" Ursus calls after him.

"Worse than that, son." The man takes one last worried look around the church. "She is completely insane."

"I just had it!"

Ursus is near tears in the cemetery. I've interrupted mass so he might look for his silver rosary, a present given him by his mother before we left Ulm, along with a pair of oversized gray boots in case his feet grow in the Holy Land. The boy's eyes and nose are red. He fears he dropped the beads into Schmidhans's open grave.

With a sigh, his father hands him his own expensive gold rosary and motions for me to continue.

You are a generous man, Lord Tucher, but are you the sort of man who keeps his promises? Do you have the courage to travel that great empty space with me? My patron puts out his fuzzy yellow tongue for the Host, and I stare deeply into his eyes. I have made you the keeper of my childhood vow, my most solemn oath; and yet the

farther east we push, the wilder the rumors surrounding her monastery become and the less you speak of your promise to me. Here,
in her presence, I command you to honor the pledge you made when
I agreed to become your confessor. Take me to her.

"May the Lord watch over our dear departed Schmidhans and
guide him swiftly through Purgatory with the help of these hundred masses we now purchase for his wretched soul."

Quickly, I confess my sins in my heart, the most recent being that
I was inattentive during my own mass, and take the Lord's Host into
my mouth.

"In Jesus' name. Amen."

Lord Tucher pushes himself to his feet and looks around for the
Franciscan. "Felix," he says, "before we take a peek at the relics,
let's see about that malvoisie, eh?"

How can he think of grapes when he knows I burn to see her hand?

"Brother Franciscan!" Tucher calls, clapping into the chapel.
"Will you help us?"

While his father profanely haggles, Ursus enlists me to crawl
around the floor with him and feel for his lost rosary. Three times
I watch the Franciscan's feet trot down to the cellar when Lord
Tucher sends him back for a different vintage. On the other side of
the wall, my beloved idly scratches a cross into the dirt floor with
the tip of her sword. She stands and paces the small room, leans her
head against the door.

"And this is a good year, you say?" Lord Tucher asks the monk.

"Friar Felix, are you married to her like Father is to Mother?"
Ursus asks, reaching under the pew near me. "Can you have
children?"

I smile at my charge's naïveté.

"No, Ursus. You know how women, when they become nuns,
are called Brides of Christ? How they call our Lord 'Bridegroom' and
wear a gold wedding band to symbolize their union?"

"Yes. My aunt is a nun. We watched her marry Christ."

"Well, when we monks take our orders, we may choose a spiritual spouse to keep us company, like nuns have Jesus. We can't very
well take Jesus because, first, he is a man and, second, he has mar-

ried all those nuns. It's wrong to presume the Blessed Virgin would have us; she is married to Saint Joseph. Saint Anne is married to Saint Joachim and Saint Elizabeth is married to Saint Zacharias, so these, too, are out. It is fitting, therefore, that a pious monk not come between the happy couplings of Heaven but take to wife some unwed virgin saint."

"And you chose Saint Katherine?"

"I like to think she chose me."

And we have been happily joined now for twenty years, since I first pledged myself to the Dominicans on the anniversary of her martyrdom when I was eighteen years old. Every November twenty-fifth I retire from the world and relive her suffering. I see again her courageous refusal to sacrifice before the pagan gods, her defeat of their Fifty Philosophers sent to break her faith in Christ. I weep for her torture at the hands of Emperor Maxentius, when he bound her to that diabolical wheel and tore her flesh with hooks. How I re-joice when the Emperor orders her head struck off by the sword, only to witness milk flow instead of blood! How I triumph as the Em-peror is forced to stand by and watch the angels translate her bro-ken body to the top of holy Mount Sinai! Katherine of Alexandria, the philosopher saint, is the patroness of young girls, scholars, and priests. I try not to take too much pride in her popularity.

"Felix." Lord Tucher bends over me, wagging a dusty green wine bottle before my face. "I bought an extra for you."

"Thank you, my lord. Might we see her hand now?"

"Friar!" Ursus cries. "You promised to help me look!"

"We are seeking and not finding, Ursus."

"Brother Franciscan," Lord Tucher calls. "We're ready."

The monk invites us back into the tight, musty sacristy. In my lifetime, I have venerated her foot in Rouen, her spine in Cologne, and now her hand in Crete. The most precious of relics, Katherine's holy head, lies where angels set her down, twelve hundred years ago, in her monastery atop Mount Sinai.

The Franciscan unlocks the sacristy closet and slowly draws from its shadows a silver box marvelously fashioned after a woman's hand. Polished rubies form the hand's fingernails, while inside the palm veins of pure lapis lazuli trace a deep lifeline, headline, and heartline. It is the left hand! The hand upon which, if we were earthly spouses, she would wear my wedding band.

The hand of Saint Katherine is a very important relic, being the blessed appendage she places upon our Lord's knee to beg favors for men. Her sainted hand holds a cool cloth against the foreheads of those with fevers, whether we suffer the physical pain of illness or the emotional distemper that accompanies too great a love. Katherine, schooled as she was in the seven Liberal Arts, with a voice so melodious it converted fifty pagan philosophers to Christ, must certainly be called upon to read aloud in Heaven. This hand, then, holds the book when she reads sweetly to God and the Holy Family.

"By the grace of God," the monk intones, throwing open the reliquary, "the hand of Katherina Martyr."

Where is it?

A cushion of blue velvet. A whiff of myrrh. No bones, no shaving of knuckle, no thumb print. *Where is my wife's hand?*

"There's nothing there, Friar," Ursus whimpers.

The Franciscan sharply shakes the box. His mouth works but no words follow. Ursus's bottom lip begins to tremble.

"Thief!" The monk shouts, sweeping up his robes and running from the church. "Thief!"

My beloved? My wife?

She knew I was coming and she allowed herself to be stolen.

An Apology

Brothers, you made me promise, that gray farewell day in Ulm, that in the event God should grant me safe passage across the sea, I would write down all that happened to me on pilgrimage, the good and the bad, the bitter and the sweet, by design or by accident, and thus make you my constant companions. Up until today, I have strictly honored that vow, recording the distances between places, the holy sites of Venice, how I found the food in Dalmatia, and much more that goes into the making of a travel book of pilgrimage. I turn to you now in my hour of need and beg you forgive me if, under the circumstances, I should transgress the realm of expected narration and turn this account, as emotional people tend to do, into some personal cogitation of my own.

Be assured. I am not upset.

I know a saint navigates the world in two ways: via translation, as Katherine was angelically translated from the forum in Alexandria to blessed Mount Sinai; or *furta sacra*—that is, by holy theft, a translation by man. If we believe the saints have power over their own locomotion, we can only reason that Katherine no longer wished to remain on Crete. Had she chosen to stay, her hand certainly would have leapt up, gripped tight the windpipe of her would-be abductor, and strangled the blasphemous miscreant dead.

My friend Archdeacon John Lazinus hovers over us, speeding our returning party up the gangplank.

"Hurry, Felix. They'll leave you behind!"

Contarini's ship has been spotted. On deck, sailors frantically hoist the mainsail and trinketum. Galley slaves, three to a bench, grasp their oars and pull; crewmen drag up the great iron anchors on either side of the prow. A word of warning, brothers: You might think, in times of bustle and haste, the sailors would welcome help or direction from the pilgrims, but in fact this is displeasing to them.

"Father John, you'll never guess what!" Ursus dodges the rigging and the swinging rope. "Someone stole a piece of our friar's wife."

"Felix, is this true?"

John's brown eyes are kind and concerned, like your eyes, Abbot Fuchs, when one of the brothers comes secretly to you in the night and lays his head in your lap. I don't want to take this turn of events personally, but I suddenly find it difficult to speak.

"I'll put the wine away," I whisper.

Seven ladderlike steps lead downstairs to the fetid, cavernous pilgrims' deck. All along the floor, in even rectangles, we chalk off our berths, side by side, with the ship's curving wall as our headboard and our trunks, placed toward the ship's center, serving as footboards. Only the Homesick stay belowdeck out of choice, and it depresses me even more to move among them. They love the dark, rotting wood that blocks this foreign sun and magnifies what few familiar Western smells remain: smoke and European piss, beer sweat, pine pitch. When the rest of us roll up our mattresses in the morning and suspend them from the rafters, the Homesick turn over and imagine their wives' hair on the pillow next to them, or the smell of their pet roosters' feathers on the windowsill, or the sound only their dog makes when his paws skid in frosty winter horse manure. They tell each other long detailed stories about their backyard cabbage gardens and their children's agues, but rarely listen to anyone's but their own.

I follow the aisle of luggage far back to my berth, where another smaller hatch opens onto the ship's belly. This third hold, filled completely with sand, is where pilgrims bury their perishables: meat, cheese, eggs. I push the bottles deep into the chilled sand and fasten the hatch.

"Felix, are you sad?"

Truly, God sent good John Lazinus to ease the pain of separation from you, Abbot Fuchs. He has been a comfort to me since we first met, at Zu der Fleuten in Venice, when the German innkeeper's black dog, who loved only Germans and loathed with an instinctual passion all Italians and Italian dogs, indeed, all Spaniards, Dutch, French, and all other races, and all their dogs—allowed Hungarian John Lazinus to teach it to dance for ham. My spirits can't help but rise, seeing my gentle friend come toward me across the field of the Homesick.

"What kind of criminal shoves the hand of a saint into his sweaty pocket?" I ask as he nears. "I keep seeing her delicate fingers spilled across some cheap inn's bedside table or peeking from an overstuffed saddlebag, tangled with twine and old raisins. Who would do it?"

"Relics are only stolen for love or profit." My friend sighs.

"*I* love her! If she wanted to move, couldn't she have waited another hour? Wouldn't she have liked to come to Ulm?"

"Felix," John chides. "Tell me you don't believe she waited until just before you arrived to grow restless. That Franciscan may not have checked the sacristy in months. She might have been taken weeks ago."

"We met a strange man at the convent," I tell John. "He was acting suspiciously, and when I spoke of God willing us to Sinai, he suggested God's will might not be enough."

"Since we've boarded this ship," John says, "I've heard only warnings against that desert. We are seeing Jerusalem, Felix. Is achieving Sinai really so essential?"

How can I answer a question that has been put to me a hundred different ways all my life? How can I explain without scandalizing you, my brothers, without appearing light-minded and impatient with the quiet of the cloister, or guilty of the sin of idle curiosity, or moved by the Devil?

"When I was a boy," I tell John, "a traveling Greek monk came through Basle, where I served my novitiate, wearing the dust of the East like a glamour. Where our habits were fine wool and silk, his was desert homespun. Where our cheeks were smooth and soft like women's, his errupted into a long, wiry beard like a prophet's. He told my abbot he had walked overland from the Sinai desert, that he was a young man when he left and now he shuffled like a grand-father. Under his arm, he carried a small carpet tied at both ends with rope, and he asked my abbot's permission to solicit funds with what was inside it."

John's serious face makes me blush at the foolishness of my story and fall silent. It was a humid day in Basle when the monk came through. The entire monastery crowded around the altar, but I pushed between the sweating bodies to be closest. With swift, prac-ticed movements, the monk arranged four finger joints to spell *K.M.*, for Katherina Martyr, and placed at the four cardinal points around them an eyelid, a toe, a vial of milk, and a piece of silk dipped in her oil. Back in the Age of Miracles, her bones used to produce enough oil for the monks to burn their lamps year round; but by the time I was a boy, oil had to be coaxed from the bones by briskly rubbing them with silk.

"Felix is in love," someone whispered behind me. But how could I not be? On our prie-dieu, Katherine stood with sword and wheel on the right hand of Mary. In our ambulatory, she smiled down from her fluted pillar on the way to our library. As one of the Fourteen Heavenly Helpers she was chiseled onto the ceiling that to my mind touched the Celestial City. Katherine was everywhere, the most popular girl in town, the scholar, the philosopher, the king's daugh-ter, the *East*—and suddenly here she was in front of me, pieces of a corporeal, human woman. I wanted to kiss that monk for bringing her to us; he had reversed the route of pilgrimage for a boy too young to leave his abbey. He brought me my first holy lust.

"If, in pieces, Katherine could find her way to me," I say aloud, "I, as a whole man, can certainly find my way back to her."

"And Lord Tucher has agreed to take you there?" John asks.

"He swore on his own life."

My friend winces and gingerly reaches into his mouth.

"How is your tormentor?" I ask. John's toothy, open smile has been troubled by a rebel molar rotting in his jaw.

"I'll get Conrad to pull it tomorrow."

"Promise?"

"Promise." He smiles.

"Is this where the dead man slept?"

John and I look up, startled, to see a man approach, hidden inside a heavy cloak of the Homesick. They hang upon his arms, wrestle with his trunk; one wipes a small flow of blood from the man's swollen lip with a handkerchief.

"What happened to him?" I ask.

"Fell down the steps," one whispers.

The man throws them off and faces me. "This was his spot, wasn't it? The drowned man's spot?"

I turn to John. I think I saw this man in Candia, shrinking back from the pale white sausage fingers of Schmidhans's sluicing corpse. He speaks the maritime merchant lingua franca with a nasal accent. Once the Homesick fall away, his long black robe and drawstring cap reveal him further as a tradesman.

"But soon we will land in Jerusalem, yes?" he asks hopefully. "Then on to Sinai?"

"My party certainly will be continuing our pilgrimage," I tell him. "I can't vouch for anyone else. There have been rumors."

"What sort of rumors?" He fingers his bonnet string into his mouth and nervously chews it.

"The captain spreads them," I say. "If we don't sail back with him—if we cross the desert to Sinai instead—he loses half his fare."

John gently unties the mattress the merchant has strapped across his back and drops it over the fat-fisted chalk scrawl, *G. Schmdhns*. Without a word, the merchant sits down, picking worriedly at one wiry overgrown eyebrow.

"I would never cross the desert." A Homesick shakes his head. "Satyrs and Fauns live there."

"The sea is bad enough, with its sharks and Troyp," adds another.

I kneel beside the merchant, who grows more pale by the minute.

"Don't listen to them." I throw my arm about his shoulder, knowing, myself, the irrational fears that accompany any new voyage. "You'll survive."

The merchant's face is close to mine, clammy and green. He lets his cap string drop from his mouth.

"None of it matters." He sighs, collecting himself at last. "If I am to ride in the drowned man's spot, I am already dead."

What a Pilgrim Should Be on His Guard Against While on a Journey at Sea

"John, wake up." I push my friend, and he rolls over onto his stomach.

Katherine came to me in a dream. She swam frantically behind the ship, her wet hair matted to her cheek. *Husband!* she cried, treading water. Between her teeth she held a wedding ring. Then she stretched out her left hand, imploringly. It was a bloody stump.

"John? Are you awake?"

How can he sleep, oblivious to the pitching boat and groaning boards, the burning lanterns that keep night from ever truly falling here? A rat gallops between us with a mouse locked between its jaws.

I have barely closed my eyes all night. The Greek merchant, Constantine Kallistos as he identified himself, kept me up for hours with his womanly puking and odoriferous unfamiliarity. Schmidhans reeked of stale beer and mutton, but it was a German reek, suspended in the national fat like ambergris. This man smells like I don't know what. Octopus? Vinegar? There's a sharp aroma that clings to him as if he's rolled in a field of onions.

O my brothers, how unquiet is the sleep of pilgrims aboard ship! As if sour, recycled smells weren't bad enough, I have witnessed whole parties of pilgrims fall upon one another with swords in a dispute over whose mattress is overlapping whose chalk line. I have seen men hurl full chamber pots at burning lanterns to extinguish them. I have heard noble knights cry like little children and call out for their mothers, only to blush in the morning at their comrades' merciless ribbing. Fleas and lice breed in our sweat; rats and mice fall onto our faces from the beams above. For a monk used to the privacy of his own cell, nighttime aboard ship is a new circle of Hell.

"John." I push him a little harder this time. "Shall we go up on deck for some fresh air?"

My friend covers his head with his pillow.

"That's a yes? You'd like to come?"

Nothing.

"I'll meet you up there, then."

While I pick my way upstairs, let me give you some advice, brothers, on what a pilgrim should guard against while moving about at sea.

First: Let the pilgrim go up and down these steep ladderlike steps with due deliberation. Twice I have made haste, and both times I have fallen, so that it is a wonder I was not dashed to pieces.

Second: Let him beware of carrying a light on deck at night, no matter how convenient it would make things, for the galley slaves dislike this strangely, being by nature superstitious, credulous creatures, and will not endure it.

Third: Endeavor not to wake these same wretched creatures, who burrow their lousy heads into their neighbors' bellies and squirm for position on their narrow wood benches, for they are also a quarrelsome, untrustworthy, easily angered lot, culled mostly from the captured peoples of Eastern Europe: Albania, Sclavonia, Macedonia. Among the slaves you will also find Bashi Bazouks, Christian apostates who fought for the Turks; Jews, Saracens, Schismatic Greeks, and Sodomites. You will never, though, meet a German galley slave, because no German could withstand such misery.

Fourth: Let the pilgrim not trust any ropes without pulling on them first to make sure they will not bring a pulley or a sail crashing down upon his head.

Fifth and last: As a pilgrim carefully climbs from one cross bench to another, let him grasp the tension lines and carefully ease himself out onto one of the horns of the ship, which is a comfortable spot to sit and think, always making sure he sits not in pitch, which substance covers almost every inch of the ship, and which would be easier to spot if a pilgrim were allowed what is forbidden in Article the Second.

I settle myself on the ship's prow, where I am wont to sit during the day, and lean my back against the damp rigging. Even alone, brothers, you are not alone at sea. The Ocean is crowded with creatures: large, round fishes shaped like winnowing fans, some with heads like dogs and floppy long ears, dolphins, mer-people, Scyllas and Charybdises that suck ships down. At night, a monster called the Troyp circles and with his long sharp beak pierces the sides of ships. Should you ever encounter a Troyp, lean as far over the side as you dare, fix it with a fearless stare, and on no accounts look away. If you grow frightened of the Troyp's hypnotic eyes and falter, he will rise up and devour you straightaway.

How Katherine haunted me tonight! I can still see the swift panic in her salt-reddened eyes, still smell her blood where it bloomed in our ship's wake. I am not a fanatic, brothers, nor am I a star-eyed prophet claiming visions from beyond. The infrequent glimpses I'm allowed of Katherine are perhaps no more than clothes I give to air, and yet only one other time have I felt her this strongly.

The night before I left on pilgrimage, brothers, a strange dread overtook me. As I lay awake in my familiar room, keenly aware of my packed trunk in the corner, my pocket processional upon it, and my clean pilgrim's costume on a nail by the door, all the eagerness I felt for touring Jerusalem and Sinai, which heretofore had been my greatest desire, suddenly drained away and was replaced by an intense loathing for travel. Those of you who had counseled me against going appeared as my truest friends, and those who encouraged me seemed to me enemies of my life. A trembling fear of the sea possessed me, and I conceived so many objections to pilgrimage that, had I not been ashamed, I would have run straight to Abbot Fuchs and begged to stay in Ulm. But then the miracle. As I lay in bed, one cowardly foot skimming the floor, a voice cut through my turmoil, pitched in the low, severe tones of a injured spouse.

Will you come when I call, my husband? it asked.

I started up, expecting to find a woman in bed beside me, Katherine's hardened face, her blond hair spilling over her shoulder like a spurned Valkyrie's. But all was dark. Only the echo of her challenge hung in the air.

Would I come when she called? Was this dream not a dream but a cry for help? No milk flowed from her severed hand tonight, only cold red blood.

What makes a saint choose a certain friend, brothers? Saint Paulinus kept company with my name saint, Saint Felix, though he knew him not in life; he built a villa by his grave, fashioned poems in his honor, was laid beside him in death. Fifty years ago, my wife Katherine, along with Saints Margaret and Michael, spoke to a young peasant girl from Domremy, encouraging her to put on knight's armor and liberate France from the English. These friendships are formed across the great gulf of Heaven; they are unlikely, dangerous alliances. We must take as much care in these friendships as we would walking about a dark ship at night.

First: We must be deliberate in our scaling of the ladder to Heaven, lest we take undue pride in our friendship and tumble painfully to earth.

Second: Like a lantern on deck at night, we must hide the light of our saint under a bushel, lest we be too tempted to gaze upon her always and slide into the sin of idolatry.

Third: We should be careful not to wake the galley slaves of the Devil, those being his demons and minions, jealous of our heavenly friendships, who will seek to disrupt them.

Fourth: We must test the ropes of our friendship by pulling on them, by which I mean through prayer. We must pray often and not fear to ask favors of our saint, for prayer and supplication keep proper tension on the ropes and stave off the pulleys and sails of Heaven's wrath, that might crash upon our heads.

Fifth and last: We must ease ourself onto the horn of salvation by remembering that Jesus Christ, not any one of his saints, is the pitch that sweetly covers this ship. How gladly we should sit in Him, brothers, that died to save us all.

So I have given you a catalog of things to guard against, both while at sea and in forming an attachment to Heaven. I will add only one more caution, and it is this: Beware of talking to strangers, or God may make a liar of you, as he has just done to me. I said we had no women aboard our ship, but I swear on my life I see one.

What a cruel joke the passing clouds play on Friar Felix, smudging moonlight and salty air, spinning silver night white hot into a hollow vessel. What I see across the deck cannot possibly be female: that flock of loose hair lifted on dark wings, the paucity of skin brushed across a face so thin it would rather wear its bones on the outside. This must be a trick of light, an Ocean mirage—there are no women aboard this ship.

And yet, without a doubt, she stands against the moon, leached of all but angular blue shadows, wearing about her neck a heavy bag, like those used to feed cattle. Could she be one of the wretched women our sailors pick up on the docks for their sport? We see them limping down the gangplanks just before the ship sets sail, twisting their skirts in their fists where the bloodstains show. Vacant, pliable women, they exist only to contain the flood of sodomy, like soft wax plugs wedged into a cracked urn. No, were she one of those women surely some sailor would be right behind her, pulling her roughly back into his hold, there to store her beside his coiled rope and his bolt of precious contraband silk, the one he carefully wraps first in straw and then in burlap to keep out the mildew and preserve its resale value in Venice.

Slowly, this impossibility walks to the ship's ladder.

And yet, what other sort of woman might she be? Mercifully, care of all the lady pilgrims devolved upon our rival, Augustine Contarini; for once one female pilgrim chose his cheaper antiquated bireme, no other dared explore our ship. Happy were we to read the ships' lists and see all the gossipy Maries and Giulias and Annes safely stowed on Contarini's galley. We aboard Lando's boat have become almost like a floating monastery of harmonious brothers, save for the cursing and brawling and lack of prayer.

Since I saw for myself no woman's name darkening our passenger list, I know she cannot have been aboard for long. What did that stranger ask in church today? Have any strange women joined your ship?

As I puzzle this out, the apparation lifts a leg and lowers itself onto the ladder fixed to the outside of the galley where pilgrims dismount to be rowed ashore. The rowboats have been hauled up and hung from the poop—does she not realize only bottomless Ocean rages below? I know what you would have me do, brothers. As you would command, I drop from the horn and follow her.

"If you don't stop me, I'll know this is what you want!"

I press my ear against the hand's-width of wall as her distraught voice, lifted on the waves and wind, sobs against the wood. She must be clinging there, arms wrapped tight around the iron ladder, her dark skirt lathered with foam. I hear a rung groan under her weight and realize she is descending, like a contradictory Venus, into the sea.

"Everything he said was true, then?" she asks plaintively. "We cannot do it without him?"

To whom is she speaking?

"Then you truly have forsaken me."

What is happening, brothers? Is there some force upon this ship that impels its passengers overboard? Have we another Schmidhans, but deliberate in her tragedy, a woman come and gone, unknown, unseen by any save a sleepless priest? I cannot allow her to destroy herself on this, a holy journey.

"Lady! Stop!"

I scramble down the ladder and stretch out to reach for her. Only the brown feedbag she wore around her neck is visible, borne up like a beaver's carcass on a bloated river. Its strap twists around her thin throat, cutting off what little air she must have taken underwater with her. I lean over, and a frantic white hand reaches up, smacking at the bag, grabbing for the last rung.

Without thinking, I hook my foot through the ladder and grasp the hand, tugging until I can snag a fistful of cold flotsam hair. Her wild feet swing around, drum against the ship's side searching for

the ladder on which to anchor themselves. Only the bag still seeks
the Ocean. Heavy and waterlogged, it snaps her head back, catching at her chin in its anxiety to rejoin the sea. I am pushing it up
and over her head, freeing her of this baleful sack, when she realizes what I'm about.

"*No!*"

The apparition twists in my arms, clutching at the bag, tugging
it back onto her shoulder. She pulls so hard I nearly go overboard
with her but manage to right us both and heave her over my head
up the ladder. When I follow, I find her prone on deck, coughing salt
water across the floorboards, clutching the bag protectively.

"Madame," I ask unsteadily, "did you fall in?"

"You do!" she cries, smothering the briny sack with passionate
kisses. "You do still love me!"

Up close, she is all hollows and bone, far thinner than any self-
respecting German woman would allow herself to become. Her dark
eyes linger on the bag, as if she both fears and expects it will rise up
and fling itself back overboard. Slowly, I reach out to take it.

"Shall I carry this back to your room for you, Madame?"

She is aware of me, I think, for the first time.

"You are her agent."

She speaks perfect Latin but utter nonsense. I am about to lift
the bag when suddenly she snatches it away.

"We owe you our lives," she says solemnly, turning to leave. "We
won't forget it."

I watch mystified, brothers, as she trails the oozing sack behind
her, stumbling wet moonlight across the galley. I watch her climb
the stairs to the ladies' cabin, where, since we had no ladies on board,
Captain Lando has stored his supplies and treasure. Above her door,
a single lamp burns in the pilot's castle, illuminating his grid maps
and compass, throwing light across the worried eyes of the pilot's
companion, our ship's soothsayer. This soothsayer is a man so
learned in his art he can read signs in the color of the waves or the
flocking of fish together, in the glittering of ropes and cables at night,
and the flashing of oars when they dip into the sea. What does he
make of the madwoman below him, looking back over her shoul-

der at the hungry water? *Madness* comes from *mene*, meaning moon. *Femina* comes through the Greek *fos*, meaning *burning force*, because of the intensity of women's desire. Even I, with no gift of prophecy, know that madness coupled with desire, glimpsed in moonlight, can only forbode disaster.

Let that suffice about what a pilgrim should be on his guard against while journeying at sea.

How Pilgrims Pass the Time on Board Ship

Unless a man knows how to redeem his time on shipboard, brothers, he will find the passing of hours very tedious. Witness: All around me, a hundred pilgrims strive to outdo one another in indolence—some nap with hats over their eyes; some, like Lord Tucher, pick splinters from the benches. Near the ship's kitchen, an especially dull pilgrim torments our poor livestock, running in circles around their corral, rapping it with his knuckles. Normally, I busy myself with prayer or observation or the making of this little book of travel; today, however, I find myself staring fixedly at the door to the ladies' cabin.

I've spent a night and a morning fashioning her a history from every account of madness I've read or heard whispered in confession. Most definitely, she is the woman sought by the stranger at the Franciscan monastery. She is his fiancée or, more likely, his new bride, gone mad upon the birth of their first child. Now she hears voices, she tortures cats, she hides in church lofts swearing she can't bear the smell of human flesh. I've frizzed her hair, ripped her clothes, and foamed the spittle around her lips, configuring the perfect madwoman: one part hysterical nun, one part seductress, her nails crusted with ripped nipple flesh from her frenzy of self-loathing.

I sketch this madwoman not in my normal, relaxed hand, for while I sat carefree among men I knew, the pen given me by dear Abbot Fuchs, that instrument which allowed me to hold a last bit of earthly Swabia between my fingers and, if nothing else, feel orthographically still tied to you, brothers, was taken.

Lord Tucher, when I loudly made public this ill usage, magnanimously bestowed upon me his favorite quill pen, along with a knife to sharpen the nib and a stoppered pot of costly murex ink. The letters that flow off this instrument are far thinner than my normal hand; are, involuntarily, reedy and excitable, like my patron's voice. It is disconcerting to have Lord Tucher insinuate himself into my private correspondence. I feel he's eavesdropping.

"Felix, did you try to wake me last night?" John asks, bringing me back to myself. He tilts back his head and opens wide his mouth for Conrad, our barber, the fifth and last member of our party.

"No."

Conrad scours his iron pincers with sea salt and wets the tip of his cloak with diluted camphor. Gently, he touches it to John's rotted molar.

"Yes, you did, Friar. I heard you get up." Constantine, my neighbor belowdeck, has assumed that geography beneath translates to friendships above and, when he hasn't been seasick, has followed me around all morning.

"Perhaps I did. I was hot."

"It's hot today, Friar," Ursus whines over the Latin text I've assigned him. "I can't concentrate."

I tap his book with my foreign pen and set him to work on the verb "to journey."

"*Peregrino, peregrinas, peregrinat.*"

"You know, Ursus," I say, "Latin is the language closest to God. It's the language of the Church and of all educated men."

"*Peregrinamus, pereginatis, peregrinant.*"

"Demons are also capable of learning Latin." I keep my eyes on his book when they want to stray to her door. "There's the story of the erudite demon who possessed an ignorant peasant. The parish priest refused to admit the demon was real unless he spoke the Latin he claimed, but the peasant's tongue couldn't form the words!"

Ursus squeals in delight.

"I know of a demon," he starts, "that possessed a girl, and when he tried to read the 'Our Father' he made all the same mistakes she usually made!"

"I know of a priest who lost his knowledge of Latin when he attempted suicide." The voice is familiar, though petal thin without the sea beneath it. "It ran out with his blood."

Conrad pops John's tooth from the socket and holds it up for us to admire. My madwoman stands beside our barber, dry and smiling, simply dressed with her hair tucked into a white cap; not a hint of the half-drowned creature I saved last night. Slowly, her eyes travel the deck, studying with a sort of fascinated awe the bald heads, the unkempt beards, the thick, corded necks that turn to watch her. Her smile falters. She realizes she is the only woman.

"I know another story of a priest who could only count in pairs. He walked through his pantry like this: 'Here is a ham and its companion. Here is another ham and its companion—'"

"Ursus," I say, "be quiet."

"Arsinoë!" The Greek merchant jumps up. "Darling, did you sleep well? Were you comfortable?"

"Yes, thank you, Constantine." She bows to the merchant.

"And will you let me go to the kitchen and have the cook prepare you some lunch?"

"No, thank you, I'm not hungry."

"Please, then. Let me introduce you to our new friends. Friar Felix Fabri of the Preaching Brothers, the Lords Tucher, Archdeacon John Lazinus with his tooth, and—"

Our barber packs the extracted molar's socket with a piece of clean cloth and smiles shyly at the woman.

"Conrad Buchler, " John gurgles around his packing. "He speaks only German."

"Conrad." The merchant nods. "Please meet the lady Arsinoë. My wife."

His wife? My elaborate construction felled like the walls of Jericho by the simple word *wife*? Can it be that she is no runaway madwoman after all but nothing more exotic than the depressed housewife of a Greek vintner?

"Friar Felix and I have already met." She smiles at me.

"When was that?" The merchant asks obligingly.

"Last night when I tried to drown myself. The friar saved my life."

In stunned silence, the entire party turns to me. What strange trick is this, brothers, to air so boldly her own mortal sins?

"It was nothing, Madame," I say, my cheeks burning beneath my beard. "You slipped and I helped you back up the ladder."

"No, Friar." She holds up her hand. "I was despairing and angry and about to destroy myself. She sent you to stop me."

"Darling, remember," Constantine blurts. "We agreed not to discuss her."

I have seen such simplicity in halfwits and the very young, brothers, but never in a woman learned in the ways of Latin and smiling so very proudly. She takes a seat beside her husband, calmly speaking of last night as if I'd pulled her stuck shoe from the mud. Perhaps this disconcerting honesty is but another facet of her madness.

"Why would you try to kill yourself, Lady?" asks Ursus.

"Ursus!" Lord Tucher gasps.

The merchant's wife opens her mouth to answer, but Constantine nervously babbles over her.

"It's a myth, you know, that Greeks love the sea. We hate the sea. Agamemnon and his men hated it; Jason and his Argonauts hated it; Arsinoë and I hate it, too."

You know I don't like to jump to conclusions, brothers, but something seems suspicious about these two. The merchant Constantine is determined not to let his wife speak, and she can barely contain herself, even on the most inappropriate subjects. What could she possibly reveal that has him figeting on his bench, forcing his cap strings once more into his mouth? We sit in awkward silence.

"We've outrun Contarini, at least," Lord Tucher says at last. He stands and paces between our benches, leaning, ultimately, where she stood last night, his back against the ship's ladder.

"Who is Contarini?" asks the merchant, relieved to change the subject.

"Captain of the other ship and bitter rival to our captain," I answer. "If they beat us to Palestine, they will bribe the Saracens to lock us out, just in sight of Jerusalem but not allowed to enter until they leave."

For the first time today, the merchant's wife's eyes lose their witless shine. She turns anxiously to her husband.

"There's another ship?" he asks. "Going the same place?"

"And if they beat us," Ursus moans, "I will have to wait weeks for my knighthood!"

"It's no matter," the merchant says tightly, patting his wife's knee. "We've prepared for that."

"Oh, no," I say. I do not think he understands the loss involved. "If we are locked out, not only do Contarini's pilgrims get to fatten themselves on indulgences while we starve like beggars at the gate, but we might miss the caravans to Sinai. There are but few months that allow a safe passage across the desert."

"Constantine?" his wife cries.

"I told you we should have gone overland." He pulls abruptly away from her. "You've forced me into a dead man's spot, and we still might not reach Sinai in time."

"In time for what?" I ask. What awaits this queer couple in Sinai?

"And what would have become of me if this friar hadn't saved you?" Constantine shouts.

"In time for what?" I repeat.

"You know we had to come by sea." The merchant's wife speaks calmly and deliberately. "It was the only way."

Without another word, she turns and strides back to the ladies' cabin. We watch the delicate spider veins flash along the back of her emaciated calves as she gathers up her skirt to scurry up the ladder. The wretched merchant stares forlornly into his lap.

"I'm actually not feeling very well," he says at last. "Will you excuse me?"

Lord Tucher waits until the merchant has gone belowdeck before launching into me.

"You saved a woman's life without telling me?"

"I certainly never dreamed she'd refer to it, Lord Tucher."

"You know this makes me responsible for her?"

"No, certainly, it does not."

He waves me off. "I am responsible for you, Friar, as my confessor. You saved a woman's life; therefore, I am responsible for her through you. It's not that I mind, I would just appreciate knowing about it."

"Pssst."

A square-jawed Greek galley slave I recognize as having carried Schmidhans through Candia hisses at me. Between his overdeveloped pectorals, a gold Saint Katherine's wheel medallion drowns in rapids of sweat. I tear my eyes away from the sailor's shirtless chest.

"I appreciate your kindness, Lord Tucher," say I, "but I saved that merchant's wife with no thought toward responsibility, yours or mine. If anyone is to watch out for her now, let it be Almighty God."

"Pssst. Friar."

"What?"

"Can you get me an audience with the lady?" the half-naked Schismatic asks. "I need to know how many more candles to light to get my father into Heaven."

"How would that lady know how many more candles you need to light?"

"She'd ask her saint."

"What are you talking about?" I demand.

"Don't you know who she is?" The slave presses his hircine lips to Katherine's wheel. "She's famous throughout the whole Levant. I bought this medal from one of the stalls outside her house."

The slave cannot believe my stupidity.

"She's the Virgin of Alexandria's mouthpiece," he says. "They call her Saint Katherine's Tongue."

"Saint Katherine?" Ursus cries. "Friar, that's your wife!"

Freeze with me a moment, brothers, and find your breath. Are your palms dripping sweat? Can you see this slave in front of you grinning, his lips locked around the wheel of your bride's torture, mouthing it like a bit of Turkish candy, and do you not have to strangle back the scream: *Stop your lies?* If you were in my place, brothers, would you believe the illustrious virgin Katherine would keep company with the likes of that insane creature plucked half dead from the water?

I am on my feet and halfway across the deck by the time John catches up.

"I told Lord Tucher this was an ecclesiastical matter," he says, slurping at the trickle of drool that leaks from his swollen mouth.

"John, attend to your tooth," I say. "This is none of your affair."

"What do you hope to gain by talking to her, Felix?" He stops me halfway up the ladder to the ladies' cabin. "The world is full of women claiming to converse with Heaven. Maybe one or two actually have."

I knock emphatically on her door.

"Is that you, Friar Felix?"

"Madame, may we come in?"

"It's unlocked."

We step into the cramped room, made even tighter by the iron-studded trunks Lando has lashed, four high, to the wall. They groan against their ropes with each swell of the sea, aggressively threatening to reclaim their freedom. Arsinoë's own trunk, a faded carnelian box stenciled with fishes, rests at the foot of her narrow pallet, fastened with a cheap lock. But you notice none of this upon first entering the dark room. What you see first are the candles.

And the icons. Everywhere.

I stumble over "Katherine Wedding the Baby Jesus." Our infant Lord presses His oval olive cheek to hers and fits a shining gold band on her left ring finger.

Every day of her life. Every hour of her martyrdom. Katherine's vita relived on wood. Here, a barb of the silver wheel gently pricks our saint's thigh; here, milk fountains up from her severed joints for the faithful to sop; here the stone of Mount Sinai gives way like softened wax to the impression of her blessed bones.

"This is my favorite," Arsinoë says, lifting "The Defeat of the Fifty Philosophers."

It is a tableau we've all seen a hundred times before: Saint Katherine defeating wisdom with superior wisdom; the fifty pagan philosophers peering out from an overgrowth of flame.

"See?" says she. "Each little man lifts his eyes to heaven. All fifty black-robed scholars stand chin deep in fire yet are not burned by it. My brother often spoke of his fellow students this way—as men kindled by books but never ignited by them. These converted scholars are as indistinguishable from one another as fifty popped mustard seeds.

"But look." The merchant's wife nods. "Behind the sculpted cedar bushes with one eye on Saint Katherine and the other on his colleagues—a lone scholar. He has not been picked to dispute with the great saint and so hangs behind, envious of his lessers' martyrdom but relieved, it seems, to be alive. Of course, he believes that if only he had been chosen, his argument would have been the one to defeat this girl."

I reach out for the unusual icon. Katherine's arguments converted the fifty philosophers to Christianity and they saw Heaven that day. The lone scholar was left among the damned.

"How did you come by these?" John croaks.

"The faithful bring them to me. Some have been in their families for generations."

"They are all of Saint Katherine," I say.

"Yes." Arsinoë clears a path for us to her pallet. "But I promised Constantine we wouldn't speak of her."

She shakes off her cap, infusing her hair with candlelight.

"I'm afraid this is the only place to sit."

John and I fold ourselves up on her bed, careful not to set the room on fire.

"We've just learned of your reputation, Madame," I say. "That they call you the Tongue of Saint Katherine. That some among the unlearned even claim Saint Katherine speaks to you."

"I only recently doubted her friendship." The merchant's wife smiles. "You restored my faith last night, Friar Felix."

I? I restored her faith? Does she attribute my rescue to the auspices of my bride? I turn to John, hoping to find mirrored my own disbelief and pity for this poor madwoman; instead, I discover my friend poring over the icon "Katherine, Protectress of Young Girls."

"Why did you come on pilgrimage, Brother Felix?" the merchant's wife asks me unexpectedly.

I give the answer that won your permission, Abbot Fuchs, the answer any right-minded dutiful son of the Church would give.

"Saint Jerome tells us we cannot truly understand the Bible until we have walked the earth that Christ walked."

"And?"

Her large dark eyes blink patiently. Does this woman's madness give her the ability to command the truth? I was able to dissimulate to you, my own abbot; I misdirected my own brothers, and, at the time, even convinced myself that Jerusalem, not the Sinai, was my soul's desire. But I am far from home now, and the truth feels less sinful than it once did.

"I made a vow as a boy to venerate Saint Katherine's body in the place God first put her," I hear myself say. "On the spot where He first spoke to Moses in words of flame. I can become a better husband by learning the land in which my bride chose to die."

Arsinoë nods, picking up a small icon of the hermit who discovered the saint's bones five hundred years after her translation. "When I was a child, I used to dream of living in the desert with the blessed Katherine as my spiritual sister. We would run in the morning, meditate on Christ in the afternoon, and study Latin by candle in our cave at night. I realize now how silly that was. How can you study if your eyes are in one town and your head in another?

"And you, Archdeacon John?" she asks quickly. "Why did you come on pilgrimage?"

He doesn't like to speak of it. I see his jaw flinch around its toothless socket as he relinquishes "Katherine, Protectress of Young Girls."

"I bound my village by a vow to resist the Turk," says John. "The entire town, including the convent under my charge, was burned."

"All these vows," says Arsinoë. "And now the mouth with which you gave the order is punishing you. Forgive yourself, friend John."

The merchant's wife stretches out her hand and brushes the Archdeacon's swollen jaw. I expect him to pull away, but he slowly shuts his eyes.

"Madame," I say loudly, "do you know that Saint Katherine's hand was stolen from the Franciscans' monastery in Candia?"

She lowers her hand to the icon in her lap. "Yes. I heard."

"If she speaks with you, as you claim, did she reveal who did it?"

"A hermit found a young girl's bones on top of a mountain and presumed to bring her down." Arsinoë carefully replaces the icon behind its candle. "Men have been taking bits of her away ever since."

"With the sanction of the Church." I hear my voice rise. "The Church Fathers approved of breaking up saint's bodies so that Heaven might seed Earth. Had Katherine's bones not come West all those years ago, we might never have known she existed."

"Perhaps that's what God wanted, hiding her in the desert." Arsinoë looks away. "Most saints are buried where they died. They perform miracles for their own communities. Why was her body translated to the most desolate mountain in the world? Why did He hide her, Friar, if He didn't want to keep her whole?"

"Katherine lets you believe this sacrilege?" I cry.

"Who do you think suggests it?"

"John, please." I rise, for things are taking a decidedly heretical turn. "We should leave this room."

John puts out his hand to stay me. How can he remain here? She's suggesting God never wanted my beloved found.

"Madame," he says, "do you have any idea who stole her relic? Whether or not you agree she should have been broken up, you can understand the horror in a piece of her having been unlawfully taken."

Arsinoë picks up the icon of the Fifty Philosophers and thoughtfully traces the lone scholar.

"Come with me to Rhodes tomorrow," she says at last. "Saint Katherine's ear is there. Perhaps she heard something."

What Was Overheard

Lando's galley anchored outside the harbor defenses of Rhodes, but the dazzled Greek slave rows Saint Katherine's Tongue ashore with John and me. He maneuvers around the sharpened wooden pikes that jut from the water and points out the high char-streaked city wall.

"They waged a war of fire," John whispers in the eerie predawn silence. "The Knights of Saint John lit quicklime, petroleum, and sulfur and poured it down upon the Turkish army. The Turks flung clay eggs filled with smoldering pinewood and charcoal that could only be extinguished with vinegar, urine, or glue."

John knows the Turks' gift for fire. The only difference between his village in Hungary and the island of Rhodes is that God fought here for the Knights of Saint John. The Christian apostates on the Sultan's payroll grew so conscience-stricken when ordered to attack the handful of warrior monks that they turned on their Infidel masters and cut them to ribbons.

The merchant's wife is strangely nervous for the ride in, scanning the ramparts of rebuilt Fort Saint Nicholas, peering into the three slowly revolving windmills that, Fate-like, haunt the harbor walls. I don't know who she expects to see; it is so early in the morning even the city's dogs are asleep. The slave touches shore and hands us out of the rowboat.

Day breaks in muddy pink puddles along the back streets to her church. We pass cremated houses, smelling of wet ash and lead, their roofs collapsed, their doors broken and brick-choked. The town's Jewish quarter was the worst hit; the Turkish cannonballs felled bakeries and crushed Jewish virgins. At the worst of the attack, Grand Master d'Aubusson ordered the neighborhood razed, and every man, woman, and child, Christian and Jew, knight and slave, worked through the night to refortify the wall, using the Turks' own cannonballs for bricks. When the war was over and the Turks repelled, d'Aubusson paid the highest honor to the valiant Jews of Rhodes. We pass by the shining new church he erected on the site of their bombed synagogue, dedicated to Our Lady of the Victories.

Arsinoë spins on me. "Did you hear that?"

I jump at her jumpiness. What does she hear?

"Footsteps," she says.

I look behind us. Yellow morning sun creeps along the damp cobblestones.

"No one is there," I tell her. "It must be an echo."

Then suddenly a young boy scampers out of the dark alley, begging for money. He puts his blackened fingers on Arsinoë's arm and chatters to her in a language I don't understand. She pats him on the head and sends him away.

"I told him if he came round to the church when we were done, I'd give him a coin."

Warily, she resumes the walk.

"Someone talk," Arsinoë commands after a moment. "I'm hearing every little noise."

"What shall we discuss?" asks John.

"Tell us about the Turk, Archdeacon. Do they really snatch Christian women and keep them as slaves?"

John is visibly shaken by this topic of conversation.

"The Archdeacon suffered great loss at the hands of the Turk," I tell her. "I'm sure he doesn't care to dwell—"

"No, Felix, it's all right," John interrupts. His speech is much clearer today; his mouth—miraculously, according to him—nearly healed.

"To the Turk, Madame"—my friend speaks with his eyes fixed on the street—"a border town like mine is no more than brush to be cleared on the way to a real city. He treats with Athens or

Constantinople or Belgrade, allows them life if they forfeit their God and kingdom, but a border town is scrub: torchable; to be consumed.

"I preached a sermon the night they breached our wall. I made every man in our town vow to kill or be killed, to die for Christ and his sisters and his crops. Well, my men kept their vows. The Turk pissed on our crops. He raped our church. He burned our sisters. I lost sixty nuns to the fire."

Arsinoë impulsively takes his hand. "How did it feel to be deserted by Heaven?" she asks, not looking at him. "Did it fill you with hate?"

John smiles. "I wouldn't be on pilgrimage if it had."

She nods, slowly.

Before us, at the far end of the plaza, ten steps lead up to the doors of a domed Orthodox church. Above the lintel, a squat Joshua blows his trumpet and Jericho's carved walls come tumbling down.

"We're here," Arsinoë says, hesitating briefly at the door. She glances over her shoulder, taking in the empty square, the closed shutters of shops. Resolutely, she opens the door.

How similar, brothers, and yet how removed from one of the True Faith, is a heretical church. Because of the shiftless nature of their religion, the Byzantines make little art that is not removable—no icons that can't be tossed in a cart, no candles that can't be snatched up. They tile their ceilings with mosaics after the ancient Romans, to symbolize their fractured, piecemeal understanding of God, and orient their churches to the East, after their friends the Saracens. A plump Greek priest trots down the aisle and addresses Arsinoë in her native language.

Does Katherine feel ill at ease here, surrounded by this Oriental splendor? Even though I know she came from the East, I've always pictured her at home in Swabia, happy to sit through our German winters in her light robes and laced sandals. She grows darker the farther we move from Ulm; on the mosaic ceiling, she has the almond eyes of an Asian princess and black, jagged hair.

"Friar," Arsinoë calls. "Come along, he'll let us see it."

The priest says a hasty mass in Greek, the only words of which I understand being *apostle* and *Christ*, those sounding the same in Latin. John and I are barely off our knees before he's scurried around the altar to the sacristy. The reliquary he removes is long and silver and hinged like a book.

"The arm of Martyr, Saint George," the priest recites in rote Latin.

We step forward and kiss it, touch our rosaries to each finger, and kiss them too. He returns to the sacristy and emerges with another box.

"The arm of Protomartyr, Saint Stephen."

More kisses. Another box.

"The arm of the blessed Apostle, Saint Thomas."

Legend has Saint Thomas's entire body preserved deep in heathen India. Whether this be a true relic or no, I let the prudent man decide.

"The head of Saint Philomela. . . .

"The hand of the blessed Saint Anne, mother to the Virgin Mary. . . .

"The arm and pointing finger of the Lord's Precursor, Saint John the Baptist."

The Archdeacon John Lazinus kisses his namesake with special reverence. The Baptist, too, knew the heat of fire. When miracles abounded at Saint John's grave, jealous Emperor Julian the Apostate ordered his bones dug up and scattered across the fields. Greater miracles then occurred, so the tyrant ordered the sacred bones scattered even farther apart. At last, when neither time nor distance seemed to slow the miracles, Julian ordered the relics recollected and burned as a whole man. Some brave Christians risked death to substitute common bones for those of the blessed saint, but they missed his right arm and pointing finger. This the Emperor could not burn, but it remained fixed, accusing him from its socket of flames.

The priest goes into the sacristy one last time and comes out with a golden box no bigger than the palm of my hand.

O, blessed virgin, like a kind friend you incline your ear to our petitions and prayers, you listen to our chests so that you might take back to Heaven our true desire for God's love. The ear is perhaps your most important organ, for it is the gate through which all language must pass. Speech would be useless without it, for even the most gifted tongue would wag in a void without the ear to catch its eloquence and translate it for your blessed brain.

On a thick pillow of purple velvet, one tiny dried apricot.

Saint Katherine's ear.

Tears stream down Arsinoë's face. "Why do they do it?" she asks. "Hundreds of years ago, under cover of a kiss, some pilgrim tore this from her head in Sinai. Couldn't they leave her alone?"

John holds me back when I want to argue. This is no place, surrounded by this crowd of saints.

"Ask her, Madame," John whispers. "Ask her if she heard who took her hand."

Arsinoë says something to the priest in Greek, and he reluctantly extends her the reliquary.

"Can you hear me?" the Tongue of Saint Katherine breathes into the ear. "Do you want this?"

The mystic uses silence more affectively than sermons, brothers, adjusting it like a compass to arc widely over a room or proscribe a tight circle of expectation. Arsinoë's silence exchanges noiselessness for a whole new language of signs: puzzled frowns and little cocks of the head, widening eyes and nodding acceptance. Neither an awkward silence nor a meaningful silence but a visceral, present intercourse that, in itself, speaks far more forcefully than words. I can tell from his worried expression that John feels it too—someone powerful and unseen troubling the merchant's wife, though whether it be my bride or the Devil, I know not.

Arsinoë gingerly lifts the relic ear to her own and frowns.

"I don't understand."

"Pater!"

The young urchin boy who accosted us earlier throws open the door, causing us all to jump. Wildly, he beckons for the priest to come away. From his frantic looks and gestures, it would appear someone is dying in the street.

Arsinoë hesitates. The priest is obviously torn between locking away the relic and accompanying the desperate boy.

"Go, Father," she says. "You are needed."

With a grimace, he sprints down the aisle and out the door. Arsinoë walks to the front pew and sits down.

"Is she saying anything?" John asks.

The merchant's wife sadly shakes her head. "There was a time, when I was a girl, that her voice came to me like sun on the water. I understood everything she said, not in words, mind you, but as a fish understands, by the warming surface of the lake, that the sun is in the sky. When my brother came and started to give her human words, it got jumbled. I needed him to tease out the meaning of what she said, because suddenly it made no sense to me anymore."

She runs her finger over the papery rim of ear.

"Now that we are alone again, Katherine and I, I almost think she prefers the language he gave her."

"*Iesu Christi!*"

A cry of abject terror comes from the street outside. It sounds like the old priest.

Arsinoë is on her feet. "He's hurt!"

John and I dash down the aisle and out of the church. A few shop-keepers, opening for the day, peer around their wooden shutters.

"*Iesu!*"

The cry comes from behind the church, down the narrow alley-way that runs between it and the city wall. The sun has not yet probed the lane, and the way is very dark.

"Felix, look!" John cries.

The fat priest lies on his side with his hands and feet bound be-hind his back. He screams much at us that we cannot understand.

I work at the knots while John tries to calm him.

"Who did this to you?"

He is incomprehensible, and his struggling makes it that much harder to untie him. He says one word over and over: *Turcos.*

"A Turk?" asks John. "A Turk did this to you?"

"Please, sir." I grasp his head to calm him, and he screams as a man tortured. I suddenly see why. "John, would a Turk do this?"

I turn the priest's head to expose the blood-soaked stones below. On the right side of his face, a tight circle has been carved around his ear.

"Where is the merchant's wife?" John cries. "Did she come with us?"

I leap up and run back to the church. The merchants are hiding inside their shops; the street is deserted.

"Madame!" I fling wide the doors.

The church is empty. She is gone.

I run to the altar, where, thank God, the gold reliquary still gleams. Her blessed ear! What madness possessed me to leave it alone?

The box is empty.

She is gone.

Confession

Forgive me, O Lord, for I have sinned. It's been six days since my last confession. I made four wretched galley slaves carry Burgher Schmidhans's heavy body in the afternoon heat to an inconvenient church so that I might, like a yokel, gape at the hand of Your daughter Saint Katherine of Alexandria. Yesterday, I listened to a woman question Your wisdom in bestowing this same daughter of Heaven's relics upon the world; and this morning, I almost believed her when, at, of all places a Schismatic church, she claimed conversation with Your most sweet daughter, the virgin Saint Katherine of Alexandria.

I confess these sins in my heart, O Lord, and on paper for my abbot Reverend Ludwig Fuchs, hoping to spare my friend, and tender shipboard confessor, the Archdeacon John Lazinus, any further discussion of the missing woman aforementioned in my list of sins. He despairs of her safety, Lord, and blames himself, in my opinion taking on a responsibility out of all proportion with the depth of their acquaintance. He endangered his own life, along with that of Your servant Friar Felix Fabri, by combing the back streets of Colossus, questioning wharf prostitutes and scabaceous fishermen as to the likelihood of a Turkish pirate attack. No one spotted a foreign ship in the harbor, Lord, yet John remains convinced the woman was stolen, as the Greek priest was mutilated, by a renegade Turk.

But I turn to You now, O Lord, and to Your Son, and to His

mother, the gentle Virgin who knows men's souls, with a heart full of shame and sorrow. I beg You, teach me, Lord, how to please You and thus earn for myself a place at Your handmaid's foot; for truly, my sins must be grievous in her eyes to avoid me so. Would that I should be devoured by the Troyp or eaten alive by lions than that Saint Katherine should, like chaste Diana, flee before me. Men grow weak in middle age, Lord, when the ambitions of youth have been harvested and old age seems not far away. In an earthly marriage, when the children have grown and money has finally been put aside, a married man might turn for comfort to his wife of twenty years and find, instead, an old and tired woman beside him. He might for the first time see in her face not the bride of his boyhood but his son's children's grandmother, whose life has been measured in blood and miscarriages, epidemics and wakes. How fortunate did I then feel, to have taken a bride of Heaven! After twenty years, I could rejoice that my love had not weighted my beloved's belly or lined her face; I could believe, in fact, that this love was a source of comfort to her in its magnification, through her, of Christ. In middle age, when I had attained, at last, the leisure to render Katherine in adoration what I had taken over the years in supplication, I fondly hoped she would welcome me to her land and clasp me joyfully to her bosom. How foolish I feel, Lord, standing before her empty reliquaries; how I blush and perspire, knowing I have made too great a show of my love, like some simple country farmer in love with the King's daughter. I tremble to remember my presumption! I rue my words! I deserve her scorn and Yours, Lord; and yet, if humility will teach me the proper way to adore a Bride of Heaven, I will be an abject student. Give me another chance, Lord. Take no more away the earthly remains of your daughter Saint Katherine. Leave me a finger, a tooth, a tongue, Lord, and I will build upon that single brick a greater, purer love, one that will be pleasing in Your eyes.

I ask this of You in Your Son's name.

Thy will be done.

Amen.

A Brief History of the Merchant's Wife

When John and I, tired and heartsore, return to the ship, Constantine Kallistos is but one in the slack-jawed circle of pilgrims that includes our barber, Conrad, and my patron's son, Ursus, watching a tragedy unfold. The object of their pity is this: a long blue fish who writhes across the floorboards, sucking daylight with its swollen pink mouth, drowning on air.

"He flipped himself on deck," Conrad tells me. "I was going to throw him back, but the merchant thinks it's a sign."

"A sign of what?"

Our barber shrugs. "Fish for dinner?"

One look at Constantine tells me dinner is the last thing on his mind. His pupils are dilated like a consumptive on belladonna and a half smile plays at the corners of his mouth.

"It's the drowned man," Constantine whispers, "come to reclaim his berth."

"Don't touch it, Friar," Ursus warns. "It's Herr Schmidhans."

This will not do. I squat down and wrap the poor creature in my black robes, feeling its muscular panic against my thighs. I climb over the galley slaves and fling the fish back into the sea.

"Friar! You've killed him all over again."

"It was a fish, Ursus, and not even a German fish. Now, run along. The Archdeacon and I must speak with Herr Kallistos."

We grasp Constantine by the arm and steer him away from the wet floorboards. His wife made a stain only a little larger the night she flipped from the sea. Up to the ladies' cabin we lead him, into the room of snuffed candles and neatly stacked icons.

"She's gone, isn't she?" he asks, looking between us. "She didn't come back with you."

"You must think, Constantine." John sits the rigid merchant upon the Tongue's carnelian trunk. "Does your wife have any enemies? Anyone who might wish her harm?"

"She promised not to leave the ship. I told her only on the ship could she be safe."

"Safe from whom, Constantine?" John urges.

Silently, the merchant sorts through Arsinoë's collection of Katherine icons, arranging them in descending order, a life lived backwards: from her discovery atop Sinai, past the Philosophers' ignition, back to her first vision of the infant Jesus. His face sags when he reaches the earliest icon, that of a haloed baby Katherine perched on the knee of her soldier father, Good King Costus.

"I brought her this one." He presses the wooden panel to his cheek and hands it to me. It is an ill-painted piece in blue and red, with a hydrocephalic father and daughter lifting stiff-fingered hands. Katherine's heavy halo has flaked away behind the shoulder.

"He looks so protective and strong, but in the end he died and left her alone in the world."

"Constantine," I ask, insisting he keep to the subject, "was your wife in trouble? Is that why she tried to destroy herself?"

The merchant leans his head against the wall, lost in the flat, foreshortened world of her icons. Sweat pills along his upper lip, and his hands lie lifelessly in his lap.

"I'm sure she did not intend to destroy herself, Friar," he says. "It's been my experience that Arsinoë always gets what she wants. She must have intended to be saved."

"Are you suggesting Arsinoë knew I would be on deck that night?"

"I am suggesting, Friar"—Constantine looks upon me wearily—"that if Arsinoë meant to test her saint, you were the means by which she received her answer."

"Please, Constantine," John interrupts, when I am about to challenge the merchant. "Your wife disappeared along with a priceless relic. Surely, this was the agency not of Heaven but of a malevolent human being."

Constantine's pallor exceeds even that of his worst seasickness. He closes his eyes.

"In the end, all became perverted, Archdeacon," the merchant says dreamily, heedless of our presence. "I should never have followed that path to her house.

"I knew when I saw the makeshift stalls hung with sharp wheel medallions and cloudy vials of Katherine milk, when I started up the long trampled mud path through the almond grove, that I had taken a dangerous road. Mostly women milled about, pulling their teenaged daughters away from the Tongue's wild hibiscus bushes, for what girl could resist picking one of those lewd red flowers and tucking it behind her ear? I asked the women why they had come, wondering if their troubles were as great as mine. 'My daughter's womb is restless,' one said. 'It migrates to her nose and bleeds during her monthlies.' I looked over at the poor girl squatting in the grass, breathing through her mouth. She pressed a stained handkerchief to her face. Another mother told me, 'We took our daughter to Saint Paraskevie's shrine closer to our house, but Saint Paraskevie told us Katherine's Tongue had to intercede for us. Paraskevie has no power over pregnancy, you see, and our daughter has been with child now thirteen months.'

"The road was crowded with fat women, unable to walk unassisted. Old men with sores. And dogs, everywhere. They ran in packs and begged food from the pilgrims. Someone said they were holy dogs, sacred to Katherine's Tongue. It wasn't true, but the dogs got fed."

John glances over at me. The merchant is rambling, nearly incoherent. What does this have to do with his wife's disappearance, or who might have wished her harm? John is about to recall him to the point when he speaks again.

"You should have seen her in her own room, Archdeacon." He opens his eyes on John. "Back then, little crowded settlements of icons flickered behind small candles, set on every table and chair, tucked into corners. In the beginning, Katherine only wanted to see herself. Most pilgrims knew and brought as an offering some small painting of the Saint, some richly plated with African silver, some smudged with eggshell tempera. You clutched your icon and walked into her hot, dark room, mingling your nervous body stench with the chamber's melted wax and incense and something else less definable: the lingering desperation of the supplicant who preceded you. All these smells Arsinoë used. She spoke them aloud as you came in, sketching you for her saint: *Vines, oak, tar*, she said. *Onions, civet, clay.* You became aware of each aroma the moment she named it, dismantling and reconfiguring your own familiar essence, startled that everything you had passed through, during a day, clung and was knowable. When she had the measure of you in the dark, she lit a taper before her, and you were granted your first close look at Saint Katherine's Tongue."

Constantine wets his lips, but by now John, at least, has no desire to stop him. My friend breathes deeply, with purpose, trying to sniff out the narrator's truth.

"The first time I saw her, she was seated on a simple chair," the merchant whispers hoarsely, "her hair virgin loose around her shoulders. Dressed for bed, in a white shift, she looked more like a fever patient than an oracle, wasted and thin with dark, ringed eyes. They said her mother died just as the child's head emerged, and when the afterbirth slithered out it formed the shape of a wheel. I never knew whether to believe such stories, but she did have the look of one whom Death had embraced.

"Behind her sat a beautiful man, whose guarded face—I remember thinking at the time—looked like one scratched out and repainted. Our church in Candia had once been a temple to Dionysus, so I had seen it before; beneath the slender oval faces of Saints Peter and Paul, you can still make out the fleshy bloating of our wine god, grape vines centuries ago straightened into haloes, and leopard skins smoothed into draped togas. Her brother, they said he was. He sat at a desk behind her, his ancient watchfulness barely hidden by scholarly dispassion, collecting the words as they fell from his sister's lips like a midwife catching drops of the Virgin's breast milk.

"'How may Saint Katherine intercede for you?' asked the Tongue. Her brother barely glanced at me but kept his protective eyes fixed upon his sister. I hadn't slept in days and could barely tell her. I shuffled forward and placed this icon at the Tongue's feet, lifting a fold of her hem to my lips. I begged her help. For weeks I'd dreamed of drowning, a cold horrible death where ropes of water snaked into my body and flushed away my soul. I should have gone to Saint Nicholas or Saint Andrew, some patron of the sea, I know, but my dream always ended with a young girl's body replacing my own, floating peacefully on to shore. I wanted Saint Katherine to take this strange, drowned girl to her and restore my sleep. I wanted not to be some creature of the Poets, nightly casting my own death upon the waters, until the day I found myself submerged and dumbfounded, raging at the will of God."

Constantine breaks off and hides his face in his hands. He must have prayed to every saint under Heaven the afternoon Schmidhans's fat, portentous body passed before him on the backstreets of Candia, fearing, yet horribly certain, he would replace that cheerful drunk on our ship. He must have turned to his wife and begged her, for the tenth time, to take the overland route to Sinai: up to Thessalonica, over the land bridge to Constantinople, down to Antioch, across the breadth of Turkey into Syria and Palestine. God would preserve him on land, he knew, against bandits and marauders, through hunger and sandstorm. *Just please*—I can hear how he begged her—*don't make me take the drowned man's place!*

"What did she tell you?" John asks the merchant. "Did she take the dreams away?"

Constantine peers at John through spread fingers, his face red and blotchy from shame. Slowly, he shakes his head.

"Her words made no sense until her brother translated them for me. *Water*, she said, almost laughing. Then, *Sleep*. At first I thought she was only repeating what I said to her, but then her brother revealed their meaning. 'You will indeed spend your eternal sleep underwater if you do not help her,' he told me solemnly. Dear God, I thought, my dreams are true! Then he came over and placed his ink-stained hands on his sister's shoulders. 'Katherine has revealed to my sister that her body is raw from too much handling. Saint Katherine told my sister she wants a new skin.'"

What could Constantine possibly mean by that? A deep and insidious fear creeps over me, brothers, leading me to wild speculation. Katherine's bones are housed within skins of pure silver and gold, encrusted with opals, emeralds, and diamonds. Flayed of these reliquaries, her sacred joints and organs would be nakedly vulnerable, wholly at the mercy of diabolical thieves like those who took her hand and ear. Twice, now, the merchant's wife has been present when relics disappeared: first at Candia, when the handsome stranger tracked her to the monastery; and then today, when Katherine's ear vanished from Rhodes.

"I later found out," Constantine says, "her brother had been giving the same response to all the pilgrims. Most, wrapped up in their own private troubles, didn't understand the needs of the saint. Some of us, unhappily—Oh, God!—some of us did."

"What do you mean by that, Constantine?" I ask the merchant sharply. "What could Saint Katherine possibly need that Heaven does not provide?"

"Oh, Arsinoë, where have you gone?" The merchant moans. "I am so afraid." Constantine throws himself over his wife's trunk and sobs like a child.

I have no idea how to comfort him, for I cannot shake my own rising horror. Is it the great waste of sea that haunts this wracked merchant, knowing it might at any moment reach into his sleep and claim him? Or is it the specter of a fish across the floorboards, harboring the spirit of a drowned German burgher? I glance at John, but he seems as confused as I, wondering, as I do, whether Constantine's fear has less to do with his wife's disappearance than with some horrible secret they hold in common.

"Do not despair, Constantine," John says, when the merchant's wails quiet a bit. "Tomorrow we reach Cyprus. If your wife is able, she will surely meet the boat there."

"We had a plan, Archdeacon," Constantine says flatly, wiping away his tears. "She would protect me from the sea, and I would make certain she reached Mount Sinai. Our first day aboard ship, and I've already lost her."

The merchant's agony is really too great to behold.

"Look on the bright side." I flounder, sounding unconvinced, even to myself. "Perhaps your wife was not stolen but merely wandered off and is even now booking passage back to Crete. She'll be waiting for you when you return with clean sheets on the bed and a spinach pie on the table. And she will laugh at how worried you once were."

"That would be quite a feat, Friar," The merchant says to me, letting his head fall back heavily against the cabin wall, "since Arsinoë doesn't even know where I live."

The Mount of Venus

I have often read in pilgrims' accounts that one should not pause long on the isle of Cyprus because the air here is poisonous to Germans. They say healthy winds get trapped behind the Caucasus and Armenian mountains and thus are not able to circulate, leaving this place both stagnant and unwholesome. If that were so, would the delightful Venus have swum out to Cyprus when she found herself unexpectedly made flesh from foam? Would Noah's son Japheth have established a new world on a noxious island? No, my brothers, discount this rumor. The air of Cyprus is not poison, merely ill-suited to Germans who are born and raised in hard, cold, consumptive air and who cannot live well in light climates where their intemperate eating and drinking may not be indulged.

I urge you to cast aside your superstition, brothers, because my patron was unable to do so. After much pleading and cajoling, he allowed Ursus and me to go ashore but elected, himself, to remain behind, far from the injurious vapors of land. Of course, his decision had nothing in the world to do with the Venetian lady-in-waiting who boarded our galley this morning.

Constantine nearly threw himself over the ship's side when he saw her small boat approach. My heart broke to watch all expectation, all hope, pool in his trembling lower lip, when Emelia Priuli, former waiting woman to the Queen of Cyprus, cousin by marriage to our captain, Peter Lando, climbed up the ladder. I'll leave it to you to determine why a woman of her youth and beauty should be ending her days in a Jerusalem convent; I'll be circumspect and say only this: She is a Jezebel if ever I've seen one, and a scheming Delilah to trim the locks of this ship! All the ringleted, earringed pilgrim swains lined up for their haircuts, and Bald Tucher was first in line.

We left my patron sitting at her side, holding her comb, while she smiled through a veil of damp auburn hair at pilgrims whose minds should have been fixed on God. I announced to the entire ship that I was organizing a pilgrimage to the holy sites of Cyprus, but, so besotted were they with the new woman, only these intrepid pilgrims came along:

Lord Ursus Tucher, a merry youth and much intrigued with the legends of Venus, whose isle this is;

Master John Lazinus, Archdeacon of Hungary, a man of principle and passion;

Conrad Buchler, our barber and cook, who pleases many with his spicy stews;

Constantine Kallistos, a depressed merchant of Crete; and

Friar Felix Fabri of the Dominican Preaching Brothers at Ulm, the moving spirit of all these.

The ancients write much about Cyprus, most of it concerning the harlot Venus and her amours. It is said she swam naked in the waves of the sea for many years until her eyes at last turned to this place. The moment she stepped ashore, the Cyprians ran after her beauty and gladly instituted the practice of harlotry in her name. They gave her the highest mount on the island for her pleasure garden and held her watering can while she sowed every herb and plant that might be used in the business of love.

You might wonder at my climbing this mountain first when across the way, on another rise, is built a church containing the cross upon which hung Dysmas, the Good Thief, crucified beside Christ. Do not fear, brothers; I have not been affected by that Cyprian air which some say keeps a man aroused the whole time he remains on the island, nor do I need to sniff the native agnus castus shrubs that dry up the seminal humors and calm the winds that engorge the sexual organs. I have a method to my madness which, God willing, will benefit not a depraved prostitute but a handmaid of Christ.

"Will we see Tannhäuser here, Friar?" my charge asks, stopping to peer in every cave and crack on the mountain. "Shall I sing his song?"

"Ursus, we are headed to Saint Paul's church. Do you think the Apostle would appreciate your tuneless howlings after the dead?"

"No, Friar." He kicks the dust. "But this *is* his mountain, isn't it? This is where he went to live with Venus?"

In modern times, the uncouth mob raves over a certain mountain in Tuscany where Venus supposedly lives and takes her pleasure with men and women. They believe a Swabian nobleman called Tannhäuser, from Tannhäusen near Dünkelspüchel, disappeared into her mountain and now lives in joyance with Venus until Judgment Day. Lo, brothers! How easily men are led into error. For Venus, hardly a goddess and no doubt damned, who never saw Europe while she was alive, they believe to dwell now and forever in Tuscany! The Germans are so demented about this Tannhäuser story that many simple people make pilgrimages to that Mount of Venus and, in fact, have so overrun it that the Italians now place rabid dogs at its entrance to scare them away.

The path up our Mount Venus, while free of beasts, is dry and hot, and we are all relieved to finally take our rest in the shade of Saint Paul's church. The locals have planted terraced vineyards here, the grapes from which I've heard are so strong, their first press will corrode a wooden cup. We overlook the whitewashed village of Paphos, no more than a web of footpaths between daub houses. On the slopes of Venus's mountain, sloe-eyed village girls forage sticks for tonight's Saint John's bonfires.

"If your wife is on Cyprus, Constantine," I say, "I'm certain she will come here."

John doubted me this morning. He wanted to wait at the docks, to ask each arriving fisherman if he had seen a woman calling for help from the hull of a Turkish galleon. He convinced Constantine that if she escaped her common sense would lead her to Cyprus, where we would surely stop for provisions. What better place to spot her than at the docks?

But John does not know the way a devotee's mind works.

Katherine's last relic before Sinai, the easternmost tip of her a pilgrim might venerate without crossing the Great Wasteland, lodges in this little church of Saint Paul at the center of Venus's pleasure garden.

Wouldn't Saint Katherine's Tongue come to see Saint Katherine's tongue?

How greatly can we praise the tongue? It is perhaps her most precious organ, even more than the hand or the ear, for with it a saint first glorifies the Lord. Had Katherine been mute, she still might have written down her love for Christ, she might still have convinced the Fifty Philosophers on paper; but the common man, the thresher of wheat, the shepherdess with piebald dog, would never have understood. Why, how else could the unlettered citizens of Alexandria have made sense of that beautiful woman's torture? Why she was beheaded or translated to Sinai? They might still be wandering in the darkness had Katherine not had a tongue.

I expect the Tongue to steal the tongue.

This part I have not shared with John or Constantine; it is a secret between us alone, brothers. As I lay awake last night, agonizing over this painful sequence of events, I realized only one possibility existed: Saint Katherine would never deliberately avoid her devoted husband of twenty years; she is purposefully being withheld by sinister forces. If someone is stealing my wife, she is in dire need of a champion.

Now, before you upbraid me, brothers, before you call me puffed-up priest and knight-errant friar, let me explain. I do not claim to understand why Saint Katherine allowed herself to be stolen in the first place. Perhaps she was distracted by long months of intercession and exhaustive charity, which selflessly led her to take fewer pains about her physical remains. Or perhaps in her dutiful humility she was fulfilling the psalm, "And God hath scattered the bones of them that please themselves," for nothing pleases Katherine more than being attentive and kind to mortals. We would slight her to believe she could not have saved herself had she only been more alert. Over the centuries, hundreds of thieves have succeeded in robbing the tombs of saints; Saint Benedict was stolen from Monte Cassino and translated to Fleury, but only because Monte Cassino was in decline and the saint no longer desired to reside there. By contrast, when a wicked monk attempted to spirit away the body of Saint Martin, he was foiled by Abbot Hilarius, to whom the threatened saint appeared in a vision. Could anything then be clearer, brothers? Saint Katherine warned me in a dream after her hand was stolen in Candia. She swam behind the boat, begging my help. I was so beguiled on Rhodes, I did not see the thief before me, though her guilty conscience had all but driven her to suicide. The woman Arsinoë took Saint Katherine's ear, and Constantine the merchant has some suspicion of it; I'm convinced. Had he not been of my same mind, if he did not suspect his wife might make an attempt on Katherine's tongue, why else would he have consented to come here? As John urged, the docks are by far the more logical place to search. But she will come, brothers, of this I am certain.

And we will be waiting.

I gather up the pilgrims and go inside. I must accept my charge and fly Saint Katherine of Alexandria's colors like a noble champion.

Inside, the church is whitewashed and bare, bereft of any decoration save a stiff, crooked icon of a shiny-pated Saint Paul. Twelve rows of plain cedar benches, split by the center aisle, lead forward to a wobbly altar. A young, well-formed priest rises from his prayers when we enter.

My first fear—that the merchant's wife might have beaten us here—is quickly put to rest. Beside the altar crucifix, the reliquary sits in plain view, a golden head with a surprised glass-fronted mouth, through which we may view the tongue. My turn comes to venerate it, and in my heart I offer up this prayer:

Like a tiny blind mouse, dear tongue, you struggled in the mouth of our infant saint. Quivering and straining, you woke her first words, rolling them off their pink, muscular bed and into the world. Shyly, you reached out for your first taste of cold melon, sadly forgot the flavor of mother's milk. You, tongue, recited pagan rhymes, thrust yourself at naughty pagan boys, licked the sweat that gathered on our saint's upper lip when she sprinkled incense before the pagan gods.

A stone in her mouth the night her father, Good King Costus, died; a wrung sponge, barely wetting her lips by her third day in the desert, taken there to learn the ways of our Lord by Saint Sabba. You tasted no flesh but her elder's webbed knuckles, no liquid but tears heated on the portal of her sunburned lips. A straining, yearning fourteen-year-old tongue against the cheek of her bridegroom, the baby Jesus, when he slipped a ring on her finger and sent her back to Alexandria.

For four years, you issued proclamations and exalted the poor, until the Emperor arrived to survey his vassalage. You, tongue, hesitated not in your answer to Emperor Maxentius; no, you touched the roof of her mouth, slid behind her teeth. *I will not renounce my husband, Jesus Christ. I will not sprinkle incense before your pagan gods.*

The Emperor followed you in your route around her mouth, watched you pause at each station of thought on your pilgrimage of refusal. He wanted so badly to take you between his lips that he sometimes felt his own mouth open and close softly, like a baby dreaming of its mother's tit. He challenged Saint Katherine further, merely to watch you savor your retort. Poor kidney-colored tongue of his wife, the Empress; the Emperor sought to replace it with you, offering Katherine his wife's place at his side for one handful of incense on an altar. Again, a slight tap to the roof of the mouth. No.

Could not fifty philosophers convince her?

You humiliated and pleasured them, first in defeat, then in conversion.

Could not torture—the Wheel, starvation—silence her?

No, you gave to God a new song, lapped nectar from the palms of angels.

Lop off her breasts, roared the Emperor, but don't touch her tongue!

Where could you rest in her rictus mouth? Could you have possibly found an idea to go with the pillows that dropped from her chest? But good came from evil: Queen Kidney Tongue was converted; jailor Porphyrius, the thousands in the square come to cheer their patroness, were converted and instantly martyred.

And when in his reddest rage, standing in the stubble field of severed limbs, the Emperor struck her head from her shoulders, his guards had to restrain him from sucking the dirt and grainy milk from your still quivering flesh. He fought hard. He had to know how Christianity tasted.

Bless me, O tongue.

In Jesus' name. Amen.

The priest stands by, while I fog the glass with my reverent kiss, and wipes it after me.

When we are done, we retire to the shaded pleasure garden, there to open our scrips and eat some lunch. Conrad, our barber, takes out a little reed pipe he has lashed together and plays festively for our entertainment.

"My brothers and pilgrims," I say, rising when all are sprawled under pine boughs and lunch is nearly finished, "I have prepared a profitable sermon on how compares this Mount of Venus to that of holy Mount Sinai: their likenesses and divergences, their places in history, and their accompanying miracles. I call this sermon Truth and Illusion. Would you like to hear it?"

"Hear, hear!" cries John, waving his water skin. "If we are to bear the heat of the afternoon, how better to weather it than with a sermon?"

Conrad pipes a little arpeggio signifying assent, and Constantine puts his head in his hands, the better to concentrate. I position myself in the pine grove so I am facing the Church of Saint Paul, there better to see the merchant's wife when she sneaks in.

"Friar, didn't we just have a mass?" Ursus pleads.

"The Sermon of Truth and Illusion," I begin. "Delivered this Saint John's Eve by Friar Felix Fabri of the Dominican Preaching Brothers in Ulm for his dear friends John, Conrad, Constantine, and Master Ursus Tucher.

"Now a sermon, like any new creature, is best begun with a birth, so before we climb the two mountains Venus and Sinai, let me first speak of a pair of births, one false and one true, that occurred in the shadow of this pleasure garden.

"When the god Jupiter took umbrage with his father and severed his genitals with a scythe, the blood from those organs frothed upon the sea until a lady was born. Does anyone know who this lady was?" I point to my patron's son. "Ursus!"

"The Lady Venus?"

"Correct. And though she was a most beautiful woman, what was she born from? That's right. She was born from a deposed god's pollution.

"Now some centuries later, another birth graced this island, even though its inhabitants were sunk deep in Venus's harlotry. A daughter was born to the vice-consul of Cyprus, before he was granted the kingship of Alexandria: a child as chaste as Venus was corrupt, as intellectual as Venus was sexual. Perhaps it was memories of her days on Venus's island that prompted her words to the Emperor Maxentius: 'If you are ruled by the mind, you are king; if by the body, you are a slave.' Does anyone know who spoke those words?" I point to my patron's son. "Ursus!"

"Saint Katherine! Saint Katherine spoke those words!"

"Correct. So, two births: one the daughter of a king on his way down, one the daughter of a king on his way up. One from pollution, one from honest employed parents.

"Let us now turn to their mountains."

I glance at Saint Paul's church, but still no one approaches.

"I think you know where the two mountains in question are situated in the world. The Mount of Venus rises up from the sea on the well-endowed island of Cyprus. It overlooks fields and streams, plowed lands and vineyards.

"The Mount of Sinai lies in a land completely opposite, in a rough, dead country, encompassed by barren rocks and poisonous snakes. A man might sail to Cyprus in the company of jolly Europeans, but to reach Sinai he would have to brave camel bite and Arab attack, perhaps then only to die of convulsive thirst in the wilderness."

Constantine shudders.

"And yet, here come into play Truth and Illusion. For all its shade and abundance, for all its accessibility and cool breezes, the mount upon which we now sit, the Mount of Venus, is a dung heap of corruption, a foul squirming pyramid of worms. It is home to a pagan prostitute who, not content with debauching her own body, had to sully an entire continent, spreading her contagion even unto Tuscany, where it might infect foolish German travelers.

"Witness, friends, how illusory then is Sinai. On the surface, it appears a forbidding, friendless rock, tempered in flame, abandoned by God. But search for Truth. You will find it in the shape of a young girl who chose *this* mount for her eternal home. For all its heat and dust, for all its scorpions, sand, and silence, Sinai is a paradise! Look with your heart and you will see blue plashing fountains, lush green groves laden with fruit. Sinai is no wasteland—no—it rewards the bold pilgrim a thousandfold with its promise of Heaven! How easy to reach inviting Mount Venus. How perilous, and thus how profitable to a man's soul, to achieve Mount Sinai. It is as close to martyrdom as a man might come in this Age of Faith!"

From a distance, I see a woman start up the mountain. She is too far away to tell for certain, but indeed she has the coloring of the merchant's wife.

"How can we tell what is Truth and what is Illusion?" I continue excitedly, keeping the tiny figure in sight.

"Item: two beautiful women translated to mountains after their deaths. One's chastity inspires Heaven; one's depravity inspires Hell.

"Item: two men associated with these women and their mountains. Where Katherine sleeps at Sinai, God spoke to the Patriarch Moses. Where Venus sleeps on her mount, be it here or in Tuscany, the deluded Swabian nobleman Tannhäuser keeps her company. Law or lust? Which is inspired by God?

"Item: miracles. On Sinai, a bush burned that was not consumed. Our Lord wrote the Ten Commandments. A virgin was translated from distant Alexandria, whose bones now work wonders throughout the world. On Mount Venus, the artist Pygmalion, disgusted with the harlotry of the Cyprian female population, sculpted a woman from an ivory block. So perfect was his skill that he fell in love with his own creation. Venus, sensing victory, granted the statue Galatea life; whereupon Pygmalion fell upon her and begat a child.

"This is how we know Illusion from Truth: Ask yourselves, my friends, 'Is the object of my affection wrought by man or God?' Ask yourselves, 'Will I be content with Venus, or will I never sleep until I reach Mount Sinai?'"

"*Sinai!*" Ursus cries. "On to Sinai!"

"Yes, my boy, my brave boy." I hug him. "You are worthy to come with us. You will live among the blessed."

"Is that her?" Constantine swivels to see the approaching woman. "Arsinoë?"

He is up and running across the garden to where she slipped inside the church. Don't stop her, Constantine, I almost shout. I want her surprised in the act.

We catch up to him on the church porch, and I put my finger to my lips to signal silence. I want to give her enough time to unlatch the glass mouth, to force her hand down my bride's throat and rip, from its bed, her perfect pink tongue.

Slowly, I inch open the door. A woman kneels before the altar, only inches from the reliquary. As I watch, she reaches up for something, but it is not my bride's tongue. Slowly the stud priest of Saint Paul lifts his cassock to this strange sloe-eyed farmgirl's hands.

It is not her at all! I slam the door. Constantine collapses to the ground in tears.

"She is gone forever, Friar Felix. I have lost Saint Katherine's Tongue."

Ursus studies the merchant, his eyes as round as saucers.

"Come on, Constantine." John pulls him to his feet. "Let's go back to the ship. Perhaps she's made her way there."

"I still believe—" I start to protest, but John silences me with a stern look.

"We've been here most of the day, Felix," he says. "She's not coming."

We walk back in silence, heartsick, defeated men. Only Ursus steps lively, practicing his skill against scorpions and poisonous snakes. He crushes the imaginary desert vermin with the heel of his oversized boot and dreams of Arab sands.

John questions the sailors when we reach the busy dock, but no one has seen a woman or a Turkish ship put in to port.

"Ursus, son!" Lord Tucher opens his arms to us when we climb up the ladder to our galley. "You look feverish. Did you breathe into your sleeve like I showed you?"

"No, Father, the air was fine."

Constantine makes his way through the thick crowd of pilgrims and wearily climbs the steps to the ladies' cabin. He curls in front of Arsinoë's door like an forgotten watchdog.

"Did you have an opportunity to meet the Lady Emelia Priuli before you went ashore?" Lord Tucher draws forth the heavy-lidded lady-in-waiting who boarded our ship this morning. We look each other up and down with mutual distaste.

"Why is she wearing Mother's Venetian comb?" Ursus asks, pointing to a gleam of ivory worked into the woman's ornate auburn hair. "We bought it as a present."

Lord Tucher shifts uncomfortably. "The nice lady lost her comb this morning, so I loaned her ours. We'll buy your mother a new one in Jerusalem."

"I think someone took it." Emelia Priuli speaks in a flat Italian contralto.

"Men are strangely apt to play the thief on shipboard," I tell her. "For example, while you are writing, if you lay down your pen and turn your face away, your pen will be lost, even though you are among men you know."

"So, you enjoyed Cyprus, son?" Lord Tucher swiftly changes the subject. "What did you see?"

"Friar Felix took us to a stinking dunghill crawling with worms."

"We climbed the Mount of Venus," I say.

"And he told us all about Mount Sinai. I can't wait to cross the desert, Father. I want to die for Saint Katherine."

Lord Tucher looks at me sharply. "There will be no dying for anyone, Ursus. And we are not going to Mount Sinai. Madama Priuli tells me they've had news at court that Saint Katherine's Monastery was attacked by Arabs. The place burned to the ground."

"*What?*" I cry.

"We all wept when we heard." The harlot wipes away an imaginary tear. "Saint Katherine's is no more."

Saint John's Fire

The sailors choke the ship with necklaces of Saint John's fire, flout the usual prohibition against lights on deck by hoisting lanterns from the benches aloft to the maintop. Other crewmen scamper barefoot across the rigging with lighted torches in their mouths, pretending, in the manner of clowns, to drop like Pentecost upon the pilgrims.

"I'm going to bed," Ursus says dully.

"You'll miss the fires," I tell him.

"I don't care."

I lean my head against the mast and close my eyes. It's been a week of thefts. My pen, Katherine's ear, Priuli's comb, my reason for pilgrimage.

I argued for hours, but what does the Betrayer Tucher care about Katherine? We've been hearing rumors of the monastery's destruction for weeks, and yet only from sources close to Captain Lando. La Priuli is cousin to his wife; of course she would willingly spread his lies! Only a man as faithless as Lord Tucher would believe them.

"Felix, you look so somber. Be happy. It's my name day."

John shouts into my ear and passes me an open bottle of malvoisie. The wine is thick and sweet, like syrup.

"I know you're upset, but you must trust God to have a plan."

I've been too deeply betrayed to be trustful. Instead, I take another few long swigs of malvoisie. Saint John's lanterns spin the whole deck red.

"Isn't that better?" John asks. I feel the wine travel hotly down my arms, swell my stiff-flexing fingers. Smoke from the lanterns grays out the other pilgrims; they cavort like insubstantial shades behind a filmy, dying scrim. Even John, with his whorling-smoke beard and fire-shadow face, seems to me beyond the grave.

We use the word *fire* to mean such a complexity of things. Fire as a deliberate combustion; fire coupled with water to represent the necessities of life; fire to destroy, as a means of torture, to eradicate a body; fire from the heavens; the fires of love. All meanings come back to the simple etymology *"ignis," qui sua omnia "ignit" natura*, fire that consumes all things by its very nature. And yet, if we go back even further, how can we separate that nature from *its* origin? Prometheus stole fire from the gods to give man his first guilty warmth; thus the true etymology of fire and destruction and love is theft.

I look back to shore and see tiny bonfires dotting the mountainside. Why do we light fires on Saint John's Eve? They say that sometimes, while flying through the air, dragons will become lustfully aroused and drop their sperm into wells or live water. This causes a year of plague. Our forefathers built smoky fires out of the bones of animals to scare off these dragons, and we continue wisely to observe this custom.

Why then, you ask, if we deplore the dragon's arousal, do we, as Christians, copulate so indiscriminantly on this day?

This, my brothers, I may not answer, for only the Devil knows why men do it. I only know something happens to a man on this the longest day of the year that stretches his passions to the breaking point.

The man who steals onto our ship, hiding behind a bright white torch, looks vaguely familiar to me. Lucifer, I think drunkenly to myself, the light bearer. He has the lithe grace and fashion sense of a fallen angel, decked out in a short black tunic and high mustard knee boots. His black curls loll across his forehead and rear in two sharp horns behind his ears. After a slow-eyed inventory of the ship, he turns back to the ladder and hands up his familiar, a fearsome creature in red felt fez, white linen tunic, and high, hard platform clogs.

"A Turk." I grip John's arm. At his waist, he wears a curving bright scimitar.

John follows my eyes, shakes his head no. "Look at his beard," he says. "It's blond."

They pretend a casual stroll, but the dark man's eyes flick sharply to the shadows, while the other's stray to pilgrims toasting Saint John. Without a word, John and I fall into step behind them.

Between the two is a slender marriage of fire and night, annulled where their heads meet to confer, where their shoulders touch possessively when they dip to peer under benches or crane behind stolid pilgrims. They move in perfect Manichaean unison, light and dark, two individuals either so completely of the same mind or so accustomed to one's thrall that they seem never to doubt their rhythm. When the dark one breaks off down our hatch, the blond stares after him like an abandoned bride.

"Ursus is down there," I whisper.

"Look at his neck."

A splinter of wood, almost as thick as my thumb, protrudes from his linen collar. Around it, an angry red mouth drools a trickle of pus over his swollen flesh.

I've changed my mind. What terrorizes pilgrims most on their ships is nothing so familiar as a four-fingers'-width of wall between themselves and the Ocean; what terrorizes pilgrims beyond their wildest dreams is to have strangers prowl their decks while their captain is leaping bonfires on shore.

The blond turns around, his hungry blue eyes fixed on us. No, not on us; on an ember that rides by my face, faints into my bottle of cold dark wine. I hear his sigh.

"*Hast du Durst?*" Are you thirsty? The dark one asks, climbing up behind him.

"*Ja.*"

"*Ihr sprecht Deutsch?*" I gasp, before John can clamp his hand over my mouth. It is the last thing I expected.

"Who are you?" The blond turns on me, his Swabian accent filtered through his outlandish mustache.

"Friar Felix Fabri of the Preaching Brothers in Ulm!" I cry. "Countryman, if you *are* a countryman, have some of our malvoisie."

His hand hesitates before taking the bottle, and I catch a swift, stolen glance at his comrade. He turns his back to us and, hunching over, drains the bottle dry.

"Is there more?"

"Ha!" His friend laughs. "Go among Christians for five minutes and you turn drunkard."

John reluctantly leaves to fetch another bottle of malvoisie. Everything sinister has fallen away. They speak German!

"What brings you aboard our humble galley?"

"Curiosity more than anything." The dark one smiles. He props his yellow boots against a bench and slowly takes in the whole deck. "I wanted to see how Lando's pilgrims traveled."

"You're familiar with our captain?"

"Only by reputation. I'm sailing with Contarini."

"Contarini's here?"

"We just arrived."

And Lando is on shore with his wife. For the briefest second, I see Jerusalem snatched away like a rug, its dust snapped in our face.

"So you're my enemy, then?"

He smiles at the absurdity of it all. "Looks like."

"John." I reach for my returning friend. "Meet our enemy . . ."

"Ser Niccolo Callegeris."

"John Lazinus, Archdeacon of Hungary." John shifts the bottles to shake the stranger's hand. "Who will do the honors?"

"Let Abdullah." Ser Niccolo passes a bottle to his friend. "He's the driest of us all."

John's eyes meet mine over the name. Abdullah on a blond man could mean only one thing.

"You're a Mameluke?" I blurt.

Ser Niccolo laughs a short, sharp blast. Abdullah pauses in his uncorking to look offended.

"Yes, Brother Dominican, I am. And I don't see anything funny about it."

Under his feminized dress, the Mameluke's thick arm muscles jump. He drives his dagger deep into the cork and yanks it out, lifts the bottle to his mouth, and drinks defiantly.

Why did this man deny his faith, I wonder? Was he, like most forsworn Christians, captured during the Eastern wars, forced to renounce Christ at cold Muslim knifepoint? Or was he, caught perhaps pants down over the interdictory loins of a Saracen woman, given the simple choice by her father: embrace Islam and marry, or suffer your spine plucked vertabra by vertabra clean of your body? It matters not. He exchanged God for Allah, and he's damned just the same.

"Don't hog, my friend." Ser Niccolo reaches for the bottle. "Oops, I forgot. No talk of the pig!"

Abdullah grimaces but passes him the malvoisie. Niccolo hands it off to me.

"Abdullah's new religion forbids him to eat pork, doesn't it, my friend?" Niccolo needles the Mameluke. "Or drink alcohol. Thank God you're among Christians."

"Thank Jesus, Mary, and Joseph." He snatches back the bottle and salutes.

Imagine, brothers, if our servants suddenly rose up and demanded the same meat we ate, to ride upon the same horses, to lead our prayers! Would we allow our servants to rule us so? Would we provide them the arms to kill us? Luckily, we are sensible Germans and not decadent Egyptian sultans, so suspicious of our fellow countrymen that, centuries ago, we surrounded ourselves with thousands of burly apostate Christian slaves to protect us. It was only a matter of time before these slaves, these *mamluks* as they are called in the Arabic tongue, looked down at the swords in their hands and thought, This will slice through a sultan's neck as clean as anyone else's. For two hundred years, Mameluke slaves have ruled in Egypt. When one is speared or poisoned or nailed to a camel—for slave kings never die natural deaths—another upstart slave steps in to take his place. Abdullah tells us that when he was still Peter Ber he was captured and sold to an illegitimate son of Egyptian Sultan Qa'it Bey and a Greek slave girl. If he kills enough people, Peter/Abdullah has as good a chance of becoming Sultan as any man on earth.

But Abdullah wants to talk of Germany.

"Yes, it's still black with forests," I tell him. "And gray-capped mushrooms grow through nets of running cedar. It rained every day of my pilgrimage, until we crossed into Italy."

"Is the beer still thick and brown?"

"With malt-flecked clouds on top."

"And the wurst?"

"Dear God, the wurst!"

"Watch the pig, Abdullah," Ser Niccolo warns. "Dwell not on the filthy pig!"

"A man who speaks perfect German mustn't joke about the wurst," I chide him, feeling the wine hot in my cheeks when I lean in for more. "Where did you learn this perfect German?"

"Ser Niccolo is a translator," Abdullah says. "He speaks all the languages of the world."

"I etymologize a bit myself"—I laugh—"but I won't translate. There are too many vernacular ideas that just won't fit any other language. The world is too full of stray words."

"Ah, there you've found the seat of the translator's power, Friar." Niccolo slaps my back with the same pride as my abbot in Basle when at seven I completed my first catechism. "It is where we have more sway than kings or bishops. It serves translators to keep mankind ignorant; the reader must trust us to think for him."

"What if we prefer to think for ourselves?"

"Then you must do as I did and learn a hundred different languages. If not, you'll always be dependent on a complete stranger's version of the truth."

"I've always thought of translators as servants," I say, emboldened by the drink. "They are slaves to genius, are they not?"

Ser Niccolo smiles, noticing the little copy of Saint Jerome's *On the Distances of Places* that peeps from my pocket. He plucks out the book and flips through it.

"Many would have it so. But let me give you an analogy: Take Abdullah, here."

He holds Jerome in one hand and places the other on the Mameluke's swollen neck. I see Abdullah wince.

"He is a slave, the servant to an illegitimate son of the Sultan. Yet if he had the genius to obliterate his enemies, he, a wretched, amoral apostate, could easily find himself ruler of the East, the most potent political and religious figure alive.

"Do you not think Saint Jerome was aware of this when he sat down to wrest the Bible from Hebrew? He knew only a handful of Romans understood that arcane Jewish language, and thus the rest of us would be utterly dependent on his Latin translation of God's Word. If the Jews were wiped out tomorrow, as many European rulers would have it, and the Hebrew language were obliterated, who would then speak for God? Only the master translator, Saint Jerome. So, I ask you, Friar Felix, who really serves in this world? Who really rules?"

John looks decidedly uncomfortable with the conversation. Abdullah shifts on his bench.

"If we're to have philosophy," the Mameluke says, "we need another bottle of wine."

"I'll get it," John volunteers.

"I'll come with you." The Mameluke follows, throwing his arm familiarly around my friend's stiff shoulders. They head into the shadows of the kitchen and ladies' cabin.

Behind us, the Saint John's festivities are beginning. A horn tosses its vibrato across the lanterns like fat into fire. A galley slave raises his voice in song.

"Are you a scholar or a diplomat?" I ask, suddenly aware of his eyes on mine.

"You have to be a little of both in my profession." He studies me as if gauging how interested I truly am in his response. "If you are introducing one language to another, you must first cajole them, get them to touch hands; it's too easy to treat translation as a rape— to usurp the meaning of the weaker language and force it into the characters of the stronger. Translation must be a seduction, Friar, with all the slow persuasions of a willing kidnap.

"I've learned all known languages but one." Ser Niccolo turns
away from me and stares deep into the ship's shadows. "I've not yet
mastered the vocabulary of madness."

Suddenly I know where I've seen him before.

"You're the gentleman from Candia! You were looking for a runaway woman!"

He studies me narrowly. "My sister, yes. Now I remember you,"
he says. "You were with a young boy."

"We found her," I cry. "She was on our ship!"

"Where is she?" His eyes follow mine to the ladies' cabin, where
I still expect to see her emerge, wet and guilty. Does her brother
suspect her too?

"She is gone," I tell him regretfully. "She ran off from Rhodes."

"Was she well? Did she appear troubled?"

Brothers, what should I do? Should I address the drowning? Should
I confide my suspicions?

"You needn't say." The translator sighs. "I can see from your face
she is still unwell. Please, Friar," he begs, gripping my knee urgently,
"if she should return—keep her for me. You have no idea what she
might do."

I do know. But dare I say?

A pilgrim strikes a tabor. Someone squeezes a bladder pipe. Ser
Niccolo releases me, looks about him in despair. All around, the
pilgrims pick up the drum's tempo, stomp their feet, clapping gaily
along. Before tonight, I had never beheld the practice of clapping
the hands for joy; I knew it only from the Forty-seventh Psalm: "O
clap your hands, all ye people; shout unto God with the voice of
triumph." I would never have imagined that the sound of many
men's clapping could kindle such emotion in my breast. Sensing
my confusion, Niccolo slides behind me, snakes his arms through
my arms, takes my hands in his, brings the four together. John comes
back with another bottle of malvoisie, but I can no longer feel my
legs, my hands under the stranger's hands. Before I know what's
happening, Ser Niccolo grabs me by the waist and swings me up and
around, wildly, until the individual lanterns on their strings above
resolve into a single heavenly wheel of fire. Like a frenzied Israel-

ite, I put my hands together and feel the vibration ring deep in my chest, shoot out through my elbows. Ser Niccolo laughs at my amazement; before I know what he's about, he slaps me with a sloppy, winey kiss of peace—full on my laugh-stretched lips.

"True translators know there is no language without persuasion, no persuasion without seduction," he shouts in Latin, Italian, German, in love with my shock and the language of stinging palms. His hands are on my body, but his eyes are out there in the night, shooting sparks into dark corners, looking, still looking. On the landing by the ladies' cabin, I see his friend, the Mameluke, wave.

I barely remember John pulling me away, his mouth on my ear— "Felix, we don't even know this man"—or their departure, as abrupt and unexpected as their arrival. I can't tell you if the tears on my cheeks, as I stand abandoned in the middle of the ship, dizzy and hot, afraid to move for fear of falling, are from shame or loss or laughter.

I only know today is the longest day of the year, and night has suddenly fallen.

A Bad Wind

"It's that merchant." Ursus's voice is like a nail in my skull. "He won't get out of bed."

A bad wind hit us just outside the Cyprus harbor. The stomach sea churns, belching fish that panic midair and plunge back down its gullet. In vain, the sailors tack, the oarsmen row, inching us laterally along. We're all seasick from last night's festival.

"Let him rest, Ursus. He'll be fine."

"I don't think so, Friar. He says he's dying. He called for a confessor."

"Why don't you run along and fetch Archdeacon John for him?"

"Archdeacon John suggested I run along and fetch you."

What choice do I have? I shade my eyes with my book and walk unsteadily to the stairs. Like a fart in the chapel, Ursus follows.

"The merchant might prefer to be alone with his private thoughts, son."

Near the prow of the ship, the Betrayer Tucher sits at Emelia Priuli's side while she throws dice with some Frenchmen.

"Run along and remind your father there is less at sea to distract God's attention away from our sinning selves."

It takes a few minutes for me to adjust to the woody darkness and fetid stench below. Wine sweat, when it pushes through the pores of several hundred hung-over pilgrims, mingling with the aroma of filthy feet and unwashed hair, is more likely to rouse a man than the loudest cock crow. Constantine must be extraordinarily ill to have remained in bed.

I know you are wondering, brothers, why I have not brought with me the Sacrament of Eucharist for a man who is supposedly dying. And yet, my brothers, this is a privation you cannot imagine until you have actually set sail, until the first storm hits and pilgrims wail and cry out for the body of Christ to comfort them. Then, frightened and seasick, you would run to the captain, only to be told, "No, Friar, the Church does not allow Christ's body to be carried on ship." What? You would rail against Holy Mother Church! Could she so abandon her needy children? But you would be wrong to accuse her, brothers. With contemplation and reflection you would realize the Eucharist might not be celebrated on board ship for five good reasons: First, because the Host is made of bread and cannot be well preserved at sea; after three days it becomes watery and moldy and melts away into liquid paste. Second, because the Host must be kept beside a burning light; and, as I said earlier, through sailor's superstition no lights are allowed to burn on deck. Third, because of want of due reverence; during a storm, sailors must run around to secure the ship, and all would be overturned, priest, sacrament, and altar together. The fourth reason the Eucharist may not be kept aboard ship is because of the folly of bad Christians: Imagine, my brothers, that a storm should blow up; were the consecrated Host on board, how easy it would be for the pilgrims to turn to the Host and say, "If Thou be Christ, save Thyself and us!" Fifth and last, the Host may not be kept on board because of the ease with which men vomit there; should a storm arise immediately after a priest had celebrated mass, he would, by force of nature, be compelled to vomit forth the Body of Christ, which thing, as some among us know, is horrible to behold.

Because of these five reasons, dying men aboard ships are denied the last consolation of the Church. If Constantine is as ill as he believes himself to be, I can do little more for him than trace a dry cross on his forehead and hear his confession.

When I reach his pallet, I'm shocked at how greatly his wife's absence of only forty-eight hours has changed him. His dirty fingernails rest beside clouded, bloodshot eyes. Next to him, a shallow ceramic chamber pot sloshes with thin green vomit. I almost gag at the smell.

"Constantine?" I kneel beside him, breathing through my mouth. "You must give over this grief."

"Felix? Is that you?" He's looking right at me. "Are we on the Ocean?"

"Yes, Constantine," I tell him. "We're in the boat."

"Felix? If my body is thrown to the fishes after I die, can God still resurrect me?"

What errors men entertain! I smile indulgently.

"Saint Augustine tells us that if a man is starving and, to save himself, eats another man, even if the eaten man is absorbed into the starving man's flesh, God knows to whom the body belongs. Should fish eat you, Constantine, God can extract your essence from the bubbles they exhale. They will only have borrowed your body for a time."

"Still," he moans, "don't let the fish borrow me. I don't want anything to make use of my body. Do you promise, Felix? Do you promise on Saint Katherine's life?"

"You're not going to die, Constantine. You are simply melancholy."

"Promise me. On Katherine's life."

His lips are white and cheesy from lack of water. Truly, he does look very ill.

"I promise," I say at last.

"I need to make a confession, Friar, and there are no priests of my faith on board."

Like an infant, he wills his eyes to focus. For the first time I know he really sees me.

"What do you want to say, Constantine?"

"I was the first one, you see. I was the first to understand what her saint wanted."

"Constantine." I brush the merchant's hair from his sweaty forehead. "I'm afraid you're making very little sense today."

"Up until I came, Katherine only asked for icons; she only needed to see herself to know she existed. I began the whole awful thing, Friar. I brought Arsinoë the first bone."

"Constantine, what are you saying?"

"At first Arsinoë was horrified, but her brother took the rib and thanked me. He said Katherine had at last found a way to come to his sister."

My hand falls away from his hair. Has the merchant lost his mind? Does he honestly expect me to believe Saint Katherine would make a pilgrimage to a mere girl?

"When other people found out Katherine wanted to come to her Tongue, they began to bring bones as well. Some were purchased; some, I know, were stolen. They were so desperate, Felix. I knew they wouldn't stop until they'd brought Arsinoë her entire saint."

I shudder at the image. A whole town lined up at the door, each neighbor holding a femur or a rib. I see a little girl with an elbow, a dog with a foot in its mouth.

"Constantine, if this horrible thing is true, as her husband why didn't you put a stop to it?"

"I have a horrible lie to confess, Friar."

Our galley hits a swell and Constantine's chamber pot sloshes onto his mattress.

"The woman Arsinoë is not my wife."

"Friar! Come quick!" Ursus calls from far away.

"What do you mean not your wife? Why is she with you?"

"She came to my shop five days ago. I know she had the bones with her."

Ursus pounds down the steps, his boots echoing through the hollow belly of the ship. Constantine rolls back on his side.

"What is it, Ursus?" I ask sharply.

"You'll never believe!" He yanks my robes, nearly pulling me off my feet.

"Just a minute."

"The Archdeacon says you must come *now*!"

Helplessly, the merchant coughs a rope of black bile into his chamber pot. He can't hold back any longer; miserable tears squeeze from his eyes. I lean over him and speak clearly into his ear.

"I will be back, Constantine, and when I return I want you to tell me everything." I wipe his stained mouth with the bedsheet. "And no more talk of dying."

The glare on deck blinds me, and I have to throw my arm over
my eyes to let them readjust. When I regain my faculties, I see, from
a distance, John and Conrad leaning over the ship's prow, gesticu-
lating wildly. Ursus drags me over.

"Is it a Troyp?" I ask. The waves are high and loud.

"No, something stranger," John shouts. He turns to Conrad.
"They won't make it from here. Send them around to the steps."

I follow my friends along the curve of the boat to where the stair
rungs descend into the sea. There, way below us, is a small two-
oared boat, very like the one we use to row ashore when we're anchored. Unfortunately for this little boat, the bad wind has agitated
the sea tremendously, so that one minute the craft is far below our
galley and, the next, feet above, completely at the mercy of the
swells.

"Here they come," John calls. "On the count of three . . ."

Conrad leans far out over the water to net a fish.

Like a trick acrobat upon the back of a great green horse, the
merchant's wife rides the cresting wave. She raises her arms to
steady herself and steps onto the rough triangle of the rowboat's
neck, nodding to her servant to dig in with his oars, so as not to
smash into the galley. Before she has perfectly gained her balance,
the wave bucks under her, lifting the small craft a good four feet
above us; I have just decided she's waited too long when suddenly,
with a cry, she leaps.

On the wall of our refectory at Ulm we have a painting of the
Annunciation. In it the Archangel Gabriel appears to the sleeping
Virgin as a blur of raised knees and frothing robes, bursting into her
room as one having just sprinted through a twilight evening to tell
glad tidings. In this suspended moment when the merchant's wife
blots out the sun with her pedaling legs and graceful arms, I too
expect a miracle. Let her change into a dove, dear Lord, and fly away
from here. Let her return to the waves like an underweight fish
caught too soon. Let her become anything she likes so long as she
disappears and no longer darkens my pilgrimage.

She strikes the deck hard in her fall, and Conrad quickly gathers
up her unconscious body. The skin under her eyes is a skein of bro-

ken purple veins, and a cut across her eyebrow has only barely scabbed over, kept soft and white by exposure to salt water. The battering of her face doesn't prepare me for the shock of her collarbones when Conrad removes her water-soaked gorget and loosens her bodice. Like a grotesque queen, she wears a violet and green necklace of mottled bruises across her chest, the pendant of which trails across her cleavage to a ragged ruby scar. Suddenly aware of Ursus staring, I dispatch him to find some malvoisie.

Her eyes snap open. "The other ship?"

Like a startled animal, Arsinoë bolts from John's lap and flings herself half over the ship's side, craning to see from where we've come. All I can make out is the receding figure of her hired boat being swiftly swept back toward shore by the bad wind. I point it out to her.

"No, the other pilgrim ship."

"Don't worry. The captain says we'll beat them to Jerusalem," I tell her, gently easing her back onto the galley floor.

"I've made it?"

"Yes," I say. "You're back among the pilgrims."

"You know I was left behind."

"We looked everywhere for you."

"A Turk." She struggles to a sitting position. "Off Rhodes. He took me."

"Shhh. You're safe now."

"He beat me, you see."

"Where is that wine?" John bellows. It's obvious that between her ordeal and this fall, the merchant's wife has sunk deep into shock. But what has happened to John? He cannot bear to touch her but stares transfixed, like a man watching his town burn. I take the small glass of malvoisie from Ursus, when he returns, and hold it to her lips. She gulps greedily.

"We must get her out of these wet clothes," Conrad tells me, helping her off the galley floor and wrapping his cloak around her shoulders. The merchant's wife is soaked and trembling.

"Were you followed?" John asks. He's right. Where there is one Turkish ship, there are bound to be others. We should tell the captain.

She shakes her head. "I'm sure they think me dead."

"Your husband was ready to follow you to the grave." I stumble on the word *husband*, thinking of the merchant's unhinged confession.

"Constantine is ill?"

"He called for a confessor," Ursus offers.

She breaks away from Conrad and stumbles downstairs.

We find her, below, watching the rise and fall of the merchant's narrow chest. His body spasms, his hand jerks from her grasp, and patiently she retrieves it, cradles it in her lap. I read once about a Celtic finger language in which each joint stood for a letter of the alphabet. Arsinoë smooths his skin, erasing her history off each knuckle of her false husband's hand. As her clothes dry, they thicken the air with the briny scent of mildew. I suggest she change, but I don't think she hears me.

"May I give him some water?" she asks at last.

John rummages through the sand belowdeck and hands her a cool goatskin. Tenderly, she raises the merchant's head, dribbles a bit of orange water into her palm, and holds it against his mouth. When he makes no move to swallow, she separates his lips and pours the water onto his tongue.

"He has a fever," she whispers.

"He thought you were dead," I say.

Without a word, our barber steps in and ministers to the patient: listens to his heart, thumps his hypochondria, lifts his eyelids. Conrad examines the bucket of vomit and the black stains on his bedcovers and sadly shakes his head.

"He is very ill." I translate Conrad's German for Arsinoë. "And this black seems more than seasickness. Conrad is afraid it is one of his organs."

Arsinoë nods. Hot, fat tears splash onto Constantine's face.

"Conrad," I whisper, "will you take Ursus upstairs?"

I wait until they leave before addressing her.

"Madame," I say gently, "your husband was confessing to me at the time you reappeared. He was very troubled and not making much sense. If I am to absolve him, I need to know the truth. Are you his wife?"

John looks up startled.

"No," Arsinoë says, almost inaudibly. "I am not his wife."

"He said you appeared at his shop five days ago and that you had on your person some bones."

"Felix!" John shouts. "What are you suggesting?"

But Saint Katherine's Tongue nods her head slowly. "Yes. I appeared at his shop five days ago."

"And where are the bones, Madame?"

"Felix, *stop*!" John orders. "She is obviously very ill."

With a sob, the Tongue throws herself over the merchant's sweating body. "Constantine, wake up!" she cries. "I need you!"

"Madame!" I pull her up, but John snatches her away.

"Come along, my lady." He encircles her protectively with his arm. "You have been through a terrible ordeal. Let's go upstairs and get Conrad to look at your wounds."

The Archdeacon throws me a disgusted look as he leads Arsinoë away. Constantine moans in his delirium and stretches out his withered hand.

At least you have a hand with which to beg, I think to myself. What have you done with my wife's?

Calm

Earlier, I mentioned several perils of the sea that plague pilgrims and terrorize them on their voyage, and yet there is one danger of which the inexperienced would never think; nor is it to be found in books. When the winds are silent and the sea is dumb, a calm comes over the Ocean that is more distressing to pilgrims than anything other than actual shipwreck. I have seen men suffer during storms, vomit, and grow weak, but many more have I seen sicken and die during a calm at sea.

When no winds blow and the ship stays fixed in its place, everything on board begins to rot. The drinking water stinks; salted meat spawns maggots, flies, worms, and lice. Men on board grow lazy and sleepy from the unrelenting heat or, worse, indulge in hatred, envy, melancholy, and spleen. On the day after Arsinoë's return, our ship suffers from such a calm. The bad wind drops and is replaced, more maddeningly, by no wind at all. Those who diced the day before, and lost, harbor murder in their hearts against their compatriots who diced and won. Abovedeck there is rage and torpor; below, stagnation and death.

Like a Christian Hermes, I conduct souls from one level to the next.

Down into the underworld, I lead the merchant's wife. John finally persuaded her late the night before to take some rest and let us watch over her husband. Just after dawn, I climb the steps to the ladies' cabin, expecting to find Arsinoë deeply asleep next to the Cypriot lady-in-waiting. Instead, I surprise her kneeling before the carnelian trunk, mouthing a prayer in the gathering light. When she sees me, she rises and silently follows me down to where her not-husband lies dying.

Up into the light of day I lead John, when the merchant's wife asks for solitude in which to bid her husband good-bye. Neither of us has slept, and the glaring sun upstairs induces in us a cranky, blinking drowsiness. To stay awake, we search each other for lice, wiping the ones we pop between our fingernails on the rigging where we sit. I stare out across the water, listening to the soft plash of ripples against the boat, letting John's fingers root through my hair. The vermin scuttle before his nails, tickling my scalp, dropping into the collar of my tunic, and swimming down my sweaty back. The Perfidious Tucher sits some feet away from us, pounding his infested shirt between two rocks he has collected for this purpose. He has endured much under-the-breath teasing for his refusal to touch the bugs, and now his exposed back is turning a deep pink in the morning sun. I run my fingers through my beard, and they come away covered in eggs.

To stay awake, we talk of Jerusalem.

In Jerusalem there will be wholesome foods to eat like new-killed mutton and eggs with cheese. Live water will bubble up from the earth to slake our thirsts, and the breezes that rustle across the Mount of Olives will dry the sweat from our swollen faces. I recite for John whole passages of Saint Jerome's letters to Paula and Eustochium, describing his life in exile. The Holy Land was perfect, Jerome has written, except that he carried his forced separation from them like a pebble in his shoe. John and I think on Jerome with selfish envy. We are a mere two days from Jerusalem, and yet it feels like God has stretched out His arm and set His palm on our ship, holding us in place like a father stays an impatient child.

John comes up with the game of putting saints to spices when, after an hour, we've grown too heartsick to talk on about Jerusalem. After all, he says, Saint Bernard wrote that saints' lives added spice to mankind's otherwise bland diet of mortality. If, as John suggests, we assign the precious saffron to the Virgin Mary and the

essential salt to Her Son, where on the palate do the legions of the
blessed reside?

Since John is the inventor, he begins. Oregano? he asks. To which
saint do we assign oregano?

I think for a moment. Saint Anthony of the Desert, I reply, reminding him of the thorny herb bushes that perfume the wilderness. During one of the dry storms over the desert, lightning might
have struck a shrub, reducing it to a cloud of thick aromatic smoke.
Asleep in his cell, the old ascetic might have dreamed of roasting
shanks of meat, dripping juice thick with flecks of the oregano bush.
He might have awaked suddenly in that sharp, smoky night and
understood the old wisdom: It is far easier to tame one's manhood
than one's stomach.

Hot pepper, I demand of John, raising the stakes. I only once tasted
this spice, and my tongue throbbed for days after. John laughs. That's
easy. Saint Dominic, the founder of your order. During her pregnancy, didn't his mother dream of a dog with a torch in his mouth?

Rosemary? Immediately, I think of Saint Agnes, whose sign is
the lamb. One of my earliest memories, before I entered the novitiate, was of my aunt's mutton stew, deliciously oiled with fat and
rosemary.

Mustard? I see the dusty road to Damascus and the yellow cloud
that rose when Paul fell to his knees in front of Christ.

Clove? John imagines the sharp black teeth of the dragon that
swallowed Saint Margaret.

On and on we name—basil, coriander, sesame—and as we play I
come to understand why Bernard chose this metaphor. Like barrels
of incorruptible spice, all the early saints traveled from the East to
preserve the West. Whether, like Paul, they came in person or, like
the blessed Katherine, as a cult and legend only, all the ancient saints
at some point boarded a ship and sailed to us. I've often wondered
how a princess martyred in Alexandria and translated to fiery Sinai
could find herself alive in the hearts of forest-dwelling inland Europeans. The returning ships of our ancestors must have brought her
legends wrapped up with their pepper and cardamom, heedless of
the peasants running along the docks, gathering their dropped sto-

ries like precious peppercorns that escaped their packaging. Once taken to market, a merchant might have related the color of the saint's hair to an Italian housewife buying cinnamon for her vats of prunes. Another might have handed over her height with a cone of green cumin. In this way, Saint Katherine was transported and reconstructed in Europe, given back her legs, and handed off the boat. Her story was told and retold in every language where ships sail, and there again she is like a spice, for thyme tastes the same on the tongue of a German as it does on an Italian, as on a Swede.

When he grows weary of his own game, John suggests we check on the merchant's wife. I take a cupful of sludgy water and follow him downstairs. It is cooler below, but moist, as though a day and night's worth of exhalations have snagged along the floorboards. As for me, I can hardly breathe for the wormy smell of the liquid I carry, and I know if the merchant is not yet dead, one sip will surely kill him. I needn't have worried. A single glance is enough to see he is well on his way to where no amount of water can slake his thirst.

During the night, after we sent his wife upstairs, the merchant began to convulse. His bowels let go just before dawn, and while I fetched Arsinoë, John had managed to soak up what he could of the watery mess. We assume that's why the merchant is now lying naked on his cowhair tick, toes to the sky, privates draped with a triangle of sheet. Arsinoë must have tried to clean him.

I stare down at his sunken chest and watch a single flea flip from nipple to groin. For a second it burrows through a gray field of hair; then, with a twist, it sails through the air in a perfect arc. On the fourth jump, it disappears for good under the sheet.

Both John and I know it is time to administer last rites, yet neither of us moves to do it. We are both keenly aware of the Church's stance on the Eastern heresy, and without a recantation we understand Constantine will have to die unshriven. While silent glances pass between John and me, Arsinoë's great brown eyes remain fixed on the soiled clothes in her lap, the garments she has stripped from her husband. Perhaps if she would turn them on John, he would put aside his scruples and ask her if perhaps she thinks Constantine might have embraced the Latin faith in his heart. If she thinks,

Perhaps, yes, why not? John might trace a dry cross over her husband's forehead and absolve him. But his wife does not raise her eyes to find John's expectantly fixed on hers. She merely examines her husband's clothing, turning it over and over in her lap, as though searching for holes.

Since I can do nothing for him as a Christian, I once more lace my winged sandals and gently lower my caduceus to Constantine's trembling eyelids. For all his delusions, he was a kindly man. It is only fitting he should have an arm to lean on as he totters off to Hell.

ii

Storage

Our wretched sheep stand in a circle with their worn velvet noses just touching. When I approach, the leader shuffles away and waits for the flock to fitfully readjust itself. Across from the sheep, with their jointed legs folded under them, the remaining assembled goats blink up at me suspiciously, watching me steal what remains of their dirty straw. These parched animals rise and stiffly follow behind where I've gathered up their grass, to lick the moisture from the floorboards with their long pink tongues.

I join Conrad downstairs, where he has already laid out the merchant; he wipes the dead man with a preserving mixture of myrrh and myrtle juice, slicking the hair along Constantine's shins, cupping a puckered foot. The pilgrims will go up to dinner soon, and that's when we'll finish him. Should the sailors discover us, they would not suffer his corpse to remain on board; but I gave Constantine my word, and on Katherine's life I won't let the fishes borrow him.

I place the cloakful of straw beside our silent barber, still as much a mystery to me as the first time we met. The Tuchers and I were hurrying through the small German/Italian border village of Botzen, afraid for our lives. On one side, Botzen is crushed against high mountains; on the other, miles of pestilent marshes bleed into its borders. Fever bred in the swamps gets trapped by the mountains; consequently, so many of Botzen's inhabitants suffer feverish symptoms that it is no longer counted a disease among them. When one friend sees another pale and shaking and asks after his health, he's answered, "Oh, thank God I'm not ill, my friend, it's only the fever that alters my looks."

Conrad stoppers his vial of myrrh and neatly nestles it in the trunk among the tools of his trade: razors, lancets, strops, antidotes, cups, and bristling brushes. He was carrying this trunk on his back when we passed him on the road out of Botzen, our noses covered against the contagion. When we offered him a ride, we learned it also housed what few possessions had not been burned belonging to his wife and small son, carried off earlier that week by the Fever that was not a Fever.

"Where did they go?" I ask, realizing John and Arsinoë are missing.

"They left as soon as I got here."

I'm relieved, actually. John would vehemently oppose this plan.

"You'll get the salt and wine?" I ask.

Conrad nods. "And a lantern."

I make a quick search under the sheets for Constantine's robe, hoping at least to cover him for the move. When I can find it nowhere, I wrap the soiled sheet under his armpits and toga him like a Roman statesman. Conrad blocks the hatch from view, while I unceremoniously stuff our senator into the shallow hold belowdeck.

Now to picture this hold, brothers, you must understand a galley is not flat-bottomed like other ships but tapers at an angle so steep that it cannot stand upright on land. Sand fills the belly of the ship almost to the floorboards of the pilgrims above, and we bury in this sea-cold ballast all our perishable goods. Once Conrad lowers the hatch, I am no longer able to stand but must crawl backward like a crab dragging a heavy log of driftwood. I must pull Constantine well beyond where any pilgrim might rummage for a midnight snack.

Only when I've reached the darkest corner of the ship, a place where no light penetrates through the floorboard cracks, where no noise reaches me, do I stop. Constantine's heels have dredged up someone's chilled bottle of half-drunk wine, and I treat myself to the rest of it. How silent and still it is beneath the pilgrims' feet. The pitching is less than on deck because the angle here is less acute, but the calm is eerier, a sort of embryonic rocking, like being nailed in a coffin when the rains flood your graveyard.

Alone in the dark, with this expired merchant between my knees, I confess, brothers, my mind misgives a bit. I know you would not have me perpetuate this fraud, and I do not want to disappoint you; but you know not the ignorance of sailors. I've provided numerous examples of their superstitions, but by far the most disturbing, to me and my promise, is their insufferance of anything ill-omened on board their ship. While at Venice, our party was shown an animal called the Elephant, a huge and terrible creature with a nose that hung to the ground and two ferocious teeth the length of a man's arm on either side, which nonetheless would perform wondrous tricks at a simple sign from its master. This master sadly told us he had owned an Elephant prior to this one, had taken it to Germany where he made much money, and then set sail with it to Britain, when a violent storm blew up at sea. The sailors, ever at the mercy of their superstitions, cast that poor gentle beast overboard, and so it perished. Hark, then: If sailors could be so hard-hearted with a creature as rare as the noble Elephant, think not that they would hesitate to rid themselves of a creature so common as a dead merchant?

But how shall the sailors be deceived, you ask? Through the fearsome power of words, brothers. With words alone, I, Friar Felix Fabri, can keep this man alive until we dock—always downstairs or having just gone above—until, once arrived at land, with more words I can slay him. I will need to whip the name of Constantine around the ship like a wandering Jew, never allowed to rest, always somewhere else, in order to keep my promise made on Katherine's life. I will have to give him sleepless nights and send him up on deck, when it's time for pilgrims to come to bed; I will have to give him listless afternoons belowdeck, deny him appetite, when pilgrims are above. I will tell the pilgrims he has not died, and thus he shall live, brothers. Wonder not at this strange juxtaposition of death and language, for Saint Augustine tells us words are like men's mortality: "Our speech is accomplished by signs emitting a sound; but our speech would not be whole unless one word pass away when it has

sounded its parts, so that another might succeed it." Thus, as speech
is predicated on dying, so sometimes dying is keyed to speech. Gently, I brush the sand off the merchant's chilled body, grasp his head,
and shake it, too, free of sand. Say good-bye to your shell, Constantine
Kallistos, merchant of Crete; you have become no more than a
breath in my mouth.

But enough. There is much to be done, and Conrad is waiting. I
follow my own trough back through the sand to the hatch we used.
Waiting for me are two bags of rock salt, two skins of water, four
bottles of lesser wine, the cloak of hay, and Conrad's trunk. But there
is no sign of Conrad. Cautiously, I lift the hatch to see if I spy him.

"There you are, Friar!" Ursus claps his hand on my shoulder.
"You're missing dinner."

"I was . . ." What could I have possibly been doing beneath the
floorboards, covered in sand? "I was saying my prayers."

"Well, come on." Ursus rolls his eyes. "The merchant's wife is
telling her story. Where is the merchant?"

"In the latrine." I practice on my charge, who seems not to doubt
my story.

I am quickly hauled on deck to the long dinner benches set up
near the animal pen. Already seated, Conrad looks up apologetically.
Arsinoë sits uncomfortably beside him, grilled by my patron.

"When he grabbed you, did you cry out?"

"No . . . I was too startled. Anyway, his hand covered my mouth."

"Were his fingernails painted? I've read they paint their fingernails."

"I couldn't see, but, yes, maybe they were painted."

"I'll bet he called on the name of Allah when he leapt."

"No, I think he was silent. Though later perhaps he called on
Allah."

I take my place at the crowded table next to Feckless Tucher, who
pays me no mind, intent as he is on the merchant's wife. She wears
the exhausted air of a guest who has arrived late at night but is kept
up talking by an oblivious host. John sits to her left, carving a picture in the table with his knife. When I finally catch his eye, his
expression is unreadable.

"Were there other women?" Ursus asks, leaning in like his father.

This seems to disturb Arsinoë. I see her knuckles whiten around her cup and she rises a little on her elbows.

"I was kept with the other prisoners. Women from all over the world: blond women, dark flaky-skinned women, blind women, and armless women. Only one thing did they have in common. They were completely naked except for a single golden manacle worn around their ankle, and they sprawled like prostitutes on mounds of embroidered pillows."

"Pardon me, my lady." Ursus giggles. "But do the Saracen women have . . . hair?"

Arsinoë drops her eyes, and Lord Tucher smacks his son across the ear.

John stares off to his left, away from the woman, toward the sea. I see his chest rise and fall in a sigh.

"They had volumes of hair, which they draped artfully." She pretends to misunderstand. "But I can't talk about it anymore. I'm sorry."

While the other diners contemplate this scene, populating their own Turkish cabins with dark bodies on embroidered pillows, I use the opportunity to put together a plate for myself. The ship's cook only slaughters animals that appear ready to die anyway, so the meat is, as usual, gamey and discolored. The boat is rocking so, it takes three tries before I can spear a piece of dead goat and add to it some grainy suet. A meager meal to be sure, but I am famished.

"I know you must be tired, Madame." Lord Tucher can not remain silent. "But how did you escape?"

She seems to have more difficulty with that, and for a second I think John is about to answer for her. He's an expert on the Turk, after all.

"I put myself in Saint Katherine's hands," she says at last.

"I'm surprised she had the strength to help you." Tucher shrugs.

"What do you mean?" asks the merchant's wife.

"First getting her relics stolen, now letting her monastery fall to the Saracens? Seems to me her influence is waning."

"What is he talking about?" Arsinoë turns, panic-striken, to me.

"Nothing, Lady," I say, swallowing the murderous rage I feel toward that most perfidious patron. "He is merely repeating a rumor told him by a faithless slut dismissed from the court at Cyprus. Pay it no mind."

"Friar!" Lord Tucher stands.

Arsinoë starts up, then suddenly collapses back to her bench, completely colorless. John leaps up to help her.

"I'll see you to your cabin, Madame." He looks at none of us but whisks Arsinoë away. Emelia Priuli angrily leaves the ladies' cabin when the two barge in and close the door behind them.

The sun is setting, and an easterly wind has whipped up. Sailors wrestle with their tarred ropes, trying to lower the sails before the strong new wind pushes us back into our wake. Above, a thick windfall bruise of clouds discolors the twilight. It's the first breeze of the day, but it brings little comfort, being the wrong direction for us. Tucher and I sit in fuming silence.

"Excuse me, Lord Tuker." La Priuli has made her mincing, harlotrous way over to our table. "I know you were speaking with that woman a few moments ago. Do you know where her husband is?"

Ursus answers, saving me the trouble. "He's in the latrine."

She curls her lip at the boy and addresses his father. "He must stifle his wife," La Priuli says. "She is making herself hateful to me."

"My dear woman." Lord Tucher rises, but Priuli refuses his seat. "What is she doing?"

"All night long, keeping me awake, nothing but prayer, prayer, prayer. And in that barbaric language of hers."

"It *is* a pilgrimage," I offer.

"For Christians, Friar," the waiting woman snaps. "I had to put up with enough Schismatics on Cyprus."

"Are you able to bear with her another few days, Madame?" I can see Lord Tucher weighing this woman's beauty against Arsinoë's disruptiveness. "We're almost to Palestine."

"I cannot endure it!" she cries. "All night it's 'Please, Saint Katherine,' 'Dear Saint Katherine,' but not a single prayer addressed to our Blessed Virgin. Not one to our Savior. She keeps that saint like a house pet."

"We're going downstairs, now, Madame," I say stiffly, "to check on her husband. We'll pass along your warning."

"Do so." She sniffs. "If she's not out of my cabin by tonight, I'm going to the captain."

A narrow flash of lightning strikes the water miles away, and thunder lows like a lost cow in the whale's belly.

"Come on, Conrad." I rise unsteadily. "Let's go tell the merchant."

The Cavity

So much blood.

I think about the world's infinite hollow spaces and how many concentric skins we all wear, while the angry Ocean wedges its fingers into the ship's belly and Conrad lifts out the stomach.

Water and blood.

"Hold the lamp above," he tells me, and I catch it just as it's ready to topple. To keep the body from rolling away, Conrad plants one knee on its shoulder, the other on its groin. He reaches under himself to unravel the long tube of intestines.

The intestines are hollow, the stomach is hollow. I dig a hole in the sand and fill it with these walls. So many borders within the body holding back the empty space.

We didn't bring a bucket to catch the blood, but Conrad thinks the worst that can happen is that it will seep down and form a thin table beneath the sand. He works quietly and calmly, detaching the heart and lungs with sharp twists of his wrist.

"A little higher, please."

The ship pitches and, in trying to catch myself, I smash the lantern against the bridge of Constantine's nose. Constantine? Did the man ever exist outside of this shadowy cave?

"Here's what did it," Conrad says, snipping away at a melted mass just above the fat-pillowed kidney. "This organ exploded," he says. "See the infection?"

He hands me an empty casing, but in the darkness I can't distinguish its green from its red. I bury this fallen wall with the ones that held.

"Hand me the water."

"What?"

Inches above our heads, frantic aimless running tells us the pilgrims have begun to panic. I hear trunks crash to the floor with each lurch of the ship, and iron pots roll across flexing feet. I needn't have worried about our voices carrying or our lantern inviting suspicion. The rough seas have completely overwhelmed us.

We flush the cavity with seawater and sprinkle it with wine. Turn him over, let him drain.

"The salt!" Conrad yells.

This part feels less unnatural to me, for I have often dressed meat for the monastery. I pour a steady stream between his ribs and spread it with my hand until every inch of pink inner flesh is lumpy with it. Since there's no water left, I run my hand through the sand until it comes clean.

Conrad is shoving fistfuls of straw up into the hollow neck, and I help stuff the pelvis, replacing the viscera with cold yellow grass up to the ribs. We work quickly, because, though neither of us has expressed our fears out loud, we are both terrified of being trapped below during the storm. Conrad unearths the merchant's buried intestine, shears off a long resilient strand with his knife, and threads it through the eye of his needle.

"Try to flatten him some, will you?"

I've stuffed the cavity too full, and now the flaps of skin no longer meet. I tug them together and hold them in place while he sews. Constantine is a lumpy hermaphroditic mess by the time we've finished, with a concave stomach and bulging hairy breasts, but he'll keep until we dock. Quickly, we wind him from head to foot in his sheet, and Conrad sacrifices his black cloak to provide an extra layer, knowing he can retrieve it when we land. Should a nosy pilgrim stumble upon the corpse tomorrow, he would be completely unrecognizable.

"Done?"

Conrad shrugs.

We sit for a moment studying the swaddled, misshapen figure, too tired to do much more than listen to the Ocean hammer against the ship's walls. Was this how it happened with Constantine? Did the force of grief rage so incessantly against his poor weak organs that one could only escape in explosion? Will it be the same for us, pulsing inside this hollow heart, when the storm finally hits?

A splintered vessel? A hundred open veins?

The Storm

Filthy bilge water has overflowed its well, sloshing stink across the floorboards. When I point this out to a wretched Homesick, he turns his lantern on his ruined biscuit, his sodden hymnal, his mattress, and I understand the time we've spent below preserving Constantine has been a time of devastation for those above. Men stumble among their belongings, trying to suspend their lanterns and baggage above the intrusive water. They make little progress, for when the ship pitches, all that aspires to height is brought low. Water cascades down the stairs from waves breaking over the prow and pours through the badly tarred ceiling in torrents. My pallet, when I push my way through the huddle of stunned pilgrims to reach it, lies like a new-risen Delos in a sea of brown water.

"Felix!" A terrified Lord Tucher sees me and grabs my robe. "The slaves say this storm is absolutely unnatural for this time of year," he sobs, "and must be the wrath of God. Pray for us!"

He pulls me reeling, off balance, into a tangle of moaning, supplicating pilgrims. See how Judas Tucher needs me now! Had he only thought of that when he kissed my dream of Sinai on both cheeks and handed it over to the Pharisees!

I will pray for him.

"'Save us, O God, for the waters are come in unto our souls. Send Thine hand from above; rid us and deliver us out of great waters, from the hands of strange children.'"

"You, O Lord, punished a wicked world with a forty-day flood when, after watching generations of perversity and wickedness come of age, You could no longer abide Your children's faithlessness. Rain fell upon them, Lord, welcome at first in their thirsty land, until the rain soaked their robes and wet their skin, tangled their dark hair into ropes against their cheeks. By the fifth day, the bottom stories of their houses flooded, and Your faithless children took their families onto the roof to wait out the storm, worried the water would rise upon them in their sleep and invade their nostrils, stealing away their babies while they dreamed of drowning. By the tenth day, the children who had held cheap their promises to You floated like pond scum on the water's surface, and still You let it rain thirty more days, just to be certain every forsworn, false friend sank to the bottom of the sea."

Pausing for breath, I can hear the sailors above us cry out one to another, each in his own language, heedless of meaning or comprehension. It seems the commonality of words has deserted them, leaving each man little more than a grunting hoarder of sense flinging chaff at his comrades.

"Again, in Moses' day"—I raise my voice over the groaning boat— "You punished betrayal with water, O wise Lord. The Egyptians, who promised the Israelites freedom and safe-conduct across the desert into Zion, went back on their sworn word. When they followed Your chosen people into the parted Red Sea, into that sea which embraces Your blessed Sinai—*the land no man should be denied*—You withdrew Your hand, O Lord, and called down the waters upon them. Like an airless mouth, the Red Sea closed over the hypocrites, sucking them from their horses and grinding them between her currents."

"I am not comforted by this prayer, Friar Felix," Ursus sobs. "Can't we have something else?"

"Let us be worthy, O God, and nothing like these false men who wantonly broke their promises," I shout. "Let us not deserve Your wrath!

"Should You come upon Your petitioners Lord John Tucher and his son Ursus, or upon their humble mouthpiece Brother Felix Fabri of the Preaching Brothers, shipwrecked and without life, I entreat You, do not let them enter Your kingdom in soggy clothes with bones exposed and eyes red from salt water. Undress them from these, their ill-fitting bodies, and translate them as shining spirits into Your house, O Lord."

A lantern crashes to the floor beside me, switching behind it a tail of darkness. Knee to knee we stand in the thick night, sweating from the closeness, grasping fistfuls of tunic and hair in the vain attempt to remain upright. The next wave flings me back against my trunk and the other pilgrims on top of me like a giant attacking octopus made all of startled mouths and slimy legs. I can't breathe, and I feel the gorge rise in my throat.

"Lord Tucher," I call, elbowing my way through the stack, "I must go upstairs for some air."

"No, Felix!" he shouts back, though I can not tell from which open mouth the prohibition comes. "You may not leave me."

I hear the splash as someone above me gives in to seasickness and know it will be mere seconds before hysteria sets in. Instantly, I give a mighty shove and am free, stumbling over fallen pilgrims, tripping over my robes. I pick myself up and slide toward the stairs, stepping on God knows what in the darkness: a loaf of bread? another's pillow? an arm? At the waterfall that was once our ladder, I plunge my hands into the icy wave, arch my neck so that it misses my face, and climb blindly.

Above, all is chaos.

Sailors fight the unwieldy mainsail and hoist in its place the short square *papafigo*, sewn of a hundred individual cloths. Lightning haloes the ship, turning faces blue and the sea dark green. The thunder that follows each bolt seeps deep into the saturated floorboards, until I imagine I'm standing on decades of dead and resurrected storms. And yet it does not rain.

"You, monk." I feel rather than see a man approaching. When he's upon me, I realize it is the ship's soothsayer who sits with the galley's pilot. "Is anyone dead down there?"

My heart stops beating. "Why do you ask?"

"You must tell me." I hear the controlled panic in his voice. "A corpse is like a lightning rod: Death seeking fiercer death. There's no other explanation for this storm."

"That's superstition," I say.

He shakes his head wildly. "It's a lightning rod."

"There's no one dead," I tell him.

"Listen to me, my friend." The soothsayer's long beard scratches my cheek. "If someone dies, come straight to me."

"I will."

What have I done?

I must find John. He understands chaos and passion and death. He'll tell me what to do. I run back to the hatch but, in my haste, trip over the edge of a galley plank. Chained to his bench, the bedazzled Greek slave who rowed us to Colossus huddles miserably in the dark.

"You, slave!" I yell, when the lightning reveals his terror-flaccid face. "Have you seen my friend, the Archdeacon John?"

"Friar Felix!" He brings his shackled hands to his face. "This is the Devil's work. Today too calm, tonight—! We're all going to die!" He yanks at the iron eyelet that attaches his chains to the ship. Should we capsize, this man and all the other slaves will dangle from their chains like grapes on a vine, tightly trestled to their wooden benches.

"No, listen," I say. "It's very important I find John."

"I've done such wicked things in my life, brother. Please, I can't die with them on my conscience."

"You're not going to die. The pilgrims are downstairs praying right now."

A sail spins loose; its sheets snap like a cave of bats suddenly terrified awake.

"We will die. Because there's already a dead on this ship. I can smell it. Only if they find it will we be safe."

I want to slap him.

"That is not a Christian thing to believe. If you don't want to spend more years in Hell than you're already set for, you must stop this superstition."

The slave to his right shrieks as a wild oar strikes him hard in the temple. He moans something in a language I don't understand and shakes the blood from his hair.

"Tell me." I grip his shirt. "Has John been on deck?"

"I saw your friend. Earlier tonight, before it is so dark."

"He's not downstairs, though?"

"No, I saw him upstairs, above, with the Greek man that came to this boat at Crete."

"What Greek man?" I ask. "Do you mean the holy woman, Saint Katherine's Tongue?"

"No, no, I saw him clearly." The galley slave crosses himself and screams when a squat emerald bolt strikes the sea not two hundred yards from our ship. "Your John was struggling with that man. The sad merchant. The husband of the Tongue!"

Constantine?

The sea goes green with fire.

Heaven and Earth

The first drop hits as I frantically push my way through the shoulders and sweating backs of the working men. For a moment, the rain sobers them; they freeze in their efforts, quivering like a pack of hunting dogs sighting a flock.

A naked pilgrim, spiraling rain, runs to the latrine. His ankles are red and his wrists are red and his flapping penis is deep, deep red. The ship moans as a yellow wave breaks over the bow, grainy with sand from the Ocean bed.

Heaven and Earth reversed.

One minute we are atop a lofty mountain, the next we are deep into Hell. The rain, black and cold, kicks me back toward the downstairs hatch. I fight to reach John.

I am responsible. I hollowed out the conduit for Heaven's rage to barrel through this ship. Constantine's empty body, his channel, his lightning rod. We've inverted the world, allowed water to become sky, fire water.

And then I see it. Against a fireball. Hell clutching a dark lantern, poised by Arsinoë's door. Hell in black flapping pilgrim's robes.

The dead and gutted Constantine.

I slam against the torrential rain, feel it jerk my shoulder from its socket, swing my arms behind me. I find the ladder steps in darkness, take them two at a time, praying to be struck and spared what I know awaits. *Don't hurt John,* I pray. *I did it. He has no knowl-*

edge. Fists against the door, wood giving way. I scream John's name, Arsinoë's name, as all God's wrath crashes upon me.

At last the door swings inward, sweeping a curtain of rain into the dark cabin. Inside, a fire has been struck and tucked into a lantern that swings maniacally on a hook above Arsinoë's pallet. Beside the door, the violently trembling frame of John Lazinus stands silent as the grave. It takes a moment for my eyes to adjust, but gradually I become aware of another figure, waiting in the dark corner. His face is partially obscured by his hood, his hands hang at his sides in fists, and if I look closely I can just make out the bulge in his chest where Conrad and I stuffed his cavity too full of straw.

"He's come for his wife, hasn't he?" I ask John, barely able to hear my voice over my pounding heart.

"Arsinoë is gone," he says.

"What has he done to her?"

"Felix, you must let us explain."

John steps in and suddenly Constantine leaps from the shadows, hurling himself at my throat. Instinctively, I grab the merchant's sleeve and fling him to the ground. The ship plunges and he rolls hard down the incline.

"If you'll explain it to him as you did to me, he's got to understand!" John shouts at the merchant. "He's not a monster!"

I felt the chill of death when he touched me.

"Tell him," John commands.

"Constantine," I ask as gently as fear permits, "what have you done with your wife?"

"We've swallowed her." The creature on the floor laughs. "She's in our belly."

"Jesus Christ." John turns away.

The hood falls back; the face comes up; I see the corpse for what it is. She is no less hideous than the demon for whom I'd mistaken her.

John paces the room, steadying her when the pitching of the ship threatens to capsize us, for she will not rise from her knees and I will not help her up.

"I will not let it happen to her, Felix." John speaks through angry tears. "She is determined to continue on alone, and I've seen with my own eyes what Arabs do to unprotected women. I will not let her leave this ship dressed as herself."

Arsinoë's hair mimics Constantine's old-fashioned Julius Caesar cut, releasing its spring around her narrow temples. Could she have possibly cut her own hair so cleanly, or did my piously weeping friend John twine his sympathetic fingers through its length, shear it away in tightening circles, until his fingertips brushed her pale blue scalp? I cannot bear to imagine what took place in this room while Conrad and I crouched in horror, working to preserve her husband's body.

"You are spitting in the face of God," I say, "to counterfeit a dead man."

"You and I have formed a partnership, Friar," the creature says loudly, over the groaning boat. "With a few simple words, you have kept Constantine alive. In his clothes, I can restore form to those words. It is the perfect substitution."

"Felix," John pleads. "Arsinoë was abducted from Rhodes. She stabbed the man who took her and left him for dead. If he's still alive, he will be looking for her. He will be looking for a *woman*."

"Friar." Arsinoë crawls woodenly on her knees to where I stand. "Call me Constantine until we reach Jerusalem. Let me borrow him for only a few days."

She reaches out her hand, but I smack it violently away.

"Enough!" I cry. "I have had enough of your pretenses! I want to know what you are doing on this ship in the first place. Why are you Constantine's wife and then *not* Constantine's wife? Why did he tell me you had Saint Katherine's bones?"

John rushes over and cradles her where she has fallen, her face angry and distorted.

"Tell him what happened on Rhodes," John orders Arsinoë. "Help him understand."

She vehemently shakes her head. Behind her, Lando's treasure-filled trunks squeal against their ropes. Unfettered, Emelia Priuli's carved ebony chest skids across the cabin and crashes into Arsinoë's. She pushes the trunk savagely away.

"He took her from the church," John tells me, ignoring the woman's refusal to speak. "He pressed her face into his robes and ran with her down to the shore. He took her, Felix!"

John hugs the stricken merchant's wife to his chest, covering her with his huge body. The boat plunges and he supports her, pressing his cheek to her shorn head.

"God should have made your hair grow to cover you, poor trespassed darling," he sobs. "Why has He abandoned His virgins?"

I do not want to hear what John says. I want only to know one thing.

"Was I right?" I tug her away from him. "Did you take Saint Katherine's hand from her church in Candia?"

"Yes!" Arsinoë screams, spraying me with saliva. "Yes, I took her hand!"

"Did you take her ear?"

"Yes, I took her ear!"

"Then what have you done with my wife?"

The ship screams under our words, spinning us heavily to our knees and across the floor. Katherine's icons break rank like terrified gilded seaside crabs, scattering across the cabin, flipped onto their backs.

"You don't understand," she sobs. "I took her to save her from a worse fate."

"What worse fate could there be than to be kidnapped and held against your will?" I shake her, catching a mouthful of Constantine's salty fever and death robe. "If her monastery truly has fallen, it is your fault!"

"It was not against her will, Friar Felix!" Arsinoë kicks away from me. "She *chose* to come to me. She told me what she wants."

"I am her husband. I know what she wants."

"You have no idea," Arsinoë shouts, backing up toward her carnelian trunk. "You only know what *you* want."

"Please!" John throws himself between us when I lunge for this evil woman. How dare she claim to know the mind of Heaven? How dare she speak to me this way when she has ruined my pilgrimage, when she has stolen from me the only being in the world that gives me joy? She throws herself across her cheap

wooden trunk when it skids across the lurching cabin, and suddenly I know.

"You have her in there!" I shout. "You have Saint Katherine's bones in that trunk."

"Felix, Constantine was delirious," John yells, grabbing my robes as I leap for the trunk. "You can't believe Arsinoë would have Saint Katherine's relics in there."

I have found her. I remember the distended bag Arsinoë wore around her neck the night she climbed into the sea, how she spoke to it lovingly and covered it in kisses. Katherine has been under my eye this entire time! Arsinoë screams when I pry her from the chest and hammer away its cheap lock with a heavy icon. I feel the wood give, the metal rip from its mooring.

"Don't touch her!" the Tongue screams, clawing at my flesh. *"She wants to go home!"*

I throw open the lid. A rush of sandalwood escapes, like Pandora's final hope.

"Felix, you should be ashamed." John reaches into the trunk and pulls out its contents. "A cloak. A drinking cup. A book. Where are your bones, Felix?"

Arsinoë shoves us aside and stares into the trunk as into a bottomless well. There is nothing there. No hand. No ear. No feedbag full of my wife's body. I turn away in tears. She is not a rival for my wife's affection; she is nothing more than what her brother said she was: a sad, delusional madwoman. How could I have been carried along? The ship pitches and our one source of light, our little lantern, smashes to the ground and rolls crazily downhill, exploding against the wall in a cloud of oil and glass.

"Come away, darling." John fumbles for her, trying to release her from where she grips the trunk. "You have suffered too much."

"You've gone over to him," she whispers into the darkness. "Why?"

"John, listen!"

A loud banging on the door to the cabin. "Open this door!"

"The ship is sinking," John says. "Constantine's blood has eaten a hole."

"That will be the captain, Madame," I say, crouching beside her. "Give yourself up to him," I urge. "He will see you get safely back to Crete. He will find your brother, if you like, and put you back into his care."

This snaps her awake. "How do you know about my brother?" she asks coldly.

"He was here looking for you," I say. "He wants to help you."

"Open this door!"

"Felix?" John asks. "What do we do?"

Before either of us can reach it, the cabin door is violently kicked open. Two figures stand before me, orange and black in a circle of lantern light.

"Where is she?" Emelia Priuli screams. "I told him this was all her fault, blasphemous bitch that she is!"

She pushes past me and bangs into the skittering trunk at her feet. Sharply, she rights herself.

"Hand over the Greek woman," the other figure commands. As he lifts his lantern to survey our dark room, I realize it is not the captain but the ship's soothsayer.

"She angered the Virgin!" Priuli cries. "I told her with all that selfish praying to Katherine she would infuriate Our Holy Mother and Her Son. She's brought Their wrath upon us all!"

I hear the hysteria in the gentlewoman's voice, but I can not force myself to speak. Arsinoë kneels by the trunk, her hood covering her face. John presses himself against the wall to remain standing.

The soothsayer approaches Arsinoë, his lantern shaking in his fist. "Sir, where have you hidden your wife?"

Beside me, John shuts his eyes. I can no longer breathe.

"She's dead," says Constantine the merchant, evenly meeting the soothsayer's eyes. "Felix buried her this evening."

The Mouths of Fishes

A cancer, Friar. You preserved a cancer.

I can't face Lord Tucher or the other muttering pilgrims when I emerge clotted with sand from the ship's belly. Nor can I stand the whispers and moanings when the soothsayer and I lift the sagging V of merchant between us and head for the stairs. I grasp Constantine's ankles and hug his feet to my chest. Despite the two layers of Conrad's cloak and sheet, I feel each individual icy toe against my ribs. Each toe is a cancer.

They follow us, those pilgrims, swallowing their vomit and fear, up the stairs, through the hatch, onto the rainy deck. I feel like an ink drawing of myself, heavily outlined in black, leading that quickly sketched procession. I have darker borders than anyone else; the eye is drawn to me.

We stop in front of the captain, who yells over the wind for the other pilgrims to stay belowdeck so as not to imperil more lives, but they are like those in a trance. The rain lashes them and the boat tilts, yet they hold their diagonal and do not fall. John and Arsinoë stand behind the captain, two brave, defiant men. I drop the merchant at his wife's feet.

Without a word, the captain summons a pair of strong sailors, men I saw scampering like cats along the rigging with St. John's fire in their teeth, to lift the body. Their arms flex and their bony hips shift and then he is gone. The merchant, the merchant's wife, arcing like a white comet over the sea. Rain catching on her tail, dragging him, cold and hissing, down.

As that body breaks the wall of water, spiraling down past porpoises and black octopi, past the beak of the Troyp, who disdains all lifeless prey, I realize I've broken the first promise I have ever sworn on Katherine's life.

The soothsayer smiles. He knew he smelled Death on board.

How We Look for Land

Washed clean by the storm, for two days every corner of our galley smells of drying salt and sunlight. Below, gathered in our little marketplace near the mast, my fellow pilgrims resume the occupations they've pursued since the moment we set sail, a solid month ago today. Some sit over chessboards; some sing songs accompanied by lutes and bagpipes. Some have their heads together discussing worldly matters; some read books; still others laugh aloud for lightness of heart. Others run up the rigging; others jump; others show off their strength by lifting heavy weights. And then there are the pilgrims who accompany all of these, looking on first at one and then another. They end their tour with me, sitting upon the horn, writing to you, my brothers. A glamour has settled upon me for my part in the storm, and these men as they pass by move their fingers in a quick gesture to ward off the evil eye. I find this treatment grievous, brothers, for as you know, I am by nature a likable fellow and not used to unpopularity.

Arsinoë, also, spends a good deal of time alone. I watch her brazenly wander the galley or read a book in the bright sunlight. She makes no effort to hide herself, and, when a curious pilgrim gathers his courage to approach her, she talks at length about the virtues of her late wife and how she will miss the dear woman's company. I am no longer afraid of her, brothers, but feel a sort of pity, for I am now certain she belongs to the genus of woman known among learned men as a *hysteric*. You might recall the time I was summoned down to Memmingen to exorcise a young woman who claimed the Devil was leaving water snakes in her bed. Upon close examination, I can say that Arsinoë, like that poor girl of Memmingen, is more in need of a doctor's care than a priest's. But that is not for me to decide. *If she returns, hold her for me, Friar*, her brother asked on Saint John's Eve. *You don't know what she might do*. Do I need any further proof of her capabilities? Did she not nearly convince me she possessed Saint Katherine? Has she not convinced John that she is sane?

John Lazinus, my poor confused friend, drifts toward the prow of the ship more often than not. He sits silently with me for an hour, sometimes two, with his eyes fixed on the same distant point as mine. It's nice to share again a single vision, and I like that time of the day best when we stretch out as we used to, on the horns of the prow, hook our arms through the rigging, and seek Jerusalem through the leaping fish. My pleasure always ends too soon, however, for John grows restless, cranes his head back toward the other pilgrims, searching out her hooded figure. Five minutes more I'll have after that, while he wrestles with his conscience. I take my eyes from the sea long enough to watch his approach, his hesitation, his desire to lean in as one does to greet a woman and the sturdy clap on the shoulder he gives her instead.

For two days after the storm I care neither for eating, drinking, nor sleeping. I can no longer read or write as before, but my only pleasure is to sit on the prow and look ceaselessly across the wide sea, that by the toil of my eyes I might quiet the fever of my mind. I can tell you a curious thing about the Ocean, one I've observed over many weeks: No matter how high or choppy the waves are surrounding the ship, the earth's horizon appears eternally smooth and composed. I've been able to think of no explanation for this phenomenon except that perhaps God wills it for the comfort of travelers. He knows men are less afraid when they believe themselves moving away from tribulation into tranquillity. From the pilot I learned that, in our approach to Palestine, we will pass by Antioch with Syria Phenice on our left-hand side. Once we reach this place, our right will directly face God's bosom, and only a matter of hours will keep us from nesting there. I begin to hate the night that snatches away my means of seeing and yearn only for the dawn, when I may sit again upon the prow, turn my eyes toward the East, and fix my gaze unflinchingly on that part of the sky where it joins the sea. *Ach, mein Gott!* How deep the love of Christ's heavenly home must be for a saint, when an undevout, wretched, sinful pilgrim like myself feels so keen and sharp a longing for His earthly one!

On the third morning, a handful of other pilgrims join me. From time to time one of the novices fancies he sees land and calls upon the others to look. A pious dispute evolves, one party seeing for sure the mountains of Palestine, the other party denying them. Through the course of this wrangling a pilgrim will inevitably lay a wager on land and call on the lookout man in the maintop to give his verdict, paying in a glass of malvoisie when proven wrong. They continue thus all day until dinner is served and they drift away.

On the evening of the third day while everyone else is eating, I keep watch despite my hunger. The sun, low in the sky, has spread its lava across the waves, making me draw my knees up under my cassock to conserve what little warmth remains. I am shivering and stiff when she sidles out onto the other horn. We have not spoken since she publicly became her resurrected husband.

"One of our philosophers wrote that those at sea could be counted among neither the living nor the dead," Arsinoë says, not looking at me. "When we can do nothing but wait, we don't even need these bodies."

Since she has taken Constantine's name, Arsinoë's face has settled into more masculine lines. I think of all the early saints who made themselves sexless before God: Marina, Pelagia, the radical virgin Thecla, who followed Paul in men's clothes and was thrown to wild animals for her pains.

"I would give every wretched bone in my body to have Saint Katherine back." She pitches her voice low over the waves and wind, but it reaches my ear like a smooth skipped shell. I will do as I promised her brother and watch her until he reaches the shore. When he reaches the shore, this will all be over.

"This man's flesh is even heavier than my own," she continues. "Once I've fulfilled my obligation to her, I can finally rid myself of the weight."

I sigh. I almost wish she could have spoken to Katherine. I have so much I want to know.

"There are so many ways to dissolve, aren't there, Friar?"

Arsinoë turns on the horn, lost already, once, inside the robes of a drowned merchant. She studies her man's hand.

"Sometimes dissolution is a woman's only way to be seen," she says.

The sun funnels into the sea, conical against two far-off purple peaks. A soft moment passes between us when neither wants to let the other know he sees; each wants to be alone with the knowledge. It is almost over.

"The mountains," she whispers.

"Jerusalem," say I.

II
THE CITY

Rules for Pilgrimage

FIRST ARTICLE: Should any pilgrims have come here without express permission from the Pope, they incurred upon themselves the sentence of excommunication and should report to the Father Guardian of Jerusalem at once. The Pope has excommunicated this Holy Land, as it is infested with all manner of Schismatics and Infidel, and will only allow pilgrims access by his blessed leave.

SECOND ARTICLE: No pilgrim ought to wander alone about the holy places without a Saracen guide, because it is perilous and unwise.

THIRD ARTICLE: The pilgrim should beware of stepping over the sepulchres of Saracens for they are greatly vexed by this, believing as they do that it torments their dead.

FOURTH ARTICLE: Should any pilgrim be struck by a Saracen, he should bear it with patience for the glory of God and report it directly to the Interpreter, who will help if he is able.

FIFTH ARTICLE: Let the pilgrim beware of chipping off fragments from the Holy Sepulchre and from spoiling the hewn stones thereof, for this is forbidden under pain of excommunication.

SIXTH ARTICLE: Pilgrims of noble birth must not deface the holy places by drawing their coats-of-arms thereon, or by writing their names, or by scratching marble slabs, or by boring holes in them with iron tools to mark their having visited them.

SEVENTH ARTICLE: Pilgrims must proceed to visit the holy places in an orderly manner and must not try to outrun one another, because the devotion of many is hindered thereby.

EIGHTH ARTICLE: Pilgrims must beware of laughing together as they walk about Jerusalem, lest the Infidel suspect we are laughing at him.

NINTH ARTICLE: Let pilgrims beware of jesting with Saracen boys, for much mischief arises from it.

TENTH ARTICLE: Let pilgrims beware of gazing on any Saracen women, for their husbands are exceedingly jealous and apt to do harm.

ELEVENTH ARTICLE: Should any Saracen woman beckon to a pilgrim and invite him into her house, on no account go.

TWELFTH ARTICLE: Let every pilgrim beware of giving a Saracen wine when he asks for a drink, for after one draught he will straightaway become mad, and the first to be attacked will be the pilgrim who gave him the drink.

THIRTEENTH ARTICLE: No pilgrim may wear knives slung about him.

FOURTEENTH ARTICLE: Should a pilgrim form a friendship with any Saracen, he must especially beware of laying his hand on his beard in jest or touching his turban, even lightly and in jest; for this is a disgrace among them, and all friendships are forgotten.

FIFTEENTH ARTICLE: When pilgrims make covenants with Saracens, let them not dispute with them or swear at them or grow angry, for Saracens know that such things are contrary to the Christian religion and will straightaway cry, "O, thou bad Christian!" which phrase they can say in either Italian or German.

SIXTEENTH ARTICLE: Let no pilgrim laugh at Saracens who are praying in the postures of their faith, for they refrain from laughing at us when we are at our prayers.

i

How Pilgrims Are Welcomed
to the Holy Land

"Name?"

"Lord John Tucher."

"From where do you come?"

"Swabia, beyond the Alps."

"What is your father's name?"

"Peter Tucher."

"So it is written. You may pass."

"Name?"

"Ursus Tucher."

"From where do you come?"

"The same place as my father, Christian Swabia."

"What is your father's name?"

"He just gave it to you."

"What is your father's name?"

"Ow!"

"Ursus!"

"Let go! Lord John Tucher."

"So it is written. You may pass."

"Name?"

"Constantine Kallistos."

"From where do you come?"

"I come from Candia in Crete. I am a merchant there."

"What is your father's name?"

Pause.

"Stavros?"

Pause.

"So it is written. You may pass."

"What is your name?"

"Friar Felix Fabri of the Preaching Brothers in Ulm."

"Failix Fabri—"

"No, no. Felix. Fee-lix."

"Faaailix—"

"No, no diphthong. Fee-lix."

"Fiiaalix—"

"Fee-lix, Fee-lix Fabri. With an *e*."

"Faielix Fabri."

"Oh, forget it."

They arranged themselves in two lines and herded us through single file. One by one, they grabbed us and studied us narrowly, recording our names in their book with long plumed pens. The Saracen who gurgled my name, substituting some word I cannot pronounce in lieu thereof, searched for something in my name, something in my father's name, that would provide him with an excuse to put me back on the boat and shove me off to Germany. I had nothing to hide, and still I blushed under that wicked man's gaze.

From our galley, we had watched these Saracens bustle in and out of two caves cut into the cliff face, assuming they were making these chambers ready for our landing. How we longed to take our rest there and kiss the very stones, for these caves are known as Saint Peter's Cellars, brothers, and it is from here that our Blessed Rock converted the port town of Joppa.

But what malodor! What putrid summer stable stink was this? When we were at last through the lists and thrust inside, my eyes confirmed what my nose already suspected: The Saracens had suspended their hairy asses over this hallowed floor; they had turned Saint Peter's Cellars into a latrine.

Imagine the dismay, brothers. Imagine the stench.

"I will not live this way!" screamed Emelia Priuli, snatching her dress off the floor. "Where is the captain?"

"Felix, over here! It's awful."

Not an inch of the cave's floor was left unbesmirched. I tried to dodge the larger piles and make my way to the back of the enormous cave where our pilgrims had pressed themselves against the wall. Lord Tucher and his son glowed eerily in the skidding green sunlight.

"Do you want to hear my first prayer in the Holy Land, Friar Felix?" Ursus asked miserably, his thin voice slicking the vault of the cave. "It goes like this:

"O Lord Jesu, with what strange courtesy have You received Your guests, men who have traveled many months, even from beyond the Alps, to visit You? Ought not Thou to have granted to those who are footsore from such wanderings, who are hungry and tired, some couch better than the steaming shit of the Infidel? Ought Thou to have welcomed us so grotesquely—"

"Ursus, let me stop you, before ingratitude is added to your burgeoning list of sins," I interrupted. "Remember you are reproaching a Host who first entered this world in a foul cow sty; whose first pillow was a stone manger smeared with regurgitated cud. Our Host could find no bed even in the rich royal city of Jerusalem, save only the gibbet of the splintery cross."

"And remember, Ursus," said Archdeacon John, newly arrived with Conrad and the madwoman Arsinoë, "the noble Job sat upon a dunghill, eaten raw with ulcers, and by his patience won twice his former glory. For as Gregory tells us, 'In the dunghill lies hid the pearl of God. Do thou then, pilgrim, search for this pearl whilst thou sittest on the dunghill.'"

The rebel Ursus was silenced, but what were we to do, brothers? We could not sit without befouling ourselves, nor could we leave, as the Saracens had posted men at the cavern's mouth. Congratulate Conrad, our practical barber, who first assailed the dung! He lifted his robe and, with the side of his shoe, pushed a pile of ordure into the center of the cave. I resolutely took up his labor, and before long all of us were clearing paths, breaking ground, erecting miniature Mounts of Venus at the cave's heart. While we were engaged in this loathsome activity, the guard admitted a handful of Saracens, poor men who had gathered rushes and the branches of trees for us to spread over our wet floor. They charged us one Venetian penny for an armful of grasses, and we happily paid it.

And lo, even while we were bargaining with these vendors, a whole different lot of Saracens entered our cave. Oh, they cried, what a foul stench! By coincidence we have here incense to burn, gum Arabic, and distilled perfumes. We have on our persons rare balsam, musk, some soap, and the whitest muslin for sheets. The pilgrims ran to these men, begging them to part with their goods. As the merchants came and went in our cave, the filth clung to their shoes and was carried outside, so that within an hour, our abode, which had heretofore been an abomination, was rendered wholesome and fit for mankind.

This is only the first degradation we have experienced at the hands of Christ's enemies, brothers; there shall be many more, and we must each learn to endure their tricks humbly, as befits an honest pilgrim.

I record this account of our landing from far down the beach, where I have wandered away from Saint Peter's Cellars and its neighboring Saracen camp, down past the rock in the sea upon which unlearned men claim Saint Peter fished and Christ called to him, saying, *I will make you a fisher of men*, etc., which thing we know from Scripture occurred at the Sea of Galilee and not here. I sit upon the highest hump in a low spine of rocks that has been bleached by sun and bird dung, just above the glistening pebble beach, from where, if I squint, I can make out our galley still listing at sea. I would wager, brothers, that there is no worse port in the entire Mediterranean than this port of Joppa. Thwarted by rugged outcroppings of stone, no boat of any size may pass through to the harbor but, instead, is forced to drop anchor beyond the infamous Andromeda's Rocks. These rocks, according to Saint Jerome in his *On the Distances of Places*, acquired their name when the hero Perseus flew over Joppa on his Pegasus and spotted a young virgin chained between two rocks in the harbor, about to be devoured by a sea monster. With a single stroke of his sword, he dispatched the feared leviathan, asked for the virgin Andromeda's hand in marriage, and flew off to conquer the land of Persia, which forever after bore his name. The Ocean now rages ceaselessly between Andromeda's Rocks, dashing broken water upon the heads of anxious pilgrims when they are rowed ashore from their galleys. Even when the rest of the sea is quiet, the water between these rocks flies high into the air in explosive, helical flumes.

We've seen no sign of Contarini's ship, which to my mind is both a blessing and a curse. Happy are we, certainly, to have attained Palestine first; even now, Captain Lando, loaded with presents, waits in the Saracen camp, hoping his bribes will convince the Governor to lock Contarini out. I, of course, have my own reasons for not wanting Lando to succeed. Not only is it uncharitable to wish upon other pilgrims a misfortune we could scarce have endured, had things been reversed but, more to the point, only when Contarini's pilgrims dock may the burden of Saint Katherine's Tongue be lifted from our shoulders.

The woman Arsinoë has taken no food since the night of the storm, brothers, and has drunk nothing but a little water. John has in no way been able to persuade her to sample the delicious puddings concocted by the Saracen merchants, nor has he been able to tempt her with grapes or sesame bread or eggs fried in oil. All of these I tested and assured her were wholesome, but to no use. She fears her enemies will use the Saracens to poison her.

Can you blame me for walking away, brothers? Have I not waited a lifetime to attain this shore, and should I be stuck inside a feculent cave, surrounded by the noisy mercantile Infidel, because of another's madness? Arsinoë has the bewitched John Lazinus to care for her, who, I believe mistakenly, looks for redemption in her folly. Sixty nuns under his charge were violated and burned alive the night the Turks took his town; John, I fear, fights the Turk once more, through her.

The sun is high in the sky above me, and the water looks cool and inviting. When was the last time I had a real bath, brothers, Venice? With soap, Ulm? Could there be a more fitting salutation to the Holy Land than to take off one's sandals, lift the hem of one's robe to one's bony knees, and recapture for a moment what it is to be clean?

I wade out, stepping gingerly over the sharp rocks on the harbor's floor, and lean forward until the perfectly transparent pane of water suspends me like a figure in stained glass. As I break the surface tension, my robes float up like a rounded fin; I swim with my eyes open, brushing small pink pebbles, furry rocks, the sharp hairballs of sea urchins. I feel purer than I have in months, brothers, pushing through this rippled world, and for the first time understand why the Jews consider unclean anything lucky enough to live in the sea that then choses to walk on land.

When the Tongue is safely restored to her brother, all will be like this water, clear and untroubled. John and I will once more take up that ease of friendship that we set aside when Arsinoë arrived; he will once more want to accompany me on outings like this, undivided in mind and loyalty. Once the Tongue is gone, I will have the energy to reclaim my patron from that snare of flesh Emelia Priuli and set his straying feet back on the path of pilgrimage. I will be kinder to Ursus; I will converse with Conrad, who speaks no language but German and thus has found few friends among our international party of pilgrims. Most important, I will have my wife back. When the Tongue is restored to her brother.

Can my pilgrimage be salvaged, brothers? I come up for air across from where the ruins of ancient Joppa start on the beach and collapse back into the desert, a sad end to this eighth city built after the flood. Joppa has been destoyed and rebuilt too many times; Judas Maccabeus leveled it when its perfidious citizens slaughtered the town's Jews; the Saracens dug under its foundations after the Christians restored it. Now Joppa's city walls are sown into arid fields, and cinnamon-colored goats roam the foundations of what were once Roman baths and echoing Hebrew temples. The dismantled city has become like John the Baptist's bones, its remains flung farther and farther apart in an attempt to weaken its formidable power. And yet, brothers, here lies the difference between a saint and a city: The Baptist may be divided a hundred times over, and still each new mote will contain his impregnable essence; Joppa, like any mortal undertaking, may be shaken only so much before it dissolves away into dust.

I stumble awkwardly out of the water, dragging sand and oyster shells in the hem of my wet robe, and climb up to the carcass of dead Joppa. You can sit upon felled Corinthian columns that once supported great courts of law; you can spread out your clothes to dry on a marble slab that once shaded a Platonic academy. To what indignities a city may be put, once it has expired, brothers: suffering, among other insults, the wet curiosity of a modern German monk. I find a long shallow marble trough and lay myself down to dry. Cicero received a letter on the death of his beloved daughter Tullia; a friend chided him out of his grief by asking what one woman's passing mattered compared to the death of Corinth. *How can we manikins wax indignant, ephemeral creatures that we are, when the corpses of so many towns lie abandoned in a single spot?* Worse even than abandonment, Cicero's friend would have wept to see how the Saracens dismember the original buildings and drag Joppa's marble away to pave their mosques. The eternal transference continues; nothing, in the end, retains its original meaning.

And is this not my deepest fear, brothers? Do I not mourn for the dying of my pilgrimage and tremble that it is being put to some other use than what I conceived? I feel so out of control, so at the mercy of my patron's fears and the Tongue's madness. He keeps us from Sinai; she keeps me in constant confusion about my beloved's desires. I know she is ill—why can't I put her from my mind?

"How can you know they are healed?"

Hark, brothers! Just above me: a man's voice, muffled by the marble walls of my trough. We know that voice.

"Because they are with her now," replies another, softer voice. "Your nuns. I see a crowd of young women behind Katherine. They wear pure white wimples and carry the slender palm fronds of martyrdom."

I ease my chin over the rim of the trough, but they do not notice me, brothers: John and Arsinoë. They take a seat upon a heap of Joppa and stare out over the harbor, past Andromeda's Rocks.

"They are not ruined?" John asks, not looking at her.

"Oh, no!" The Tongue shakes her head vehemently. "They are overjoyed to have stepped out of those bodies. Without skins and muscles and organs to impede them, your nuns can finally achieve true heavenly dispassion. Where there is no passion, there can be no ruin."

They sit too closely together, their fingers tracing the shallow flutes of the same fallen column. Arsinoë has dared to take off Constantine's bonnet, and her profile for the moment appears almost a woman's. She seeks desperately to comfort my friend, looking upon him with that determined hopefulness I've seen too often on the faces of soft-hearted deathbed confessors. I should reveal myself and put an end to this intimacy. She should not look at him that way.

John turns to her suddenly. "How did Katherine first come to you?"

Without thought, I duck back into my trough. Arsinoë takes a long time to answer.

"We had an icon of her in our family chapel, as big as I was when I was a girl. Saint Katherine painted tall and long-limbed, holding an open book in one hand, a heavy golden sword in the other, her hip resting lightly against her wheel. I used to measure myself against that icon. I fit myself to it as to a grave: Was my hair as long and sable as Saint Katherine's? Was my foot arched as gracefully? Did my eyes, almond and dark like hers, recall pain so exquisite it read like euphoria?

"I would press myself against her portrait and imagine us deep in the desert, alone in a shallow cave, with only icons of ourselves for decoration. She would touch me as a woman touches, not tousling my hair or pinching an arm, but firm and confident, kissing my face before sleep, washing my arms and legs in the stream."

John's eyes stray to her legs, where she has propped them on the column's pedestal. They are naked and brown in the sun, tight, like those of a distance runner.

"The night my brother left for university," she continues, "I took all my sorrow and fear and loneliness to that icon. I worshiped him, you know. My brother taught himself a thousand languages, he *understood* things, and, as men do, he was leaving me behind. I went to Katherine, begged her to do something, anything to bring him back, when suddenly her eyes began to vibrate, like a rabbit's or a bird's. I couldn't break away from them. She left her frame, Archdeacon. She bent over me, where I had fallen to the ground"— Arsinoë brings her face closer to John's, until not an inch of sky shows between them—"And she blew into my mouth."

John hesitantly licks his lips. He is trembling. *Please, John*, I pray. *Don't.*

"The Saracens call Christ the Breath of God," the Tongue whispers. "I became her breath that night, her voice, her sighs, her indignation. I was no longer a little girl in a big house. I was someone important. And no one could prove I wasn't."

Her mouth is so close to his, I am afraid for him to breathe, lest by his inhalation he should draw them together. *A woman is more bitter than Death, John; she is a snare, her heart a net, her arms are chains.*

"How can we love a saint who reveals herself to little children"— Arsinoë searches his face—"knowing full well she has perverted us for the rest of the world?"

John closes his eyes and surrenders to the Tongue. I cannot bear to watch.

"Look, Archdeacon." Arsinoë stiffens, sighting something over his left shoulder. "The mast."

I glance over, to discover the miracle that has saved my friend from certain damnation, and spy a tiny twig bobbing in the Ocean way beyond Andromeda's Rocks. Certainly it is Contarini's ship. Our enemy. My salvation!

"That is my brother's ship," she says.

"The brother who transcribed your visions?" asks John, his voice hoarse and shy. He is remembering Constantine's description of brother and sister together, Arsinoë's hair falling loose over her sheer nightdress.

"The night she first came to me, I prayed." The Tongue laughs softly. "I begged Saint Katherine to do anything to bring my brother back.

"This was the price. He did come back, but not for me. He came back to study *her*, to learn *her*. Sometimes I wish he had stayed at his university. He belonged there, among like-minded men, not locked in a girl's bedroom listening for saints. My brother thought I was worthless because I could not manage to communicate directly with God; he said I was merely some freakish vernacular dialect. Katherine was the translation, God the true Words. He couldn't bear to be God three times removed."

Her brother the translator, the man who taught me how to clap on Saint John's Eve. I have only to hold her until he comes ashore.

"No matter what, Archdeacon"—the Tongue turns forcefully on John—"I cannot allow him to find me. I must reach Saint Katherine before he does."

"If that is the only way you believe you will be safe," he says, "I will do anything to help you."

Reach Saint Katherine? What is John Lazinus promising?

"Tonight, before they dock," she says. "I must get away before Contarini's pilgrims come ashore."

"Let's go back, then." John rises, staring worriedly out to sea. "If Lando can lock them out, you have plenty of time. If not . . ."

She stands and slips her hand in his. "Your nuns are smiling, Friend John."

Oh, God! What fresh betrayal is this, brothers? I watch them walk down the beach, hand in hand, until they come in sight of the Saracen camp, where Arsinoë reties Constantine's cap under her chin and squares her shoulders into a man's. Like a senseless animal John has fallen into her pit, has become food for her madness. He would truly help her escape? He would free her to dog my pilgrimage, to keep me in perpetual fear for my wife's well-being? Who knows what this creature might do if, God forbid, she should reach Sinai? No, John. Climb out of the pit! Fill it in so it swallows no others! I will help you, my dearest friend, the only way I know how.

I stand up and quickly brush myself off.

I must fetch Arsinoë's brother.

Aboard Contarini's Ship

The hired Arab who pulls the oars of our small boat studies my monk's robe with its great red cross, listens to our friendly German; slowly he shakes his head at my companion, Abdullah the Mameluke.

"Fucking Arab dog." The Mameluke seethes. "They're always looking at you as if you're going to slip. Look, Friar, I can call him a fucking Arab dog and he doesn't understand a thing."

Abdullah smiles at the rower, rolls his eyes at me.

"Fucking Arab dog."

Behind us, on the shore, tiny sandpiper pilgrims hop in and out of the surf. My patron and his son are among them. They must wonder where I am.

"I'm the only one allowed to leave the ship," Abdullah says proudly. "Contarini sent me to petition the Governor. Lando's trying to lock him out."

"Is Lando having any success?" I ask.

"Not much." The Mameluke laughs. "The Governor told me that if your captains don't agree to tour Jerusalem together, he'll send you all right back home."

There's not much chance of that; both captains are so greedy they would sooner climb into bed together than lose a florin between them. That Lando is having little luck, however, means I have even less time to accomplish my task.

If meeting the Mameluke is any indication, fortune favors my mission, brothers. When I was certain John and Arsinoë were out

of sight, I started purposefully back to Saint Peter's Cellars, resolute in my plan but confounded as to how it might be executed.
Could I hire a Saracen to row me out to Contarini's ship and back
before our guards locked us in for the night? Could I be certain
Lando would not start for Jerusalem while I was away, leaving me
bereft of patron and possessions? As I fretted, I came upon the
donkey pen of the Saracen camp, where the restless brown beasts
we'll use for our peregrinations through the Holy Land grazed upon
thistles and reached with their lips for the sweetly scented terebinth flowers above them. I confess, I was distracted from my plan
long enough to move among those donkeys and gather for myself
an armload of terebinth, as this plant's red-tipped thorns, brothers, crowned the greatest king of all: the poor mocked King of the
Jews.

As I was contending with the donkeys for their dinner, suddenly
I heard behind me a loud and imperious shout. I dropped my thorns
and tried to scramble over the fence, but it was too late. A hand on
my shoulder pulled me back and spun me around.

"Monk of Ulm!" The infidel cried in German. "Are you taking
those back to sleep on?"

Behind me stood, of all creatures, Ser Niccolo's Mameluke, the
former Peter Ber of Swabia. He was on his way back to Contarini's
galley and agreed to take me with him. Now he sits across from me
in our little boat, ruefully massaging his pustulant wound.

"How is your neck, Abdullah?" I ask. "Is it healing?"

Gingerly, he prods the splinter, sucks in his breath at the pain.

"It's fine as long as I don't poke it."

"Why don't you have Ser Niccolo remove it for you? It can't help,
leaving it in."

"Ser Nic?" The Mameluke hoots. "He is a man who likes to see
a person suffer."

"When we get back to shore," I say, "come have our barber look
at it."

The Mameluke, as I spend more time in his company, reveals himself to be an odd combination, brothers. Sly and mocking, as if real
Saracen blood ran in his veins, and yet at the same time kindhearted

and funny. He obviously misses Christendom deeply and wishes himself back home. Perhaps he is not completely lost after all.

"So what do you have of Ser Nic's?" the Mameluke asks. "Did he lose something on your ship?"

"In a manner of speaking," I say. "I'd prefer to discuss it with him."

He shrugs. "That's fine, just don't take too long about it. I absolutely have to be back by sunset for evening prayers." Abdullah glares at the small Arab oarsman. "If all the converts don't show up, there's hell to pay."

"I have to be back by sunset as well," I say. "That's when I'm told they lock us in for the night."

All conversation ceases when the current spirals into chaos around Andromeda's Rocks. Abdullah's rower digs his shoulder into the right oar to keep us from spinning completely around and smashing onto the rocks. Caught in sea and harbor's aquatic lovers' quarrel, our little boat is spat back and forth, battered and wet, until a sharp barb lands in the sea's breast, and we are through. Before us, Contarini's and Lando's galleys roll on the waves.

O brothers, if only the prideful Venetians back home could see how these captains flinch into Palestine like dogs with tails between their legs, groveling to the Infidel for safe-conduct, they would blush for shame. Like Lando, Contarini has furled all his colorful sails, lowered his fine silk banners, and altogether made his galley naked before the Saracens. We row around to the ship's rickety ladder, sunk in wood pustular with barnacles and pocked with green rot holes. Abdullah helps me up and orders the rowboat to wait for us.

"It's a rat pit, isn't it?" The Mameluke shivers as we climb aboard.

Five minutes upon Contarini's ship and I remember why I elected to sail with Lando. Before us, two black rats race like Atalanta and Hippomenes but fall upon each other in vermin passion, tearing fur and flailing bald tails. Beneath our feet, fat white worms wriggle across the floorboards, seeking in their cunning way to crawl up the hem of my robe and suck my leg blood. Though many filthy creatures live on damp ships, thank God nothing venomous can breed here: no toads or vipers, no poisonous snakes, spiders, or scorpions.

Had not Divine Providence thus ordered it, no man might survive one of these large old ships.

I walk directly to the galley's horns, the one spot on board a pilgrim ship where I know a man might sit and keep his own thoughts, and there I find him, writing diligently in his book. The sinking sun is behind him, and he holds his page at an angle to catch what amber light remains of the day, purposefully marking the page, referring to a sheaf of notes tucked into the back of his manuscript.

"Ser Niccolo." The Mameluke taps his shoulder. "See who has come to visit."

The translator looks up, startled, and almost spills his pot of ink.

"It's Lando's friar." Ser Niccolo leans down awkwardly to bestow the kiss of peace. *"Wie Geht es ihnen!"*

Why do I find such pleasure hearing my language on his lips, brothers? I blush in confusion.

"Friar Felix Fabri from the Preaching Brothers in Ulm," I say.

"I remember you." Ser Niccolo smiles, then, noticing the Mameluke hovering, gently touches his elbow. "Thank you, Abdullah, for showing our guest over. I'm sure we'd love some malvoisie."

Reluctantly, the Mameluke backs away to fetch a bottle of wine, leaving us alone on the prow.

"What are you working on?" I nod at his book, suddenly shy about my reason for being here.

"I'm translating the life of a saint whose vita has only recently come to light."

"Which saint is that?" I ask, for, as you know, brothers, I pride myself on my familiarity with lesser-known holy lives.

"She's very obscure." He smiles.

"Is it Saint Withburge, one of four Saxon sister saints?"

"No."

"Is it Saint Julitta, who was boiled in tar along with her three-year-old son, Saint Quiricus?"

"No, it's not Saint Julitta or Saint Withburge."

"Is it Saint Concordia, whose body was tossed into a Roman sewer and mucked out by Saint Ireneus?"

"No, Friar." He laughs. "She is a Greek saint, of the Orthodox religion."

"Oh."

"I've devoted a good portion of my life to rescuing saints from obscurity," he says. "Usually their lives are hidden from the world for no better reason than they were written in some arcane language no one remembers anymore. I liberate the saint from her forgotten, anonymous community and settle her in a flourishing modern neighborhood."

"You write in Greek." I touch the wet ink on his page, then quickly smudge it into my cassock. "I would like to learn that language."

The translator studies his book and smiles.

"There was a time when you as a churchman would have thought these letters from the Devil. Greek was lost to the world for such a long time, Friar. It was the language of dark gods and pagan idolaters, of mystery cults where frenzied women dismembered their own sons. Now look at it."

He turns the book so that I may see, but to me it looks like strands of black hair tangled across the page.

"These same letters are now the language of light," he says. "They hold the rebirth of knowledge. Some men say this old language, with the philosophy and science it unlocks, ushers in the New Age of Man. That soon we will have no more use for God."

"Surely you don't belive that?" I ask, shocked.

"Of course not." He flips through the book. "What is a world without a rival?"

Is he as prideful as his sister? I begin to wonder. He seems as committed to these lines on a page as she is to the body of her saint, and together they speak far too familiarly of Heaven. I try to steer the conversation back around.

"Tell me about this saint you are translating now," I say. "How does she die?"

Ser Niccolo shakes his head and closes his book. "I've only just started this one, Friar. But, I'll tell you what. When I'm done, I'll dedicate her life to you."

I nod my thanks, but I can see his impatience rising. I have interrupted his work, and he cannot fathom why I have come.

"Ser Niccolo." I crawl awkwardly out onto the other horn of the prow so that he no longer has to crane to see me. "You might be wondering what I'm doing on your ship."

"Since you risk being locked out, yes, I am curious."

"When last we spoke, you told me you were endeavoring to learn the language of madness, that you might better track your lost sister. I am afraid I am a better linguist than you, for I have mastered that tongue."

"I don't understand, Friar."

"The last few days I have lived on the edge of dementia. I have tried to believe what I cannot believe; I have suffered doubts and confusions wholly antithetical to my nature. Now she boasts she will run away before you dock, and I can only shudder at the damage she might inflict either on herself or on my beloved's body. It is time to put an end to this nightmare. I have come to give you Saint Katherine's Tongue."

"Here's your wine."

Abdullah the Mameluke returns with a cold green bottle of malvoisie and three cups.

"Thank you, Abdullah," Ser Niccolo says tightly. "Would you mind swilling your share over by the slave benches? I need to speak privately with the Friar."

Abdullah pours himself a cup and thrusts the half-empty bottle at me. I take an unsteady swig as he walks away.

"You know where my sister is?" Ser Niccolo's feverish eyes fix me to my spot.

"She returned to our ship after Saint John's Eve."

"Where had she been?"

"She didn't say." I exclude her lie about a Turkish attack and the saga of Constantine's death. "She is quite brainsick, Ser."

"You can't imagine what it was like growing up with her." The translator leaps from the horn and paces before me. "The plays for attention, the tyranny. Katherine said she didn't have to wash. Katherine said she might speak out in Church. Katherine said she should have a tutor. Katherine said marriage was out of the question. We lost our mother early, but luckily Katherine moved in and ran our lives for us.

"Our father finally asked me to come home from university to watch her. She'd become so erratic he couldn't handle her alone. Has she tried to harm herself in any way?"

"I pulled her from the Ocean," I say. "I think she intended to drown herself."

Ser Niccolo shakes his head. "Before he died," he says slowly, "our father urged me to put her in a convent, where she would be safe. She's attempted to destroy herself before, Friar. Two months ago, I found her unconscious in a pool of blood. She tried to hack off her own breasts."

Brothers, you cannot appreciate my flooding horror as Niccolo reveals the pattern of Arsinoë's insanity. I understand now her despondency and mania, her delusions of Turkish women in chains, and her feelings of persecution. Do you not remember a certain brother at Ulm who, some years ago, suffered from the same tribulations as Arsinoë? He believed that Abbot Fuchs was putting ground glass in his food and would only eat after three of us had tasted each dish.

"It's getting late," I say. "I have to be back before dark. If we can get the Mameluke to row us both in, you can take charge of your sister tonight."

Ser Niccolo instantly agrees. He collects his book and papers and walks with me to the ship's ladder.

But the Mameluke is nowhere to be found.

The little rowboat Abdullah and I left rocking on the waves is gone, but no one saw it leave. When Niccolo queries the galley slaves, more wretched and begrimed even than Lando's, they shake their heads like simpletons and point to the sun. Niccolo finally gets a response from a Syrian slave, sitting near the ladder.

"The sun is setting," Ser Niccolo translates, disgusted. "He said he'd miss the call to prayer."

The wretched apostate! So cowed is he by his Saracen masters that he abandons a pilgrim—a fellow countryman, too! What if he does not ever come back and I am locked out with the rest of Contarini's luckless company? What if Arsinoë runs tonight?

"Are there no other boats?" I ask.

"Abdullah has one. We lost the other in the storm," he says, then is struck by a sudden fear. "Will my sister be safe—without you to watch her?"

Will *she* be safe? I am far more worried about John.

"Yes," I say at last. "A friend is watching her."

The translator nods seriously while, behind us, the traitor sun capitulates to the sea. We are as far from Palestine as we were in Venice, still at sea after months of travel. Contarini's defeated, lifeless pilgrims shuffle up to dinner, each one looking over his shoulder to flagellate himself with the unattainable shore. Back there, in beshitted Saint Peter's Cellars, my pilgrims unroll their pallets and lie down for bed. Without thought, they arrange themselves as though still at sea: heads to the wall, feet stretched out toward the cave's center, small trunks touching feet. All down the row, they feel the floor gently undulate beneath them, that tide in their blood after months at sea still rocking them to sleep. Groups of friends lie together in the low light, talking and swearing, flicking dung and laughing. Ursus, my patron's son, pulls his father's sleeve and begs him: Please, can't we go look for Friar Felix? What if he is hurt? But my patron sets his lips and shakes his head. He will not wander the Arab darkness and risk his own life for a friar who cannot make it back by bedtime.

"Are you hungry?" Ser Niccolo asks.

I shake my head.

"Come downstairs, then." He gently guides me away from the ship's side. "I'll show you where we sleep."

I write to you, brothers, from the unsettlingly familiar sleeping quarters of Contarini's ship: identical to ours in configuration, stench, confusion; different only in the particulars of the sins each pilgrim carries. Most of the pilgrims have retired, but Ser Niccolo's lantern still burns, attracting clouds of hot, peppery gnats. He leans against his trunk and scratches away at his translation, oblivious to the snores and moanings of his fellow passengers. Earlier, he confided to me that he believes the most noble thing a man might do is to make public something lost; and that he hopes, once his sister is safely taken care of, to return to university and have his new vita accepted by the library. He is a fine specimen of modern manhood, brothers; as open as his sister is closed, as jovial as she is melancholy. He is like a secular Felix, translating Heaven for the scholarly community, while I reconstruct an earthly pilgrimage for you to whom the world and its customs are as foreign as saints are to scholars. And yet, one thing still troubles me.

"Ser Niccolo?"

"Is your pallet comfortable, Friar Felix? I'm afraid the other pilgrims think it's cursed. A man expired upon it just before that awful storm, and the sailors blamed it all on him."

"A man died on this pallet?" I have to keep myself from leaping up.

"You're not superstitious, are you?" He raises an eyebrow and returns to his writing.

"No," I say. "Ser Niccolo?"

"Yes, Friar?"

"Why do you think your sister's madness fixed upon Saint Katherine of Alexandria? Certainly there are other young virgins to whom she might have turned."

He thinks long and hard before answering.

"I've often wondered that myself. We had a large icon of Katherine in our house that was part of my mother's dowry. For years it hung in the room where my tutor taught me Latin and classic Greek, mathematics and geography. Arsinoë was a smart young girl and sometimes sat in with us. I wonder if her fixation did not begin there."

"If you knew Arsinoë was mad and a danger to herself," I ask, "why did you allow your sister to believe—and, worse, allow foolish pilgrims to believe—she was Saint Katherine's Tongue?"

He is silent for a long time, regarding me over the lantern.

"If you can seduce a madness, Friar," he says at last, "you can control a madness. It was wrong, but it was my way of coping. I believed if Arsinoë's Katherine grew dependent on me, I could protect her from herself."

"And the bones?"

"Did she show you bones?" he asks, startled.

"No," I admit. "A man named Constantine told me devotees brought them."

"A man named Constantine brought them is more like it." Niccolo puts down his book in disgust. "This merchant showed up one day with a cow's rib and claimed he had it from Katherine's church in Hania. It seemed to greatly disturb my sister so I buried it, and the others they continued to bring, in the yard with the carcasses from our slaughterhouse."

"So those bones were not holy?"

"You be the judge." He shrugs. "Where would peasants and zealots have gotten true relics, Friar? Heaven itself would have had to provide them."

He is right, brothers. Unless I am willing to concede that Saint Katherine willingly put herself into the hands of a madwoman, I have no reason to believe the bones Arsinoë claimed to possess— the bones I never saw—were real. And her confession of theft, as much as I want to solve that hurtful crime, cannot possibly have been more than prideful hollow boasting.

"Thank you for your honesty, Ser Niccolo," I say, putting aside my book and pen. I am suddenly very tired.

"Thank you for your trust, Friar," says he, and, noting my exhaustion, considerately blows out the light.

An Unrestful Night

Back at sea, my mind inevitably misgives to monstrosities, brothers. The Troyp is replaced by struggling Andromeda chained between two rocks, about to be devoured by the personified gullet of her mother's pride. For many centuries after Perseus set up house with his rescued Andromeda, the bones of that slain sea monster rested on Joppa's beach. Men say the skeleton was 90 feet tall and 200 feet long, and no one man owned it so it was enjoyed by all. Children swung from the sand-pocked ribs; poor families stretched fabric between the bones, creating a peaceful community of tents. As he terrorized in life, so this creature sheltered in death, a sort of Noah's Ark to Joppa's poor.

But as men covet the famous Ark, seeking it in the land of the Turk and in Aethiopia, the Emperor Vespasian, when he came to Palestine, coveted the bones of this sea monster. He ordered his men to drive spears into the Joppian tents, fling the children from their perches, and load the frame of this monster on a boat for Rome. For centuries it swung like a baby giant's mobile, suspended above the public square for all Romans to enjoy, until at last Saint Sylvester had the bones dismantled. He knew full well that pilgrims in the Eternal City spent more time gawking at the carcass than at their prayers.

I've been sitting upon the horn of Contarini's ship for the last few sleep-denied hours, brothers, watching the movement of torches on what used to be the sea monster's shore. Nighttime still belongs to

demons in a heathen land: Christians must content themselves with
spiritual illumination, for they are kept in abject darkness, denied
the comfort of any light whatsoever; while those wanderers in darkness, the wretched Infidel, have before each of their comfortable
tents a pole lit with six bright lamps in honor of their accursed
Mahomet. Some time ago, a phalanx of lanterns broke off from the
Saracen camp, moving quickly toward dark Saint Peter's Cellars.
Now the cellars are ablaze, and a hundred smaller dots of light bob
up the hillside.

My worst fear has come true, brothers. They are leaving me behind. Lando has succeeded with the Governor and given the order
for his pilgrims to arise. Tomorrow will be spent in Holy Jerusalem,
friends, he tells them. If not for Andromeda's Rocks upsetting the
water between us, I might certainly hear the joyful shouts of pilgrim thanksgiving, the bustle of rolling up pallets and repacking
trunks. Ursus's cry would reach me—*To my knighthood!*—and
Arsinoë's sigh of relief; she would be on her way inland long before
Contarini's ship disgorged its passengers. What have I done, brothers? She is escaping, and I am abandoned; she is on her way to Sinai,
and I am still at sea.

O wretched Felix! O prideful Folly that led me to act so rashly!
Would I had stayed asleep and not been taunted by those retreating
torches. Would I had awakened tomorrow morning to find them
gone, Saint Peter's Cellars housing no more than footprints and half-
eaten apples; better that than to wonder, tonight, which torch is
John's and if two shadows mingle in its light. Certainly, it is prefer-
able to die in one's sleep, brothers, than to be tortured, slowly, to
death.

And here is the sea monster. In the pale moonlight, I spy his
uneven wake making its way to us from Andromeda's Rocks. He
slithers over the waves, his long flippers propelling him forward. In
a matter of moments the monster will be upon us, and this ill-lived
life will be snuffed once and for all. Denying me His Holy Land, God
has at least sent a swift and merciful death. I close my eyes and
prepare to be devoured.

"Ser Nic? Is that you?"

A voice from the dark water. The sea monster—could it be?

"Abdullah?"

"Friar Felix?"

"What are you doing here? Why did you leave?" I whisper roughly. "I got locked out because of you."

"Prayers, Friar. I had to grovel before Allah. What are you doing on the horn? That's where Ser Nic sits when he cannot sleep."

"Listen, Abdullah," I say, "you must row me back to shore."

"Forget it. I just came from there."

He wedges his paddle in the galley's side to keep from floating backward.

"Are they leaving?" I ask.

"The pilgrims? I don't know." He shrugs. "It's all confused."

"Now you listen to me, Peter Ber. If I am left behind, I will make your life a living hell," I threaten, infuriated almost to tears by his casualness. "I will make certain not one more drop of wine passes your wretched Mameluke lips. I will witness to you night and day, calling upon our Lord and all his saints to bring plagues and boils upon your irresponsible apostate head. I will convert you back to Christ and then I will cast you into the pits of Hell—"

"All right, Friar." The Mameluke holds his hands up in mock surrender. "For Chrissakes, come around to the ladder."

Once in the rowboat, I can let out my breath. Up close, the Mameluke looks and smells like the drunk he is, disheveled and red-eyed, reeking of pilgrim malvoisie.

"The Governor clapped Lando in jail," he tells me. "After a few hours, he was begging to have Contarini's pilgrims come ashore. There's no more lockout; Ser Nic will be right behind us."

I glance back over my shoulder at the retreating galley. Ser Niccolo will be angry I have left him behind, but what choice do I have, brothers? I cannot deliver his sister if she gets away.

The sky above is white with stars, and I lean back under the infinite Milky Way. Even if they have started, I can catch up. I can still make it.

"So, did you and Ser Nic talk about me while I was gone?" The Mameluke pulls unevenly on his oars and steers the boat crookedly.

"No," I say unkindly.

I see the constellations Cepheus and Cassiopeia enthroned over their daughter's looming rocks, and I offer to take over rowing as we approach.

"Don't you trust me?" The drunken Mameluke waves his oars in the air. "After all I'm doing for you, countryman?"

"Of course, I trust you," I snap. "I just thought you might be tired."

"You never get tired when there are two of you," he shouts, over the roaring water, as we approach Andromeda's Rocks. "When Peter's exhausted, Abdullah takes over!"

I feel the swift current suck us closer to the stones, then thrust us back into the sea. I can only distinguish the outlines of the rocks in this lactic starlight, but the weighty nearness of them curves above us, recycling cold waves over the bow of our little boat.

"I wondered if you and Nic spoke of me, because I've been looking for his sister for days, and there you had her all along. It's so lucky!"

I grip the boat's sides tightly as Abdullah digs in his oars and thrusts us mightily into the channel. Water squeezes into the pass and hurls itself against the rocks, crashing down upon us, nearly sweeping me from my seat. Abdullah heaves once more and spears us through.

With Andromeda's Rocks behind us, the harbor quiets, and it is only a short ride to the beach. Under cover of darkness, while the Mameluke pulls the small boat onto shore, I kneel down and kiss this holy sand. I will never risk you again.

"Looks like you were right." The Mameluke points to a troop of bobbing torches. "Something's going on."

I push the Mameluke aside and race up the slope, stumbling over my soaked robes. A black, agitated cloud of pilgrims swarms outside the cave. They are still here, brothers! Thank God I have not lost them.

"*Friar!*" My patron's son, Ursus, stands apart from the crowd, his hands twisted in his father's beads. When he sees me standing dumbstruck on the path, he rushes forward and buries his tearstained face in my robes.

"It was so awful. She slept right beside me, and I'm the one who smelled her."

"Ursus, calm down," I say, suddenly aware of a thick, sweet fog hanging over the cellar. "What happened here?"

"Where were you, Friar? We needed you so badly, and I thought you were dead in this awful country."

"Shhhh." I kiss the top of his sweating blond head. Behind him, our pilgrims stand in postures of disbelief. Some hide their faces in their hands, some chew their fingernails worriedly. For the first time I realize the torches around Saint Peter's Cellars might spell something besides our departure for Jerusalem.

"Take me to the Archdeacon, son," I say.

"What happened?" the Mameluke asks, his eyes wide.

I shake my head and leave him to gather his news from the Saracens.

Ursus pulls me through the crowd of disoriented, weeping pilgrims, past where his father leans against the cavern wall, staring blankly before him. Two Homesick, as tremulous on land as they were at sea, hover around him.

"It was the Archangel Gabriel, I saw him myself," one says. "He touched his flaming sword to her hair."

"No," the other argues. "I saw an imp creep in, as black as could be, and piss a stream of fire across her face."

Ursus pulls me past them, down the hill to a flat square of land just beyond the shore, and points to a figure kneeling in the moonlight.

"Thank you, son." I squeeze him tight. "Why don't you check on your father? He looked like he could use you."

Ursus runs back and I walk down the hill.

Someone has twisted two palm branches into a spiky cross and thrust it down where the earth has been recently turned. As though offended by the smell of its charge, the cross bends away, rustling its fronds woefully in the night breeze. Tendrils of smoke escape the earth like steam from a piecrust.

Before the grave, my friend sits silently. His eyes are swollen and caked with dust; his hands pat the hot earth. He looks up to see me and flings himself into my arms, where we rock like two old Jewish men over their dead.

"She's gone, Felix." John's grief drips down my neck. "I loved her. I loved her even as I watched that woman's face peel back from the bone."

"What happened here?" I ask. He shakes his head.

"I don't want to believe it."

"Did Arsinoë harm herself? Is that what happened?"

"No," he whispers.

"She's a very disturbed young woman," I say.

"Felix, Arsinoë did not harm herself. She set Emelia Priuli on fire, and she ran away."

Have I heard him correctly? This body is Emelia Priuli's? With both hands I brush away the sand that covers her face, flick off the russet crabs that already nibble her pink-black flesh.

"Why would she do such a thing?" I ask in disbelief.

He shakes his head and will not answer.

"John." A horrible fear grips me. "Did you know she was planning this?"

"How can you suggest such a thing?" He shoves me away from him, confirming my suspicion that, if nothing else, he guessed at her intentions.

"I heard you this afternoon."

"Since when did you become a spy?" John asks angrily.

"Since everything I held sacred became threatened by this woman."

"She is not a monster!" he shouts. "She was kidnapped. She was raped. Someone is trying to kill her. Can you blame her for trying to protect herself?"

"How is murdering someone else going to protect her?"

"She knew her kidnapper would be looking for a woman, so she made the only woman present unrecognizable. She has a mission."

"John!" I cry. "Listen to yourself!"

"Oh, God, Felix!" John presses Emelia's grainy black fingers to his lips and weeps over them like a child. "In how many graves has Arsinoë left her body?

"She needs her assassin to believe this talon is her hand. 'But wait,' say the pilgrims, 'doesn't her hand lie off the coast of Cyprus where the sailors threw her dead body to stop the storm? We saw her sink ourselves.'

"I tell you, Arsinoë will never die, Felix, she will just go on and on, borrowing the deaths of others. And on the Last Day, she'll appear before God with a whole regiment of identities behind her and she'll say to Him, 'But I thought I could die in the body of another and still live myself. I thought I could exist as a poem in a hundred corrupt translations and still retain an honest meaning.'"

Only now, brothers, do I fathom the true extent of John's feelings for the merchant's wife. Someone, somewhere, believes the hand he holds to be Arsinoë's, and that will suffice. If he cannot embrace her, he will embrace the perception of her, the hot echo of her against dead skin. I gently pull the stiff fingers from his mouth and cover them with pebbles. He is, after all, still a priest.

"Come away from this place." I pull John to his feet and lead him up the hill. Dawn is only a few hours away. I will need to find the strength to tell Ser Niccolo that his sister is more disturbed than we thought. Not only is she a runaway and liar, now she is a murderess.

And, God help us, now she is gone.

How Someone Finally Came to Us

Sometime before sunrise, the Saracens, tired of being ignored, pushed the pilgrims back into the cellar, locking us in with the rotted-melon fog of burned flesh and our escalating theories. No one truly witnessed anything, except, I learn, my patron's son.

Emelia Priuli had flirted too democratically to feel safe sleeping next to any one pilgrim, so she positioned her pallet between the wall and the unthreatening young Ursus Tucher. He takes me by the hand and walks me to the ember upon which she slept, showing me the buzzard streaks that blacken the wall behind her pallet and his. His face is pale and troubled, and he tries to speak several times before I ask if there's something on his mind.

"Friar, do you remember when we arrived you told me to look for the pearl in the dunghill?" He draws me back into the corner of the cave, digs in his pocket, and deposits something cold and smooth in my hand. Five angular bits of red light. Five perfect bits of polished glass.

"Where did you get these?" I ask.

"Did you see that young man I spoke to for so long, when the Saracen merchants came? He's the son of a very strict Saracen lord, and he'd gotten himself into a scrape gambling. It's quite unfair, really; these jewels came off his father's shabbiest coat. Anyway, I drove a hard bargain—and he was desperate to sell before his father found out. Friar, have you ever seen such rubies?"

"Have you shown your father these stones?" I ask, rolling the glass in my palm.

"No, I bought them with my own money. It took almost all of it, but think of what we would have paid for rubies this large back home!"

"Ursus—"

"Only now they are ruined, Friar." Ursus looks ready to cry. "I can hardly bear to touch them. I think these rubies killed my father's friend, the Lady Emelia."

"Son, how could that be?" I ask.

"She slept right next to me, Friar," he whispers. "What if that Saracen wanted his jewels back and set fire to the wrong person by mistake?"

"Ursus, child"—I smile—"Priuli is a woman, hard to mistake for a young man like yourself."

"But it looked like him, Friar. In the dark, it looked like the man who sold me the rubies."

Did Ursus see someone bend over La Priuli? Did he wake up and see Arsinoë's robed figure light the fire?

"I thought you were asleep, son," I say. "I thought the smoke woke you up."

Ursus shakes his head miserably. "I was too scared to do anything. I thought he wanted me." Ursus turns away, and I see his hand go to his running nose. "Will they still let me be a knight of the Holy Sepulchre?" he asks. "Even though I let a lady die in my place?"

My poor Ursus, happily dreaming of hairless Turkish women in chains, suddenly strangled awake by a genie of smoke and melting flesh. I cannot let him believe La Priuli died for him.

"Ursus, look at me." I lift his hanging head and smile into his eyes. "That man, if it *was* that man, was not after you. I'm afraid you bought nothing more from him than a few worthless chips of glass."

I place a ruby between my teeth like a cherry pit and bite down hard. When it cracks in two, I cough it up and hold it out to him. I watch the boy's face shift from fear to relief to righteous indignation.

"Faa-ther!"

Lord Tucher strides across the cave at the sound of his son's cry. He takes one look at me and snatches Ursus away.

"We are angry with Friar Felix," my patron tells his son sternly. His eyes are red from crying. "Come away."

"I'm very sorry for having wandered off, Lord Tucher," I say, as contritely as possible. "It was wrong of me."

"Thank God we learned Saint Katherine's Monastery burned to the ground. I can see you just 'wandering off' and leaving Ursus and me to die in the desert."

"I was cheated, Father," Ursus cries.

"We were both cheated, son. Putting our faith in such an irresponsible priest."

"That's not fair, Lord Tucher, I got locked out."

"I wanted *my* friar to bury Lady Emelia Priuli. I wanted her poor body put into the earth by a friend. Where were you, Felix?" my patron yells, his voice breaking painfully. "Where *were* you?"

"Gentlemen."

Like the snapping of a holy wafer in an echoing church, this dry, crisp word stills us. The desert speaks in our archway, in the guise of an ancient Saracen man.

"I know you have suffered a loss. I am here to see it redressed."

He does not yell or even speak loudly, yet his words reach every teeming, wet crevice of the cave. This venerable Saracen must be near to eighty years old, upright in posture, trim of beard, cleanly dressed in white robes with a crisp white turban. Someone has finally come to us.

"My name is Elphahallo," says he. "I am the Calinus, interpreter to the pilgrims. From this hour forth, you shall entrust your physical bodies to my keeping so that you may concentrate solely on your spiritual selves. I understand one among you has gone early to God. Who saw her attacker?"

If the patriarch Moses appeared in our archway, I don't believe he could have been more commanding. The Saracen rakes the cave with abrasive eyes, rooting up the truth, commanding our consciences. With a red face and an aching throat, I open my mouth to confess, to say, Yes, it is my fault. I deserted my patron in his hour

of need. I committed the worst sin a confessor could commit. I left
his son to carry the guilt of this woman's death; I abandoned my
dearest friend to an unholy obsession; worst of all, none of it helped.
She still got away. Had I only been here, I could have watched her.
I could have saved Priuli's life.

"I did it!" A Spanish pilgrim on the far side of the cave flings himself to the floor. "I killed my mother as sure as if I'd burnt her alive!"

His sobs echo through the cave; we watch horrified as he forces
mouthfuls of grassy feculence into his mouth, rubs it through his
hair, into his eyes.

"I needed the money. She never understood how desperate it was.
Mother, why else would I have married a Jew?"

The pilgrims part silently to allow Elphahallo into the cave. He
holds his white robes scrupulously above his ankles and picks his
way to the shrieking man.

"Christ, I've come to make peace with you! You took my mother,
you left me with that stinking convert Jew wife and her devil
father. Take me back! I need you!"

"You married a Jew?" someone beside him marvels.

"Stand up, my son," says Elphahallo, careful not to let his wide
sleeves trail across the man's shit-smeared face. "You must not
speak that way of your wife."

The Saracen addresses him in hushed tones for what feels like
an hour, but try as I may I can make out none of it. He shows the
pilgrim how to wipe his hands and mouth on his robe, demonstrat-
ing the procedure on his own pure white caftan. Soon after, the guilt-
stricken pilgrim quiets and Elphahallo addresses us once more.

"Each man must make his personal peace with God, and I know
many of you have journeyed to this place to do so. It is not my concern what baggage you brought with you from your separate homes,
unless in it you packed ill will against your brother. My sworn duty
as Calinus is to see that you stay safe while in my care, so I ask again:
Who marked that woman's murderer?"

"Excuse me, sir." To my surprise, Ursus speaks up. "I might have
seen something."

"What's that, child?"

Across the cave, John catches my eye, asks the question. *Did he see? Will he betray her?*

"Yesterday I bought what I thought were precious gems from a despicable unclean Saracen—no offense, sir—only to discover this morning that they were glass. Is it possible that same lying Saracen came back in the night to set me on fire so that I wouldn't tell and, in the darkness, killed the person beside me by mistake?"

"It's quite a theory, young man."

Lord Tucher boxes his son's ear, but Ursus will not be stilled.

"I only—" Ursus raises his voice over the laughter of his fellow pilgrims, straining his neck to be heard—"I only mention it—*please*—I only mention it because I thought I heard the lady scream while she was burning, 'It wasn't me!' I thought she screamed, *'It wasn't me!'*"

"I understand you discovered her, son, and I know that has been very hard on you," Elphahallo says at last. "I'll keep what you said in mind."

"What about that man? He took most of my money. Don't you want to know what he looks like, what he said?" Ursus demands.

"I know who he is."

"You know? And you let him prey on innocent pilgrims?"

"You bought gems off a desperate man for a fraction of what you would have paid back home, did you not? Who exactly, son, was preying on whom?" Elphahallo bows to us and turns to leave.

"I want my money!"

Ursus's scream shakes the cave, and that's all it takes.

"Wait! When are we leaving?"

"Our captain! Let us see our captain!"

"Why are we being held prisoner in this stinking shit hole? Why aren't we in Jerusalem?"

"I want my—"

"Will we have a guard? You're in league with them, aren't you."

"—money!"

Elphahallo answers no one but waits like a patient camel against a raging sandstorm. When at last he is certain to be heard, he touches his white turban respectfully.

"The other pilgrim ship is debarking at dawn. I'll ask you to remain inside until we've registered them and spoken with your captains about this tragedy."

And with a duck under the archway, he is gone.

Oh, the tedious hours.

Conrad found a dead tortoise yesterday, and in between the times we are lined up, counted, and checked off by the Saracens he sits by our lantern, hollowing the beast out with his knife. The meat he sets aside for stew; the muscle he shears as he did Constantine's intestine in the belly of the ship. I watch him bore two holes at each end of the shell, thread the sinew through, and tie it off at the bottom. He plucks the string. A lyre.

Disaffected Ursus consoles himself by stacking shells he collected on the beach one on top of the other. Clams and angel wings, scallops and oysters, he builds his little Tower of Shellfish Babel, then blasts it with his fist, sending it clattering across the cavern floor. Lord Tucher watches his son sorrowfully, while John stares intently into space. I want to see if Ser Niccolo has arrived, but the guard will not allow anyone outside, not even to pass water. There is nothing to do but wait. As we were born to wait.

When Christ walked the earth, so near and yet so far from this port of Joppa, He was wont sometimes to take his ease in the comfortable home of the sisters Saint Mary Magdalene and Saint Martha. Now, once when blessed Saint Martha was running herself ragged—going to market, chopping sweetmeats, setting places at table, spicing wine, ordering the servants about, tidying her hair, stirring the soup, sweeping the floor, and seeing to all else that must be done in honor of such an important guest as our Lord—she chanced to see her sister, Mary, sitting at His feet, listening calmly to His Word. Martha wiped the sweat from her brow, straightened her apron, and stepped out of the kitchen. "Mary," asked she, "can you be comfortable sitting while your sister goes crazy making all things happen?"

"Martha," said our Gentle Lord, touching the Magdalene's head, "Mary has chosen the best part, which shall not be taken away from her." By which he meant, Mary has chosen a life of contemplation over a life of action. When I have departed this world, she will have heard me, while you will have been bustling.

As you know, brothers, those of us in religious orders have chosen Mary's part. We have retired from the world to meditate upon Christ and devote our lives to prayer. But woe unto me! At the heart of my Mary life I am still a Martha! Try as I may, this enforced inactivity is more grievous to me than any amount of effort could possibly be.

I rise and tap our Saracen guard on the shoulder. Will he not, please, let me go outside? Again he shakes his head, gestures for me to return and sit with the other pilgrims. I sneak a quick peek over his shoulder and see Contarini's rowboat unloading six pilgrims onto the beach. They will soon have their first look at Saint Peter's Cellars, recapitulate our labors of yesterday, and scrape their own Mounts of Venus to the cave's center.

"Contarini is here?" John looks over my shoulder. He has not spoken since we left Emelia Priuli's grave, and his voice sounds small.

"Yes," I answer.

Had that wretched Mameluke not left me behind on Contarini's ship, none of this would have happened. We would be on our way to Jerusalem by now. My friend John looks ten years older than when we began our pilgrimage, as haggard as Constantine before he died. Does the Tongue have this effect on all men?

"I am glad she got away before they docked," he says.

Until recently, brothers, I had mistaken John Lazinus for a man of good sense. He had been nearly destroyed by the tragedy that befell his convent, that I knew, but his faith was intact; he was on pilgrimage to make peace with his past. Something must have changed the evening he spent alone with the Tongue in the ladies' cabin; while Conrad and I worked to preserve Constantine, Arsinoë was busy replacing one protector with another. John's heart was secured by the time we put the last stitch in the merchant's chest. By Christ, brothers, if I cannot get outside to warn the translator, I can, at least, get to the bottom of John's fixation. Without speaking, I lead the Archdeacon away from the cellar's mouth, back to that smudge of ash that was once La Priuli's crimson dress. I feel his resistance the closer we get to the spot.

"In this place," I say sternly, "a lady was killed. I had no fondness for her. She bewitched my patron and undermined my pilgrimage, but she was one of God's children. She was about to take her vows as a Bride of Christ. She would have been one of us."

"Why are you doing this?" The Archdeacon turns his face away, pretends not to smell the roasted-pork crispness of the flesh that melted into the cave floor. He cannot defend her, his Tongue, here in this place.

"I want to know what Arsinoë said to you the night of the storm."

"What do you care about that night?" he says protectively, as if it could be stolen from him, like a hand or an ear. "Didn't you do enough?"

"I care," I say slowly, "because that's the night you ceased being my friend."

I do not mean to say this, brothers. I do not mean to increase the distance growing between us. He is the only one who understood my need to reach Sinai, who never teased when I stopped in every church that had so much as a carving of Katherine in the nave. He accompanied me to Rhodes, to Cyprus; he sat with me over Constantine's voiding, exhausted body; why do I need to wound him? Why did he have to give his heart to her?

"You said last night that you loved her, even after she set Emelia on fire," I prompt. "Why, John? What did she promise you that night?"

"Don't you understand, Felix?" John Lazinus whispers angrily, pointing to the thin skin of ashes on the floor. "Don't you see this is my punishment? How many women have I already watched burn? Do you not think God saw my sin and set alight another?"

The Archdeacon throws himself into the corner of the cave, still sticky with the Saracens' filth. Several nosy pilgrims approach us, but I wave them off impatiently. Cautiously, I crouch beside my friend.

"I am still your confessor if you want me." I take his hand, as I saw Arsinoë do on the beach, and prepare to hear the worst. "I can still absolve you if you desire absolution."

"I was so weak that night," he says, so softly I have to bend down to hear him. "To have used her after she had been violated."

So it is true. I try to swallow my bitter disappointment.

"John, you are a man," I finally say. "And chastity is a nearly impossible vow."

He turns on me horrified. "You think that? My God, Felix, what sort of fiend do you take me for? Listen to me." He laughs ruefully. "What right do I have to be offended when what I did was so much worse?"

"What did you do?"

He shakes his head. "She was exhausted. She was sick. I forced her into it."

"Into what?"

"Into calling Saint Katherine!" he yells, furious at me for goading him into this. "I believe in her because I *saw*. Katherine was with us the night of the storm."

Can he possibly be telling the truth? To have withheld this from me, when he *knew*; when he, of all men on earth, knew the anguish I felt at having lost her. I stare at him, speechless, sickened, mortified.

"At first she said Katherine wouldn't come without her brother present." John speaks, but I look at anything but him: Conrad giving my patron's son his first unnecessary shave, two French pilgrims arm wrestling; a Saracen merchant pleading with our guard to let him enter and sell us yogurt. Though life continues in the cellar, I am numb to all but John's relentless voice.

"When she saw I was about to leave her, to go find you and give her up, she pulled me back into the room. 'Wait,' she said, in a voice beyond all human exhaustion, 'what do you want to know?'

"I looked on her then, Felix, with wolfish eyes. Not on her bruised and battered body newly covered with Constantine's robes, nor on her aching, uncertain face, nor on her eyes, filled with the pain and humiliation I'd seen in sixty other pairs of eyes when, God forgive me, they still had eyes. I ignored every part of her that was still a woman and searched for that place beyond her that I needed to find, if I was to believe.

"'Prove she speaks to you,' I ordered. 'Ask her what has become of my sixty nuns.'"

John drops his head into his lap and covers his face.

"Are we not each of us greedy for Heaven's attention?" he asks. "Is it not greed that sends a young girl to a fortune-teller or a duke to an astrologer? Was it not greed that made me force Arsinoë open, even after she had already been pried apart by a force larger than herself? A man is not allowed the luxury of remorse like mine unless he has already gone too far or taken too much. We are the plunderers of Heaven, Felix, we greedy mortals."

And yet, I think to myself, you at least, John, have seen the riches that are to be had. You have heard Katherine with your own ears, looked upon her with your own eyes. I cannot plunder if I am no more than a beggar at the gate, and it appears that is all I am ever likely to be.

"What did Katherine say?" I ask roughly.

John's eyes fill with tears, and he swipes them away. "That she had gathered my poor slain daughters to her. She was tending their burns with sweet heavenly ointments; she was brushing their hair to encourage it to grow. They were not restored yet, but they were on the mend."

My need to know is as great as John's, and yet I almost choke on the words. "What was she like, Saint Katherine?"

"Like fire on a mountain," he says.

"Damn you, John Lazinus!" I shout, rising to leave. Across the cave, Ursus's troubled eyes are on me, wondering what has made his friar angry now. I have been convinced of Arsinoë's madness since we opened her trunk to find it empty, since she took on the life of a dead man and walked the ship in his clothes. Now my own friend, a man I have trusted and depended upon, says he saw Heaven through this woman, that my own wife spoke to him through her. What am I to believe?

"Come back, Felix." He pulls me down to him by my robe. "Katherine commanded us to help her. We were to make certain Arsinoë conveys her relics safely to Sinai. It is her will."

"How can it be her will if there are no bones?" I snap. "This is
further proof of the Tongue's madness, don't you see? Her brother
told me all the bones those crazy peasants brought were buried
behind their slaughterhouse!"

"When did her brother tell you this?" he asks sharply.

I feel my face turn red. For the first time since I boarded Contarini's galley, I feel the furtiveness of what I've done.

"Last night," I say finally. "I was on his ship."

"What?" John's voice is fierce.

"I overheard you talking of escape. I thought her brother should
know."

"You were going to turn her in without telling me?" John cries.
"Just hand her over to her brother?"

"You were going to help her run away!" I accuse him, just as
angrily. "I certainly was not consulted about that."

"She was terrified of her brother." John has leapt to his feet. "She
thinks he is trying to kill her."

There is a scuffle at the entrance to our cellar. Our Saracen guard
steps aside to admit two men; the first is the short Saracen yogurt
seller, who wiggles in under the guard's armpit and immediately
withdraws ramekins of his cool white dessert for the pilgrims' in-
spection. The second is Ser Niccolo, the translator.

"What is he doing here?" John gasps.

"I told him to come for his sister."

He picks his way through the crowd, searching, no doubt, for me.
He is a good head taller than most of the pilgrims, and I watch his
curly black scalp, like a snake on the water, wind its way closer.

"Felix, Arsinoë has had only a night's head start." John clenches
my arm. "You can't tell him she's fled."

"What am I supposed to tell him?" I ask the wild-eyed John, whose
grip is bruising my arm.

"Tell him she set herself on fire," John says.

"Are you out of your mind?"

Ser Niccolo bends familiarly over my newly shaved patron's son,
Ursus. The boy smiles and points me out to him.

"Katherine wills it," John insists. "Arsinoë is doing her will. Do you know for sure she is not?"

What am I to believe? Ser Niccolo bears down upon me, his eyes troubled and dark. Surely Contarini's pilgrims have heard the tragedy that took place here last night. Surely Niccolo knows a woman went up in flames.

"You must help her, Felix," John whispers, as Niccolo steps up to us. "For me."

The translator does not even glance at my friend; he has eyes only for me. What do I do? I am all confusion.

"Abdullah says the only woman in your party was found in flames last night," the translator says. "Tell me it is not true."

John's hand is on my arm. I may be damned for all eternity for this. I may have sold my wife for a slave.

"It is true," I say, and, just like that, Arsinoë has stolen another life. "Your sister, the Tongue, is gone."

Asses

The sun set by the time our captains, not wanting to slow the pilgrimage with an investigation, declared Emelia Priuli's death an act of God. We stepped out of the cave to find a half-moon rising. I pulled my damp robes around me and breathed in the cold shore smells: rotting crab claws, driftwood, picked bodies, rock.

"She's over here."

I led the translator to Emelia Priuli's grave. He would take one look at this charred body and recognize the fraud. He would call me irregular priest and false friend, beat me to within an inch of my life, I thought, and all this I would deserve.

Niccolo knelt and gently touched the earth over Emelia's face. Long strands of melted hair stayed fixed to the scalp. Surely, I thought, he would recognize the hairs.

"Will you take her body home to Crete?" I asked softly.

He slowly shook his head. "I have business in Jerusalem. I don't think I have the means to preserve her."

"I'm sorry," I said. "She was more self-destructive than I thought."

The translator nodded slowly, rocking back on his haunches. I was about to help him up when, without warning, he fell upon the grave and tilled up the body, harrowing the charred joints like stones in a field. The baked head separated from the torso, but he embraced the jumble, breathing deeply as of a bouquet of roses.

"Do you smell anything, Friar?" he asked.

"No," I replied.

"Neither do I."

Niccolo dropped the bones and walked away.

"There's a translator's quarter in Jerusalem." He spoke more to himself than to me. "Maybe they will let me study with them until I can find the strength to go home."

"That's a fine idea." I dug into the earth with my hands and slowly began to reinter Emelia Priuli.

"Don't you find it awful, not understanding?" he asked me, gesturing to the hundreds of pilgrims milling about with their luggage. The Italians from Contarini's ship had sought out the Italians from Lando's; French had found French; the women, no matter what nationality, stuck close together.

"Not understanding what?" I asked.

"What people are saying all around you. All these private conversations in all these private languages."

"No one can speak all of God's tongues," I reminded him gently.

"The Donestre can. They can speak all the languages of the world, Friar Felix. But we'd do well to stay far away from them." His eyes welled with moonlight, overflowed his cheeks.

"Who are the Donestre?" I asked.

"A race of men I met in the Red Sea. If you were to go to their island, Friar, one would call to you in an accent so subtle, you'd believe he grew up in the next parish over.

"*Felix . . . Felix Fabri . . .* he would call. *Good Abbot Ludwig Fuchs commends me to you. Come and eat with us.*

"You would walk up the path to the rock where he sits, holding out his arms for an embrace, and you would be so delighted to find someone from Ulm in the middle of the troubled sea, you'd happily fling yourself into them. The Donestre would kiss you on your cheeks and eyes. He would murmur in the voice of your favorite aunt and remind you of your boyhood summers in Zurich. You wouldn't feel his teeth on your leg until it was too late. First your knees would be gone, then your thighs. Your trunk would be eaten and then your shoulders. The Donestre would devour you, all but the head. And then he would sit and weep over the head."

"Felix?" John approached with a lantern. "Everyone is moving down to the beach."

"I got away with my life." Niccolo rolled down his thigh-high yellow boot and pulled up his slashed hose to reveal a deeply churned red scar. "Because he recognized me for what I am."

John tugged my robe, glaring at the translator. "Come on, Felix. They'll leave without us."

"A kindred spirit."

I let John lead me away from this man, this friend of monsters. We unhinged him with our lies. As we walked back to the cave to collect our trunks and roll up our pallets, John smiled wanly at me. I could not look at him. What we did was wrong. I saw again the despair on Ser Niccolo's face as he pressed that woman's remains to his face. Was he sniffing for sanctity, for the holy scent of myrrh? Did the translator believe, in his secret heart, that his sister had talked to Heaven?

But enough, brothers! I can bear no more to examine my sins. I promised, when I left, to keep a balanced account of my pilgrimage: the sacred and the profane, the serious and the absurd. What befell the pilgrims next may not be omitted if you are to experience, first hand, what we endured that night.

Like ants on a stick, we walked single file down the path to the beach, each pilgrim hefting his trunk in his arms, each praying not to collapse under its weight. Upon the beach, the shadowy donkeys blended with the sea, a few white-capped backs moving restlessly among them, as anxious to convey us to the Holy City as we were to mount them. Finally, we were on our way, brothers. I stood looking about for the rest of my company when, without any warning, a dark calloused hand reached out and grabbed my arm.

How I screamed, brothers—like a girl! My trunk bumped along my spine as it slid to the ground; my shins slammed against sharp rocks. Because my captor had grabbed my right hand with his right hand, I was dragged awkwardly, stumbling, twisted like a kite's flapping tail behind him.

"Stop!" I screamed, digging in my heels and trying to reverse our momentum. Where was he taking me? All around, pilgrims were

grabbed, fought over, yanked like wishbones. Where was Ursus? My
Saracen tugged harder, pulling me off balance while repeating many
words I could not understand. I fell and he helped me up, barely
missing a step.

When at last I realized what was going on, I was too out of breath
to protest. My Saracen shoved me astride a black donkey and pat-
ted her thick neck frenetically. *"Gut! Es Gut!"*

The donkey whinnied softly and pushed at his hand with her nose.
In fact, she *was* a good donkey, her spine not too sharp, her flanks
not too barrelish.

"No. Not *gut.*" I leapt from the donkey and mimed myself dragged
like Hector behind Achilles' chariot at Troy. The Saracen bowed
low before me and clasped my hands repeatedly, I think in a show
of apology. Evidently, more ass drivers from Joppa arrive than pilgrims, and thus the drivers must fight for business. This rough and
squinty Saracen gestured behind him to a noble member of his faith,
beturbaned and sitting astride a purebred horse. The mounted
Saracen held aloft a torch, touched me gently with his staff, and said
much more to me that I could not understand, but which I took to
mean:

"Stay, Christian pilgrim, and accept our ass. My name is Galela,
and this is my slave Cassa. If you have need of him on your wanderings, call Galelacassa; he will come to you and serve you faithfully
without overcharging you or mistreating you in any way."

Looking over the broken asses foisted upon the other pilgrims, I
reluctantly agreed to stay with Cassa. He ran back for my trunk and
affixed it to the saddle behind me.

So here I sit, astride my donkey, brothers, waiting for the other
pilgrims to be settled on other asses. The Saracens take a school-
boyish delight in annoying Christian pilgrims, and even Cassa, who
seems a good sort, peers over my shoulder like a monkey and wonders at my letters, even as I put them on the page. I cannot say I am
unhappy to leave Joppa behind. I have committed many sins for
having been only one full day on holy soil, and I am carrying into
Jerusalem a heavy heart. Pray for me, brothers, pray that things may
change.

The moon hangs low in the sky, and dawn will break in a few hours, Elphahallo announces. We must prepare ourselves for an arduous journey to Jerusalem. We may encounter rough Arabs on the way, and if this occurs we are to stay calm and let our Saracen guides protect us. On no account are we to draw weapons.

Elphahallo addresses the pilgrims who have, for piety's sake, elected to walk across the burning desert into Jerusalem. "Know you that you walk of your own volition," says he, "and if you cannot keep up, you will either be left behind or you will have to find your own ass driver. Do not return to your homelands saying that Saracens will not suffer Christians to ride through their country but make them walk in the heat. Witness this is not so. Are you so resigned?"

Two walking pilgrims slink away from the group and procure drivers. The rest, perhaps twenty in all, remain. Elphahallo surveys the pocket of barefoot walkers, the legion of donkey drivers, the Mameluke and Saracen guards, armed and on horseback. Asses stamp their impatience, guards joke, but when Elphahallo raises his staff high above his head and shouts, we Christians fall as silent as the grave.

"Pilgrims, set your hearts for Jerusalem. We are off!"

ii

Prayers

"Do you hear it? That tapping?"

"Yes, I think so. Look, it's moving."

My patron and his son stare fixedly at the back wall of our room, here in the well-appointed pilgrim's hospice of Ramleh. After a weary night and day of traveling, we've finally put to rest at the man-made oasis left us by Duke Philip of Burgundy, of blessed memory. My party has taken a room off the loggia that opens onto a court-yard complete with marble fountain and spreading green fig trees. All eyes are turned away from Nature's beauty, however, riveted on a single large block of stone, waist-high from the floor, that appears to be wiggling its way toward us.

"What do you suppose they're doing?"

"Repairing the wall?" Conrad ventures.

"I think they're trying to break through." Lord Tucher paces. "To rob us."

I snort, perhaps too rudely.

"After what happened in Joppa, Friar Felix, I'm not about to take chances with my son's life." Lord Tucher picks up the weapon of war he wrought after Emelia's assassination, a sea urchin on a stick.

Fellow pilgrims, lured by our intense concentration, stop into the room, depart in search of boards and stones—as we are forbidden by Article Thirteen to wear daggers slung about us—and return to wait. The mood in our cell has grown so black, I fear for whoever is working to reach us. I hope for his sake he is a bad man—a robber or an assassin—because, good or bad, he will not escape a braining.

The stone teeters and drops to the ground.

"All right, dog!" Lord Tucher shouts at the hole. "Show yourself!"

A thick brick of setting sun replaces the missing stone, confirming that the culprit bored through from outdoors. Ursus leans down to put his eye to the hole, but his father yanks him back.

"Whoever you are," Tucher calls, his voice cracking, "come out."

We all breathe shallowly, each man with a different threat before him: demons, Turks, red poisonous gas from the East that saps the will and leaves us slaves to the Sultan. The tension is unbearable. I have to look.

"Felix, don't!" Lord Tucher grabs for my collar, but I throw off his hand. Momentarily blinded by the pink light, it takes a second for my eyes to find their subject, and when they do my confusion is so great it takes another for my mind to process it.

"Don't!" I pull back. "Don't look!"

But it is too late. She sticks her head through the hole for all to see and calls to us in her heathen language: a Saracen woman, swathed in the black crepe veils they wear, and behind her, in a mirror courtyard to our own, five of her wanton sisters. They gyrate with gloved hands, these mute Lorelei dipped in tar. A rough grip on my shoulder pulls me away from the hole.

"Let me see!"

"No! Me!"

All the male pilgrims want to spy on the Saracen women, and together they cause a great push, as when flesh arrives in times of famine. I back away frightened. Tenth Article: Let the pilgrims beware of gazing on any Saracen women, as their husbands are exceedingly jealous and apt to do harm. Eleventh Article: Should any Saracen woman beckon to a pilgrim and invite him into her house, on no accounts go. Two articles against such behavior, and yet they will not stop.

Ursus struggles to the front.

"What are your names? Are you married?"

"Are you attracted to us? Is that why you broke in?"

"Are you in trouble?"

These knights and pilgrims query the women as if expecting them to suddenly reply in the German tongue, and the women answer nonsensically to whatever it is they suppose we say. Throughout this fruitful conversation, the pilgrims trade places so that each can gaze upon the women in their natural hareem, not out furtively shopping or disappearing into doorways as has heretofore seemed their wont. Never have we met such brazen women in the East, but assumed them all to be chaste and frightened of their men, as commanded by their Alcoran.

"If only we had some way of talking to them!" Ursus wails. "I want to ask them about their hair!"

As I have no desire to see how this folly plays out, I quietly take up my mat and book and walk up the marble stairs to the hospice's flat-tiered roof, there to take advantage, in the Saracen fashion, of the cool night air. A Minorite friar, one of the monks assigned to watch over us in Ramleh, rushes past me with a bowl of mortar and a trowel. I can hear the lecture he will give our ungovernable pilgrims now, for if a Saracen man catches them making sport with his women the punishment will be conversion or death.

Below me, across the city of Ramleh, a hundred Saracen steeples puncture the twilight. Flat-bedded donkey carts, hillocked with boughs of cherries, roll through the dark streets; behind them walk slow, sandaled men, bone-weary after an afternoon's harvest. Are they headed home to discover that their wives have been soliciting lusty Western pilgrims through chinks in the wall? Do they have to fear, every time they leave the house, that their spouses will reveal themselves to others?

Is there any faith left in women, brothers? As much as I have tried to push it from my mind, the night of the storm returns to me again and again: my friend the Archdeacon John writhing on the Tongue's pallet, bent over the aching girl who slowly becomes my wife. He held her and looked into her eyes and asked questions of her like a familiar; and she answered him. Every time I look at John, I feel her betrayal. Today, in a church outside of Gath, the city that bred Goliath and the Dog-Headed Saint Christopher, John stopped to point out a carving of Saint Katherine I had overlooked. She stood between Saint Christopher, who only became a man after he ferried Christ across the river, and Saint Nicholas, whom some in our country depict as a child-eater. The mason had been careless and had carved Katherine's sword so that it appeared to pierce Saint Christopher's flat bare foot. The smile on her face was full of satisfaction and, worse, brothers, drew into an almost carnal smirk, pressed as she was between two male saints. I could not bear to look on her, and when John came around to see what disturbed me, I could not look on him either.

Farther out, our Calinus, Elphahallo, with several of his companions who have also made their beds on the roof, talk among themselves, sharing bread and melons. When he sees me, Elphahallo beckons for me to join them.

"Friar Failisk"—he smiles—"come lay your bed near us."

I smile but shake my head no, preferring, instead, to spread out my mat a little higher up.

"Will you not at least take some fruit?" The Calinus extends a juicy pink wedge encased in green rind. I want no more to think on women, brothers, so I walk down to sit with the Saracens.

"Thank you," I say, gingerly biting into the melon. Oh, what ineffable springtime sweetness! Like crunchy new-scythed grass and honey on the tongue. I accept the second piece he offers and, cautiously, eat that as well.

"The name of this town, Ramleh," Elphahallo says, "means lofty. Look how far you can see, Failisk. And over there, the patch where they grow your melons."

Indeed, brothers, Ramleh is a green, fertile place, and everything here is cheap, sweet, and exceedingly good, save only its citizens, who are evil-minded and bear an especial hatred to Christians. When we arrived, they would not suffer us to ride our donkeys into town but commanded us to dismount and carry our luggage on our backs like pack slaves. Bad boys sat on the hospice rooftop, while we celebrated divine service in the courtyard, and hindered our worship by hooting and laughing and twisting their fingers with an ill meaning. We looked in our turn with serious countenances at these boys and signed to them to go down, which only after much joking did they do.

One cannot appreciate the foreignness of the Saracens until one has dwelt for a few days among them, brothers. They wear hermaphroditic clothing, so that from the back it is difficult to distinguish their sex, and upon their heads turbans, after the fashion of the drunken god Dionysus, who bound his head against the headache after too much drinking. The Saracens' false prophet, Mahomet, followed the tradition of Dionysus, both in turban wearing and in excessive imbibing, until one day he committed homicide while inebriated and forever after swore off drink for himself and his followers. The turbans, however, he allowed to remain.

Elphahallo, Cassa, and the many Saracens we meet, from the Sultan's officials to the humble food merchants who feed us every day, seem genuinely helpful, yet we mustn't forget their manifest heresies. Elphahallo and his kind declare that God cannot have a Son, because He has no wife, and that He does not live because He does not eat! Cassa believes Christ was not God, only a good man, and calls him merely Rucholla, the Breath of God. Our food merchants might be accomplished in their cooking of eggs, but as for their understanding of Creation, they are mooncalves! Imagine believing that Heaven is made of vapor, which is called an exhalation of the sea, and that in the Beginning there was no distinction between night and day! Saracens also enjoin a plurality of wives and do not scruple to recognize sodomy.

Beside me, Elphahallo rises, and as if to keep the world in balance the last kernel of sun drops behind the hills. From the high round steeple tower across the street, a long atonal howl startles me from my third slice of melon. I once read that Saracens fear the twilight and will bellow to keep the sun awake so he won't oversleep and forget them in the morning. I ask Elphahallo if this is true, and he laughs.

"No, Failisk." He orients a red rug away from the setting sun. "That is our priest, and he is giving us our call to prayer. You must excuse us for a few moments, while we give thanks to God."

And lo, brothers, even while I watch, these Saracens bow their heads and bodies down to earth and remain awhile in this position, while their priest stands atop his tower and performs the office of bells, uttering his profession of faith. Such a noise you never did hear, but that it sounds like goats and calves, for it is known the world over that Easterns cannot sing. In musical notation, their prayer goes like this:

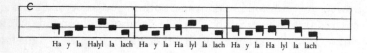

Watching these Saracens pray together like monks all of one order, I grow sad and disquieted of heart. I compare these utterly lost men who only aggravate their damnation with the gravity and devotion of their prayers, provoking against themselves the wrath of God by methodically dishonoring His saints and angels with their blasphemous prayers, to the wretched Christians downstairs who, though redeemed by Christ's blood, would rather consort with wanton Saracen women than keep their faith! And when compelled to pray, how often do they offer those prayers with levity and unspeakable lukewarmness and wandering thoughts? I fear many Christians pass the whole day without any adoration of God or prayer to Him, which thing you would never find among the Saracens, Turks, Jews, or Barbarians.

"Calinus," I ask him, when the Saracens are finished with their prayers, "are you not worried about damning yourself even further with your great seriousness of faith, understanding as you do that your people are consigned to Hell for not knowing the Savior, Jesus Christ?"

Elphahallo shakes his head and hands me yet one more slice of delicious melon. "You are not the first pilgrim to fret over my immortal soul, Friar Failisk. I once escorted a good German knight to Sinai who loved me so dearly, and worried so much about my damnation, that he kidnapped me and took me to the court of your Emperor and Pope. I will tell you what I told the vicar of your

Church, before he grew so frustrated by my stubbornness that he
sent me home.

"A man might only be saved in the faith to which he is born, I
said, provided he keeps it pure. To me, the only men worthy of damnation are those who become enchanted by what they are not: those
Saracens who embrace Christ, or Christians who embrace Mahomet.
Though the Mamelukes have converted to Islam, the faith of my
father and grandfather, in my opinion every one of them is damned,
because, as I see it, the renunciation of one's own native God is the
only unpardonable sin."

"You said that to the Pope?" I wonder that a man more than eighty
years of age, an upright Saracen of seeming moral virtue, could have
so little knowledge of the truth.

"Yes." Elphahallo smiles at his Saracen companions as though
sharing a rich joke. "Then he weighed me down with presents and
sent me back to my family."

I pensively chew my melon. "Calinus," I ask, "you say you escorted that pilgrim to Sinai? What do you know of Saint Katherine's
Monastery there?"

"I know a good deal," he says, gently wiping away a black melon
seed that was caught in my beard. "I have crossed the desert many
times in my life."

"And you have survived," I marvel.

"Many times I thought I would not." He laughs.

"What do you know of the monastery's current condition?" I ask.
"We were told it has been burned to the ground."

Elphahallo confers with his Saracen companions, who shake their
white-turbaned heads emphatically. Several of them look upon me
kindly, and one holds out a plate to collect my stack of gnawed
melon rinds.

"My cousins confirm what I thought," Elphahallo says. "We heard
the monastery was attacked last year, but no one believes it was
destroyed. If you have vowed to go, Failisk, you may keep that vow."

I thank the Calinus and agree, out of courtesy, to take several
more slices of melon back to my pallet. I eat them mechanically, in
a quandary of self-doubt, brothers. Here I have been presented the

means of fulfilling my most solemn vow, and yet for the first time in my entire wretched life I wonder if I still have the desire to go. No one else knows that Saint Katherine's Monastery still stands, that it is attainable with the help of this Calinus, and so it would be no public shame to abide by Lord Tucher's wishes, returning with the other pilgrims to Swabia. It would require only my silence, which, you, Abbot Fuchs, remind me I indulge all too infrequently.

O God, save me from these doubts.

Why, when now I think upon Katherine, the chaste bride of my youth, do I see her as some pawed village slut, swinging her allegiance from one grimy man to another? Why does she expose her flesh and invite any and all to handle those delicate bones I have venerated for lo these twenty years?

I lie back under these strange stars in this strange country and wonder what has become of Felix Fabri, husband to Katherine, brother of Ulm, son to Abbot Ludwig Fuchs, that he could think upon Sinai without the slightest excitement—that he could think upon it even, I blush to confess, with dread.

A Holy City

Cassa, my ass driver, points out many things along the tooth-jarring, dust-choked, arduous ride into Jerusalem.

"*Shoof,*" he says.

A palm tree split in two by lightning.

"*Shoof.*"

A large rock shaped like a sheep.

"*Shoof.*" On and on, he points. Objects that need no language. As the sun rises and the day grows hotter, Cassa and I devise a game to help us forget the heat. He points out an object—say, a fence or a statue—and says its name for me in Arabic. I repeat what he says, adding its name in German, whereupon Cassa gives it back to me in German and finds a new word in Arabic. In this way, we braid together a conversation of sorts, though I often feel bad for Cassa in his inability to reproduce our sounds. I have no problem at all with his language, but say each word correctly on the first try.

This morning we took our leave of the comfortable hospice at Ramleh and fixed our sights on the blessed road to Jerusalem. Once more, we hefted our trunks and shuffled through the dusty streets, kicking up a cloud so thick we could not have recognized the man next to us, be he our own brother. I suffered especially from having committed excesses in eating too greedily of melons the night before, which thing I did to my own hurt. How grateful I was to see Cassa and my comfortable ass at the edge of town!

Now we have been traveling in the hot sun for hours, three abreast, flanked by Mameluke and Saracen guards. The heat and crush and rocky terrain have conspired to incite the tempers of the duller pilgrims, for to those unread in Scripture, Palestine appears a nation cursed by God. I will provide but one example of how the Devil grabs hold of our donkeys' tails and rides with us into Jerusalem:

"Augsburg is a much better place than this," complained one very belligerent knight, a man whom I had often seen, while still on the ship, lift above his head heavy casks of the cook's vinegar, merely to advertise his strength. "At least you see a fucking stream every now and then."

Abdullah, the German Mameluke, who rode next to me as part of the regiment assigned to protect us from Arab attacks on the road, cut his eyes at this new sacrilege. "How can you compare a reeking German cesspool to our Lord's land of milk and honey?" asked he contemptuously.

"By Lord, do you mean God or Allah?" sneered the knight. "Show me the Lord's milk. Show me His honey! This land is as dried up as your mother's apostate cunt."

See, brothers, how the Devil dogs this pilgrimage?

Contarini's ladies, several rows ahead, pricked their asses and trotted ahead. Abdullah spun his horse around, logjamming the rest of us.

"What did you call my mother?"

To my horror, the Mameluke leapt from his horse and unsheathed his sword. Pilgrims scattered, breaking ranks with their asses, knocking their drivers to the ground. Only one pilgrim retained his countenance; from the corner of my eye, I saw Ser Niccolo standing apart, silently observing the riot. As if about to lay a wager, he sized up the combatants: the Mameluke was certainly the more fearsome of the two, with his wild blond mustache and blue-veined neck. The knight of Augsburg met Abdullah's sword with a ludicrously small branch, prohibited as he was by Article Thirteen from carrying a blade. Though greatly overpowered, he would not keep silent.

"If there is any manna falling from these heavens, it's Allah shaking his prick on the likes of you, Mameluke," he said, or something equally obscene.

"You impious fuck!" shouted Abdullah. He lunged and jabbed at the knight's shoulder. Knight Augsburg spun, and the sword just missed Cassa's eye. To his credit, my ass driver barely flinched, believing, as do all Easterns, that his day of dying is set and is therefore unavoidable.

O contentious, murderous, sinful pilgrims! Even at the gates of Jerusalem you desire to shed blood! What is it about this land that inspires violence, when minds should be fixed on peace; that breeds intolerance when Christ selflessly died upon it to save each one of you? I know now why the word *pilgrim* is translated "stranger," for you are all strangers to the Truth, trespassers against God's commandments! All this and more I said in my heart, praying not to have another homicide before we reached the Holy Sepulchre. Even as Abdullah took a second pass, Ser Niccolo maneuvered his donkey between the combatants and put his mouth to the Mameluke's ear. What he said, I still do not know: perhaps having just lost a sister, he pleaded not to lose a friend; perhaps he impressed upon the Mameluke the holiness of this site and the great damage that his soul would endure should he profane it. Whatever the case, Knight Augsburg used this opportunity to slash Abdullah across the cheek with his feckless stick.

And even as I thought the end had come, that Abdullah would return blow for blow and our pilgrimage would be stained with yet more wasted blood, a miracle occurred. The Mameluke, having listened intently to what Ser Niccolo had to say, sheathed his sword and angrily remounted his horse. Knight Augsburg was left flailing his branch, cursing at no one, until several of his companions stepped in and led him away.

Ursus Tucher trots up beside me to glower at the still-seething Mameluke.

"Ursus." I smile, realizing the boy has never met this strangely dressed creature beside me. "Let me introduce you to Peter Ber. His Mameluke name is Abdullah, but he is from outside of Augsburg."

"How do you do, Herr Mameluke?" murmurs Ursus.

"Fine, thank you, son." The Mameluke in his turn ignores the boy, straining to find Ser Niccolo in the surging crowd ahead.

"If I were a Knight of the Holy Sepulchre," Ursus says suddenly, rudely, "I would have to fight you as an enemy of our Faith."

"That you would, son." Abdullah agrees, and spurs his horse to overtake the translator.

"Wretched Infidel." The boy practices his swagger on me, but I am unimpressed.

Lo, my brothers! Even as I am about to list for Ursus the proper sentiments a knighthood of the Holy Sepulchre should inspire, the boy turns his eyes eastward toward the swelling land and puts his hand upon my arm. Perched upon the next high mountain's top, we spy an octagonal marble church, whereupon we marvel and call to Elphahallo, asking what place of worship that might be.

"Behold, pilgrims," says this venerable Saracen, "though nearer to you than this mountain, you cannot yet see your holy city. Your first glimpse of Jerusalem is the Mount of Olives, and atop it the Church of the Ascension, from which your Savior was translated into heaven."

Oh, God, Oh, God, my brothers! We spring from our asses, two hundred exhausted pilgrims suddenly rejuvenated, and pray toward that holy mountain: Jerusalem beyond maps and others' accounts; Jerusalem transcending portraits, icons, books. My fat tears wet her holy cheeks, my spittle drips onto her bosom. We leap back upon our donkeys, kicking our heels into their sides like bad children, and beg our drivers to make haste for the city. We've gone less than half a German mile when we stop again.

"Cassa, why are we still?" I demand, ready to combust at the delay. He points to where the pilgrims up ahead have dismounted and are wandering toward a dry stone wall behind an abandoned castle.

"What's this?" I race up front, peering over the heads of Contarini's old ladies.

"Castle Emmaus," whispers one of the white-hairs. "The inn that received our Lord on the day of his Resurrection."

What a welcome for the bone-weary traveler! Here the resurrected Jesus, disguised as a pilgrim, broke bread with his disciples Luke and Cleophas, who knew him not. We feel Christ, in the same dusty pilgrim garb as we, has come out of His city to greet us. *You go in,* He says, embracing us. *Witness my passion. I have my own pilgrimage to make—I'm off to my Father's house.* How we kiss this spot, my brothers, and here receive indulgences. (††)

For the duration of my stay in the Holy Land, brothers, I will use the symbol (††) to designate the places we prayed and thereby received indulgences.

After marveling for a while at this place, we remount our asses and climb up out of the Valley of Terebinth toward the south. Gradually, the earth becomes greener, and even the Augsburg knight finds vegetation in which to delight. We trot past terra-cotta pots of herbs set out to sun atop a stone fence and into an orchard of ripening fig trees. I reach up for the boughs above my head to pluck a green fig when Cassa shakes me suddenly.

"*Shoof!*"

We see it, all at once.

Blue-and-white Jerusalem, shining in the sun.

How to describe the most Holy City, my brothers? Can I even see it through my tears? It is a wavy city, a blurry city, one obscured by salt and wet lashes and thick-coming sobs. It is a city seen from the ground, seen in shy glimpses through the fingertips of hands that cover an open, shaking mouth. Only birth and the winning of hard races bring about this sort of unconsolable joy. From halfway across the world we've run to this place—Germans, Italians, Hungarians, Spaniards—we outran death and seasickness, anger and intrigue, to finish our race at Christ's home on earth.

"*Te Deum laudamus.*" I struggle through the tightness in my throat. "*Te Dominum confitemur.*"

Up ahead Lord Tucher joins in, softly singing Saint Ambrose's hymn of thanksgiving. John Lazinus feelingly begins the first few chords before realizing his order in Hungary sings the *Te Deum* to a different tune. No matter. His voice joins ours cacophonously, encouraging other monks, from other orders, to weave in their melodies, each according to the notation of their choirs at home. Never have you heard such a joyous, polyphonal, heartfelt song, for even the laypersons join in—some knowing the tune but not the words, some knowing neither but humming loudly some prayer of their own. How the sight of Jerusalem changes these contentious, grasping, chatty men! I see pilgrims lie powerless on the ground, as by an excess of devotion, sapped of reason. I see others wandering among the asses, beating their breasts like those pursued by evil spirits. Others drop to their knees and extend their arms in the shape of the cross; others shriek aloud as though in labor. A few pilgrims lose all command of themselves and, out of immoderate zeal to please God, make strange and childish gestures, jabbering in a language that I think not of this earth.

My brothers, had you been through the hardships we've endured, and gazed for yourselves upon the longed-for Holy City, I do not think you could have stanched a flood of tears. Witness: Some young Saracen shepherds who left their flocks to mock us, when they saw the deep earnestness of the pilgrims, went quietly away. And some of them remained and wept with us.

Here Follows a Brief Description of Our Procession to the Holy Places on and Around Mount Sion

After unloading our luggage at the Hospital of Saint John, a vaulted, ruinous building far more squalid than our accommodations in Ramleh, we joined the venerable abbot of Mount Sion's Order of the Brothers Minor, Father Guardian, as we call him, for a tour of the nearby holy sites. If I told you of all we saw, my brothers, this account would encompass eight books, for every stone holds a story, every street a chapter and verse. I will take you with me, then, a little ways, at least until my hand cramps up and I am forced to set aside my pen.

THE PLACE WHERE SAINT THOMAS, BEING DOUBTFUL, TOUCHED THE LORD'S WOUNDS

Having heard mass in the noble Church of Mount Sion, built over the spot of our Lord's Last Supper, we descended a flight of steps and came to the Chapel of Saint Thomas, who by his most profitable curiosity won the privilege of touching Christ's wounds.

Many saints have taken their refreshment at Christ's side: Saint Bernard, Saint Francis. Saint Catherine of Siena, that holy maid, was once changing the bandages of an ulcerous woman when, overcome by the stench, she vomited the contents of her stomach. Angry at the weakness of her own flesh, Catherine straightaway collected the pus and bloody bandages and, going off apart, swallowed the whole. That same night, Christ appeared before her and, laying His right hand upon her neck, guided her mouth to the wound in His side, saying, "Drink, my daughter, whereby thy soul will be filled with sweetness. As you have gone beyond your own nature, so I will give thee a drink beyond all that human nature is wont to receive."

The iron spear with which Christ's side was pierced is kept in Nuremberg; I have both seen it and handled it. I now stood on the spot where Thomas reached out his hand to prod that spear wound, and thereby received indulgences (††).

The Burial Place of David and Solomon

Outside the Church of Sion, but not outside its gates, we found a small door leading into what appeared another church. As it was shut tight and iron-bound, I asked the Father Guardian if it could be unlocked for us. No, he said, this is the burial place of Christ's forefathers David and Solomon, yet it exists within the confines of a Saracen mosque, where you are forbidden to go.

We were quite saddened by this, for the place is often mentioned in the books of Kings and Chronicles. When we asked the Father Guardian how this place came to be covered by a mosque, he informed us that long ago the Jews and Christians had fought over the site so publicly that the Sultan, to thwart them both, seized it for himself. I understand the Jews are pleading for its return, even to this day.

We stood outside the door and prayed earnestly, and there received indulgences (††).

The Tabernacle of David, Where the Lord Jesus Preached and the Blessed Virgin Listened

We left that court and entered the old choir of the Church of Sion, which is utterly destroyed but still worthy of veneration. The Jews especially honor this place, because they believe, as we do, that here David deposited the Ark of the Covenant, amid songs and great rejoicing. Jesus, in his youth, preached here, which spot is marked with a stone, as is the place where the Virgin listened proudly to her intelligent son read from the holy book. We kissed these stones reverently and received indulgences (††). While the other pilgrims were paying their respects, I spied a crumbling staircase leading to what remained of the choir's broken vault. I climbed these stairs and, by hoisting myself up, was able to sit atop the roof and thus look out over the mountain. Far below, in the courtyard, some Eastern Christians gathered around a square stone that juts out of the old choir, apparently rolling dice upon it. They would pick up four pebbles from the yard, roll them across the stone, and foretell the future by the pattern they formed: the nearer the figure is to the cross, the luckier they will be. I marveled at their behavior for some time until the Father Guardian yelled at me to come down or he would leave me behind.

The Kitchen Wherein the Paschal Lamb Was Roasted and the Water Heated for the Lord's Supper

We wandered a little farther until we came to the spot where the disciples roasted the Paschal lamb, pounded the bitter herbs, and heated water for washing the dirty dishes. This place is not with-

out holiness, for as we read in the twenty-second chapter of Saint
Luke, Saints Peter and John were the cooks of that sacred Passover
feast. We pilgrims merrily pictured these two worthies burning the
meat and overboiling the water, fighting between themselves over
seasoning and technique, arguing over who had to do the dishes.
Here, also, Peter and John heated water with which Christ washed
his disciples' feet. Granted, nowhere in Scripture does it say that
Christ washed his disciples feet with *warm* water, yet warm water
takes away the dirt better than cold and refreshes the feet and legs.
Warm water also shows greater piety, for it is no great proof of friendship to wash a man's feet in cold water, just as it shows no great
affection to offer a man lukewarm water to drink. We cannot suppose Christ would withhold any sign of perfect love, whereby we
can also assume, though it not be in Scripture, that his water was
not only warm but steeped with fragrant herbs, strong-smelling
roots, and aromatic cordials as well. Profiting by this pious conversation, we knelt and here received indulgences (††).

THE PLACE WHERE SARACEN WOMEN
SUPERSTITIOUSLY WORSHIP JESUS CHRIST

After walking about a good deal more in the heat, we caught our
breath at a spot outside the Brethren's cemetery, where Saracen
women had set up a heap of stones stuffed with prayer rags they rip
from their linen clothing to display piety. Around this altar they
bury loaves of bread and claim that here, not in the Holy Sepulchre,
our Lord Jesus is buried. These women say that the man hung upon
the cross, whom the Jews call Jesus, was not Jesus but some other
man put in his place. Jesus, the Son of God and Mary, was able to
escape and lived a long holy life, dying peacefully here, where they
now propitiate him with sandy loaves. This is to be added to the
list of the Saracens' many errors. They also believe Mary to be the
sister of Aaron, putting her a thousand years before she was born!

Though not believing in the Seven Sacraments, they still often bring their sick babies to be baptized, thinking Christian priests can perform the same magic with water that Thetis did when burning off Achilles' mortality in the fire. I made sure no one was looking when it was time to leave this place and with my foot scattered the women's stones, rooting out the offending loaves, and so left signs of my vengeance there.

Lunch

"Felix, may I bring you more water?"

"Yes, thank you, Lord Tucher. Would you mind fetching the bread? And salt?"

How satisfying it is to order my patron about for the good of his soul! When he realized several other nobles had volunteered to wait on the pilgrims and humbly serve them lunch, he leapt up from his place beside me and grabbed a water pitcher. Ursus takes even greater pleasure in the situation than I, purposefully dropping food on the ground for his father to pick up.

As we had eaten nothing since our arrival in Jerusalem, the Father Guardian kindly invited the pilgrims to his Minorite convent before we returned to our lodgings at Saint John's Hospital. We sit crammed together around three long boards, shaded by an embroidered cloth depicting the Descent of the Holy Spirit. Where the sun comes through its loose weave, I feel my scalp as much on fire as the twelve stitched apostles, each capped with a tidy orange flame.

"Friar"—Ursus fidgets, anxious for sunset—"tonight I am made a Knight of the Holy Sepulchre."

"Yes, that's true, son."

"None of Count Eberhart's other pages are likely to be Knights of the Holy Sepulchre, are they?"

"Not likely," I say.

He sits across from me, his too-long arms awkwardly bumping Conrad every time he reaches for his food. I can hardly imagine what it must be like for his father, knowing our pilgrimage will soon end, leaving him only a few more precious months with this boy. Whenever Ursus brings up his apprenticeship, I've noticed my patron inevitably steers him back to some shared funny moment from his babyhood: how Ursus once put a spider in his mouth or fell asleep in the chicken house and had the whole manor searching for him. They will laugh together, and for that moment, at least, Lord Tucher has Ursus for eleven more years.

"If only we could have crossed the desert to Saint Katherine's Monastery. Certainly dying for Saint Katherine would count for more than a knighthood of the Holy Sepulchre." Ursus Tucher sighs.

"Listen to me." I reach across the table and grip his arm more tightly than I mean to. "I don't ever want to hear that sort of talk again. Saint Katherine is nobody compared to the One who died upon the Cross to save your soul. Now I want you to say thirty pater nosters for insulting our Lord in His own city."

"Friar!" Ursus cries. "You are the one who told me Sinai was the holiest spot on earth!"

"Since when do you listen to what I say?" My anger comes out of nowhere, brothers, and I am ashamed of it. Have I really filled this boy's head with such nonsense? "Speak no more of Saint Katherine, she is a weak, irregular saint."

The boy pulls away, and I cannot blame him. I have been an irresponsible, besotted friar, unworthy of entering this majestic city, as cheaply as I've held it. The Archdeacon John, having witnessed the scene, looks over worriedly. I am saved his concern, however, as Father Guardian is about to speak.

Father Guardian thanks us all for dining as his guests and reminds us that, should we feel inclined to leave a donation toward the church's upkeep, we might find the Brother Bursar standing within the cloister. He offers our thanks to Calinus Elphahallo, standing regally beside him, and blesses him as a friend to all devout men who wander far from home. Once more, the Father Guardian stresses the sixteen articles we heard in Joppa, adding to them rules for our upcoming night's visit to the Holy Sepulchre. Every pilgrim must buy for himself a candle to take, pilgrims should not waste time

within the church trafficking with Eastern merchants, the priests
among us should not wrangle over who gets to celebrate mass inside the Sepulchre, we must not lie down or leave our property about
because of theft, etc., etc. We listen attentively, and when he is finished, those who are of the means to do so set off to find the good
Brother Bursar. Elphahallo approaches me and puts his hand on my
shoulder.

"I hope to see you at my house when your stay in Jerusalem is
over, Friar Failisk." He smiles. "I only have a few more desert cross-
ings left in me, but one belongs to you."

I return his smile uncomfortably and thank him again for the
melons I ate, even as my intestines rise up against them. Behind
the Saracen, my patron waits anxiously, signaling me to hurry
Elphahallo off.

"Lord Tucher, how may I help you?" I ask, after I've shaken the
Saracen's hand and wished him good day. I have celebrated mass
for my patron as a dutiful friar, but, between the Tongue and the
Temptress Priuli, we have lost the easy familiarity we had on setting out from Ulm.

"We are keeping vigil in the holiest church in Christendom tonight," he says, not looking at me. "I have a serious sin I cannot
take into that sanctum unconfessed."

Abbot Fuchs warned me of two things when he allowed me to
become Lord Tucher's confessor: first, that my patron was easily
whipped into frenzies of faith, and second, that these paroxysms
passed as swiftly as they hit. Lady Tucher's confessor, who, by rights,
should have had my place on this pilgrimage, flat out refused to
come. He claimed it was impossible to know when his lady's husband might fancy to outfit them all with chains and hair shirts for
a day, and he didn't want to risk the rash. Clearly, this holy city
has tweaked my patron's conscience. Lord Tucher still holds the
heavy water pitcher with which he humbly served the pilgrims. The
red cross on his chasuble needs to be restitched where it is peeling
back from the fabric; without thought, I smooth it into place before
leading him into the church.

We settle ourselves inside one of the six wooden confessional boxes set into the wide aisles for use by the pilgrims. Three were already occupied and I could hear soft murmurs of Spanish, French, and Italian as we passed, worried men sharing their private sins, saving themselves from future shame by present shame. I sit upon an embroidered purple pillow and face Lord Tucher through a trefoil-patterned grate.

"Forgive me, Father, for I have sinned," says he, his thin voice shaky and self-conscious. "I have not confessed since the night of the storm."

"What sins do you have on your conscience, my son?" I ask.

"I know you think I committed adultery with the woman Emelia Priuli, but I swear, Felix, I did not."

"I am not Felix in this confessional, my son," I remind him. "I am the Ear of God. If you want the Lord to know you did not sin with the waiting woman, He already knows."

"I did not commit adultery with her, but I am responsible for her death, which is even worse."

I observe my patron through the flimsy grate. He sits erect behind the water pitcher he forgot to put down and directs his confession straight ahead. Surely Lord Tucher had no part in setting that fire?

"What was your role in her burning?" I ask evenly, trying not to betray my mounting concern. "Did you strike a flint?"

"No," he says miserably. "But had she not found this among my things, she would have slept beside me, and her assassin would not have dared to touch her."

My patron digs into his pocket and pulls out a carved ivory comb. A perfectly formed tiny Dionysus extends his hand to diminutive Ariadne, left behind on the shore of Naxos. Why is he showing me a woman's comb?

"It is Emelia's," he says, holding it against the grate. "The one she lost her first day aboard ship."

"You took it?" I stammer, remembering now all the petty thefts, the incidental items that disappeared at sea, where they could not

be replaced. Lord Tucher magnanimously substituted his own gold
rosary for his son's lost silver one; his wife's costly Venetian comb
for Emelia's ivory ornament; a fine nibbed pen for the humble instrument I had as a gift from dear Abbot Fuchs! Why steal in the first
place? My patron was the richest man on Lando's ship.

"I don't know why I took those things," Lord Tucher moans. "I
didn't need them. I wanted so badly to be generous, but no one has
seemed to need my help."

"You know theft is a serious sin," I say, inwardly marveling at
the tangle of this man's deception. To what lengths may a man
rationalize theft, brothers? Tucher steals from his fellow pilgrims
so he may be known as a giver of gifts; Arsinoë steals the identities
of the dead so she may survive to feed her mad mission; it is truly
only a matter of time, as Ser Niccolo says, before we are baldly stealing from God, taking away His creative force and shaping it for ourselves. Is this not what I have done? Is that not what this new Age
of Man is all about?

"I am ready to accept my penance," Lord Tucher answers, "however severe it may be. Let me be bowed under a great weight when
I pass through the doors of the Holiest Sepulchre."

My patron looks upon me expectantly. How best to handle the
man who takes pride in his own punishment? Will I make him fast
on bread and water? Will I encourage him to buy that black scourge
I saw him eye covetously today, that he might cut a fine, remorseful figure before Christ's grave?

"In the Alcoran," I say at last, "Mahomet commands: 'As for the
man or woman who is guilty of theft, cut off their hands to punish
them for their crimes.'"

Lord Tucher hugs his pitcher and sputters. This is not what he
was expecting.

"But that is the Devil's book," he says.

"Then be thankful we are happy Christians!" I cry. "For Proverbs tells us, 'There is no great sin in theft.' Your confession is its
own punishment, my lord. Say three Hail Marys and an Our Father,
and go about your way."

Frustrated tears spring to my patron's eyes. He has no penance with which to accessorize his pilgrim's garb. He goes practically naked before Christ tonight.

"You are indeed a merciful priest, Felix." Lord Tucher turns away from me chastised. "It is more than I deserve."

He slides back the grate and leaves with a weak shake of my hand. Into it, he slips my stolen pen.

The Holy Sepulchre

The tomb of our Savior sits at the heart of the Church of the Holy Sepulchre; the church occupies a square on what was once the Mount of Golgotha; the mount rises now in the center of the city of Jerusalem; and from Jerusalem, brothers, the entire world radiates. The miracle of Christian faith, and its ultimate paradox, is that the center of our world is hollow. Jesus Christ rose from the dead; his tomb is empty. We have no physical relics of our most precious Savior to fight over and steal. He exists as pure love, everywhere and nowhere, a corona of light from this dark, buried grave. To this eternal tomb, the pilgrims who boarded Lando and Contarini's ships—in fact, the pilgrims who for the past one thousand years have set sail to this place—bring the sins they've carried from the ends of the earth. Centuries of trespasses—adultery, fraud, regicide—find their way into Christ's tomb, and yet it is never full. There will still be plenty of room for the sins of our grandchildren's grandchildren's grandchildren.

Before you can enter the Church of the Holy Sepulchre, however, you must run the gauntlet of merchants that feed off it. One bustling candle stall features an emaciated wax Christ, tall as a church door, dripping crimson wax blood from real thorns pressed into the taper; a Mary-in-agony candle worked with gold leaf beaten so flat it would melt like the sacrament on your tongue; thin tallow-yellow tapers that clump together like a fistful of underdone spaghetti, a dozen of which Lord Tucher buys to light inside, blow out, and take back to Swabia, believing, like many, that if his wife holds a lighted candle from the Holy Sepulchre in childbed, she'll be delivered safely and without pain. Next to him, the Greek proprietor measures Ursus with string and snips the string to use as a wick, pouring hot wax into a mold to match his height.

Strolling merchants hawk amethyst rosaries, thick corked vials of River Jordan water, fistfuls of tin medallions, and clay ampullae pressed with an image of the Holy Sepulchre. A man may get the Holy Sepulchre in any medium he fancies: etched into a cameo, stenciled on napkins, or, in direct contradiction of Scripture (paying unto Caesar what is due unto Caesar), minted on a coin whose flip side depicts the three crosses of Calvary. Our pilgrims trip all over themselves to buy sepulchre gilt back scratchers and old bits of sepulchre candy, wrapped in paper that has touched the Edicule. I buy a simple sketch to put in my window back home and compare it against the original.

My sketch does not indicate the four elderly Saracen guards set at the doors to represent the overlordship of the Sultan. Elevated on a stone dais, they sit cross-legged like vigilant tailors, gazing sightlessly upon what once was the church's bell tower—before bells were outlawed in the Holy Land—a five-story structure capped with a parqueted wooden dome. Behind these guards, the church's white marble facade, crowned itself with the dome of the Anastasis, absorbs the eerie blue shadows of pilgrims moving through torchlight. Only last year, the Saracens began the practice of locking the pilgrims in for the night. It is an honest hardship to spend all day walking in the heat, only to remain awake all night in the Sepulchre and then walk all the next day, once more in the heat.

Two by two the Saracens let us in, scrutinizing us like convicts. It is said these solemn guards are so greatly skilled at physiognomy that as soon as they look upon a man they can determine his station in life, his disposition, and his desires. I am filled with confusion and covered in blushes passing before them, not from guilt but from having to endure their power over us, even at this holiest of Christian sites. When we are all counted and herded inside, they slam the doors upon us, as guards are wont to do with robbers and rapists, turn the key, and lock us in until sunrise.

What joyous imprisonment, my brothers! What delightful detention! Now that we are rid of the Infidel, we rush to and fro about the church, seeking holy sites as we find them, led only by what attracts our eye. Pilgrims elbow each other out of the way to kiss the pillar where Jesus was scourged in the house of Pilate (††), where the bad Roman soldiers cast lots for his robe (††), where he appeared to Mary Magdalene after his resurrection (††). This area once lay outside the city limits until the Emperor Hadrian commanded the walls be rebuilt to include it, erecting upon the spot a temple to Venus, purely out of spite. Not until Empress Helena journeyed here some hundred and eighty years later, discovering the True Cross and casting out the pagan icons, was Calvary reclaimed and rededicated to Christ.

With some difficulty, the Father Guardian lines us up, makes certain our tapers are lit, and begins our more orderly procession to the holy places before Christ's actual tomb.

We sing and progress and receive indulgences on practically every stone in the church, kneeling before small shrines themselves bowed under the weight of candles. We weep over the stone brought here from Pilate's house, whereon Jesus sat to be crowned with thorns, and take turns sitting there to imagine for ourselves His pain and humiliation (††). We circle around the stone altar marking the "Center of the World" and dispute piously among ourselves if this is indeed the true center. Lord Tucher says it must be, for he was told that at noon the sun shines so directly upon a man's head that his body casts no shadow; he points to a steep flight of stairs leading to a hole in the dome, where, during the day, men are allowed to test this theory. Now I draw the name of Doubting Felix upon myself, by informing them that the casting of shadows in no way determines the centrality of a place. We are told by Dionysus in his third book of Antiquities of a Southern Island, wherein no midday object casts a shadow; likewise, Peter de Abano says the same thing takes place in Athens. Some men believe any spot of ground can be the center of the world, because they believe men are spread all over

this earth, with their feet opposite to ours, and each with his own
zenith. No, I tell Lord Tucher, in this case Science only confuses
us, and we must look to Scripture for the truth: Ezekiel, Leviticus,
and the Seventy-forth Psalm all proclaim Jerusalem to be the center, and thus it must be so.

From the Center of the World we climb eighteen steep stone steps
into a vaulted, airy, lamplit chapel, its dome adorned with vertigi-
nous mosaics of David and Solomon, Abraham drawing his knife
across the lamb's throat. We had entered this chapel singing *Vex-
illa regis prodeunt*, but upon seeing the structure before us, like
uncanny birds sensing a storm, we cease all psalmody.

Rouse yourselves up now, lords and brother pilgrims, lay aside
sorrow, dry your tears, refrain from lamentation, for we have come
through a toilsome Lent into a happy Easter day! Sing alleluia, somber Abbot Fuchs! Break your fasts, brothers one and all! Jesus Christ
after His scourgings and torments, after His sponge of gall, after His
piteous crucifixion, after His dolorous burial, after He had descended
into Hell, after He harrowed the Prince of Darkness and set free all
the chosen patriarchs, rose resplendent and triumphant from this
darksome tomb. In this sepulchre the phoenix renewed its life, Jonah
came forth unharmed from the fish's belly, the sun shone forth from
behind a cloud, the stag again put forth his horns, the green of spring
broke through the snow, Joseph came out of prison and ruled in
Egypt; and besides all this, our toilsome pilgrimage and weary wanderings are here ended and brought to rest. Come then, brothers and
pilgrims, feel with your hands, see with your eyes, touch with your
lips the place where Christ lay; and receive upon this rock entire
and plenary indulgences for all your miserable sins (††).

As one, we fall to our knees in front of Christ's burial chamber
and kiss the ground. On our bellies we crawl like the lowliest snakes
to the Edicule, the chapel that rests above the tomb's hewn stone.
The Father Guardian lets us slither, four at a time, down into this
most sweet cave. My eyes water as much from the smoke and oily
stench of nineteen burning lamps and a hundred candles as from
piety; their smoke has blackened the whole marble interior of the
tomb, though the outside is gleaming white. Under the soot you can

make out hundreds of overlapping crosses, initials, and shields, for not an inch of Christ's tomb is bare of graffiti. As I prepare to give up all my sins and begin my life anew, I confess my trespasses thus for our Redeemer:

I confess that I put a woman before You, Lord, a saint before my Savior.

That I cavorted with Schismatics.

That I attended to my pilgrimage with a wandering mind.

That I, Friar Felix Fabri, usurped the power over life and death by preserving a merchant and gave out that Constantine lived.

That I, Friar Felix Fabri, usurped the power over life and death by turning a blind eye on a murder and gave out that Arsinoë died.

That I thought on Sinai with more desire than Jerusalem.

That I took more pleasure in saints lives and pilgrimage tales than in Scripture.

That I hoodwinked Abbot Ludwig Fuchs into allowing this pilgrimage by appealing first to the Pope, so that my prior might find it impossible to say no.

That I took personally the vagaries of Heaven.

That despite my deep sense of shame, despite the betrayals and deaths of the past few weeks, I cannot help wishing things were as they once were and that I had Katherine back as the wife I have loved for lo these twenty years.

All these sins and more, I lay at Christ's feet. Blessed be my Salvation who lifts them from my shoulders and allows me a second chance at life. I am in sore need of His consolation.

The knighting takes place just before midnight, here in this very chamber. Ursus holds the third highest rank among the pilgrims, but because of the confined space, he has to wait outside in the Angel Chapel for the first two, unable to see what is expected of him before his turn. When his time comes, John, Conrad, and I squeeze ourselves into the tomb with the Tuchers, ducking so as not to catch fire from the ceiling of lamps. Lord Tucher perspires heavily, smoothing his son's damp blond hair. Ursus, dear brave boy, looks ready to vomit.

The Father Guardian speaks, his voice loud in the small chamber.

"Do you"—here he consults a paper whereon all names of those wishing to be knighted are written—"Ursus Tucher of Swabia, swear to defend the Catholic Church, its Pope and its bishops, its monks, nuns, widows, and orphans? Do you swear in your lands not to make treaties with the Infidel, to agitate constantly on behalf of a Christian Palestine, and to urge your princes at every turn to rush to her aid?"

"I swear."

"Then lift up your leg, Ursus"—he consults once more the paper—"Tucher of Swabia, and receive the spurs of Godfrey de Bouillon, the first Crusader to liberate Jerusalem."

Ursus solemnly places first one and then the other of his oversized boots on the lip of Christ's tomb, while the Father Guardian ties Godfrey's golden spurs around his ankles. He raises his arms, and the Franciscan girds his waist with the Crusader's golden sword. What a bold warrior he will make, brothers, this boy who, before my eyes, becomes a man. I find it difficult to contain a flow of tears.

"Kneel over the tomb."

Ursus drapes his arms over the tomb and presses his soft cheek reverently against its sooty marble.

"I knight thee, Ursus Tucher of Swabia, in the name of the Father and the Son and the Holy Ghost."

Unsheathing Bouillon's sword, the Father Guardian smites the boy three times on his shoulders, raises him up, and kisses him on both cheeks.

"Let it be for thy good."

Now there are many reasons why a knighthood of the Holy Sepulchre is better than any other knighthood in the world, and while Ursus divests himself of his golden spurs and his sword, I will share them with you, brothers.

First, a knighthood of the Holy Sepulchre is more sacred than any other because the dubbing is offered only here, in the holiest spot on earth, on the spot where Christ rose even from the dead. Second, it is purer than all others because no blood is spilt in attaining it, whereas most men gain knighthood through shedding the blood of their Christian neighbors, which thing is abhorrent to God. Third, it is more noble, being conferred by our holy Father Guardian rather than by some petty viscount on a limb-strewn field. Fourth, it is more dangerous, because it is no great feat to ride a horse into battle five miles from your own house, whereas it takes great courage to cross the sea and brave the Infidel. Fifth, it is more established, in that it frequently happens that those who are made knights in one place are not recognized by those made knights in another, but are laughed at and called pussy-cat knights and lady knights, whereas Knights of the Holy Sepulchre are recognized by all. Sixth and last, those of our knighthood are wiser than knights of any other order, and the reason is this: A man who sets out for Jerusalem gains more experience of the world, of honest men and liars, of believers and Infidels. More important, he gains knowledge and an honest estimation of himself—for on a pilgrimage no part of a man's character can remain concealed. Few things would make me as proud as having a son of mine be invested with the Holy knighthood. Beside me, Lord Tucher sets his lips to keep from crying; he must be reflecting on the inevitable separation this knighthood prefigures.

Young knight Ursus joins us, trembling and smiling, his face positively Moorish with soot. I spit on my cassock and wipe his cheeks clean.

"Friar, did you see me? I had a hard time getting my leg up on the tomb, and then I almost fell over. I prayed so hard not to embarrass us! And I didn't! I didn't fall!"

"You were very brave, Ursus." I shoo him up the stairs. We have to leave the chapel immediately, as nobles Four, Five, and Six are waiting to be knighted. Outside, we all suck in deep breaths of clean air. The lamps in the Rotunda hang safely high above our heads.

It is late, and we left Ramleh well before dawn. Even as our new knight lies down to sleep, curled around his wistful father, and John and Conrad quietly share a bite of cheese, I move restlessly around the chapel. As tired as I am, there is too much still to see. I leave behind my companions and retrace my steps to the more solitary underground chapel called after the Invention of the Cross.

It barely registers in the shadows, this low door, which appears
to lead outside but which actually opens onto thirty narrow stone-
hewn steps. I feel along the wall with my left hand, pushing back
the darkness with the light of my narrow candle. If I weren't aware
of what miracles took place in this subterranean cavern, I might feel
like Orpheus groping his way toward Hell, listening for snakes and
three-headed dogs. But this is the chasm where blessed Saint Helena discovered the True Cross, a splinter of which has been translated to nearly every major church in the world. Here, she dug with
Judas Quirinus through the refuse of two centuries, casting aside
layers of history with rotten food, glass, pottery, and bones. She dug
through the beads and beaten gold of Byzantium, the straight pav-
ing stones of Rome, the phylacteries and scorched scrolls of Jewish
Israel. This queen picked through the garbage, unearthed Christ's
sponge, His crown of thorns, His nails, the plate that bore His name.
In her chapel, she ordered two caves hewn and a chair carved out of
stone that she might sit and gaze upon the pit of her triumph. I
believe that if she hadn't found the cross when she did, she would
have dug even to the center of the earth.

Five unlighted lamps hang in the twenty-foot chamber, dark
through the poverty of the Georgians who own them but can't
afford their oil. I sit upon Helena's cold stone chair and gaze into
the cavern below, where one lamp burns. Shadows own that place,
backed up against the rock like jealous tyrants defending their petty
kingdoms. I am at last alone, and I bow my head to pray.

Dearest Saint Katherine, this is the last time your dismissed
servant Friar Felix Fabri will entreat you. I have just come from
my patron's son's knighting, where he swore to defend
Christendom, its widows, virgins, and children from the Devil's
campaigns on Earth. As I watched Father Guardian buckle the
Crusader's spurs around Ursus's thin ankles, such envy possessed
me, the likes of which I've rarely known; for at that moment I
realized those still in the world have a right to fight for Heaven,
while those of us who have retired from it have only our own
impotence to war against. Knowing you were on my side these
past twenty years, stengthening my feeble faith by your steadfast

example, living a quiet life beside me, allowed me to walk the
contemplative path even when I longed to stray from it. Now it
appears you have, all along, secretly favored those who take up
the sword for Heaven, as John did against the Turk, or who are
familiar and rough with it, as is the woman Arsinoë. I have
struggled so long and so hard to be good, and yet you choose the
Cains over the Abels, clutch God's problem children to your
breast, and push aside His dutiful son. I desired only to honor
you, Blessed Saint; never once did I consider threatening your
relics or desecrating your altars, as some irreligious men do when
their prayers are not answered. I believed you would reveal
yourself when you were ready, and it was wrong to force you.
How do you suppose I feel, then, when I learn you are appearing
to every Hungarian who entreats you? That you speak through
that wretched Tongue to any peasant girl with a question about
her monthly cycle? Was I so bad, was I so undeserving, that in all
those twenty years of prayer, of supplication, of need, you could
not show yourself unequivocally? *Will you come when I call?*
you once asked me—but at night, when I was half asleep and
terrified of coming to this place. I have no idea if that was really
you or some coward's trick of my own to keep myself from
turning back.

If you can hear me now, in this place, where Christ has relieved me of my sins, let me know what you want. With my fresh
start, I will take up a sword for you. I will fight with sweat and
steel the enemies of Heaven if you desire, laying aside my quiet
prayers. I will be your creature to command, if only you will say
the last twenty years of my life have not been a pitiful lie.

Katherine, Blessed Katherine, come to me now. I can no longer
live in this uncertainty. Have pity. Wife. Beloved. Come to your
unhappy Felix.

The room is so still I can hear my own heavy breathing and the
soft plash of water dripping from the six holy sweating pillars that
support the ceiling. Not even this is a miracle, as some men who
say these pillars weep for the innocence of Christ crucified would
have it, because back home we have similar stones that, due to their

coldness, condense the air around them and thus drip water. The room is quiet. The room is so very empty.

But wait. Below, something stirs. Deep in the precarious pit, wherefrom protruded the Holy Cross, thin shadows like undulating seaweed move in the lamplight. I take up my weak candle and charily descend the sixteen steps deep into the narrow cleft. Rocks hang overhead, threatening to fall upon my head. I hold my candle aloft to see what moved, when it becomes sickeningly clear.

Crackling, acrid smoke. A brush against my cheek like hovering flies. I spin around at the touch, hearing my own caught breath echo off the chasm walls.

Scorched hair. On fire.

The walls sprout burning hair.

My candle brushes the strands, sends them spinning back to the stone, melting red embers extinguished even as they ignite. I pull the candle to my face, nauseated by the smell. The walls are covered in hair. Black fistfuls stuffed into the cavern's crevices, coarse red bunches spread on the floor. I cross to the back of the cave, where a deep hole marks the actual Cross's Invention. It is filled with blond beards and brown bangs, greasy tresses in long-outdated hairstyles.

"They bring it to cure the headache."

Her voice echoes off the overhanging rock, comes to me from four directions. I swing the candle around, inhaling a mouthful of feathery clippings that blow past and stick to my sweaty cheeks.

"Christians and Muslims both, when their heads are splitting, they shave off their hair and offer it here. I understand the Egyptians used to do the same thing."

I see the tonsure first when she ducks under the overhang, it catches the light like a dull ivory plate. To my horror, the black-and-white robes of a Dominican monk cover her malnourished woman's body.

"That's mine, over there. I didn't have a headache, but I thought I could use the blessing."

I lift the short brown curls she points to and let them sift through my fingers. This is the answer to my prayer. It is over. I have no more hope.

"Where did you get that habit?" I ask flatly.

"From a monk I met with no desire to go home." Arsinoë looks about uncomfortably. "Let's go upstairs where we can talk. I'm all cramped from hiding beneath this rock."

My candle has gone out, so I blindly follow her up the stairs to Helena's hewn bedchamber. A stone shelf that would have once supported a feather mattress provides us enough room to sit, but I cannot bear to be near her. I pace the small room.

"I know you are upset, Felix," she says. "I booked passage with a caravan leaving tomorrow night for the Sinai. The Calinus might be looking for Constantine, and I couldn't very well go as myself—"

"Dominican. That's *my* order."

"I know."

"You are going to Sinai in my clothes."

"Please, Felix. I've been waiting all night to talk to you."

She knew I would come back here. I didn't even know myself until my feet touched the stairs. Why does she think she knows me?

"Perhaps you should have stayed with us instead of killing Emelia Priuli." I turn on her. "How could you murder an innocent woman?"

"I did not kill Emelia," the Tongue cries. "Does John believe I killed her?"

"Everyone believes it."

Arsinoë rises and drifts anxiously to the far wall of Saint Helena's chamber, where a small conch-shaped basin, back in the Age of Miracles, caught perpetually dripping holy water.

"Come listen, Felix. If you put your ear to this shell they say you can hear the souls in Purgatory."

I join her by the basin and put my ear to the shell. I hear low moans and ancient creaking waterwheels, the loud rush of a thousand arrows released into a storm cloud. I suspect it is the noise of pilgrims walking about above us, but I don't say so.

"Poor Emelia." Arsinoë sighs. "She was everything I am not. She commanded love just by being alive."

"She commanded lust, Madame," I remind her, "which is an entirely different affair."

"Is it?" she asks. "I find it hard to love something for which I don't also feel lust."

"And do you lust for other people's lives?" I ask angrily. "You seem to love usurping them."

"I did not kill Emelia Priuli," she insists.

"Yet you disappeared at the very moment of her combustion!" I shout.

"I did not kill her!"

"Then who did?" I demand.

"My brother!" The Tongue spins away from Purgatory and faces me like a distorted mirror. She is my height, she wears my clothes. She will take me if I let her.

"When our guard let him in, I knew my time had come," she says softly, her hands involuntarily going to her new-shaved tonsure. "He lifted his low lantern before every pilgrim, obviously searching for someone. When he got to me, I felt his eyes on my short hair, my merchant's robes, my woman's leg. I saw him hesitate, look around— at me, I closed my eyes—at your patron's son, at Emelia Priuli. She slept on her stomach with her face pillowed in her arms, her skirt fanned out over Ursus, asleep with all the proprietariness of her waking self.

"He melted toward her, the only woman in the cave. I watched him lean down, place his hand on her back, and whisper something into her ear. She didn't stir, and after a moment he moved on, completing his circuit of the cave, slipping out as quietly as he sneaked in.

"We smelled the smoke, and I used that chance to run away. I knew he made a mistake."

There is no John here to shield her or manufacture excuses. She is finally exposed for the fraud she is.

"I was with your brother, you liar, the night Emelia caught fire," I tell her. "Your brother was asleep on Contarini's ship."

"My brother would not have mistaken me," Arsinoë says contemptuously. "He sent the man who took me from Rhodes."

"Why would your brother want you dead?" I snap.

She shakes her head miserably. "I don't know. I didn't think he would be so angry I took the bones."

This delusion again! I can take no more of it.

"There are no bones." I grab Arsinoë by the shoulders, and my hands burn from her heat. "This is your madness speaking. The bones Constantine brought were cow bones. You brother buried them in the back yard."

She looks upon me with eyes full of pity. "Would my brother chase me halfway across the world for cow bones, Friar?"

I fling her away from me. Truly, my hands burn.

"First he stole me from the church on Rhodes," she says. "Then while I was captive, he came on board our ship and stole Katherine from my cabin. But he underestimated me, and I escaped."

"Why would your brother want Saint Katherine's body in the first place?" I argue. "He is a scholar."

"Nikolas commanded the relics and they came. 'Katherine wants a new skin,' he told people. Oh, God, I remember that awful day so clearly. Constantine held out the first one like an apple. He told me I'd ordered him to bring it while I was in a trance. It was a rib, and it was real; I recognized instantly the smoky amber bonfire of her. Less than a month later, another came, this time with no provenance."

Arsinoë wraps herself tighter in her Dominican robes and looks away.

"Katherine used to ask for icons," she says wistfully. "You saw them, Felix, as if she needed a constant reminder of how she had lived, in her flesh. I remember her desire for those images. I remember her telling people, through me, to bring them. But when Constantine told me I had commanded him to bring a bone, that I don't remember. It was the first time Katherine *used* me without my knowledge; for the first time I was truly just a tongue."

"If what you say is remotely true," I counter, not wanting to give her even that inch, "what will he *do* with her? Sell her?"

"He is a translator, Friar." She leans against the far wall. "He kidnaps languages and holds them hostage. My brother can't bear that Heaven won't speak directly to him. He wants to force it."

I want no more to do with these people. I have remission from all my sins. My slate is clean. I throw up my hands and start for the stairs.

"You believed once," she pleads. "The night of the storm, the night I discovered her missing; you knew I kept her relics inside my trunk. You smelled the myrrh. You, Felix, saved our lives the night I despaired of making it without him and tried to drown us both. Why suddenly do you no longer believe?"

"I no longer believe," I cry, trying to keep control of my voice, "because I no longer care. You destroyed whatever bond Saint Katherine and I had, if in fact there ever was a bond. You have made me doubt my entire life."

I can see it from her face: She never once considered the toll her pretenses were taking on my faith. In her robes and tonsure, she looks like nothing more than a worried, remorseful Friar Felix. I have not even my own shame to myself anymore.

"Do you honestly believe that?" she asks, stricken.

"I do," I whisper.

"I do not want you to doubt," Arsinoë says, reaching into her pocket. She gently places into my hands the book I'd last seen in her trunk the night of the storm, called *Wonders of the East*, a collection of oddities and mirabilia from the edges of the world. Inside, the pages have been glued together, hollowed out with a knife, creating the kind of false box used by smugglers and nervous ladies of the court.

"The caravans for Sinai leave only once a week. My brother's name is on the list to go tomorrow. If I have a head start, I can save her—but I have to have a head start. It's your decision: Will you detain my brother for me, Felix? Will you make sure he misses tomorrow night's caravan?"

I turn the book page and am suddenly back in Ulm on a drizzly summer morning eight years ago. Abbot Fuchs ordered our convent treasurer dug up when we learned he'd died swallowing alms money. Decomposed flesh so soft, Abbot Fuchs could push through his chest and extract the thirty coins he'd ingested. All I saw was his mouth, however—his maggoty lips, his mossy teeth, his slippery pink pallet.

In the hollowed-out Book of Wonders, a little leathery patch no bigger than my largest toe.

A human tongue.

I look up for the woman Arsinoë, my eyes streaming with tears, but she has gone. Under the tongue she has left a note, just a single simple sentence.

Will you come when I call, my husband?

Confession

Forgive me, O Lord, for I have sinned. It's been six hours since my last confession. I am in possession of a stolen relic, the tongue of Your daughter Saint Katherine of Alexandria, and I know not what to do.

Is this a mockery or a miracle, Lord? The woman who placed this tongue in my care behaves like a crazy person; she has no self of her own but assumes the bodies and souls of others, confusing the very notions of Life and Death. She speaks with Saint Katherine's voice; she moves now in Friar Felix's clothes. In the brief duration of our acquaintance, already she has expired twice.

And yet. . . .

The only piece of Katherine I *knew* was safe, that I saw with my own eyes secure within its reliquary, this woman has just put into my hands, using it as a pledge of her good faith, as one might put up a goat or a silver candlestick. She asks me to believe, but everything in me rebels, Lord! Saint Paul tells us that to work Your miracles, You have chosen what the world holds weak, so as to abash the strong; You have chosen what the world holds base and contemptible; nay, You have chosen what is nothing, so as to bring to nothing what is now in being. I think upon the Apostle's words as I study this thin, withered bit of girl cupped in my palms. Is anything weaker than a snip of displaced muscle? Is anything more contemptible than a human being not only dead but disassembled? My desire to walk away from Saint Katherine and the conspiracy surrounding her is what is now in being, Lord; You have chosen this frail tongue to bring my resistance to nothing.

As I see it, I have two choices. I can either deposit this relic in the capable hands of Father Guardian, who will see it safely returned to Cyprus, or I can take it as a token of Saint Katherine's faith in my abilities and do as Arsinoë begged: Keep her brother from reaching Sinai.

Which is the correct path, Lord? I have never been so uncertain in my life. One road leads to safety, losing me in the process Katherine's trust forever, should Arsinoë truly be performing her will. The other road leads to more lies and subterfuge, glory or perhaps to Hell. I am caught between the Tongue and the Lone Scholar, between faith and reason, and I am too weak a man to choose my own salvation.

Grant me, O Lord, a moment of illumination as You did Your beloved son, Saint Augustine, when he too struggled against his destiny. In his deepest despair, that dear man heard a child's voice from the house next door sing, *Take it and read, take it and read,* and, seizing the Bible in his lap, fell upon the passage *Not in reveling and drunkeness, not in lust and wantoness,* and so knew Your will. I have nothing with me but a collection of Jerome's writings, Lord, his *On the Distances of Places* and a few of his letters. I am opening my one book, Lord, dropping my finger on the page, and I pray, in my deepest humility, that You send me a sign as you did Saint Augustine.

I am reading the words, Lord:
Avoid men whom you see with braids:
their hair, contrary to the Apostle's admonition,
is worn long like a woman's.

Is this Your revelation, Lord? But Niccolo's hair is short, as is Arsinoë's. This message I will take to be a false message and will try again.

I am dropping my finger again, Lord, and reading the words Jerome translated from the Book of Genesis:

Look not back, neither stay thou in all the country about;
save thyself in the mountain, lest perchance thou be taken
captive.

Save thyself in the mountain.

Look not back.

Thy will be done, Lord.

In Jesus' name. Amen.

The Quarter

I walk down David Street, avoiding the sluice of dung, butcher's entrails, and dumped chamber pots from the windows above, every manner of blood and runny thing. In winter, rain purges the streets like Hercules' Augean stables, but when it is hot, like today, the liquid in these trenches bubbles and dries up, forming pestilential pools at the low parts of the city.

By checking the sun, I know I am still headed south, away from the Holy Sepulchre and Saint John's Hospital, toward the Armenian and Jewish quarters. Ser Niccolo told me he would be staying in the al-Rishah section of the Jewish quarter, but as the hovels grow more and more ruinous, the people more and more abject, I wonder if I heard correctly. By order of the Sultan, Christians in Jerusalem are ordered to wear blue turbans, Jews must wear yellow, like the yellow patches they wear back home. To further spite the Jews, this Sultan ordered an open abattoir built in the middle of their neighborhood, across from one of their synagogues, so that while they pray they might breathe the stench of death. The whole quarter reeks of blood and punctured bowels.

At dawn the Saracens woke us, banging the doors of the Holy Sepulchre and practically pulling them off their hinges when we didn't leave quickly enough. Frantically, the pilgrims ran around kissing the holy places as if they'd never see them again, when in fact we are scheduled to return for a second vigil later tonight. The Saracens entered with sticks and ran us out like cattle. I saw

Arsinoë no more and assumed she escaped in the stampede. The more I comtemplated her confused theories, brothers, the more they made a chilling sort of sense. I remembered the translator's bizarre behavior on Saint John's Eve: the Mameluke's appearance by the ladies' cabin, and their sudden departure. Did Ser Niccolo come onto Lando's ship with the express purpose of stealing Saint Katherine from Arsinoë's trunk? Did he distract me with talk of translation and lessons on clapping, while that thief-in-the-night Mameluke snatched up the brown bag Arsinoë had worn around her neck? There is only one way to find out. Today I will learn, once and for all, the secret of Saint Katherine's body. Or if there is any body at all.

Ducking under the low archways and flattening myself to let others pass, I can see into the small shops. Ancient men in rolled velvet sleeves draw straight lines across parchment. They dip their brushes into jeweled pots and trace the letters YHWH until their soulless, vowelless name for the great Jehovah fills a page. This is the al-Rishah quarter, named for their feathers and quills, a quarter of timeless writers and illuminators and scholars. Dogs run free through their shops, licking gilt from the floor with their pink tongues. Only when I see so many dogs in one place do I realize I had been conscious of their absence. A few streets west, in the Muslim quarter, I am told dogs are clubbed to death, considered unclean by the followers of the Proto-dog Mahomet. A curly-tail trots past me with a donkey's hoof in his mouth. I follow him down three flights of stairs before I remember I am here for a reason and turn back to the Via David.

I have no idea of Ser Niccolo's exact address along this street but hope I may stumble upon him or someone who has seen him. I try to imagine what kind of friends he would have in this infected area, equidistant from the abattoir and the city's leper colony. I dare not venture toward those melting milky reaches where the most envious and lustful creatures in the world dwell. We have all heard the rumors back in Ulm that lepers are creatures of the Jews, who are themselves in the employ of the Sultan of Egypt. Together they are planning the overthrow of Christendom, first by poisoning the wells and then by invasion. I paid the rumor no mind, especially as it seemed spread by men of the lowest character who could not keep gainful employment anywhere in the city. Now, trapped in a triangle of leper, Jew, and Infidel, I shudder and pull my robes tightly around me. Everyone looks suspicious. Yellow turbans touch, beards wag; plots are hatched in every stall and tea salon I pass. The tailors whisper to the shoemakers, the cotton cleaners, tossing white clouds into the air with their bows, signal to the butchers. *That monk is spying on us. Keep silence, compatriots, silence like the bottom of a black and icy well. Go home, my leper friends, pretend we've never met—*

"Christian." A hand on my shoulder. I jump and spin around.

Yellow turban. A Jew.

"What?"

"Come into my shop, my friend."

He speaks heavily accented Latin. I barely understand him.

"No. I don't want to."

"No need to be afraid. I'll pour us a glass of wine."

Bushy black eyebrows arch up toward his yellow bulb, and his chin beard salutes the sky. He lays hold of my sleeve and tugs me behind him, down the street, into a cluttered shop. Dusty codices line the shelves, figurines, red glass lamps. He clears a stool of papers and gestures for me to sit. I pull away and jar a tray of loose wooden splinters.

"From the True Cross," the merchant says solemnly.

"Really, I'm not here to buy. I am looking for a friend."

"And look at this: crocodile heads."

On the shelf to his left, fifteen monstrous lizard heads, glittering eyes, gaping jaws, teeth painted red to give the impression they've just torn human flesh. At least I think they are painted.

"Only the finest, from Crocodopolis on the Nile." He takes an enormous triangular head from the shelf and swoops down on me. *"Gra! Gra! Gra!"*

"Really, I must find my friend." The crocodile teeth catch my nose.

"I am going to eat you!"

"Please!" I push past him and find the door. The Jew's cat screeches when I step on her tail, trying to get out.

"Wait, come back!" he calls after me. "I'll make a good price. I have many things for Christ!"

"Pssst, listen."

I swing right and almost collide with another Yellow Turban lurking in the shadows.

"You want Christian stuff? Don't go to him. He'll cheat you. Come to my brother."

"I don't want Christian stuff. I'm looking for an Greek translator who is staying on this street."

"Come to my brother. We have Greeks there."

Two women carrying baskets pass. I notice one's kerchief has slipped from her forehead. She is bald.

"Come."

He pulls me hard and the alley swallows us up. A white chicken flutters against my chest and flaps around us, chased by a young barefooted girl. I feel my arm yanked from its socket.

Yellow Turban leads me in a wide semicircle until we come back to the Street of the Quarter of the Jews, a few shops down from where he grabbed me initially. Just outside the doorway, a familiar-looking towheaded man leans against the shop, playing idly with his donkey's tether. The beast in front of him is packed for a journey, saddled and loaded with a trunk on its rear end. Where have I seen this man before?

"Go in," urges Yellow Turban, pushing me into the dark doorway. "Greeks."

"Wait." I pull away from the merchant and walk over to the waiting man. Dressed in somber pilgrim's garb, he wears a coarse brown robe with belt, heavy black boots, a flimsy white chasuble stitched in what looks to have been great haste, from the crookedness of its red cross. He is clean-shaven and weaponless, but there can be no mistake. This waiting pilgrim is Abdullah the Mameluke.

"Abdullah?" I marvel.

He sees me and for an instant contemplates flight. Why on earth is he dressed this way? Certainly, if the Saracens discover it, he will be thrown in jail or even killed.

"Peter, please," he says, cutting his eyes at the impatient Jew. "How are you, fellow pilgrim?"

"Fine," I say. "*What* are you?"

The Mameluke throws his arm around my shoulder and leads me away from the shop door. From the open second-story windows above us, wide-eyed Jewish children, their mouths crusty with goat's milk, their arms albino with dust, lean out and sing the word, "Biscuit!" I reach into my scrip to give them some bread, but Abdullah smacks their grasping hands away.

"I am *battal*, Friar," the Mameluke says, checking to make certain the children are not spies. "Do you know what that means?"

I do not and say so, brothers.

"It means I disgraced the Mamelukes. I was caught enjoying myself like a Christian once too often and they dressed me down, exiled me to backwater Jerusalem, where I was to petition Allah's forgiveness for the rest of my days."

I have heard of these outcasts, brothers, though I did not remember the word. They are considered unclean by the Saracens and no longer live free lives. Some are penned up in stalls to meditate on their sins; some are merely followed wherever they go by stern Saracen priests who scowl them to an early grave.

"Ser Nic knew my status when he met me and offered me a way out," he says. "I perform a few odd tasks for him, and he, in his turn, promises to take me home."

I know very little about the Mameluke lifestyle, brothers, but I do know it is not possible to simply bid it farewell when it chafes. The Saracens take their Allah very seriously, and to insult him, as Abdullah seems bent on doing, is a capital offense.

"Peter, are you sure?" I ask. "Have you weighed the risks?"

"Do you know what it is like, living divided against yourself?" Abdullah asks. "When I came here as Peter Ber, God how I envied the Mamelukes, their fine horses, their rugs, their huge Damascus swords! I came with seven other Germans, all of whom dropped dead, one by one, of dysentery. What was stopping me from slipping into the East, Friar, from picking up one of those fine swords or stretching out on one of those gorgeous scratchy carpets? Only once I renounced Christ and became Abdullah, Slave to Allah, everything changed. Then I wanted only what I couldn't have: ham and wine and hot Christian virgins."

I remember Elphahallo's words to me on the roof at Ramleh; he believed the only men in this world who were truly damned were those who lived an unfamiliar faith. Still, this Mameluke stands before me, ready to be welcomed back into the flock. The least I can do is bless him.

"You will have much to atone for." I hug the new Peter Ber. "But you have made the right choice. Christ Jesus will welcome you, prodigal son, with open arms."

"Great," says the Mameluke, and looks away.

"Where is Ser Niccolo?" I ask, releasing my fellow pilgrim. It is time to get what I came for.

"He is inside with those grave robbers." Peter fidgets. "I've been watching his stuff for an hour, and I'm getting thirsty."

"Grave robbers?" I ask.

"You should see that place." Peter snorts. "Full of legs and eyes and mummified cats and every other dead thing you can imagine. Christ," he says, wiping his brow. "It's really hot out here."

Treachery comes easier and easier these days, brothers. I see my chance and take it.

"Why don't you step off and get yourself something cool to drink, my friend?" I offer amiably. "I am happy to watch Ser Niccolo's things until you get back."

He looks at me uncertainly. "He's very particular about them."

"Who can he trust if not a priest?" I ask.

Peter Ber considers this briefly and nods agreement. With a brief look back to the donkey, he starts down the street.

"I'll just pop into the tavern for one," he reassures me. "Won't be long."

"Take your time." I wave as he disappears down the alley.

A donkey and a trunk. My entire life comes down to this combination. She is a white donkey with big soulful mandorla eyes that seem almost to be encouraging me in the words of the Apostle Mark: "There is nothing hid, which shall not be manifested; neither was any thing kept secret, but that it should come abroad." This trunk upon my rump has obviously come abroad, she says. It is only right that its contents should be manifested.

I duck my head quickly into the relic shop's back door and check for Ser Niccolo. This back room is well organized, if nothing else. The jar of Christ's foreskins sits alphabetically next to the stack of girdles dropped from Heaven by the Virgin Mary. Boxes of fingers sit next to caskets of hands, and toes go with feet. I shudder at how these men make their living, preying on the gullibility of desperate Christians. Is Niccolo inside, right now, rummaging through the assorted paste reliquaries, looking for a set of Saint Katherine's ruby lips? Suddenly a horrifying thought occurs to me, brothers. What if Niccolo is not here buying? What if he is here to sell?

A strange calm always descends upon me in moments of greatest sinfulness. The resolute hand of the murderer, the slow heartbeat of the thief, the liar's cool head are all mine when the Devil's work is to be done. With only a swift glance around to make certain I am not noticed, I walk back to the trunk and sink my pen deep into its cheap lock. I will not name names, but one among you may congratulate yourselves for my acquisition of this useful skill. It requires only a bit of jiggling before the shoddy lock drops open. The donkey's skin twitches with horseflies, and her tail slaps my hand, shooing them away. She takes a short step backward, jarring the trunk from my grip.

Katherine, give me the strength to deal with whatever I find here. I fling open the lid.

The myrrh. You smell it first, brothers. The heady sandalwood, jasmine flowering of Heaven. A thin unguent of this scent oiled the empty reliquaries of Crete and Rhodes; a wispy column escaped the night of the storm when I threw open Arsinoë's trunk, expecting to find it full of bones. It was this celestial perfume Niccolo was sniffing for when he plowed up Emelia Priuli's bones on the beach of Joppa.

Ask your nose how something so pitiable can smell so sweet. Then ask your eyes to make sense of the jumbled hostage that is your beloved saint.

I spread open the burlap feed bag that once embraced the neck of drowning Arsinoë and find inside what must be a hundred pieces of Heaven. Narrow ribs comingle with a thigh and a wrist, recalling some ancient runic alphabet written all in sharp angles and joints. There is the left hand from Candia. Dear God, there, with no velvet to cushion it—clenched, in fact, between two bony toes—is the ear we lost on Rhodes. My hand goes instinctively to the money pouch next to my heart, where I have had to bunk her tongue in a bed of filthy lucre to keep it safe.

You were imprisoned in this trunk the night I slept on Contarini's ship. You were bound and gagged, before that, in a waterlogged bag around Arsinoë's neck. How many times I could have saved you, had I only known! Forgive me, dearest spouse. Forgive a foolish, wrong-headed, inflexible husband.

I gather the oily bones in my hands and bring them to my mouth. John once remarked that relics were only stolen for love or profit. Niccolo left her outside a relic shop, when he could have taken her inside and made a fortune. If he did not kidnap her for profit, what sort of ungodly love does he indulge for her?

"Abdullah, let's go!"

A shout from inside the shop. I drop my beloved back into her bag and slam shut the trunk. With frantic, fumbling hands, I try to snap the lock back into place. I broke it with my pen.

"Friar?"

Ser Niccolo the Translator steps through the doorway as I pound the lock with my fist. The white donkey leaps forward at my violence, and the trunk slips precariously. I lunge to right it.

"What are you doing?" he yells, pulling me away from his ass. "Don't touch that!"

"Some children tried to steal it," I gasp, my voice breathless with fear. "Abdullah . . . I mean Peter . . . ran after them. That way."

I point down the alley where the Mameluke disappeared and pray Niccolo does not decide to follow. He eyes me suspiciously, but says nothing.

"I'm sorry," I stammer. "It's my fault, really. I distracted Peter. We were speaking of his conversion, when these children—"

Niccolo has noticed the lock won't close. He turns on me angrily.

"The children I suppose picked this lock?"

"They had a stick," I say weakly.

"What are you doing here, Friar?" the translator asks, not believing a word I say.

I haven't thought that far ahead. What am I doing here?

"I was headed out to Aceldama when I found myself on your street. I thought I'd stop in and see if you'd join me for a bite to eat."

"I am leaving the city tonight," he says, opening the trunk wide enough to satisfy himself that nothing is missing. "I'm afraid this will have to be good-bye."

"You are leaving already?" I ask. I have thought of no way to detain him. "You mustn't leave Jerusalem without visiting the Holy Sepulchre. Come with us tonight."

Niccolo shakes his head. "I'm sorry, Friar. If I miss my ride, I'll be here another week."

He bends over, tightening the saddle around his white donkey's flanks, and repositions the trunk. Should I confront him here on the street and demand Katherine's body? He will get away unless I can convince him he absolutely cannot go.

"Would it be so bad to stay here an extra week?" I ask with a smile. "We are planning a short trip to the River Jordan. You could come with us."

"Actually, I've been extended an invitation by a lady friend," he whispers conspiratorially. My stomach turns over. "You know women don't like to be kept waiting."

I laugh like a man who has not sworn a vow of chastity and grope for one final lie.

"Ser Niccolo . . . " I hesitate, petting the donkey's flat white head. There must be something, something he desires badly enough to turn aside from Sinai.

"Is something troubling you, Friar? Surely you can't crave my company that badly?"

My voice comes to me from far away. "It's just that I've been disingenuous with you, and now I'm embarrassed."

He pats the donkey's rump and straightens, tugging his tunic into place. "Yes?"

I can't look at him, but absently comb the burrs from his donkey's mane with my fingers. She whinnies and bumps my hand with her nose.

"The night of the fire," I say slowly, "my friend John and I found something on your sister. Something that wasn't consumed."

"Yes?"

"It did not belong to a cow, nor do I think to a mere mortal. Your sister, Ser Niccolo, was in possession of Saint Katherine's tongue, stolen from Cyprus."

For the first time he looks upon me with something besides outright suspicion.

"When Contarini's ship reached Cyprus"—he measures his words—"I learned Katherine's tongue had been taken from a church in Nicosia. I was afraid it might be her."

"We kept it safe until we could decide what to do with it. John wants to take it to Sinai and hand it over to the monks there, but I fear my patron will not let us go. I believe it should be returned to Nicosia, where it belongs."

"I would be happy to return it for you, Friar," Ser Niccolo offers, swinging onto his donkey. "I feel responsible for its theft in the first place."

I breathe a loud sigh of relief. "How I hoped you would say that, Ser Niccolo! I know you will reach Cyprus before we will. I am so anxious to give it back."

"Certainly. Do you have it?"

"John has it," I say, a bit too quickly.

"Shall we go find him?"

"He's gone off to Mount Olivet," I say. "And I'm on my way to Aceldama. We are supposed to meet in the Sepulchre courtyard at dusk. Could you join us there?"

"At dusk?" I can see his desire war with his common sense. The caravan leaves at midnight, but if he wants her tongue, what choice does he have?

"If it will make you late, we can always return it ourselves," I suggest.

"I don't see why I couldn't stop by on my way out of town," Ser Niccolo says at last. "Wait for me in the courtyard. I'll be there at dusk."

I am sealing our appointment with a handshake when the tipsy Mameluke Peter Ber swings around the corner. He is lifting a bottle of small beer to his lips when he spots the translator and flings the bottle aside, smashing it against a Jewish door.

"Peter!" I cry nervously. "Did you catch those bad children?"

He has not been a crafty Saracen for nothing, brothers. Immediately he assumes I have told a lie.

"Yes, I did," he shouts. "And stomped their necks."

Ser Niccolo spits in disgust and spurs on his ass, leaving me coughing up fine red dust. He slaps the Mameluke painfully on the neck as he canters past.

"Let's go, Abdullah," he shouts over the ass's hooves. "We have much still to do."

The Mameluke trots resentfully after the translator, and I watch them disappear into the bowels of the Jewish quarter. I have much still to do before tonight as well, but first I must see what Niccolo purchased in this shop. I slip in through the back and startle the shopkeeper, who bears more than a striking resemblance to Yellow Turban, who brought me here. His turban is blue, however, and I realize to my surprise he must be a Converso.

"That man who just left." I speak slow childlike Latin, hoping to make myself understood. "What did he buy?"

The shopkeeper nods his comprehension and takes me by the hand to the back of his counter. There in miniature jars and boxes he stores parts of the face: cloudy eyeballs rolling in vinegar, noses wrapped in cotton, teeth that have been stained with tea to falsely age them. Three tongues are lined up, nestled in brightly painted tortoise shells. In a tidy Latin hand, they are labeled *Saint Lucy, Father Abraham, Queen Zenobia of Palmyra*. He is about to walk past them.

"Wait." I reach out and stop him. "These tongues. I know they are not real."

He feigns insult in his Hebrew language, ordering me out of his store until he sees I prefer the tongues to be false. Then he smiles.

"Are they Christian? Saracen?" I ask. I need to know what poor soul had her grave disturbed and her tongue pulled out by the root.

The shopkeep chortles to himself. "*Mamluk.*" He snorts. "Who cares?"

I think about the open pits outside the city walls we saw on our approach to Jerusalem, the common burial apostate slaves are given in communal, rat-infested graves.

"I'll take this one then," I say, pointing to Queen Zenobia.

He wraps up the tongue in its tortoise shell and works out my total on a scrap of paper. Was Ser Niccolo honestly fooled by these laughably false relics? Does he so desire to collect Saint Katherine that he is willing to insert a corruption into her otherwise pure body?

"What did that man before me buy?" I ask again, distracting the merchant from his addition. Spread out before him on the counter are sheafs of paper stamped with what appear to be authentic papal seals. He sorts through purchasable Indulgences, Bulls, Dispensations for Marrying Nieces and Nephews, until he finds the paper Niccolo put his signature to. He turns it around to face me as he hands me my tongue.

Ser Niccolo, I read, purchased a hundred masses for his dead sister's soul.

Relics

I find the story of the Donestre in Arsinoë's hollowed little book, *The Wonders of the East*. The glue that held the pages together has loosened, and, toward the back, a few single leaves are free and readable. Before the light deserted me, I read of the Iron Gate erected by Alexander the Great at the edge of the Immense Desert, where the foothills of Paradise begin. He penned in the flesh-eating Dog Heads, the Sciapodes that hop on one foot, the unnatural Blemmies who wear their eyes in their chests, and all the other monsters who haunt the edges of maps. The Donestre, Ser Niccolo's monsters, live on an island in the center of the Red Sea, where no barricade can contain them. They are the worst sort of monster, brothers, because even as they devour you they tell you what you want to hear.

It is too dark now, though, to read. The street traffic around the Sepulchre is thinning, Saracens head home to eat dinner on their roofs and watch the sun set. They walk so slowly, these Eastern men—time is no more than a shallow pleasant footbath to them. I see, through the slotted window in the thick-walled tower beside me, an old Saracen priest start up the steps. When the sun disappears and he announces the call to prayer, the Sepulchre guards will lock us in. Or out. I glance behind me. Only five pilgrims left in line.

Truly, the East is full of Wonders, brothers. That an honest monk could leave home and become a liar, picklock, and handler of false relics seems wondrous enough to me. That he might, in a single day, have laid up such a huge store of new sins after being granted complete remission almost surpasses belief. Deceiver that he is, will he even be allowed to enter the Holiest Sepulchre, or will the hand of God strike him a blow across his mouth and stop him on the threshold? I suppose only time will tell.

The Saracen priest's white beard bobs up the staircase, in no more of a hurry than the men drifting home to dinner. Two pilgrims left in line. The priest climbs onto the wooden platform just below the minaret's roof and floats to the very edge.

"Allaaah . . ."

"Felix, there you are."

I close my eyes. He has really come.

Ser Niccolo strides across the courtyard, leaving his loaded white donkey tethered to a sheepish Peter Ber. The Mameluke looks uncomfortable out in public in his Christian clothes.

"Peter," I call, "watch Ser Niccolo's things for a moment. We'll be right back." I grab the translator's hand. "John's inside," I explain. "I told him we'd come find him the minute you arrived." As we sprint to the doors, the Saracens rise to shut it. I thrust my last ten ducats into a shriveled fist and push Niccolo in ahead of me.

"What's the rush?" he asks.

"I just don't want to make you late. You are doing us such an enormous favor."

The pilgrims stray into the processional, but John is not among them.

"I told him not to wander off," I lie. "This is very rude."

"It's fine." Ser Niccolo smiles. "I'm sure it won't take long."

For several minutes, I honestly can't find him. At last there he is, praying under a hanging lamp in the Lady Chapel, just beyond the Edicule.

"John." I bend over and tap his shoulder. "Do you have the tongue?"

The Archdeacon looks up, startled by my question. When he sees who I brought, I expect him to slap me across the face.

"Don't say anything," I whisper. "I'll explain later."

I feign a transaction with my friend and produce the hollow book from my pocket. John grips my robe, but I shake him off.

"*The Wonders of the East.*" The translator turns it over and smiles. "She stole this too. It's from my library."

He carefully unlatches the book on Queen Zenobia's tongue. Behind me, John catches his breath.

"'Death and life are in the power of the tongue,'" the translator quotes.

"Proverbs Eighteen," John says tersely. I quickly cut him off.

"We mustn't detain Ser Niccolo any longer," I say. "He has been kind enough to come so far out of his way."

"I'll see this reaches Cyprus safely." Niccolo drops the little book into his pocket. "Now I must go, or I will miss my ride."

"Certainly, certainly." I keep pace as he starts toward the doors. Precessing toward us, the pilgrims cup their tapers against the drafts. One staggers under the weight of his self-sized candle like Christ beneath the cross.

"So good-bye, my friend; perhaps we'll meet again." Niccolo stretches out his hand.

I say good-bye in the vestibule, happy to get away before he tries the door.

While I wait for Ser Niccolo to discover he is locked in for the night, brothers, I want to interject a brief word here about resurrection, so that you might pardon the sin I committed this afternoon at the relic shop of the Jewish quarter.

In their benighted faith, the Saracens believe that at the End Times an angel called Adriel will slay all creatures, including the angels, and, having performed his macabre task, will turn his sword upon himself. When all are dead, Allah, as they call God, will raise up every creature, saving only Death. This they hold as a tenet of their faith, and this they believe to be true.

As you know, brothers, in reality the End Times are quite different. When the Day of Judgment comes, all the peoples of the earth will gather together in the Valley of Jehoshaphat, there to be tried for their sins. I know many simple countryfolk worry of nothing more than "How will I have a place to sit in the valley, if we are to share it with all other nations?" This is not a fear so foolish as it might seem, for the Valley of Jehoshaphat is barely large enough to contain all the Swabians who currently *are*, not to mention all that were or will ever be. Several countryfolk gave me money to set up a small pile of rocks in the valley and thus mark their place for the Last Judgment, which I shall do to humor them. All learned Christians understand that in the last days the world will be rent and the valley elongated, past the Mount of Olives, past the River Jordan, so there will be room for all to stand and hear the word of God.

In any event, wherever we are buried, on the Last Day we will stand bodily before our Lord. For this reason, grave-robbing, be it for scientific or artistic purposes, is anathema to most Christians. How if after death someone takes one of our legs? Shall we approach the throne a cripple? How if someone takes our eyes? Shall we approach blind? How if, even as we are growing cold, a surgeon or undertaker's assistant takes our maidenhead? Shall we cry out to God for the return of our virginity?

So, you see, in both Saracen and Christian faiths, a person must preserve his body for the Day of Judgment. Had I stumbled upon a tongue of either faith, I could never have purchased it. I take it as a miracle that my bride steered us to one of Abdullah's wretched race, neither Christian nor Saracen, reviled by both, a tongue that has no voice before our Lord in the first place.

"Open up! What's wrong with this door?" It took even less time than I imagined for the pounding to begin.

"Why is this locked?"

"Ser Niccolo?" I take a deep breath and run back to him. "What's wrong?"

"This door is *locked*, that's what's wrong. How am I supposed to get out?"

"What? Why would it be locked?"

"Let me out!" He shouts into the wood. *"Somebody!"*

"There must be some mistake," I reassure him. "Let's find the key."

Of course, Father Guardian is unavailable, leading the procession. Any number of Heretical Christians mill about, relaxing at their own shrines, cooking their dinners behind heavy red altar curtains. The translator explains the situation to one scrawny Copt, who slowly shakes his head. There is no way. These guards won't even accept bribes, he tells us, can you imagine? We quickly circle the whole church, searching for an alternate exit—a forgotten door, a low window. As I know from last night, the Saracens have walled up every opening so that no one may enter without paying the proper fee. The only way out is sealed until dawn.

"Ser Niccolo, this is all my fault. If only I had known!" I am on the verge of very real nervous tears. Perhaps my distress communicates itself to him.

"It's not your fault, Friar. It is just unbelievably stupid." The translator lets out a slow breath, looks around him as if noticing his surroundings for the first time. "So this is how I finally see the famous Sepulchre?"

"If only the stone would be rolled away once more, to let you out! I am so sorry, Ser Niccolo."

"There is nothing to be done," he says tightly. "A caravan leaves next week. I've gotten so used to rushing, I forget there's no longer any need."

I relax a little. My urgency on his behalf was much greater than his own—but, after all, what *was* the rush with Arsinoë buried on the shore of Joppa? Then I remember.

"Peter," I say.

"Peter." Niccolo had forgotten. I feel his swift panic. The bones are with Peter.

What was I thinking? I've locked Niccolo inside but left her body in the hands of an erratic apostate. I can only pray he will protect them.

"Will he steal your things?" I can barely hear my voice through the throbbing in my head.

Niccolo is silent for a moment. "He knows I'll always find him."

I'm not sure if that's meant as a reassurance, but I try to take it as one. After all, Peter has had the opportunity to steal them ever since they disappeared from Arsinoë's cabin on Saint John's Eve.

To take our minds off the Mameluke, I suggest we walk through the Holy Church. I want to resuscitate the reverence I felt last night, but all I see are despoiled mosaics, the Virgin Mary's tiled limbs pried up for souvenirs, her Son's face acned with graffiti. Most pilgrims don't even bother with the procession tonight. They lounge around in knots of six and seven, gossiping over rice puddings and bottles of contraband Cretan wine.

". . . Agincourt, when I was only thirteen . . ."

"My mother used to make it—just take day-old rice, a handful of raisins, sugar. . . ."

"Back home there are no fleas in the churches. Back home the fleas stay on the dogs. . . . I wish we were home. . . ."

The hoots of laughter, the audacious snores. I see a cluster of nobles kneeling and snickering together by the Stone of Christ's Anointing. When I look closer, I notice one is chipping his initials into the rock. Unheeded by them, a battle is brewing over whose turn it is to say mass on that spot. Pilgrim priests swear at one another and tear at the surplice, pulling it in five directions at once, slapping each other like girls. I blush to see them carry on so, each determined to say mass at Christ's tomb so he may boast of it back home.

Yet, how am I any better, inviting a murderer and a thief into His temple? Mary of Egypt, even in her days of debauched prostitution, still trembled and went limp before the doors of this holy place. A depraved whore showed more reverence than I, one who has consecrated his life to God.

"You look ill, Friar. Would you like to rest?"

"If you don't mind, I'll leave you for a while and make the round of holy sites. I feel I should repent the sin of presumption that made a fool of me and stranded you here."

"I understand," Niccolo says. "I'll take a look around myself."

I make my circuit, praying halfheartedly at each shrine. All I want is to sit in the dark, but I can't bear returning to Saint Helena's Chapel, where this disgraceful plan was hatched. No matter where I pray, John the Archdeacon kneels pointedly in my line of vision, obviously waiting for me to explain myself. I know he is furious, but having him upbraid me is equally unbearable right now. Instead, I walk to Calvary, where the Crucifixion stone juts up like a shrugged shoulder, drop to my knees, and bury my arms and head in the empty socket as far as they will go.

It is dark in here. And sweet. I smell the myrrh from where Christ's True Cross once filled this hole, even as my own breath bounces off the rock, hot and melony. If I never emerge, I could start a whole new order of Reverse Stylites—monks who burrow in the postholes of pillars rather that perching atop them. Men who direct their asses toward Heaven while they bury their brains.

A little lamplight filters in through my armpits. Inside, the socket is a flickering topographical map of shields and crosses, names and dates. I run my fingers over the trenches. *Here, Christ died for me: Johann Niebur, Frisia, 1413. Here, Christ died for me: Guy de Lorraine, 1101. Here, Christ died for me: Julia Maximilla. My* name lives now where Christ died, so that all may know He died, not for humanity, but for *me,* and *me,* and *me.* As I'm backing out, I notice, in hasty red chalk, Christ also died for Ursus Tucher, Swabia, 1483.

Lord Tucher's confession must have stirred his conscience, for he, unlike most, is sunk in prayer, bent low against the Edicule. Ursus, I don't immediately see, until I notice another red autograph on the Center of the World. He's talking to Ser Niccolo.

"Friar!" Ursus shouts when he sees me. "Tell Ser Niccolo what you told us when we were locked in last night. About all the other places where there's no shadow at noon."

Ser Niccolo's face is absolutely unreadable. Involuntarily, I begin to tremble, brothers.

"Our friar is the smartest monk alive, Ser Niccolo," says Ursus. "He knows all about Germany and Italy, Jerusalem and Egypt. He wants to cross the desert, but Father won't let him."

"Is that so, Friar Felix?"

"Is what so? That I want to cross the desert, or that I'm the smartest monk alive?"

"Obviously you're not the latter. Why do you want so badly to cross the desert?"

"To save Saint Katherine." I feel my chin tremble. I am not afraid.

"She needs saving?" The translator's eyes are pinpricks.

"Ursus, will you excuse Ser Niccolo and myself? We need to have a grown-up talk."

He looks between us, confused. "What did I do?"

"And give me the chalk." I hold out my hand. Reluctantly, he deposits it and sidles away.

"Now suppose you tell me why you trapped me here?" Ser Niccolo says through clenched teeth.

We step into the Prison Where Christ Was Confined Before the Crucifixion, a darksome cell, having no windows and only one small altar. Four thin new candles have been stuck in the sand, wedged in between hundreds of melted stubs.

"I won't let you kidnap her."

"Who?"

"Don't pretend. I know everything: the kidnapping, the lies, the murders. I didn't believe it at first, but now I know."

"What do you think you know, Friar?" He towers over me, and my left leg shakes uncontrollably. I put my weight on it, but the shiver leaps to my voice.

"That you are a liar. You said they were cow bones, but they are not! You are holding Saint Katherine hostage."

He shoves me into the candles, and I slide to the floor.

"Goddamn it!" Niccolo slams his fist hard against the hewn wall, pounds it like a mortal foe. I tense my knees, ready to kick when he turns that rage on me. A female pilgrim sticks her head into the chapel, sees one man sprawled on the floor, another in tears, and abruptly leaves. My shoulder aches from the fall. Oblivious, Niccolo turns.

"I don't know why you'd believe that of me, Friar. Have I shown myself to be a fanatic in any way? Have I seen visions, heard voices? I am a scholar, Friar. I'm no bone merchant."

I see the resemblance between brother and sister now that he stands accused. Arsinoë's wide flashing eyes, her shallow breath, her strong, dewy forehead.

He regrets his eruption. "Did I hurt you?"

I shake my head.

He takes up the narrow yellow taper that fell at my feet and replaces it in its tray. I watch it sag and melt into the other stubs.

"I lied to you, Friar," Niccolo says. "I don't know what those bones are. The men and women who brought them believed they were real; they certainly paid enough for them. My sister believed they were real. As for myself, I just don't know. How many believers does it take?"

This chapel is so small, I feel like I'm sitting in an upended coffin. The guards used to give prisoners who waited here for execution a special cup of wine. It was unmixed, to get them drunk so they wouldn't mind Death so much when it came.

"It doesn't work that way, Ser Niccolo," I say at last. "A body is either a saint's or it is not."

"You forget, I rescue saints' lives, Friar." He shakes his head. "I translate their stories where I find them. How many times have I read of holy greed: two towns claiming possession of the same saint's body? They scream, they argue, they write false histories; one says the saint was born in his town; the other claims he died in *his*. They are ready to tear the coveted body to shreds when lo! the saint, not to disappoint either town, provides a second body! Which is then real? Does Saint Nobody now have two right hands and twenty toes? Or did some clever monk sneak into the local graveyard, unearth his uncle who died of the pox, and put him in the saint's coffin? Does it matter? Does God not work miracles around *both* bodies? Are both towns not happy?"

"This is not about happiness, Ser Niccolo," I cry. "This is about Truth. If, as you say, a common man might falsely become a saint, does it follow by the same reasoning that my bride, one of the most powerful saints in Christendom, will become a cow? Relics are not abstractions to be played with by sophists. They are the living splinters of Heaven. They have shape and heft and presence in the physical world. They are true *or* false; not true because we say so, or false because we deny them."

"Who found Saint Katherine's body, Friar?" Ser Niccolo asks me.

"What are you talking about?"

"Who found it and how?"

"You know as well as I do," I chide. "A desert hermit had a dream that led him to climb Mount Sinai. There he found the body of a young woman floating in a pool of oil, and God said to him, 'Behold. The first Katherine.' And God revealed to him the story of her martyrdom."

"And he was one man?"

"Yes," I snap.

"And his proof of her identity was his dream?"

"What are you getting at?" I ask.

"Only that it is possible for a single clever man to take up an alphabet of bones and translate Heaven. This lone hermit, while other monks were busy supplicating the known crowd, climbed a mountain, found a skeleton, and put a skin on it. *His* dream alone gave us Katherine's wheel, her milk, her Defeat of the Fifty Philosophers. Once he provided her history, his job was done; he walked back into the desert from which he came, secure that no matter how her body was broken up, each limb would be called Katherine, the name *he* gave her, knowing that should each limb be smashed to dust, every particle would still have once been strapped to *his* wheel, beheaded by *his* sword, and translated to *his* mountain."

Ser Niccolo's eyes glow in the candlelight.

"There must be nothing in the world so exciting as finding a blank saint." He sighs.

"Your sister told me you were jealous," I counter. "That you couldn't bear not having Heaven speak directly to you."

"What did Heaven gain my sister?" the translator asks. "The only power she ever had in this life lay in giving herself away. Nobody wanted Arsinoë. They only wanted the saint that spoke through her."

"Yourself included?"

Ser Niccolo studies his hands. "I lived in a house with a body part. It was hard to love the tongue as much as I loved the words that fell from it."

Constantine clung to Arsinoë to keep from drowning; John pursued her to assuage his guilt. I try to see Arsinoë as that little girl in a big house, measuring herself against her saint, but the Katherine she presses herself against is a rosy German fräulein, a Katherine for me.

"Don't feel sorry for her, Felix." Niccolo stands and paces the small room. "My sister understood what true saints understand: that a person cannot live in Heaven until the self is annihilated on earth. It's the law of translation: One language must die to be reborn in the next."

"She wanted to die," I say.

"You are only fortunate she died before she could put her mad plan into effect," Niccolo says. "Had she escaped with those bones, all the priests and scholars and young girls of the world would have found themselves without a patroness."

"Arsinoë told me she believed Katherine wanted to return to her monastery at Sinai," I say.

"Oh, Friar, how like a monk you think!" Niccolo laughs. "My sister believed Saint Katherine wanted to go *home*. Not back to a comfortable crypt to be venerated by pilgrims. She wanted to return to oblivion, hidden in the desert, lost forever, as my sister believed God wanted her."

"She wants to make Saint Katherine disappear?" I ask, suddenly more nauseated than I have ever been in my life. Oh, God, what have I turned loose on the world?

"Why do you think I went to all this trouble to get her back? If Arsinoë had reached Mount Sinai, Saint Katherine's body would have vanished as abruptly as it first appeared."

"Felix!"

I look up. John is panting in the doorway.

"What's wrong?"

"You have to come with me."

"I can't right now, John."

"Felix. It's serious."

Niccolo extinguishes the dying candles on Christ's altar with sand. "I'll be right back," I tell him.

After the chapel's midnight, I am blinded by the wheel of candles hanging from the Anastasis. An angry crowd has gathered around the Edicule. Father Guardian is furious.

"It is a crime against God and your fellow pilgrims, and not one of you can plead ignorance because the rules have been read to you now three times."

"What's going on?"

John steers me around to the back of Christ's tomb. A hunk of marble, big as my fist, has been hewn away. Where the chisel struck looks like teethmarks on an apple.

"Someone has stolen part of the Holy Sepulchre?" I ask.

"Not just someone. Lord Tucher."

I swing around to find him. He's leaning against a pillar with his hands tucked inside his sleeves, calmly listening to Father Guardian. He catches my eye and smiles.

"Why do you think it was Lord Tucher?" I whisper. I have whispered not a word of my patron's confession to anyone.

"He's been kneeling back here all night. He gets up, and a few minutes later we notice half the Sepulchre is gone? It must have been him."

"People steal from here all the time. There's not much we can do about it."

John stares at me in exaggerated disbelief. "That's all you have to say? You're not going to try to get it back?"

"What am I supposed to do, accuse my patron when I saw him do nothing but pray? John, I was in the middle of an important discussion with Ser Niccolo."

John stares at me horrified. This is obviously about more than the Sepulchre. I would tell him how I tricked the translator if I weren't increasingly more convinced I have made a terrible mistake.

"What has he been saying to you?"

"Nothing." I look away.

"He's trying to turn you against her, isn't he?" John grabs me by my robes.

"Leave me alone, John." I shake off the Archdeacon. "You don't know everything."

I rush back to Christ's prison, but as I expect, Niccolo is gone. He stands with his lips pressed against the main doors, murmuring for someone to release him. My God, brothers, Arsinoë wants to make my wife disappear.

"Pilgrims!" Father Guardian's voice booms. Flanked by two important-looking Eastern Christians, he threatens like a street

prophet. "We will not leave this place until the stolen piece of the Holy Sepulchre has been returned. That means everyone, Eastern, Syrian, Latin alike."

A great protest goes up. Shouting and pushing and name-calling. Anyone seen with a metal instrument tonight is suspect. The bickering priests accuse each other; the graffiti artists swagger, defiant. Through it all, Lord Tucher maintains his equanimity. He is such a bad liar, is it possible he can be responsible?

Father Guardian commands silence in the church. "Please, pilgrims, we don't want the Eastern Christians to think badly of us. Give back the stone anonymously, and all will be forgotten."

Lord Tucher listens politely, then turns his attention to John, who I'm sure is reciting the Ten Commandments.

Hours pass. Father Guardian pleads, allows no one to sleep. "Through the actions of one, we all stand accused," he admonishes. "Give back the stone and pardon us all."

All during the night, Niccolo wanders the church like one of the earth's dispossessed. He returns to the door every few minutes to try it, speaks against it as though his breath will animate the wood and cause it draw back before him. From where I sit nearby, I can tell the hour by the thickening stubble on his cheek. Rich sable, it must be close to morning.

"They won't let us out till daybreak; you're wasting your time," I tell him sharply. His constant attempts at the door are wearing thin. "Why don't you relax and wait it out?"

He ignores me and pulls on the door handle with both hands, curling his body like a strung bow.

"You've already missed your caravan for the Sinai, what's the rush?"

Niccolo turns and looks at me sharply, both hands still on the handle. "What caravan to Sinai?"

"Don't play dumb. The one you were to be on tonight."

Niccolo releases the door and crosses to me.

"Who said anything about the Sinai? I was headed to Alexandria tonight."

Now it's my turn to be shocked. In truth *he* never had mentioned the Sinai.

"What's in Alexandria?"

"A ship back to Greece. I was going home. That's why you gave me the tongue. To take back."

"But she said you were taking the bones to Sinai."

"Who said?"

"I saw Saint Katherine's bones in your trunk."

"Yes, but they don't belong to me. I'm taking them back to Italy and Rouen and wherever else her mad devotees got them."

"You are not going on to Sinai?"

"How many times do I have to say it? Who told you I was going to Sinai, Abdullah?"

I shake my head slowly.

"Who?"

"Your sister."

"My sister is dead," Niccolo says slowly, deliberately. "You told me so yourself."

"I lied," I whisper. "She lives."

Before I can move, Niccolo seizes me and slams me against the door. Once. Twice. I feel the bones in my back separate and crack.

"All this time, you've let me think my sister was dead? What kind of sick priest are you?"

"I believed her," I choke. "I believed that lying Tongue."

"You trusted a woman with no self of her own, Friar?" Ser Niccolo breathes in my face. "Reason it out: If she has no self, she suffers no pain. If she suffers no pain, she has no feelings. If she has no feelings, she is without a soul. A soulless creature is a monster, Friar. You sold your saint to a monster."

Next to me, I hear a key move in the lock. From halfway across the church, Father Guardian hears it too and is beside us in an instant, his mouth against the crack. He barks something at the guard and the door slams shut.

"*No one, I repeat no one*, will leave this church until the stone is returned. I don't care if we all turn cannibal. There will be no food or water or any hope of outside air until I see that stone."

"I have to get out." Niccolo catches Father Guardian's cassock. "I'm not supposed to be here."

"Tell that to the thief." Father Guardian shakes him off. "He is responsible for your suffering, not I."

"Felix, do you realize what you've done?" Niccolo pulls on the door like Samson working the pillars at Philistra. "She has gotten away. You will never see your saint again!"

It is all my fault. The monster Arsinoë is on her way to Sinai and no one can stop her. I leave Ser Niccolo and run through a crowd of fighting pilgrims for Lord Tucher.

Chisels drawn, fists raised, the pilgrims lunge at each other, connect knuckle to bare skin. *Criminal*, they scream. *Despoiler. Cunt.* Ursus watches wide-eyed, as if it were a drunken brawl in Ulm's main square instead of the blackest kind of sacrilege. Calmer heads rush to break it up, but the rage is too hot.

I am sick with fear and disgust. When John runs to separate the combatants, I grab Lord Tucher by the arm and drag him away from the melee.

"Look what you're doing." I hold him by the collar as if he were my child rather than my patron, turn him toward the fight. "You're turning brother against brother, fostering strife in the holiest church on earth. These men are damning themselves—all because of you."

His pupils flick between the fists and my face. Ursus has joined the fight, swinging a thick Mary in Agony candle at people's knees. I see him wince when Ursus takes a boot to the neck.

"I'm the only one who knows what you really are." I speak into his ear, crowding out the shouts and curses of the pilgrims. "Seems as good a time as any to inform Ursus his father is a thief."

I drop his collar and head toward the fray. Wounded, Ursus has crawled outside the tangle, dragging himself on his elbows. He looks up and sees me.

"Make them stop, Friar Felix," he sobs.

"Ask your father to make it stop, Ursus," I shout, loud enough for Tucher to hear. "He's a far more powerful man than I."

"All right!" Lord Tucher grabs my shoulder, pulls me away from his son. "I took the stone. But I can't give it back."

We spin around behind a thick choir column, into the indigo darkness of an abandoned chapel.

"You must give it back. We have to leave here."

"I won't. I can't."

"You stole it."

Lord Tucher draws himself up to his full height. He reaches in his pocket and holds out the stone to me.

"You do it," he says.

Without thinking, I grab his wrist and pull him back toward the Anastasis.

"Let me go!" he screams, in absolute terror. He twists his body against my grip, struggling back toward the abandoned chapel. I have him too tightly, force his arm straight like a flagstaff, his hand full of Christ's tomb. I want everyone to see.

"*No!* Don't!" He tries to draw in his arm, but I snap his elbow sharply, lock it into place, press my mouth hard against his ear.

"Let's let the other pilgrims decide. Let's ask John and Conrad and Father Guardian and Ursus." I wrench him toward me and push him toward the light. He struggles with more strength than I knew he possessed.

"Don't expose me!" The flailing man drops to his knees, pulling me down with him. "I'll do anything you say, just don't shame me in front of my son!"

Lord Tucher sobs against my knees. I squeeze his bloodless wrist and the stone rolls to the floor. A perfect diamond. A golden cup. Nothing on earth has more value than this hacked bit of stone.

"Get up," I command. "I will return this rock for you, and I, Lord Tucher, will name your penance. I will brook no whining, no resistance. You will do as I say, or you will be revealed as a thief and a coward before the whole Church. Do you understand?"

He nods slowly from where he lies.

I walk to Father Guardian, who still tries in vain to part the fighting pilgrims. Drawing him aside, I slip the stone into his pocket, tell him I found it near the Adam Chapel, that the thief must have repented but was too ashamed to come forth publicly. Father Guardian studies me to determine if I am that ashamed thief, but I hold his eye, refusing to stand accused. At long last, he breaks away and pounds twice upon the locked doors. They swing open as if by magic.

"Get out of here, you wicked men," he shouts. "You're lucky I don't excommunicate every last one of you!"

Niccolo and I rush through the doors, each bent on the same creature. We find him sprawled out in the courtyard, the white donkey tethered to his ankle. At first I think he's dead, but then I smell the grapy syrup on his labored breath.

"Peter, wake up." Niccolo shakes him roughly. The donkey turns up her head and brays. "Wake up, you idiot."

"What happened to you?" The former Mameluke struggles upright, rubbing his tongue across his mossy teeth. "I waited all night."

"I got locked in. Are my things safe?"

"That's a nice hello." Peter throws his arms over the donkey and pulls himself to his feet. "I spend all night here in the cold, and all you care about are your things."

"Peter, you're drunk," I say.

"Thanks to that friend of yours." He squints. "And I thought I was the most wicked sinner you knew."

"What are you talking about?"

"The fey little Dominican who recognized me from Joppa. He said he was looking for you, Felix, to make you a present of some Cyprian wine. When I told him you were inside, we drank it ourselves."

"What time did he leave?" Niccolo demands.

"Can't really say. That's some strong stuff from Cyprus."

Niccolo shoves Peter aside and throws open his wooden trunk. On top is the woven feed bag that Arsinoë wore around her neck the night I saved her. Niccolo unties the drawstring and looks inside.

"My sister has fulfilled your prophecy, Felix." He flings open the bag, and a hacked, gristly cow's head bounces across the marble.

"My money is gone too." He slams the trunk lid shut, grabs the fallen Mameluke, and slaps him hard across the face. And again. And again.

Peter stretches out his arms to me, weeping, begging me to save him. But I cannot. I must find Lord Tucher. It is time for him to learn his penance.

III

THE MOUNTAIN

i

Wonders of the East

After two weeks in the wilderness, brothers, after the betrayals and the violations, the thefts and recriminations—when suspicion threatens to bury this pilgrimage more completely than any desert sandstorm—Fortune, festively arraying herself for our wake, sends us a caravan.

At first, we bristle. Easterners and Westerners do not usually look upon one another save with loathing and, if reason did not hold them back, would rush at each other like angry dogs. The caravan's advance guard, comprised of hired desert savages only one degree less nakedly wretched than their cousins, our camel drivers, sniffs our flank warily. Surely the Arabs scent nervous German blood and the ethereal ichor of a duplicitous Greek translator. Or perhaps their noses are even sharper, and they detect the redolence of madness that serves as our own advance guard. Let them engage our dementia like the practiced desert veterans they are; surely they will have better luck quelling it than we.

The Arabs are royalty for hire, brothers; offer them only a few pence or a handful of hardened biscuit, and they will walk miles before your caravan, defending it against other tribes as if you carried the floating tomb of Mahomet on procession. They will take your hand and lead you to the pearls of the desert, those secret wells swallowed by oyster crags of wadi, underground caverns that bubble salty rust water you would sell your own mothers to drink. The Arabs suffer such poverty and want as not even a dog could bear among us, and yet they carry their filthy bodies regally, dress their wives in gold, and style themselves Lords of the Desert. Cross them at your peril. Should you disdain to pay them toll, they will bar you from these same wells. They will conspire with your own servants to steal from you in the night and with them gnaw holes in your provision bags, help themselves to your onions and flour, and murder your chickens while you sleep. The desert Arabs say that, of all peoples, they alone are the true nobles, for they live by plunder and not by work. So this advance guard of nobles sniffs our flank and scowls, and Elphahallo, our Calinus, motions us to be perfectly still.

We meet the caravan on the great wide avenue of Hachseve, a flat caesura between the sand mountains of Magareth and the terrible white wilderness known as Minschene. These are names in the desert for realms that to our eyes, brothers, appear interchangeable wastelands, identical in their uninhabited desolation, and yet are privileged with a name because of their proximity to water. The thousands of other parched wadis and hilltops that compose the Great Desert wait out their eternities in anonymity; we scale and cross them, carrying their dust on the soles of our feet, but we know them not. Water is the only bestower of fame in the wilderness.

Hachseve, Minschene, Meschmar.

Hallicub, Ramathaym, Machera.

These valleys and rises are still to come, these names and more, before our party reaches the Mountain of Saint Katherine.

It was in the sand mountains of Magareth that Lord Tucher finally collapsed and first saw his dream church. On a night when a storm blew up from the quarter of the Great Sea, pushing before it roiling waves of sand, our young Lord, Jesus Christ, pointed out to my patron a limestone cathedral high on a mountaintop. *Tucher*, said He, *seek my church, rededicate it to the Martyr Priuli, and all your sins will be forgiven.* The air was black with dust that night, brothers, sharp glassy sand like sea spray stung our cheeks, and we could barely open our eyes against the flying dirt. From the quarter of the Great Sea, thick blue fissures of lightning rent the sky, and the troubled sand rained down upon us, threatening to drown us where we camped in the foothills. Conrad, at last, wrapped his nose and mouth with a cloak and pulled the penitent Tucher in from the storm. My patron had been kneeling with no food or water for six hours, by the time he saw his dream church, and was delirious for another twenty-four. Ser Niccolo cared not but ordered him set upon his donkey when the storm lifted, when we again set course for Sinai.

Our secretive translator heeds not Elphahallo's warning to remain still and quiet upon his donkey, but now jumps down to treat with the desert Arabs in their own tongue. Behind the dark-skinned spear-wielding men, their women wait, some large with child, some bent and old, as shabby and naked as their husbands. They peer at us from beneath indigo ink tattoos, faces swirled and dotted with outlined waves of blue, their palms marine and mermaid undulate. Around their grimy necks, the women layer gold and silver necklaces that jangle rhythmically as their babies take suck. What avarice can gold spark, brothers, when water is the only currency in the desert? I have learned over the past weeks to no longer value valuable things. In the wilderness there is safety in simplicity: a tent over my head, a fire at night, a drink of water from a red, salty skin. In the desert, the nomad Arabs place stone piles on the mountaintops to mark a path through the pathless wilderness. If they did not, no man could keep to his course but would wander too far from water and lose his life. I have come to value markers, brothers, when all around is mysterious land.

"What is he saying?" John Lazinus leans over my shoulder, attempting to decode the translator's conversation with the Arabs. Far more mistrustful than I from the beginning, John has leapt from suspicion of Ser Niccolo in the desert to outright hatred.

"I can't tell," I say.

Our venerable Calinus dismounts and joins the discussion. After a few tense moments, he walks back to our camel drivers and orders them to unload a sack of biscuit.

"Toll." Elphahallo smiles apologetically at us. "We may not cross the plain until the caravan passes."

Ser Niccolo will be none too happy about that, I know. He already resents being burdened with pilgrims and priests; we lost two days in Gazara securing enough camels for the Tuchers' luggage, souvenirs, bags of spice, bedding, and tents; two days in which Niccolo's sister put a plain and a mountain range between us. When Lord

Tucher lay feverish and exhausted by penance in his lowly tent, the translator pulled him up by an arm and thrust him upon his donkey. And yet, what choice does Niccolo have but to travel with us, brothers? He is penniless in this world.

Young knight Ursus leaves his donkey to stand with John and me and marvel at the caravan that lurches up the hill past us, now that toll has been paid. It is East traveling from farther East, bearing goods that will one day make their way to us in farthest Europe. It slices across the Sinai peninsula, linking the ships of the Indian Ocean to those transports of the Red Sea, a great flexible spine of craftsmen and merchants and tax collectors and customers connecting Cathay to Cairo to Venice to Hamburg.

"Look, Friar!"

Ursus points out the first wave of men after the desert Arabs pass us by. I start at the sight of blond heads and hunched pale shoulders, heavy iron shackles around unconditioned ankles. Ahead of us, Peter Ber, the renegade Mameluke, draws in a slow, loud breath. These men are destined to become what he leaves behind; they are the captured marauders of the Spice Islands, second sons to petty European nobles who found careers among the Eastern pirates; they, my brothers, are already learning their Arabic alphabet. They are Mamelukes-to-be.

Peter slouches lower on his donkey, uncomfortable in the presence of other slaves. Since Niccolo forbade Conrad to swab the Mameluke's neck, it has become blown with infection, so that now his sore perpetually oozes, drying in clumps of his greasy blond hair. I cannot say the Mameluke did not deserve the humiliation he had at Niccolo's hands for allowing Saint Katherine's bones to be stolen, but the translator has been harsh to the extreme with him, in these already difficult days. I have no idea why he wanted him along, unless he actually intends to honor the promise he made—to take Peter home. I wonder if the Mameluke will last that long; his infection has made him increasingly unpredictable.

Before us, brothers, the Great Caravan continues past: a ptolemy line across a map, the tail of a comet, a snake's belly trail in the sand. Do these trajectories care about the lives they cross? A cara-

van? A pilgrimage, brothers? Was it naive of me to view this journey as anything other than a straight line, bisecting countries and
lives and time but, ultimately, a path unto itself, with no more sen-
tience than that path marked for us through the desert by godless
savages? Each time I strive to find a meaning in these deaths and
betrayals, I am thrown back on chaos. Katherine eludes me. I can
only follow the scent lines she has laid down and hope they lead to
some humble destiny.

"Friar, look." Ursus grabs my arm. "The camels."

Behind the novice Mamelukes, a flotilla of aubergine and orange
carpet-saddled camels, each bearing a different wonder upon her
hump, hitches past hypnotically. This one carries a wooden cage
of grass-green parrots grackling happily to each other. The next
conveys a cask of acacia wood carved with leopards and starfish.
Aquamarine silk shot with silver thread spills from the third camel.
The fourth transports jasmine-scented rice. We have traveled in
the company of camels for two weeks and have often praised God
for their ingenuity of form. The camel is a kindly if deformed creature, brothers, with a long neck and legs and a humped back upon
which to balance burdens. She seems always to be a sorrowful and
troubled animal. She has big and terrible eyes in her too-small head,
and when a man walks up to her she begins to tremble, for God
fashioned the camel's eyes in such a way that she might perceive
men to be four times as large as they really are. Had our Creator
not ordained it so, no camel would allow herself to be driven or
burdened. A camel may live a very long time, even to one hundred years, so long as she travels not to some cold, wet country
where she would contract a disease. Her memory is as long as her
life, and she bears a natural hatred for all mules, horses, and asses
because they sometimes bear burdens the camel believes belong
to her alone. Our camel drivers spend many tedious hours in the
mornings loading and reloading these beasts, for our luggage must
be perfectly distributed over their humps, or the camels will not
budge. Easily a hundred caravan camels stretch like a painted ribbon across the plain.

"Failisk."

The Calinus, Elphahallo, approaches our little trio and draws me aside.

"Will you walk with me for a few moments?" he asks.

I turn away from the procession and allow him to lead me along the wadi's ridge until we are out of earshot of the other pilgrims. Ser Niccolo has joined our camel and ass drivers and jokes with them in their language, making the best of this new delay.

"One of my men came to me last night with a disturbing allegation," Elphahallo says, fixing his gaze on the driver who has his arm thrown around Ser Niccolo's waist, laughing at a caravan camel ridden by a spider monkey. "A rumor is circulating that your Lord Tucher has hired Christian spies to steal the camel drivers' children while they are away."

"What?" I cry. "Surely, Calinus, you can't believe that?"

"Of course I don't." He brushes a bit of sand off his still-white robes. "But I thought you should know, since every rumor has a source."

Calinus lets his eyes linger on the translator before they drift over to the maligned Lord Tucher. Truly, brothers, when I laid penance upon my patron, first that he should fulfill his pilgrimage to Holy Sinai, the seat of all law, where God decreed *Thou shalt not steal*, and second that he should assume the financial obligation for our entire party, I never expected him to take his mortification to such an extreme. At first, we all considered his contrition a rich joke and waited for it to exhaust itself, as every fancy had before. While his father knelt motionless, arms extended in the shape of the cross, young knight Ursus would pelt him with stones to make him flinch. Tucher held his shape, though, brothers, and begged forgiveness hours on end for his desecration of the Holy Sepulchre. Now Niccolo is stirring up suspicion against this repentent man? I don't understand what such a rumor could accomplish.

"Are you well, my friend?" Calinus asks worriedly. I shake my head that I am not. Since we left Jerusalem, lo these two weeks ago, I have felt altogether altered in mind and body, brothers. I have been plagued by fever and troubles in the bowel; truly, I feel like a subtle poison is making its way through my body, affecting first my sense of smell, so that the very essence of an object crawls within my nose;

and then my eyes, taking away the natural colors of this world and replacing them with a gray cloud of tears.

"Do what you can to quiet the rumors, my friend," I say at last, addressing Calinus as "my friend" in the Saracen fashion. "I will warn Lord Tucher to be on his guard."

"Rarely have I seen a procession as majestic as this." Elphahallo sighs as the final camels trek by, loaded with indigo and yellow bags of mastic, cardamom, and pepper. "With the Venetians opening more sea routes east, these will soon be a thing of the past."

The proud merchants touch their turbans to Elphahallo as they pass, and our Calinus bows low to the ground. At the tail end of the caravan, bringing up the very rear, ten strapping Saracens heft a cloth draped litter, its bed marvelously constructed of sturdy red-laquered wood worked with gilt, its carpet canopy woven with scenes of sea battles: spouting whales sundering bireme ships; dolphins taunting voracious giant squid. Surely this is a litter constructed for a true marvel, brothers, an enormous pearl or perhaps coral formed into the shape of a horse. For the briefest second I think they have my wife under that shroud, a perfectly preserved effigy of Katherine, sunlight streaming through the carpet's weave, gently warming her set jaw; thick blond hair poured over her breasts, her two hands meeting in prayer over a just-cooled heart. They plucked her from Constantine's dream, after she replaced the drowned merchant and floated serenely to shore. Shrouded against the sun and sand, this final Wonder of the East remains veiled to us. Whatever sleeps inside serves as a reminder that no matter how far afield our wanderings take us, be they to Sinai or India or to the threshold of Alexander's Gates, there is always an East beyond us, unknown and unknowable. In that East, the sun rises and monsters dwell, there the Ages of Men are born and demons are fought, and it is all the same place, brothers, the same East; let no man tell you otherwise.

"Calinus! They are getting away!"

My patron's son, Ursus, grabs Elphahallo by the sleeve and tugs him toward the retreating caravan.

"We want to see what is under that veil!"

It is not for us to know what prize the Saracens carry across the desert from sea to sea. I tell Ursus to leave it be, but he runs for Ser Niccolo.

"Please, Ser, ask the Saracens to let us look!"

Of course this bad boy finds his champion in the translator, whose impatience is only matched by his curiosity. Niccolo, too, wants to know what is so precious that ten men would carry it on foot across the burning sand. He halts the Saracen merchants with blandishments and speeches, smiles winningly, and asks them, for the sake of the child, won't they please expose the treasure on their litter?

Calinus and I join John, Conrad, Lord Tucher, and Peter Ber where they wait nervously on the wadi's rise. Below, on the plain, Ursus capers next to Niccolo, eagerly collecting another wonder to vaunt at Count Eberhart's court. The Saracen merchants are proud of their find and want the Christians to see what it is they possess that we do not. Look upon this and marvel, they seem to say. Look into the eyes of Death.

With a flourish, Niccolo and a Saracen merchant uncover the red lacquer bed to reveal the Wonder of the East.

It is a fish, brothers, captured in the Indian Ocean. Monstrously long and thick, it spans the length of two men laid end to end, sports a wing upon its back and a ferocious swordlike beak. Its scales reflect all the colors of marine life: green for the moss that grows upon the wreckages of ships, purple for the ticklish finger anenome, blue like a sky distorted by the waves, the yellow of the Ocean bed. His beak is sharp and threatening, but it is by his eyes that we know him: two violet, searing, magnetic eyes, weakened in death, but not completely. Close upon this creature, I see he holds a man fast with a very simple trick of reflection. The fish before us has no pupil, no cornea, no second lid. In his enormous eye, you may see only yourself, set shamefully inside the head of a monster.

Look not away from the dreaded Troyp, brothers.

When you can bear to see yourself no longer, that is when he devours you.

Water

We fight over everything, but nothing more so than water.

We fight over how much of it we are allowed, how far out of our way to go to find it, if it is drinkable, if we need it. We fight incessantly with our camel drivers, who disdain to load the four enormous sealed earthenware jugs of pure water I purchased in Gazara to drink in case of emergency. At first they refused to carry the water at all, calling it foolish and heavy, and raised such a hue and cry that Elphahallo, in disgust, commissioned two more beasts simply to transport the jugs. I can only console myself with dreams of those camel drivers, their tongues swollen and black, crawling across the parched plain to beg some of Friar Felix's cool, clean Gazara water. Shall I laugh to scorn at them, brothers, tilting back my head to let the life-giving liquid trickle through my beard? Tempt me not, for a good Christian struggles mightily sometimes to turn the other cheek.

But now we wait anxiously for these same drivers, here in the white valley of Minschene, where burned lime cliffs hide like a secret leper colony inside the red desert. We have seen no live vegetation all day, brothers, but our camel drivers swore there was a marsh some few miles away and, taking with them our animals and water skins, have gone off in search of it. It is getting dark, and they have not yet returned. We are counting on that water for dinner.

"Gather your branches and eat cooked meat while you may," said Elphahallo, who, seeing us fret, dispatched us to scour the chalky torrent bed for firewood. "Soon you will find not another living thing to burn."

He sent us out to take our minds off the water, brothers, for Calinus knows we worry each time the Arabs leave us that this will be the night they don't come back; tonight they will leave us stranded in the desert. A few yards beyond me, Lord Tucher weakly searches the torrent bed for sticks, sifting through the albescent sand. I have not had the heart to tell him the Arabs believe he has hired Christian spies to kidnap their children. He would merely smile beatifically if I did.

"Think they'll be back soon?" Conrad joins me by the spot we have cleared for the anticipated fire. I throw upon it the confection of dried vine I found.

"Elphahallo said the marsh was several hours away," I reassure him, pretending a confidence I do not feel. "And the animals must drink."

Conrad glances at me worriedly. "You don't look good, Felix," says our barber. "Really, we should open the water jars."

I look over at the four huge earthenware containers jumbled together with our other bedraggled possessions. These four jars, brothers, are far more precious than the bolts of red silk the Tuchers bought in Jerusalem, or the silver inlaid trays, or the august bags of cloves, cinnamon, and mace they intend to take back to Swabia. Without water, a man would die inside two days, for the heat in this desert reaches deep into his body and steals water from wherever she finds it. A man's two eyes, like islands in a dredged marshland, sink back into his head; his open mouth, no longer lubricated with saliva, fills with sand; his every organ dries up, brothers, and blows away.

"They are only for emergency," I tell Conrad. "They must get us to the mountain."

"Take a sip of wine then," he orders. "You need to keep your strength."

I agree to taste a little from our precious store of wine, well hidden from the felonious Arabs in a burlap bag of salt pork, for in fact I do feel very dizzy. This malady that has gripped me, brothers, comes in waves, like seasickness, leaving me barely able to stand.

"Did you move it?" Conrad asks, rummaging in the bag of salt pork.

I reply that I did not and join him to more closely search our baggage.

Our flagon of wine is nowhere to be found, brothers, and this is a serious matter. Water we need for survival, but wine we need for health. To cross the desert with no medicinal spirits is the height of folly; ask any doctor you know. I resolved where to hide the wine when I recalled the story of Saint Mark's relics being spirited out of Alexandria under layers of pork. The scrupulous Muslims would not touch the barrels to inspect them, and thus the clever Venetian thieves made away with their patron saint. I cannot believe our Arabs would be so undevout as to rifle through the filthy pig for a few swigs of alcohol, and yet it is well known they become terrible drunkards whenever they are able, being denied by their faith even a sip of the stuff.

Conrad looks grim. He has been nursing Lord Tucher back to health with three sips of wine before bedtime. Behind the camp, our guide, Elphahallo, drives the tent poles deeper into the earth with his shoe. I storm over to confront him.

He nods to me as I approach. "Failisk."

"Calinus." I frown. "The camel drivers have now stolen our wine."

Expertly, he reties the tent flaps, brushes away the creeping sand. At this news, he straightens up.

"Are you certain?" he asks. "It is prohibited by our faith."

"They are thieves, Elphahallo," I tell him. "Every night some bit of food goes missing, and now our wine. I want it back."

"I will speak to them, my friend," Calinus reassures me. "Try not to make a scene. Things are tense enough as it is."

Remembering the rumor spread against Lord Tucher, a terrible fear strikes me, brothers.

"You don't suppose they will get drunk in the wilderness and forget to come back?"

Elphahallo laughs, I think inappropriately.

"There is little chance of that," he says. "If you are thirsty, my friend, drink this. It will make you feel better."

Elphahallo holds out his own tanned water skin, but I shake my head. I have seen the water that comes from these; not only is it red as blood but it smells as if it has been stored in an animal's stomach for three days, then spit back out. The Saracens slurp the stinking stuff with relish, but I am not so bad off, brothers. Elphahallo shrugs, but before he can move on to the next tent, we hear it. As one, Calinus and I prick up our ears.

Han na yo yo an ho ho oyo o ho! Han na yo yo an ho ho oyo o ho!

The camel drivers' song comes over the torrent bed like a throaty bird call, the rhythm of our traveling. A camel will not suffer herself to be goaded or scourged, brothers; the only way to move her is to sing soothingly as to a child.

"Friar!" Ursus clambers down the other side of the wadi from where he has been looking fruitlessly for sticks. He too has seen the camels return. "The water's here!"

We will not assail them, as much as we would like to rip the water skins from their saddles and greedily gulp their contents. We watch the camels pick their way down the torrent bed, tentatively advance a spindly leg, shifting their weight behind them. Conrad joins us, and we wait like a party of angry yet lascivious wives for our husbands back from the tavern.

Elphahallo helps the last camel driver encourage his beast into camp, where we pounce upon them. The beleaguered drivers toss us our skins.

"It's white!" Ursus shrieks when the liquid hits his cupped palms. "Friar, look!"

I examine my own handful and sniff. Indeed, brothers, the liquid they have brought us back is thick and white, more like milk than water, and gives off the gag-inducing aroma of rotted plants! I show it to Elphahallo, and even he wrinkles his nose.

"There is nothing to be done about it," he tells us, after a long conversation with the drivers. "They say the marsh was almost dry and they had to dig even for this.

"And," he adds, "they swear they did not even know you had wine."

"We can't drink it!" Ursus cries.

"Perhaps we should open the jugs," our barber suggests.

"No," I say firmly. "Calinus says we will soon come upon much harder times. When the others come back with firewood, we can boil this."

We have another eight days ahead of us, brothers, traveling through a land cursed by God. Calinus tells us wells are few and far between in this, the deepest part of Sinai; they are guarded by tribes of fierce desert nomads, where the heat allows, and by venomous snakes where no human can survive. We can only wait for firewood.

We have a long time to wait before the next pilgrim makes it back to camp. Ser Niccolo hobbles down the torrent bed, crutched upon a single large stick. When he reaches us, he empties his pockets of some more tangled vine and a few twigs, barely enough for kindling.

"What happened to your ankle?" Conrad asks. When Niccolo removes his boot, we see it has swollen to twice its normal size.

"Snake holes, everywhere." He touches the sprain tenderly. "It was like walking across a sieve."

"You saw snakes?" I ask.

"Hundreds of them. And thousands of holes."

"I have read of a certain snake that lives in the desert called *dipsades*," I volunteer. "Its bite causes intolerable thirst."

"Don't talk about snakes," Conrad says.

"Where *is* the water?" the translator asks. "I am thirsty."

I explain about the dry marsh and how, unless we have a fire to make it drinkable, we will have no water tonight.

"Let's open the jars," he says.

Can no one think to conserve except for me, brothers? I am dripping with sweat even though the night is cool, my stomach cramps, and my bowels rebel, but at least my head is clear enough to know we will need this water far more, later.

"No," I say. "We are saving that."

"Saving it for what?"

"For the dangerous days."

"Those days are upon us, Friar," the translator says, stumping off to his tent to retire for the night.

"Don't you want to wait for John?" I call. "He might bring wood and we can boil what we have."

"He will find nothing in this valley," Niccolo says over his shoulder. "And I have work to do."

A lantern always burns inside Niccolo's tent, brothers, sometimes even until dawn, and I have no need to spy to know he is hunched beside it, frantically scratching away at his lost saint's vita. Every night when the others have sat around the campfire trading stories of home, and I, keeping company, have perhaps scribbled in this little book for you, Niccolo has retired to his tent to add another chapter to his secret translation. It is no use asking to read it, brothers; he only shakes his head and says, "Soon, Friar. Soon."

The translator's prediction proves sadly correct. We wait another hour, until the mountains have soaked up the last of the sun, and John comes dragging home, defeated, with not a single shrub. There is nothing to do but gnaw some hard biscuit, wash it down with our own saliva, and go to bed.

Dejectedly, John and I retire to the close leather tent we share with Conrad, whose turn at watch it is: there, to strip as we did each night at sea and pick our gelatinous vermin. Before we might lie down, Calinus warned us always to check for biting sand fleas and their far more lethal cousins, the Pharaoh's Lice. These black worms, about the size of a hazelnut, crawl up from the ground to suck a man's blood like gruesome ticks. After their bite there remains a scar, a livid blue mark streaked with a red cross, about the size of a penny. If this scar is not immediately anointed with lemon juice, it will turn into an incurable foul wound.

While John checks himself, I strip down to my breeches and money pouch, remove Saint Katherine's tongue, and kiss it. This token is the only piece of her I know is safe, this voiceless instrument, this unpaired fifth of a mouth. I thought I understood her desire when I read the words of Saint Jerome, but now I know not whom to trust. Even my old friend John watches me suspiciously from across the tent, certain I betrayed the Tongue when I accepted this organ in her stead. John Lazinus joined our party in Venice, brothers; he was under no obligation to come to Sinai. Sometimes I believe he accompanies us solely out of spite.

I set the tongue before our lantern and close my aching eyes to say my silent prayers.

Lord, I used to have such deep desires. I yearned for enlightenment, for peace among our brothers, for a German Pope in Rome; and every night I devoutly prayed for these. Sometimes You heeded my prayers; sometimes, as is Your will, You chose not to grant my idle supplications. Once when Abbot Fuchs had fallen down the stairs and it seemed unlikely he should live, I prayed with such frightened coursing tears that You took pity and spared our gentle Abbot. I have no tears tonight, Lord, for there is no water in my body to offer up, but if there were, You should see it streaming down my cheeks. Your servant Lord John Tucher needs water to recover, Lord. He is ill from excesses of devotion and even now lies weakly in his tent. Your servant Friar Felix Fabri suffers on again and off again with fever, Lord, and nothing seems to hold his interest long but the idea of cold, clean water. I fear there is trouble brewing in our camp, O gentle Father, and water might be the only antidote. We snap and bicker over water; our numbers grow weak from the lack of water; friend sides against friend over a simple swallow and soon will come to blows. O Lord, let this simple tongue before me act as a divining rod and lead us on to water. It is all I ask, the most elemental prayer. In Jesus' name.
Amen.

When I open my eyes, brothers, our divining rod, Saint Katherine's tongue, is gone.

John smirks at me, his hands cupped like a child's holding a squirming toad.

"John," I say. "Give that back."

"Not until you tell me what is going on."

"This is not funny."

"I haven't laughed in weeks."

"I mean it." I lunge for him, feeling the fever surge behind my eyes. "Give it back!"

John kicks out and hits me in the chest, sending me sprawling across my pallet.

"No. I want Katherine to whisper to me tonight," he says. "I want her to tell me why she is putting us all through this. What's that you say?" He holds her tongue up to his ear. "You don't know whom you love?"

"John!" I command. "Give that back—you are damning yourself to Hell."

"I don't see how Hell could be any worse than this constant unknowing. We used to be friends, Felix. We used to confide in each other. Now you have betrayed Arsinoë, and I don't know you anymore."

"I did not betray her, John. She lied to us."

"Why did she come to you?" I can't tell whether John is asking me or the tongue. "Why did she trust you? I never would have sided against her."

Outside, the night wind pushes against the tent flaps like a woman in labor, grunting sand through the joints and laces. John is holding the tongue carelessly. Little grains of stone and earth stick along the tip, as though she has licked a city street.

Why do we do it, brothers? Why do we struggle over bits of women? Even John and I, who have renounced the sex completely, are not free. I want Katherine's tongue; John wants Arsinoë's heart—no, no, more than that. He wants that small, pulsing piece of absolute trust that no man ever truly wins. But he knows Arsinoë has long ago given that to another woman. John cannot bear that we are both more devoted to the tip of this tongue than either of us are to him.

"Felix. John. I think you should see this." Conrad, our watch, sticks his sandy head through the tent flap. For a second John is distracted; he loosens his grip on the tongue. I snatch it and thrust in into my money pouch before I grab our lantern and follow Conrad. I must be more careful from now on.

Down the torrent bed, unevenly lit by the half-moon rising in the sky, staggers our final pilgrim, the Mameluke Peter Ber. Even before he breaches the ring of camels surrounding our camp, I can smell his reeking breath.

"I guess we know what happened to our wine," Conrad says.

"Everybody! Everybody wake up!" Peter shouts, stumbling over a tent brace. "Guess what I found."

Heads emerge from the other two tents. Ser Niccolo raises his lantern and scowls in disgust at the Mameluke's condition.

"Peter," I say sternly, "that wine was our medicine. You had no right to take it."

"This is the thanks I get," he scoffs, throwing his heavy arm around my shoulder, "when I traveled miles for these?"

Ursus creeps outside his tent, hoping not to wake his exhausted father. He too wants to see what the Mameluke brags about.

With a flourish, Peter unfurls his robe, and like Venus's golden apples they roll out: four perfect spheres.

"Fruit!" Ursus cries. "Herr Peter, where did you find it?"

"Way, way down the torrent bed." He gestures behind him, opposite to where the others searched. "There must be an underground spring. I found no water, but a whole patch of these apples."

"Can we eat them?" Ursus reaches for one, but Peter pushes his hand away.

"Cut them, son. We mustn't be greedy."

Like a good anatomist, Ursus cleaves them, working his knife through firm flesh and flicking away seeds like small chips of bone. The apples bleed clear juice onto the sand, fall vivisected into his palm, to be passed between us. If our earthly Paradise is truly to the east of here, brothers, it seems some kindly prelapsarian took pity on our thirsty party and rolled us the fruit of Eden. My fever has gone down several degrees just at the sight of them.

"Enjoy!" the Mameluke cries and collapses to the ground.

Before my teeth even touch the apple wedge, my lips have shriveled into my skull. A tongue crashing against my palate to get out, a dry desert vacuum in my mouth! I try to swallow, to raise saliva, but it is impossible. My mouth has turned in on itself.

"Oh, God! Oh, God! You should see yourselves!" The drunken Mameluke practically pees with laughter.

Ursus thrusts handfuls of sand into his mouth, scrubbing his tongue and screaming.

John, Conrad, and I spit again and again at the ground, but for nothing. Our mouths are bitter, arid, puckered bladders.

"Must be what Adam felt like when he bit into *his* apple, eh, Felix? *Oh, no, Evie! Ye vile shriveler!*" Peter coughs raucously and points to his phlegm on the ground. "Look. The spit comes back."

"Why did you make us eat those apples?" Ursus cries like someone numbed with alcohol.

"I didn't *make* you, son. I offered, just like Mother Eve. I bit into one myself a few hours ago and knew I couldn't deny you the experience. Just drink some water."

Elphahallo comes running from his own tent at the sound of our wild screams and stoops to examine the apple Ursus spit out. I move my tongue inside my mouth and feel only the cracked, uneven salt flat of a cheek.

"Oh, Failisk!" Elphahallo shakes his head sadly and holds up the fruit for the awakened Arab camel drivers to see. "Don't eat these! They are wild gourds. They are poison."

The Arabs convulse and hold their throats, pantomiming our deaths from the gourds. Did I spit out my piece or did I swallow it?

"Elphahallo," I beg, "our mouths are filled with poison, and we have no water. I beseech you, let us have some of yours."

"You mean our stinking red water?"

"Please, my friend." I feel my desperation rise. I *did* swallow the gourd.

"I don't know, Failisk. I have no water to spare for men who will pick anything off the ground and put it in their mouths. These men lack the proper humility to make it across the desert alive. I would be wasting my water."

"You can be assured, we are the lowest of all men. We are at your mercy, Elphahallo."

Elphahallo turns back to his comrades and confers with them. After much incoherent wrangling and jabbering, he extends his water skin.

"Though red and salty, this water is medicinal, Failisk. Drink, and pass this among you. When you have emptied this skin, come back and I will give you another."

I could kiss the ancient Saracen, but instead I solemnly do as I am told: drink and make the others drink. Little by little, the poison gall washes from my mouth; patches of my tongue retain the metallic imprint of the gourd, souring each mouthful, but at least I am able to swallow. We all glare at the abashed Mameluke.

Peter kicks the dust. "It was just a joke."

Ser Niccolo, the only man not to taste the fruit, strides to Peter Ber and smacks him sharply across the face.

"You think that's funny?" Niccolo growls. "Here—in this place where there is too much to die from already?"

The Mameluke's spirits, in the manner of drunken men, change instantly from levity to belligerence.

"Don't you fucking hit me!" He shoves the translator hard in the chest.

"You are a stupid slave, Abdullah," Ser Niccolo sneers. "I should have left you in Jerusalem to rot."

"You couldn't very well do that, now, could you?" Peter spits. "You owe me."

"Shut up," the translator warns.

"You lied. She wasn't even worth it. Like fucking a corpse."

With a cry, Ser Niccolo tackles the raving Mameluke, battering his face with his fists. I grab Ursus Tucher, who looks on wide-eyed, and press his face into my robes.

"You fucking animal!" the translator screams, banging Peter's head against the ground. "I never told you to do such a thing."

"You only told me how pretty she was," Peter shouts back, wrapping his beefy fingers around Ser Niccolo's neck. "How weak. You only sent me to steal her for you."

"Goddamn you!"

The Arab camel drivers dive upon the foes and fearlessly pull them apart. Niccolo and Peter claw the air between them, eager for more blood, but the Saracens won't allow it. A skinny camel driver walks the Mameluke one way down the torrent bed, gibbering at him in Saracen, while another steers Niccolo in the opposite direction.

What could Niccolo have been thinking, brothers? It is not as though he was unaware of the sort of man he sent in search of his sister. He knew Abdullah to be a dissolute, erratic apostate, pledging allegiance to no faith or country; worse still, *battal*, a disgrace even among the most depraved Infidel. How could he imagine a man of this sort would not take liberties with a defenseless woman and, after she stabbed him and escaped, later seek revenge upon her? It was Emelia Priuli's eternal misfortune to have slept in a woman's skin our first night in Joppa. I can only imagine the drunken Mameluke saw only one female form among our slumbering pilgrims and extracted his payment from it. Thank God, brothers, that Lord Tucher sleeps through the Mameluke's tirade. Happily praying inside his dream church, he has no idea Peter Ber set fire to his beautiful Martyr Priuli.

"Go back to bed," Elphahallo orders us solemnly.

It is my turn at watch, and while the others reluctantly head back to their tents, I miserably take up my post to walk the concentric camps of Animal, Infidel, and Christian until dawn.

Elphahallo falls into step beside me, stopping to pet the distressed camels, who lift up their necks and roar. I am truly the most wretched of monks, brothers, stumbling through this darkness. I try not to let Calinus see my emotion.

"Do you see that star that has just risen?" The venerable Saracen stops me and points to the dark southern sky. "That is called Saint Katherine's Star, and beneath that star is the Mountain of Sinai. When we must travel at night, as we will soon, we will go no other way than toward that star."

I study that tremulous bit of light assaying the vault of Heaven. Beside me, Elphahallo says no more, offering up no comment on what we just witnessed. For once I do not need to talk, brothers. For once, it is enough to know I am not alone in this strange white desert. It is enough, in this darkest night, to have been given a star to follow.

"I say let's make haste through the mountains. Three days is not so long to go without water, and there is no guarantee we will find it on the longer path. If the wells are dry, and they may well be, we will be farther away from our destination and worse off. I would rather be a little thirsty for three days than take such a risk."

Ser Niccolo's motives could not be more brazen. Arsinoë's caravan will naturally stick to the known wells. If we cut through the mountains, we will have at least two days' jump on her. All the pilgrims, myself included, fear to cross Ser Niccolo. After last night, there is no telling what he might do.

"I beg pardon, but we would suffer more than a little thirst." Conrad bravely speaks up. "I have seen men in the fields, under a much weaker sun than this, faint dead away through lack of water. Their heads throb, their fevers soar. Lord Tucher almost succumbed to this heat, and we had ample water to revive him then. We are men of differing ages and conditions. I think we must take the route of water."

"Felix." Niccolo turns from Conrad in disgust. "You are Lord Tucher's spiritual adviser. Wouldn't you counsel him, for the benefit of his soul, to assume the extra hardship of the mountain journey—sparing himself none of the desert fathers' privations?"

"Yes, Felix," Lord Tucher says. "I want to be a desert father."

Niccolo's eyes bore into mine with an unmistakable meaning. He will uphold the pretense that this pilgrimage is about Tucher's sin, if I will publicly show my allegiance to him. Can I weigh the lives of a dozen plus men against the health of Christendom? Niccolo knows I understand the consequences. A wheelbarrow's trip of bones between our group, inert, heavy clubs, piped with spongy marrow—what would the world care if any in our party left his corpse on the desert floor? But to bear the responsibility of losing Saint Katherine forever? Could I live with it? Wouldn't I rather slowly turn to sand, my eroded bones mingled with this chalky dust, than inform Europe I had lost the Bride of Heaven?

"I don't think our friend Calinus would present a route that he knew would spell death for us," I offer at last. "If he thinks it is possible, perhaps we had best take the shorter path."

How Easily Implacable Enemies
Are Made in the Wilderness

We travel the whole next day without a word between us, so our throats are tight, not only from thirst but also from disuse, when Elphahallo stops and puts our route to a vote.

"We have a choice to make," Elphahallo announces, while our donkeys mill, pressing their juiceless noses together.

"If we take this left path through the mountains, we will reach the monastery in three days. The way will be hard, and I know for a fact there are no wells before we reach our final destination. Our water supply is almost exhausted as it is.

"If we take the path to my right, down along this torrent bed, across the black plain, and back into the mountains farther in, we may find water, or the wells may be dry, or warlike desert Arabs might surround them. I know wells exist along this path, but I cannot swear to their condition.

"I put it to your decision, gentlemen. Which way shall you go?"

Young knight Ursus looks back to me for advice. His father no longer cares about water or food; he talks of nothing but his dream church. Until today, I had not noticed how filled with concern Ursus's eyes had become when they rested upon his ailing father. Not yet fully recovered from his excesses during the sandstorm, Lord Tucher might not survive a three-day press. The only safe way, grievous as it may be, is to take the more circuitous path.

Niccolo's voice surprises us all.

John gasps at my rationalization. "I am surprised at you, Felix," says he. "Our desert fathers never strayed far from water, for they knew nothing displeased God more than suicide."

I wish I could say John's reaction was solely about water, brothers, but he would do anything at this point to gainsay the translator.

Ursus Tucher speaks before I can argue. "We shall not take the short path," says he. "I forbid it."

He speaks simply but forcefully, in the voice of a knight. "I know we vowed to be ruled by you, Friar," Ursus continues, shifting awkwardly on his donkey, "but my father is delicate right now, and I will not risk his health, not even at the cost of damning my own soul."

"But I want to go into the mountains," Lord Tucher says. "My church is in the mountains."

"Felix." Niccolo's face is set. "You should command that boy."

"Am I a child?" asks Lord Tucher.

"It is not Friar Felix's place to command anyone." Ursus squares off against the translator, his voice shaking only slightly. "You, Ser Niccolo, my father hired out of love for our confessor. We could just as easily pay an ass driver to escort you home."

"Do so, little boy," Ser Niccolo flares. "Nothing would give me greater pleasure than to move at my own pace."

"Stop!" commands Elphahallo. "No man will go alone into the desert. We will decide this now, fairly. Show me by your hands: Who wills we take the longer path?"

Ursus, John, and Conrad raise their hands.

"Who wills we journey through the mountains?"

Lord Tucher's hand shoots up, Niccolo nods his head, and after a second's hesitation, a hung-over, battered, deeply abashed Peter Ber joins him.

"Failisk," says Elphahallo, "you have not voted."

What am I to do, my brothers? We might beat Arsinoë to the monastery, but we would certainly be useless to Katherine should we perish along the way. My dry throat aches with thirst and fear and indecision. Niccolo's eyes are cold upon me, Lord Tucher's plead. I look into the grown-up, worried face of my charge Ursus, who has seen far more on this pilgrimage than any boy of his age should have to see.

I vote for water.

And that is how easily, brothers, implacable enemies are made in the desert.

Lord Tucher's Dream Church

It is blazing afternoon when Lord Tucher comes to me with news of the church. After crossing the sulfurous black plain called the Elysian Fields, Calinus sets up the shady tents and tells us to rest; we will camp during the heat of day, he says, and press on by moonlight.

"Don't you know the story, Friar," Lord Tucher asks excitedly, "of the hermit who recognized Saint Katherine?"

I glance up from my book, brothers, to find my patron breathlessly pointing out a high craggy hill perhaps an hour's walk away. Backlit by blue sky, a spiraling limestone church teeters atop it.

"That is his church! That is where the hermit dreamed Saint Katherine."

"How do you know that is his church?"

"I overheard the translator speaking with a camel driver," Lord Tucher explains. "Ser Niccolo was angry his swollen ankle kept him from making even this short walk. When I asked him if we should go venerate it, he said I should be ruled by you."

In the two days since we argued over water, Niccolo has spent even more time in the accursed Arabs' company. They laugh in the Saracen tongue, whisper, trade secrets. These Arabs know the desert like we, my brothers, know the alleys and back lots of Ulm. Is the place this driver named truly holy?

Elphahallo says no. Rumor and legend put the hermitage there because heathen desert people have for millennia worshiped that place as holy, but the Catholic Church grants no indulgences on the spot. By the time I learn this of our Calinus, it is too late. Lord Tucher has enlisted intrepid knight Ursus for his pilgrimage.

"The boy Jesus sent my father a vision," says Ursus. "A church on a mountain."

"Elphahallo says there is no church on that spot," I tell him.

"Do you doubt your own eyes, Friar?" Lord Tucher points to the squat structure with its vaulted spire. "What do you think that is?"

He pulls his scrip over his shoulder and shoves in a goatskin half full of water, all that remains of our last supply. I have not seen him this spiritually determined since he strode through the streets of Candia to dispose of Schmidhans's bloated body.

"Come on, Friar. Look. It's not far."

"I don't think we should go without consulting Calinus," I say.

My patron laughs, and I get a glimpse of the old Tucher.

"Do you expect me to ask permission of my own servant when our Lord commands?"

And so we set out, led by our faithful companions Boredom, Pride, and Idle Curiosity, to seek the mountain of Ser Niccolo's hero, the hermit who, with a single dream, altered the course of Heaven and joined our destinies to Sinai forever.

Deep, deep in the desert, brothers, a hermit lies asleep in his cramped cenobic cell, dreaming of a mountain. It is a red, forbidding, impossibly tall mountain, untouched by human feet since Moses took off his shoes and walked beside God there, a millennium ago. Across from the mountain, separated by a fiery plain, the hermit sees a dark, beautiful chained woman: Jerusalem, the lovely daughter of Sion, looking back over the red stones and waterless hills to where she stumbled in her journey, to that place where her love for a golden calf first tugged her from her Lord. She turns her eyes to the pinnacle of Sinai, remembering how God willed her into being, put the desire for her into every Jew's heart, and then, after the rebellion, denied her to them for forty years. Now, in her stead, she sees another, an adopted daughter sleeping on her Lord's bosom: a young Christian virgin, the child of His old age. Jerusalem studies her temples and churches, her invader's mosques like heavy bracelets on her arms. It is as Isaiah said, she thinks: I, the daughter of

Sion, am left as a cottage in a vineyard, a lodge in a garden of cucumbers, a besieged city.

The hermit rolls over, troubled in his sleep. Upon the dream mountain's top, he sees another young woman, a blond virgin, herself turning over in a new bed, herself dreaming, but of her bridegroom here in His father's house. Of all the saints and all the martyrs, of all the patriarchs and all the prophets, Sinai chose her. An intellect to replace a passion, she keeps Him company, helps Him forget the daughter He lost. He smiles at her pagan philosophy; she listens politely to His tales of wrath and slaughter. She loves the Son enough to put up with the Father's war stories.

Who is this beautiful virgin? the dreaming hermit asks. Why does she lie in a bed of scented oil? Why do angels sit at her head and feet like kindly duennas, protecting her reputation, still, after five hundred years?

And the Mountain says to this hermit, Come to Me. Upon My summit, you will find this virgin pressed into stone as to a fit grave. Take her down and give her to the world. She is the first Katherine, who died for Me in Alexandria.

The hermit awakes, brothers, in a trembling sweat of indecision. Should he ask permission of his Abbot to leave the cenobium and walk alone across the desert to the mountaintop, or should he roll over and go back to sleep, hoping to dream safely of a fresh loaf of bread and plenteous rain?

Unknown to the hermit, on the other side of the desert, at the foot of Mount Sinai, the Abbot of the Monastery of the Transfiguration is also dreaming. Surely there are some hermits in these mountains, the Abbot's dream suggests, who have lived holy lives and died unknown to us. Surely, we should climb the hills and search out their relics, to bring greater glory to our monastery. So this Abbot seeks out his fellow monks, who are praying piously in the Chapel of the Burning Bush, and sends them into the wilderness, with a directive to bring back the bodies of any holy hermits they should find there.

And lo, brothers! The monks of the Monastery of the Transfiguration climb Mount Sinai and find upon its pinnacle the body of a young girl, floating in oil, and they marvel not a little. Woe unto us, says one monk, for our Abbot has sent us to search out the bodies of holy hermits, and here we have found the bones of a virgin, surely devoted to God. If only we knew her name, if only we knew her legend!

And at that moment the clever hermit, having heeded his dream after all, appears on the mountaintop.

She is the first Katherine, says he. Patroness to scholars, priests, and young girls. She was tortured on a wheel and beheaded under Maxentius in the year of our Lord 307, and angels translated her here, to Mount Sinai, where she has remained, uncorrupted, for lo these five hundred years. Take her, brothers, said the hermit, and when your monastery knows her, let it throw off its old name and be rechristened the Monastery of Saint Katherine.

Seven hundred years later, and we are still dreaming in the desert, brothers; for man loves nothing more than to hang his legends upon the dead. We privilege our martyrs with mystery and strength and the power over monsters, but who is the greatest martyr of them all? Surely, it is the desert, this plot of ground so beloved by God that it had to die. Before I left Ulm, I believed no place on earth could please me more than our dripping evergreen forests rising along the Danube. But then I had not guessed at the spiritual euphoria of true emptiness. We travel this desert with the same automatic veneration reserved for our holiest saints, as though our minds and bodies have been melded in this crucible, irrevocably binding prayer to locomotion. We travel as we dream and pray, to make shape of the eternal emptiness.

"Look, son." Lord Tucher points to a trinity of rocks made roundly irregular by weather. "Doesn't that look like the Holy Family?"

Tucher's strides are long and purposeful, and Ursus manfully keeps pace beside him. For the briefest moment, brothers, I put away my reservations. Lord Tucher and his son hum the song that we, like centuries of Germans before us, sang as we set sail from Venice, the happy *In Gottes Namen Fahren Wir*, We Go in God's Name. Barely a month after he gets home, Ursus will enter the service of Count Eberhart, and begin his apprenticeship. He will return to Ulm probably only upon his father's death, to pick up the reins of the household, console his weak-eyed mother, and, perhaps, come across his father's faded pilgrim's chasuble wrapped up in Jerusalem silk, tucked among processionals and vials of evaporated Jordan water in the back of a sea-warped trunk. He will remember, then, this day, when his father set off bravely to find his dream church, when a Saracen goatskin passed between them felt as natural as the sharing of a pint of beer; and, if I know Ursus, he will tell his own young son not how bitter the water tasted but how his father swore he wasn't thirsty, so that Ursus might drink his fill.

The mountain is farther away than it looks, brothers. We scaled the first rise, expecting to find ourselves, easily, halfway there. The camp already lay far behind us; from the summit, I could make out tiny Elphahallo, waving his arms to call us back, but when I turned again toward the mountain, the church seemed in no ways closer.

Just one more hill. Lord Tucher has said it now eight times, and each time his voice gets tighter, more querulous, as though daring us to disagree. Ursus lags behind, dragging his oversized boots in the sand, sitting down suddenly and refusing to get up.

"Father, are you sure Jesus wanted you to walk this far?" Ursus asks. "It's getting dark."

Lord Tucher sets his jaw and says, Just one more hill.

My patron, who nearly died of exhaustion and heat and sand only days before, now has more energy than Ursus and I combined. The longer we walk, the more I feel the gourd again in my veins, brothers, weakening my legs, tingling my lower back. Our water gave out an hour ago, and since then, the desire for it has filled my world. Water follows all the rules of love, brothers. When it is plentiful, you take it for granted, waste it, pass over it in favor of intoxicating spirits. When you are without it, though, your body aches for water; it recalls the particulars of each sip upon your tongue, from the rushing streams of your heady adolescence to the thin infertile drops squeezed from a Saracen's goatskin in middle age. My mouth is so dry, it would hurt to swallow, even if I did not feel the bite of gourd lodged still in my throat, slowly pumping its heated poison.

Beside me, my patron's son chews his tongue, trying to raise what soothing saliva he can.

When at last we come to the mountain's foot, brothers, we have walked three hard hours from camp. Long shadows slant around us and the evening wind picks up, fanning the desert's tide into skittering waves. It has been decided that I will quickly say mass, reconsecrating Lord Tucher's dream church to the Martyr Priuli; then we will walk purposefully back to camp, hoping to make it with an ember of sun still left in the sky.

But there is still a mountain to climb.

We follow a corkscrew path worn in the dusty granite, until the slope becomes too steep and we are forced to hand each other up the headland. Digging for toeholds, scraping our chins and elbows against the flinty rock face, we, the most miserable of men, painfully scale the hermit's mountain.

I would consider this exercise pure folly if not for what Lord Tucher whispered in my ear, three quarters up the slope, when Ursus demanded to rest and entrenched himself upon a flat outcropping of stone. My patron drew me aside, under the pretense of straightening my tonsure, and breathed into my ear what sounded remarkably like a thank-you.

"Soon all my sins will be forgiven me," said Lord Tucher softly, "but while I am still a thief and a miserable man, let me ask your forgiveness for my behavior in the Holy Sepulchre."

I assured my patron there was no need to seek my forgiveness when our Lord God had forgiven all.

"Still," said he, "had Ursus begun his knighthood with that cloud over him, I could never have forgiven myself. A son should not think ill of a father, Friar. Thank you for not exposing me."

Brothers, a feeling of peace unlike few I have known came over me then, and impulsively I kissed my patron on both cheeks. I confess I had questioned his dream church as I questioned my own visions of Saint Katherine, as something born more from fear and need than piety. Now I see God has truly worked a change in Lord Tucher. He has set my patron on the path of redemption, and I blush, brothers, for my own dogged skepticism.

Full of love for each other and for our Creator, Lord Tucher and I make short work of the summit. Lord Tucher tugs my robe when I climb ahead of him; Ursus, rejuvenated by his rest and delighted at his father's sprightliness, kicks out stones to slow us down. I fall behind, still weighted by a heavy syrup of poison gourd, and so am the last to behold the cenobium of Saint Katherine's hermit, that soon-to-be rededicated chapel to the murdered Emelia Priuli, the Church of Lord Tucher's inspired Dream.

My patron stands in disbelief before it, at a total loss for words.

"Father, turn away," says Ursus softly.

His church is no more than a marker, brothers, an inverted ark of uneven stones, stacked up to blaze a path through the wilderness.

I look out around me, onto the boundless wilderness, broken up by mountains, white and red hills, torrent beds. From this vantage, a hundred dream churches stretch into the desert, marking a winding road across the mountaintops for nomads to follow. Some are great cathedrals, some tiny little shrines; some look unlike churches at all but, to a tired, dehydrated pilgrim, resemble clumpy hunkering lions and horses, whose raised hooves displace the sky.

"Why would Ser Niccolo tell you there was a church here when there are only rocks?" Ursus wails. "Father, why did we come?"

But Lord Tucher has been betrayed far more deeply. The boy Jesus commanded him to endow a church in the desert. He sent a sign. Tucher strides to the pile, where Saracens have stuffed rags, torn pieces of robes and shirts—as is their wont to mark some natural spot, high in the desert, that they consider holy—and flings them away like startled doves caught on the wind. He wrenches a sharp stone from the cairn and, double-fisted, scratches upon his church a shallow, flyaway cross.

Like a recording angel he scores, leaving his wrath upon the place. *I will be back, and where once there was a phantom church upon this rock, I will build a stone cathedral even unto Heaven.* Ursus and I watch him passionately claim each rock for Christ like a tomcat marking a doorpost, scoring cross after cross, until at last his son steps forward and says, *Father, please, I want to go.*

A deep chill settles over me with the passing of the light, broth-ers. I do not see our camp from up here, nor in fact do I see any man, bird, or beast, only the vista of that scorched, sulfurous plain called the Elysian Fields through which we passed this morning, hurrying the asses so that their hooves might not burn. We climbed so hap-hazardly up the mountain, finding handholds where we might, that I am completely turned around. In the end, I suggest we take the less steep path down the hill, on the opposite side from where we climbed up but certainly safer in the encroaching dark. If night claims us, we are Children of Death, brothers, as that godless trans-lator intended by sending us here. And who shall be our brothers and sisters? Goat-legged satyrs and prying demons like those who attacked Saint Anthony as he lay alone in his sepulchre? Scorpions and the crackling ghosts of dehydrated Arabs? Other pilgrims who have strayed from the path and gone insane from *adiaphoria*, wan-dering the wilderness naked and raving, living off the shells of locusts and their own hot piss? I feel them out there, waiting for darkness, anxious for their element.

Ursus tugs his numbed father by the hand and pulls him down the path, where we walk without speaking, each of us alone in his own desert. Light, like water and love, abandons a man too soon. Let me never again, brothers, take for granted a long purple sunset over the Danube, or cease to esteem that stalwart orange ball as it struggles to remain above water, denying quarter to the oppressive night. How I yearn to fashion all my unappreciated sunsets into a single day, like a fishwife adding scraps to her ball of twine. We might travel in perpetual pink twilight for twenty-four hours, no matter, so long as day did not desert us.

"Father, look! A cross!"

Without warning, Ursus peels away and disappears into a black fissure in the mountain's side. His father and I stand transfixed, neither knowing what to do.

"Maybe it's your church!"

The young voice escapes the cavern in wreathed echoes. Cau-tiously, Lord Tucher and I step through this pitch into dusk, into a long narrow downhill shaft that disappears into darkness, a shaft filled with the fresh-blood smell of metal. Lord Tucher trips and, reaching down, retrieves an irregular conglomerate of shiny stone and porous gray rock, the refuse driven out when refining gold. Slag.

In the days when Antony was besotted with Cleopatra, the Romans struck illegal coin in mines all over the Sinai. When Rome abandoned her veins, Christian hermits moved in, as Saint Jerome tells us, settling the old shafts like underground cities. Saint Katherine's hermit may very well have lived here, brothers: hungry, thirsty, holding off demons with the iron lining of his empty stomach. Lord Tucher points to the wall and the faint ochre need graffitied there: *O Esau, my brother, Give me lentils, for I will surely die.*

"Ursus, come out," I call. "We don't have time for this."

A rustling deep in the cave. What else lives here?

"Ursus," his father calls. "Let's go!"

I test each step the deeper in we press. We seem to be walking more steeply downhill, into the very heart of the mountain. The sun trails behind us like a carpet runner, just a thin orange band lighting our feet. From deep in the shaft comes a low, inhuman growl. Are there wild dogs?

"Ursus! Come on!"

My voice shimmies through the shaft, drops off somewhere just ahead. I put my foot out, and it falls into nothingness.

"Ursus!" I scream, grabbing Lord Tucher to keep from tumbling into the pit. "Ursus, dear God, are you down there?"

The pit is deep, brothers, and it is full. Stuffed with the twisted length of my patron's whimpering son and a scuttling, hungry darkness.

Alexander's Gate

It is night and there are monsters at the gate.

I know because I heard them stirring: the quiet shiver of a head-less Blemmy who wears his eyes in his chest; the thumping run of the one-legged Sciapode, the soft whinny of the captive Centaur. Alexander the Great built the iron gate to pen them along the edges of maps, in the mountains on the other side of this desert; but I worry about gaps. Who is to say the Dog Heads aren't, at this very minute, sniffing the air, kicking up dust on their way to devour us? The gourd. Perhaps they smell the poison gourd.

I hear it again, that awful howl.

Is the Desert as hungry as we are, brothers? Are the monsters?

Even if we could light a fire, we wouldn't dare, not knowing if we would attract our party or murderous strangers. I take the first watch in darkness. Saint Katherine's Star floats like a drop of milk on black suet, but I am so turned around I don't know whether we are east or west of it.

I only know we passed the Elysian Fields today.

A scorched rock plain where no grass grows, smelling of sulfur and char, its smoldering eternity separates us from Alexander's Gate. We kept this plain on our right-hand side all day long and never saw the end of it—Elphahallo says a man might travel ten German miles a day for two months, never meet another human, and find neither food nor water. And yet all the ancient heroes made their home here, living an afterlife one layer of fame more substantial than the dim multitude of common shades. Ulysses, that best known of pagan pilgrims, who wandered far from home for twenty years, traveled to the Elysian Fields to learn what would become of him. He dug a pit and poured black blood, and the ghosts crowded round, unable to move, unable even to communicate without a sip of it. Have any of you died, my brothers, since I went away from Ulm? If you are here in the night, circling me, I won't scare you away; you may drink as much of this dwindled bloody camp as you can stomach. So long as it is you howling, my good dead brothers, and not the Dog Heads. Or the Flesh Eaters. Or, as I fear, murderous Arabs, less merciful even than either of these. It comes again, low over the sand, a vibrato lamentation of pain and agony, neither human nor animal— a hybrid scream.

Monsters at the gate.

"Friar, what is that?"

Poor scarred Ursus turns over next to his sleeping father. I tried to bind his wounds the best I could, ripping the hem of my robe into long wide strips. He mumbles through the bandage covering his lower face.

"It is probably dogs, child, a long way off."

"It's not our men?"

"I don't think so."

"I am so thirsty, Felix. These burn." He pulls at the bandages that cover his purple lesions and asks again, "Why would Ser Niccolo have sent us here?"

There is only one answer for Ursus, and I will not give it to him when we are so close to fulfilling the translator's desire. Ser Niccolo sent us here to die.

I look upon Lord Tucher, brothers, corpse-pale in the starlight, his fear and bellicosity having finally exhausted themselves in sleep. He has been a millstone around my neck all night, dragging me away from the direction I knew was right, running toward footprints that were no more than wind pocks on the sand. If only I were comfortable with the idea of an orphaned Ursus, I would club his father over his head with the chunk of slag he insisted on bringing back, the relic of his dream church.

But I must think of Ursus. I must bring back Conrad so that Ursus's wounds won't go another minute untreated. I must bring a donkey, as he is no longer able to walk, and a full water skin to slake his thirst. I see those creatures on him still, chewing the lenses of his eyes, black plague buboes fixed to his jaw, his neck, shins, groin. He was unconscious by the time I reached him in the shaft, face down in a nest of starving Pharaoh's Lice. Lord Tucher screamed like a woman while I pried each one loose.

I can't shake the feeling that our camp is nearby. Nothing concrete tells me, brothers, only a slight heaviness in the night that feels like the weight of men. I listen for an argument, for the crackling of a fire, for camel roars: that welcome nightly noise I railed against and grit my teeth over and swore I could go a lifetime without ever hearing again. And I think.

What if they have left us?

Who would want to wait? John, my friend, whom I have banished from my confidences? Peter, the apostate, who would desert his own mother if she lay bleeding before him? Niccolo, our murderer? Conrad is our only champion. He would defend even Lord Tucher— but will anyone listen to a lowly barber?

I am almost positive our camp is just over that hill.

Quietly, I leave the sleeping Tuchers and pace out under the stars. The penitential Seventeenth psalm has always calmed me, brothers, and I sing it now, loudly, with all my heart. *Domine, exaudi,* I sing:

"Hear the right, O Lord, attend unto my cry, give ear unto my prayer, that goeth not out of feigned lips.

"Hold up my goings in thy paths, that my footsteps slip not.

"Keep me as the apple of the eye, hide me under the shadow of thy wings,

"From the wicked that oppress me, from my deadly enemies, who compass me about.

"They are inclosed in their own fat: with their mouth they speak proudly.

"John!" I call, for the hundredth time tonight. *"Conrad!"*

John? My voice comes back to me bounced off the invisible mountains. Conrad?

My sandals push hard against the sand. I will only go as far as the next rise, for surely the pilgrims must be camped beneath it, protected from the wind by this promontory's stiff back. They will have retired to their tents by now, and soon I will spy their lanterns like the glowing hearts of three animals kneeling around the campfire that still sizzles with fat from a skewered white chicken. Surely, John will hear the strains of *Domine, exaudi* on the wind and know only one man in the desert could be singing that psalm.

"They have now compassed us in our steps: they have set their eyes bowing down to the earth;

"Like as a lion that is greedy of his prey, and as it were a young lion lurking in secret places.

"John, Conrad!"

Lemon juice. What we need is lemon juice to anoint his wounds.

The howl. And its echo. I am sweating in the cold air. Can the monsters smell me?

"John!"

"Felix?"

The heat lightning of a woman's copper voice in the night. It could not be her, could it, brothers? Could we have overtaken her caravan where they paused for the night? Dear God, will the Tongue be our salvation?

"Arsinoë?" I cry.

"Felix?"

She is calling as to a lost dog. Mournful, anxious, impatient. *"Meine Liebe?"*

"Who is there?" I spin, for now the voice comes from behind me.

"Felix, komm du zurück, ich brauche dich." Come back, I need you.

My stomach seizes in fear. Arsinoë speaks no German. There can be only one woman.

"Katherine?" I ask.

"Mein Mann?" My husband?

"Where are you? Oh, God, I knew you would come!"

Hill after hill I climb, but her voice is like the hermit's mountain, forever in front of me. How far I've strayed from my patron I don't know, until I see the orange melon moon slowly bubble up from the plain. I am back at the Elysian Fields.

"Mein Gatte, ich bin hier, komm zu mir." I'm here. Come to me.

Across the smoking region, she stands, her head thrown so far back that it appears stricken from her shoulders. She is not looking at me but she knows I am here, hesitating as if she had asked me to walk upon water. *Have I never shown myself to you before because of your imperfect faith?* I can hear her wonder. *Am I mistaken now?*

No, it is my turn, here in the wilderness, to be the single frond on her palm branch. East and West float away like two unmoored islands, revealing the core of the earth. This desert. This woman.

"Help us!"

I run to her and fall to my knees in the burning waste dump of Elysium. The bloom of her hair, Heaven on her lips, she bends and gently lays me flat as for an anointing. My head is on fire, clouded by green sulfur; my body shakes as from a high fever, the gourd in my throat, though perhaps it is only the terror of proximity. Over her shoulder I see the discarded wheel and her sword driven into the ground as through a steaming heart.

Like a wife, she takes my leg and slowly brings it to her lips.

"I will chew away the man in you, so that you may approach my bones."

It hurts, the teeth going through sinew, the grinding molars on my ankle. Is this a gift, I ask?

Her delicate teeth tear into my knee. I feel them pop the joint out of place and scrape along the cupped patella.

"We who have eternal life in Christ must expect a dismantling from time to time. Fragmentation is Man's natural state."

I feel nothing below the waist, not even the phantom limbs of an amputee. I am simply missing. Her jaw dislocates to fit itself around my pelvis and, like a mighty lion's, snaps my body in two.

Up the torso she rips, building speed, spitting ribs like broken teeth; pared ringlets of skin make a beard around her working mouth. She is getting closer to my money pouch, to the piece of her inside it. Will she reclaim herself?

Katherine's incisors taste the leather, lift the pouch from my neck.

"What is this?"

"Your tongue," I gasp through the blinding pain. She must know where they left her pieces.

"Saint Katherine's tongue?"

Even in my delirium, brothers, I am instantly wary.

And then the howl, the human-animal frenzy of a thousand impaled infants flung to a thousand starving wolves, makes all things clear.

I jerk back on my stump of torso to see the Donestre's jaw snap furiously around my shoulders, my arms, my neck. He hisses at the pouch but is unable to sever another limb.

Green egg-stink sulfur chokes the field. I dig my elbows into smoking earth and fall into the stench, frantically trying to get away.

What has he done to my body?

"*Stop!* Felix!" Her voice like arms around my neck, hugging me back. I can't move and he cradles me, snapping my shoulder joints until I am a paralyzed bust of myself staring up from his heated lap. He sees the pain of betrayal in my eyes; he sees, so much more than any physical disassembly, how completely he has broken my faith in myself.

"Oh," says the Donestre, gently touching the corners of my eyes. "Oh."

I remember only snatches.

"Felix?"

I remember my hand like a swollen starfish.

"It is. Felix. Oh, God."

And only one eye, scabbed with sticky yellow sun.

"He is covered in sand. Help me!"

I remember German voices, but that language was no longer a tongue I trusted, brothers. I remember the worried blue eyes of my friend John Lazinus, whom I realized at that moment would love me even if I were no better than a melon head, a cartographer's globe, an orb. My one eye wanted to cry, but I had no water left in what was once my body.

"Roll him over, he can't breathe."

And Conrad was with him. Our barber who loves bodies for what bodies do: bleed, ooze, swell, char. If anyone could put my broken body back together, this barber could.

But did he leave the pieces? I spoke the words in my head but was unsure if I had said them aloud. In answer, a palm slipped under my neck and tilted my head forward.

"Here, drink this. It's all we have left."

If I have a neck, I remember thinking, I must have shoulders. And if shoulders, arms; the water slid down my throat and into my stomach, which meant I must have a torso.

"John," I remember saying.

"Oh, God, Felix. He tried to make us leave you behind."

"Feel my legs."

The weeping Archdeacon crushed me to his sweaty chest and my back gratefully cracked. Over John's shoulder, Conrad paced out into the plain, scanning the ground before him. *What is he looking for?* I remember thinking.

"We thought we had lost you forever," John cried, glancing behind him to where two glowering Saracens helped Conrad look. He lowered his voice.

"The drivers have gone over to Niccolo. Elphahallo threatened to slit their throats and drink their blood if they mutinied."

"Where am I, John?"

"You are southeast of the camp, just on the edge of that cursed Elysium. Felix, how did you get here?"

For a moment, this was the one piece I could not remember. I recalled gases and howls, a beast with a glowing heart, an orange bubble moon, but nothing else. I was on my way to find something, this much I knew, to bring back something absolutely necessary.

Lemon juice.

"Ursus!"

I sat up too quickly, brothers, and that is all I remember.

Ursus

He weighs as much as the medicine chest, two carpets, and a bag of browning, thin-skinned lemons. He swings at eye level—my eye level, because I am the one walking next to him now, trying to keep his mind off the heat and burning—and balances out the makeshift pannier Elphahallo has slung over a camel's hump. I am describing our view for him, keeping my eyes away from the daubed white lemon paste Conrad made from mashed pulp and what juice he could wring from the stringy fruit. As though he walked into an acid spider's web, the lesions have left a red net over Ursus's entire face.

"You can feel us walking uphill, can't you?" I ask him. His pannier is rigged so that no matter the inclination, he hangs flat.

"Yes," comes the muffled voice from deep in the shaded pannier. He can see only the canvas sides of his hammock and the slab of sky directly above him.

"Elphahallo tells us that when we reach the top, we will have our first view of Mount Sinai. Would you like to sit up for that?"

"Yes, thank you, Friar, it's hard to breathe in here."

I pull the sides apart, holding them against the tension of his sagging body, to let in some air. I get a glimpse of his poisoned knees, feeding like swollen ticks on his legs. The red streaks from them run down to his ankles.

When John and I finally retraced my path to where I had left them, brothers, I thought we were too late. Lord Tucher sat like an ineffective seamstress, trying to keep his skein of son from unraveling.

His hands worked methodically, clearing Ursus's sticky wounds of the gnats that crawled through them, his mouth buried in the child's salty hair. I was stricken with a sharp pang of guilt at having left them alone, even though I had inadvertently brought help; it was obvious Lord Tucher had prepared them both to die.

And now he rides before his son, his eyes fixed between his donkey's ears. Lord Tucher has spoken to no one since our camp was reunited. Elphahallo ran out to berate us, but one look at Ursus silenced him immediately. He has ridden quietly beside Lord Tucher all morning.

I have told no one but you, brothers, how I mistook a monster for a martyr on the Field of Elysium. I have no sense if the Donestre was real or an apparition sent by the Devil or a product of the poison gourd firing in my brain. My body is whole, I know that, and, except for a few scrapes I received dragging myself across the black volcanic plain, is unmarked. And yet, brothers, I still feel disassembled. If my corporeal self is intact, my faith has been snapped into a hundred little pieces and left like a trail of bread crumbs across this pilgrimage. Have I the strength to follow them back out of the wilderness? I do not know. The Donestre has left me a nomad in the desert, and I must teach myself new markers if I am ever to find my way home.

"I see a stone that looks like a pouncing lion," I tell Ursus. "It is yellow with jagged claws."

"There are lions in the desert, aren't there, Friar?"

"Certainly used to be. A lion dug the grave of Saint Mary of Egypt."

"That's unusual, isn't it?"

"Yes, son, highly."

Ursus is a marker, brothers. This thin, vulnerable boy is a reason to go home. He will recover and take his scars back like scallop shells from the beach, to stir the envy of other pages. I will not be there to see him pull up his tunic and display his wounds, but I will know he flourishes, a man among boys, and surely that will be enough.

John, too, is a marker. My friend will take me as far as Venice, where, needfully, we will have to part ways: he home to Hungary, me back to you. His donkey trots beside me now with my own ass's lead tied around its pommel. I cannot fathom being divorced from this friend, brothers, as much as I long to see you again. His faith is the only thing that stands between me and despair. When my saints have been replaced with monsters, is there any reason to maintain a pilgrimage? John says, Yes, Felix, keep moving forward. Go farther so that you may, at last, go home.

The way up the torrent bed is steep, and we have to climb on hands and knees from time to time. The driver leading Ursus's camel tugs the beast to make her clamber up. By nature, camels prefer flat sandy ground, but there is no flat land for miles.

"I wish I could see."

"I know, son. Say your prayers."

Ahead of us, the traitor Niccolo rides with the other camel drivers. Last night, the translator had demanded the camp move out at midnight as usual, even though there was no hope of us finding a moving camp in darkness. He made them load the camels, but Conrad and John pulled their things off and set out to find us. Niccolo fumed all morning as Conrad dressed Ursus's wounds, not even bothering to hide his disgust at our return. Hourly, brothers, I berate myself for having ever trusted that perfidious translator, for having been wooed by his reasonable voice and artificial logic. And yet perhaps he too is a marker, like the stones sailors set up on bluffs to keep ships from sailing into a Scylla or Charybdis. A whirlpool of pride, Niccolo rescues and condemns at will; snatching obscure saints from oblivion while at the same time sending Christian pilgrims to their certain deaths. Once, at the beginning of this folly, when we were on better terms, Ser Niccolo said that articulation was the only weapon we had against God. If we can order our own chaos, Friar, said he, what use have we for a Higher Power? Perhaps Niccolo is a marker to warn me away from my own chaos, brothers. I stumbled into it last night, and it has nearly spun me apart.

Of course, they reach the top of the torrent bed first, Niccolo and his friends, and wait upon its sharp rise impatiently for the rest of us. In the blue heat of day, no star shines to mark it, but I know where to look. Off to our left, brothers, a deep red mountain, angular and cropped, raises its head above all the rest.

"Ursus, sit up," I whisper. "The holy mountain!"

He struggles against the confining material and rests his chin on the canvas side.

What does he see, this sick child, straining to focus his eyes? Does he see the young Midianite Moses, sitting upon one of the mountain's terraces, scratching the neck of a shaggy gray sheep, or does he imagine that stern patriarch staggering under the injunctions of twin stone tablets? Is Sinai's burning bush made all of blooming desert thorns for Ursus, or does it resemble the white rosebush in his mother's garden at Ulm, the one he could smell from his bedroom window? The pale smile Ursus gives me is far away, brothers, a smile that comes from a happier part of his brain, where the mountain hasn't even registered. Slowly, he sinks back into the pannier.

"Gebel Musa." Elphahallo slips off his donkey and touches his forehead to the ground. *"Allahu Akbar."*

It takes us three times as long to descend the wadi as it did to climb its bank. The camels refuse the precarious footing, balking at almost every step. Our donkeys are only marginally better; their hooves skid over the slick stone, dislodging pebbles that collect more pebbles in their fall. I can tell time by Ursus's pendulum pannier, six counts from the apex until he almost smashes against the rock face, six counts more until he hangs suspended over nothingness. I am glad his father is in front of him, concerned with his own lack of balance, and doesn't have to watch.

We make it safely down a little before sunset, and Elphahallo steers us to the right, hurrying us along. Something feels wrong.

"Where do you think you are going, old man?"

Niccolo's shout stops us cold. He has not moved from the torrent bed.

"This is the way to water," Elphahallo states. "We have a sick child who must drink."

"This is the way to the mountain, though." Niccolo points off to the left, where from above we saw Sinai's peak.

"That way is too difficult. We must approach it through the pass that lies behind the mountain and to the right."

"Too difficult for whom?" Niccolo asks frostily. "Strong men, or grandparents and children?"

Elphahallo draws himself to his full height.

"I don't think you should suggest putting your benefactor's son at any further risk," he says quietly. "You don't hold the purse to this expedition."

"Then I think it is time I did. Calipha, Ibrahim." Niccolo nods to two of the camel drivers, and before I know what is happening, brothers, these two treacherous Arabs have drawn knives, cut the money pouch from Lord Tucher's neck, and tossed it to the translator. As one, the Arabs, including our ass drivers, turn their bows and arrows against us.

"I have promised to pay them double their wages to come with me," Niccolo says, smiling at their raised weapons. "Will you really drink their blood, old man?"

Elphahallo says much to the drivers in their heathen tongue, but the traitors make their black eyes into those of uncomprehending strangers and hear him not. John, Conrad, and I crowd around a stunned Lord Tucher.

"And I'll take those provision camels too, please," Niccolo orders. "A man has got to eat."

"You mean to strand us in the desert with a dying child and no food?" John stammers.

"You may keep the wretched water. For all the good it will do you." Niccolo nods to the drivers standing at the loaded camels' flanks, who cut the water loose as they have been dying to do ever since we set out from Gazara. At least they have left us that.

"Pardon me." Peter pushes past, leading his donkey over to the translator's camp. "To the left then?"

Niccolo extends his boot into the Mameluke's chest.

"Not you, my love. I won't profane Saint Katherine's church with the man who raped my sister."

"But," Peter stammers, "you promised to take me home."

"You deserted God. You deserted Allah. It seems to me you are most at home in the desert. Die here like the dog you are . . . Abdullah."

Niccolo turns his donkey, and the drivers, mounted on their own animals, trot swiftly after him. Between them, they lead off all our goods, save only the donkeys we ride and the single camel transporting Ursus Tucher. What are we to do? Beside me, a small choking noise builds in Lord Tucher's throat, a hybrid catch between rage and impotence, fear and decision. Before I can grab him, brothers, he twists away from my arms and sprints madly after the translator.

"You fucker! You have murdered my son!"

It happens faster than you think it possible to happen: An arm reaches back, finds an arrow, bends its bow, releases. Tucher is felled before he even reaches the translator's donkey's hoofprints. The Arabs, who are violent and cruel but who rarely kill, glance nervously at Ser Niccolo. Waving his creatures on, the translator gallops swiftly across the plain, followed by our men, the loaded camels lumbering after in a cloud of carmine dust.

"Father!"

We did not see him struggle up, the blanched, frightened boy. He has wriggled out of the pannier, upsetting the balance, causing the camel to wag her neck and roar. He is on the ground, crawling toward his father like the pieces of a butchered mother snake instinctively making toward her orphans.

"Ursus, stop." John scoops him up under the armpits and pulls him to his feet. "Let us handle it."

Conrad is the first to reach Lord Tucher. He has pushed up my patron's tunic and is pressing on the wound with both palms, raised up on his knees to lend more body weight. The arrow entered his chest between his fourth and fifth rib, just below the heart.

"Get the water, we must flush this wound."

Water saved Lord Tucher once, Dear Lord, let it save him again. Let the cool, clean Gazara water restore him, Lord, let it wet his lips and cleanse his wound. Take not away Your servant John Tucher when his child needs him so. Take him not away. I pray as I struggle with the massive terra-cotta jar, twisting the cork stopper between the crook of my arm and my chest. It comes off with a sucking pop, and in that terrible moment, brothers, when my nose understands this water, I know why Ser Niccolo hesitated not in leaving it with us.

Rotted fish, human ordure, leprosy—nothing could smell worse than this jar of spoiled water. I pour some into my hand, and it splashes out chunky white with maggots and decay. You can trust no one in this land! The thieving merchants in Gazara swore that if we kept the jars well sealed this water would last the entire trip.

"Where is that water?" Conrad shouts.

I kick the jars over near where our asses are tethered. They lunge to drink it, but even they find it too loathsome, and prance away like spoiled colts. I kick the jars again and again, shattering their worthless shells.

"Felix!" our barber calls over his shoulder. I walk back to where he has wrapped his robe around the feather and is tugging straight up. The arrow comes out covered in gray tissue and blood.

"The water was corrupted by the heat," I say.

"Press, then," Conrad orders. "I'll get the medicine chest."

His heart. I think the arrow punctured my patron's full heart. Blood oozes between my fingers and they slip off the wound. I press harder.

Conrad returns with a vial of brandy that he pours into the wound, followed by a vial of oil, then a stuffing of clean rags. There is nothing more to do than wrap his chest and press.

"Let me see my father!" Ursus screams, struggling against John. At last John half walks, half carries the sick child over to us.

"Lord Tucher?"

He is surprisingly gentle, lifting his father's head into his lap. His own face is so distorted with infection that it is impossible to tell whether or not he is holding back tears.

"Father, if you can hear me," Ursus whispers through his swollen mouth, "thank you for taking care of me in the desert."

He wipes Conrad's bloody handprint from his father's brow and gives it a tiny kiss.

"I know you took the silver rosary Mother gave me before we left home, but it's all right. You can keep it."

Like a tender thief, Ursus rummages through the pocket tied next to Lord Tucher's heart and draws out the bloody silver cross stolen a lifetime ago, the day we buried Schmidhans.

"See?" He swings it above his father's sightless eyes. "I knew you had it all along."

A Lion

Ursus asked to dig and we let him, cupping his small hands in our own to help him scoop. It exhausted him, and now he lies asleep, wrapped in the canvas pannier next to our only remaining camel. She guards Ursus like a giant sad-eyed dog, holding back the desert monsters with her hypnotic chewing.

We have settled for the night, brothers, on the warm ashes of a caravan that passed before us. Their dried camel dung fuels our campfire, burning clear and blue, though we have nothing to cook over it. Niccolo took with him the onions and biscuit, the flour and dried meat. Our chickens died of heat exhaustion days ago—they stopped eating the millet we pushed through the bars, settled down in their own shit, and squinted themselves to sleep. Now, unless we eat our donkeys, we will have nothing until we reach Saint Katherine's.

I sit between the fire and the boy and use the thin edge of the recovered silver cross to clean the dirt from under his nails. A boy shouldn't sleep with his father's grave dust on his hands, even if there is no water to wash them. I separate the limp fingers, define the crescent on each one, and relax them into a fist.

"How long had you known your father was a thief?" I asked him after we weighted my patron's grave with rocks so that wild animals might not dig him up again.

"He prayed with my silver rosary the night of the storm," answered that most wise Knight of the Holy Sepulchre. "It seemed to comfort him."

Ursus wanted me to bury his father with those silver beads, but I snatched them back when the boy was not looking. The rosary, by rights, belongs to Ursus, and he has great need of it, brothers.

"Failisk, you should go to sleep." Elphahallo rolls over and sees me sitting up beside Ursus. We have to push on soon, but I cannot close my eyes.

"How is the child?" he asks groggily. His face slackened by sleep, Elphahallo appears to have aged thirty years in the last few hours. I did not know, before today, that he traveled the desert with ruptured genitalia; his hernia is acting up, I can tell, for I see him wince when he lifts up on his elbows.

"He is asleep," I say.

"Perhaps it is a blessing. In a few days, the father would have had to bury the son."

My hand steals out to blot the boy's face, where one of his wounds is weeping again. Ursus feels the pressure and starts to cry in his sleep.

"I am so sorry, Failisk," Elphahallo is saying. "Never in fifty years have I had men turn on me."

I nod.

"I knew that translator was stirring trouble," he says. "I finally convinced my drivers Lord Tucher had not sent Christian spies to steal their children, when one of them came to me saying Lord Tucher had been seen casting spells over their water."

We sit silently, absorbed in the fire and her blue hem. I trace her flame skirt up to her sharp orange arms—she throws them out to me, up to Heaven; out to me, up to Heaven.

"Go to sleep, Failisk."

"Soon, Calinus."

Around the fire, our exhausted pilgrims sleep: Conrad still streaked with his patron's blood, John shivering against the cold hard earth, Peter curled into a tight ball as though expecting someone to plunge a knife into his back. I have my boy all to myself, brothers, to study as I would a child of my own.

I comb his dirty blond hair with my fingers in a vague memory of how he wore it when we set out from Ulm. Ursus and his father

appeared at our convent, despite the gray rainy weather, clean and
bright and smelling of borax. These two will be my family for the
next year, I remember thinking, as you, brothers, hung about my
neck, crying for my certain death at sea. Will this surrogate family
be kind or cruel? Will they become annoying in their worldliness
or will advising them bring me closer to my God? The Tuchers were
by turns generous and attentive, frustrating and proud, and yet I
could never have guessed how like a real son this child Ursus would
become to me. We decide for life or death in life at such an early
age, each one of us, brothers. Surely I am not the only one among
you who found he needed a family enough to borrow from the dead.
What harm could come from playing husband? Does Katherine not
already belong to Christ? What harm from playing father? Will my
son not return home with another man? A coward's family, surely;
a saint and a monk and another's child, but my one chance to pretend I was a man like any other.

Ursus stirs in his sleep and calls upon his younger brother, Henry,
to shut out the lamp.

The single fierce ember in our guttering fire is the one piece of
wood abandoned by the caravan that preceded us. John Lazinus read
this square as a pledge, brothers, and a token of faith. I am not so
sure the icon that I threw into the flames means the Tongue is alive.
It could just as easily have been tossed aside by thieves. Throughout the night, I have watched the Fifty Philosophers slowly melt
into one, separated by a hedge of dripping green from the Lone
Scholar; it took the scholar longer to combust, but when he did his
end was long and lingering, a flame through his heart that slowly
ate away his head. John did not argue when I set Arsinoë's token
alight. He too is exhausted by Heaven.

"We should get ready to go." Elphahallo sits up. "The wind is
blowing stronger."

Indeed, brothers, another storm seems to be brewing off to the
east. I sigh and breathe in a mouthful of flying pulverized stone,
chilled in the cold night air. Sand sticks to Ursus's lemon paste, but
if I wipe it clear, it will hurt him more, so, helplessly, I watch the
uneven bunkers amass across his cheeks.

Elphahallo shakes the others awake. We need to cover as much ground as possible before the heat of the day, and, moreover, we must find water. My body feels the lack of food, the strain on my back from digging and sitting on cold earth. And now we must suffer the fierce sand that, like a ghostly horseman, gallops over the plain.

Ursus won't be budged. John and I wrap our arms around him, but he shudders like a lamprey and slides back to the ground. At last I pull him into my lap while John scours the soiled pannier with handfuls of sand. We don't want him riding all day in his own filth.

How we complained of driving rain aboard ship, brothers; how little we were prepared for the deluge of sand that falls upon the wilderness. We remount our donkeys and turn our faces toward the quarter we hope holds Katherine's Star, for we can barely see the man beside us, much less make out the heavens. A fierce wind blows off the Indian Ocean, pushing the desert sand always before it, so that, hour by hour, entire mountains melt away under our donkeys' feet.

We hunch our way through these mountains, shoulders drawn around our ears to keep out the bitter winds. My stomach shakes with cold and hunger, and I can feel my trapped heart beat sideways against my lungs. From time to time we sink in pits of sand, when pilgrim and camel, Saracen and ass must struggle up as through deep snow. Just as we are about to lie down and abandon ourselves to Death, brothers, the landscape gradually changes. Hard rock replaces loose sand, and the storm, like fire denied its air, slowly dies. A warm dawn breaks over the flinty mountains, buying us ten minutes of comfort. Our shoulders relax, our stomachs unclench, and for the brief morning we are human.

But hour by hour the heat's gentle fingers on our shoulders tighten; the sun clamps down on our backs and necks, the ridges of our ears, our calves. Soon sweat slides across our upper lips, drips down our inner thighs, and the frozen, stormy hours of Erebus are forgotten. We are back in Hell.

The thirst is unbearable, brothers. We have had no water to drink now for a full day and night; my lips bleed freely, my nose membranes crack like brittle bug wings. I notice, ahead of me, Peter is sucking on his fist.

"What do you have?" I ask, trotting next to him. He takes his hand from his mouth.

"A lemon," he says. Its feathery flesh looks like the poison lungs of a she-crab.

"Those are for Ursus." I slap it from his hand, send it spinning.

"How much longer do you think he'll need them?"

I lick the sweat from my lips and move ahead.

Elphahallo has tied the camel's lead to his pommel and trots beside Ursus. He is telling him the story of Albaroch, Mahomet's steed.

"He was a bit bigger than an ass, with the feet of a camel, and a fair face like a man's; his hair was fashioned all of pearls, his breast made of emeralds, his tail hung all with rubies, and his eyes were brighter than the sun. Albaroch would let no man mount him unless the Archangel Gabriel vouched for his goodness. 'I have met no man on this earth better than Mahomet,' said Gabriel, and offered to hold the prophet's stirrup. Together, Mahomet and his steed came swift as the wind to Jerusalem, where all the patriarchs and holy men did them homage."

"I had jewels once," Ursus says.

"I know, my child."

I drop back.

What can we do to slake this thirst? The mountains are too sharp against the sky, and their red throbs painfully against my broken eye veins. The smells of our company, usually so muted, separate themselves into deities: Lord of the Camel's Breath, Master of the Unwashed Crotch, Hierarch of Piss. Standing Godhead over all odors is the Whiff of Lord Tucher's Punctured Heart—I smell it every time I scratch my cheek or brush the hair off my brow. It lingers like the first fish I ever skinned as a boy, impossible to keep my knuckles from my nose, realizing that salty foreignness had been absorbed into *me*. Each sniff explodes my headache until I have to ride with my eyes closed.

At last Elphahallo stops us. "Here it is."

Another dusty, arid torrent bed. Has he lost his mind?

"No," Elphahallo says. "Climb down. The river has dried up, but some water remains standing in pools."

We dismount our donkeys and skid down the wadi's steep face. Blessed Jesu, brothers! Elphahallo is right. In shallow clefts, like molten alexandrite, stands warm green water. I cup handfuls into my mouth, gulping like the greediest swine. I drink until my cleft is half empty, until my swollen belly strains against my navel, and then, only when I am completely satisfied, are my eyes opened.

I have been drinking worms.

Above us, Elphahallo shakes his head. See how the donkeys drink—he gestures to the animals sucking only the top inch of the water, straining off any parasites with their careful tongues. See how the men drink—more like beasts than their own asses.

All the little pools are writhing with flat white worms, but what can we do? We must drink. I strain the water through my handkerchief into my empty goatskin and toss the loaf of worms aside.

"Felix, over here!"

John has found a deep blue hidden spring at the bottom of a narrow ravine. He slides his way down and plunges in, popping up like a sleek brown otter. Soon we are all bathing, brothers, and baptizing each other as though we swam in the River Jordan. When our Calinus sees what we are about, he sternly warns us against diving under the water, but we heed him not and so enjoy ourselves for the first time in weeks. At last, naked and clean, we lay ourselves upon the hot rocks and feel our hair slowly stiffen and our skin tighten across our cheeks and chests. We all clamor to spend the night at this torrent bed, but Elphahallo will hear none of it. When we are dry, he forces us back onto our donkeys to make for a protected plain just through the mountain pass. Arabs, again. We're always guarding ourselves against these Arabs.

I ride next to Ursus, who is looking much stronger for his swim. Conrad reapplied the lemon paste to each bite, and it has hardened into a pulpy mask over his face, evening out his features. His eyes are bright from the exertion, and he is smiling for the first time since his father died.

"My legs don't hurt anymore, Friar," he confides. "They feel like a fishtail."

I think Elphahallo and Conrad are wrong about his condition; I am not at all convinced the infection has spread as far as they. A monk of our order once chopped his wrist while cording wood and I witnessed the gangrene that set in; this child's skin does not pump that rotted-melon stench and does not break open along the same juicy jags. His web is almost beautiful, as if the insects had constructed an intricate highway between the stations of his bites, paths as straight as Roman roads, colonizing his body in order to restore order. I ask him if he feels like a flourishing province, and he tells me fish can swim upside down if they want.

God, brothers, our bodies smell so good!

I had forgotten what clean people smell like. Ursus smells like lemon verbena, and John behind me smells like tin spoons. I can't quite place Elphahallo, but I imagine him as blue Iznik tiles or black calligraphy ink—some repeating pattern, simple and Saracen and interlocking. I left Lord Tucher's heart in the torrent pool, floating like fat on the surface, and made sure to step out of the water far away from the slick. I can't have that smell clouding my reason at a time like this.

For the first time today, my hunger feels like a blessing. Unpolluted by food, my mind is sharp like a Hindoo's or a Brahmin's. I think I may have picked up Arsinoë's scent, her briny trail over the rocks. I peek back at John to see if he has noticed it, but he is surreptitiously sucking the inside peel of one of Ursus's medicine lemons.

Those are for him!

I push us to move faster.

A fish out of water, that's her scent, and when we squeeze through the superhumanly narrow mountain pass that leads to the Field of Machera, we must keep our cheeks from scraping her cod-liver oil off the rock walls. The growing evening shadows throw each stone into high relief, and, like a miracle, dew begins to sift from the sky, brothers, like the softest, sweetest rain. Elphahallo laughs quietly to himself and sticks out his tongue to catch the moisture. Our donkeys shake it from their bristly manes, blinking it from their eyelashes. They stop of their own accord, then gallop through the pass down onto the sunken grassy plain as though home to their own stables.

While the donkeys rip at the monkey grass, we clear stones for a night's rest. I have just smoothed a spot for Ursus when Elphahallo puts his hand on my arm and points up.

Above us, where the ground swells toward Saint Katherine's Star, a squat animal stands on four thick legs. She is the color of box-wood, brothers, with small pig eyes that watch our work and, most amazingly, a single horn upon her head.

"What is it?" I ask Elphahallo.

"It's a unicorn," says Peter.

"It is a rhinoceros," answers the Saracen in a whisper. "Very few still live here."

"What's happening?" my patron's son asks anxiously. "Friar?"

I move to where Ursus is still attached to the kneeling camel and lift him in my arms to see. His scalding, light body is all moist on the bottom.

"Look there, son, do you see that creature?"

"Is it a lion?"

"No, sweet, can you see the horn?"

"Did it come to dig my grave?"

He twists in my arms so sharply that I lose my grip and drop him, hear his head hit the stones I cleared like a heavy fish slapped against a table. A fish out of water. A fish.

"Oh, God!" Conrad is above him, returning his head to its proper place on his neck. I walk swiftly away from the camp, hard through the twilight. The rhinoceros started at Ursus's scream; I find her four solid footprints, her streak across the sand where she ran away. In her flight, a tiny stunted tree was crushed; it glistens with fall-ing dew. How simple it is, just to kneel down and lick the moisture from its leaves, savor the ineffable sweetness, better than any honey, any syrup. Between the fronds, I spy a hardened droplet, translucent as amber but dusted with white. I sniff it, then put it between my teeth. Pure heaven. It is the child of the moon and the air, dried in the hot afternoon sun. Manna.

"Manna!" I cry, weeding the tree of it, prying droplets from between adjacent stones. I have got a double handful, enough for us to feast on, enough to turn this night into a party, a proper thanksgiving. I run across the plain, dribbling candy like a breathless, drunken Santa Claus.

"Ursus!" I pelt him with fistfuls of treats. "Look what I found for you!"

The pilgrims stare up at me, from where they kneel beside my broken, lifeless boy. My legs can hold me no longer; I drop beside his body, gathering this fallen knight to me. Surely there is one more miracle left in this wretched Age of Man.

I rip the tongue from around my neck and touch it to his eyes, motionless beneath their lids. I place it on his mouth, the gate of breath, upon his heart, so still and quiet beneath my hand. I touch her tongue to his useless legs, to his wasted arms; I press it tight against his nostrils to seal his loosened soul inside.

This fraud, this worthless piece of flesh.

Ursus, child. I have killed you too.

The Other Mountain

No matter what cartographers say, there are only two mountains in the world: the Mountain of Truth and the Mountain of Illusion.

Mount Illusion, I have learned, is, in fact, a chain; a jagged spine that originates beneath our monastery in Ulm, swells across the Mediterranean into the Holy Land, and spikes under us, here in the wilderness. Upon this range, brothers, saints intercede for men, churches in our dreams are churches in the flesh, and brave young boys are buried by lions that come down from the hills to paw the earth. Here upon the range of Illusion, a stern Asian princess might once more become the sweet fräulein I believed I married; she might stand beside the sad-eyed lion and rub his head as he roars over an open grave.

Love truly does own Illusion, I have learned, and I blush to remember how I reviled her on her island of Cyprus. Were I a skilled Pygmalion, I too would take up a chisel to carve something familiar and kind from the ossified creature my pilgrimage has become. As it is, with no such talents, I can only sit here, on Illusion's last rise, remembering happier times, knowing I must soon cradle the Truth of Ursus Tucher's putrefied body and walk it to my wife's monastery below.

How small her house looks from this vantage, brothers. It would disappear into the desert, were it not for the defining green spit of olive and cypress trees planted behind it. Her church sits behind a thick military wall, erected almost a thousand years ago by the

Emperor Justinian to protect the monks who dwelt beside Moses'
Burning Bush. A trained eye can read the history of the complex in
its buildings, as one might divine the seasons of a felled tree by the
rings in its trunk. Fat, prosperous years yielded the lead-roofed Byzantine church and the verdant garden, heavy with olives and purple
aubergine. Lean, parsimonious years converted the monks' guest
house into a Saracen mosque, to placate its Turkish invaders, and
bricked up the entry, so that the only remaining way into the monastery is via a basket drawn up into a suspended gatehouse. This
monastery has endured by its very isolation, keeping close its Ara-
maic Bibles and Pancrator Christs, texts and images as old as Christianity itself. What Emperor, King, or Sultan would not want to own
this rough-hewn jewel? But which of them can be bothered to lo-
cate it somewhere, out there, inside that brutal desert?

Brothers, as we know that it is not Truth's nature to remain for
long unassailed, so now we arrive to find the monastery choked by
new invaders. Garotted by traitorous criminals like the ones who
deserted us. Or their naked cousins. Or their naked cousins' bas-
tard stepbrothers. On camels and asses, tethered with jangly silver
coin bridles and saddled with carpets. Armed.

Wild Arabs, at last, at the end of our journey.

From where we sit, we can count almost two hundred of them
spread out around the monastery. Our ship's captain warned us
against these nomads, and Elphahallo did all in his power to avoid
camping by their wells. Next to these men, the Saracens in Jerusalem, whom until now we had regarded as scarce human, seem civi-
lized and almost as ourselves.

Disquieted, we drink the last of our leftover crevice water, remount our asses, and pick our way across this final field. John
reaches out to steady the collapsed body of Ursus Tucher as he sags
from my saddle. Mercifully, the Archdeacon did not argue when I
insisted on burying my patron's son on holy ground. Ursus wanted
to die for Saint Katherine. The least she can do is provide him a bed
in her church's graveyard.

The nomads watch our approach with interest. Their cousins who
led the merchant's caravan, for all their filth, carried themselves like

princes; these savages, brothers, mill like desperate, hardened guer-
rillas. We wind slowly through their ranks, past dark-skinned men
who rise in their stirrups to scratch unself-consciously at their naked
buttocks; beyond chieftains in filched European helmets, sharpen-
ing their arrowheads with flint. The scrawny nomad children hide
behind their unclothed mothers and reach out imploringly to us.
Surely, brothers, these hands are too small to hold a coin, should
we even have one left.

Cautiously, Elphahallo approaches the most intricately tattooed
and fiercely armed of the savages. I see our Calinus touch his turban many times, gesturing back at our bedraggled party and the dead
boy I hold across my lap. A few moments later he returns to us in
defeat; we may not enter the monastery, he informs us, unless we
pay their toll.

For a second I am tempted to employ the Turks' strategy against
Rhodes and hurl the maggot-eaten, stinkbomb body of Ursus Tucher
into their crowd. The horror of corruption transcends all language
barriers, brothers, and that would be payment enough for their
betrayal, their comfortless desert, their white-green worm water.
We have no money to pay them, no treats to bribe their children.
We cannot have traveled so far and endured so much to be halted
for lack of a rucksack full of biscuit.

Instead, I swing my patron's son over my shoulder like an elop-
ing suitor and push against the crowd. A hundred lions fought over
my carcass in my dreams last night, so tell me what I have to fear
from these conscienceless, masticating, unclean lower beasts? My
valiant charge takes me no farther than ten paces before a hundred
spears are aimed at me, one point landing like a delicate butterfly
upon my neck. Elphahallo pulls at me to come away. There are
other ways, he says, but I don't care.

"Let me pass," I order the uncomprehending savages. "I command
you."

And just when I believed no wonders remained in the East, my
brothers, these violent Arabs turn aside. In fact they more than turn,
they run away from me, back to the monastery gate.

"Aeysh! Aeysh!"

The nomads shove me to the ground in their hurry to reach the palm-frond basket that slowly descends from the monastery's gatehouse. They raise their hands to it, as if in worship, and leap for it when it drops not quickly enough. Their children, brothers, squeeze between the adults' legs and reach the basket first, emerging in triumph with, of all things, round white loaves, each one stamped with the image of the virgin martyr Saint Katherine. The young boy before me hungrily rips Katherine's head from her impressed body, leaving the decapitated saint idly holding a cross and a palm branch, floating on a stack of books. These wretched nomads are not here for plunder, I suddenly understand. They are here for bread.

"Felix! Where are you going?" I hear John's voice through the mob but pay it no mind. I have spied my one chance to enter the monastery, and I run with Ursus, brothers, straight for the basket. Flinging the remaining Katherine loaves at the crowd, I dive in, cover myself with Ursus's putrid body, and yank on the rope. To my amazement, the supple basket jerkily ascends, leaving the Arab feeding frenzy far below.

"Who are you?" An angry monk asks in Latin, when I step out of the basket into their spare wooden gatehouse. Behind him, three more Greek monks rest against the wheel winch they turned to raise me. All four wear faded black habits, patched many times over and held onto their bodies by hanks of rope. Their uncut gray hair has been tied back into ponytails in the fashion of Eastern Christians, and their long beards, like the wandering monk who first brought Saint Katherine's relics to a young boy in Basle, grow wild and wiry from their cheeks.

"My name is Friar Felix Fabri of the Preaching Brothers in Ulm," I say. "My party has no toll to pay those Arabs; we were robbed in the desert."

The monk who speaks Latin eyes Ursus suspiciously, his nose crinkling in distaste.

"I'm afraid we cannot help you. Only eight of us are left at the monastery, and we barely have time to even say our prayers, much less look after you. The Bedouin have us too busy baking bread."

He nods at the body I am still holding.

"You should have buried him in the desert," he says.

"I want him on holy ground."

"Our cemetery is out behind the Bedouin, but even if you reach it, the earth is so hard we only have five graves. When a sixth monk dies, we dig up the bones of the first and stack them in the ossuary. There is no place for this boy."

I lean my head against the daub wall. It could not have come to this, brothers, that the very heart of the desert is hardened against us. Below, I hear the Arabs screaming *aeysh, aeysh!* What does that word mean?

"It is their word for bread," the monk answers, before I even ask. "It means *life*."

Nothing is as I expected it, brothers: not this besieged monastery, not this graveless earth, certainly not these Eastern monks, who care no more that we have come weeks across the desert than if we had ducked into Ulm from Wiesensteig. I cradle my unburied boy and try to imagine where we might put him.

"May I have some water, please?" I ask at last.

The monk reluctantly leads me down an exposed, banisterless wooden staircase into the complex proper. The walls of the monastery have been razed in places to the height of a man's head, and I can see from here that the right bartizan has completely collapsed. How can eight monks hold off a hoard of Arabs when their defenses are little better than a child's fort? Do they really think this munitions of bread will protect them? The monk leads me around a corner to a stone well.

"Cross yourself, brother," the monk says. "This is where Moses drew water for Jethro's sheep."

Absently, I kiss the stones, not even bothering to ask if indulgences are attached to this spot. For the first time in the Holy Land, I can appreciate a place for its present over its past: Yes, our Lawgiver drew from this well, but it matters more to me that the water inside it, now, is ice cold and pure. I drink gratefully, brothers, cleaning the desert from my mouth. With heavy tears in my eyes, I pour a handful of clean water over my patron's son's mangled face. I will find a place for you to rest, Ursus.

"I must return to the kitchen," the monk tells me, "but I will be back."

Across from the well, two immense wooden doors, the sturdiest features I have seen in the complex so far, stand ajar. They frame the entrance to a small granite lead-roofed church.

"Don't touch anything," he warns.

Carved partridges flock along the door lintel, flanked by stylized lions, winged cherubim, and vines. The early Christians favored animals over people, brothers, in their sacred art. How far away they were from this new Age of Man, which desires to put its own face on every post and pillar! In the old days, a saint's very manhood was disguised; of the Evangelists, Saint Mark became the lion, Saint Luke the ox, Saint John took on the mien of the noble eagle. Saint Matthew alone retained his human form but even then was granted cherubim wings, so one might not mistake him for the common flesh. The ancients understood the more we searched out ourselves in God, the more easily we would get the two confused. Do our modern painters not dress up saints as wealthy ladies of the court and set the apostles down in colonnaded dining halls for their final supper? Is the desert of Saint Jerome not painted as a pleasant glade in Tuscany, stocked like a duke's preserve with stags and curious ostriches? It is no wonder, brothers, that foolish pilgrims have no idea what real saints suffered until they come to the testing ground of this cruel East. We have grown too used to keeping company with our saints as ourselves.

I carry Ursus Tucher through these massive doors and into the cloister. Upon the ceiling, painted white against the deep carnelian paneling, Katherine wheels alternate with bony fish and pelicans. Twelve hollow pillars support the ceiling, representing the twelve months of the Christian calendar, and inside each pillar the monks of Saint Katherine keep the relics of any saint who, according to his legend, died during that month. You may reach into the little doors cut into each column and rummage around in martyr's bones, brothers, for they store them haphazardly inside, careful only not to mix up saints from different months. Nailed to each pillar, an icon representing all the saints, martyrs, confessors, and abbots of January,

February, March, and so on lets the unlearned know which of the blessed repose inside which column. Truly, brothers, these icons are a marvel of overcrowding; tight clusters of saints, wedged shoulder to shoulder, three and four deep, are all painted together. Some saints look stern, some joyful; some roll their eyes in fits of agony. Some hold crosses; some read books; some stand with lions or allow birds to perch upon their shoulders. Do they bicker when this church is empty, I wonder? Do they jostle and push to the front, or is the secret to Heaven that each saint has found his place and is comfortable there? I carry Ursus to the November pillar to search out Saint Katherine, but she is not present. These icons were painted while Katherine slept in oil, unknown to the Christian world.

Ursus and I walk down the right-side aisle, equally crammed with altars. Cosmas and Damian, Anne and Joachim, Antipas, Marina. Saint Marina lived her life as a nameless monk in the desert. Only when they washed her limbs for burial was she discovered a woman. I pause at none of these shrines but walk to where I know she must be, under the archway to the right of the front chancel. I hesitate on the step. A single olive-oil lamp casts red light over the Byzantine capitals and granite slabs mortared with broken rock that make up her pedestal. When they brought her down from the mountain, they laid her once more upon stone.

Slowly, brothers, I approach Saint Katherine's tomb.

"Katherine, virgin of Alexandria, erstwhile wife, saint." I begin my prayer self-consciously in this quiet room. "Forgive me my constant incomprehension, for I am but a foolish priest. For twenty years I dreamed a spouse, a gentle virgin to share my life. If I could have any wife in Heaven or Earth, I wanted it to be you. When I learned you gave yourself freely to John and Arsinoë, I sadly put on my cuckold's horns, wept bitter tears for the dying of this dream—but then suddenly my life was given back: You spoke to me through the Tongue. I learned you were a captive, held hostage, your body folded inside a box. I vowed to take up the sword for you, my true wed wife, and lay down my life to regain you for the world.

"Now, with the passing of this boy, I know, Katherine, you are not the saint I dreamed you were. You have shown yourself nothing but a cold, remote princess who has forgotten her human life. You have ruthlessly demanded Constantine and Emelia and Lord Tucher, and now this child, when all your tormentor Maxentius requested of you was a handful of incense upon an altar.

"Was Arsinoë correct? Are you lost without the images of your own destruction? Does Heaven truly forget its earthly struggles, the further it moves from Art? You were tortured, Katherine, but you forget the feel of the wheel tearing at your muscles. You were humiliated, and yet you cheerfully subject your servants to far worse shame. Is it that without the picture of your degradation always before you, you turn loose the memory? Have you forgotten what it means to die?

"Take this child, Katherine. I had meant to come to Sinai and fulfill our marriage vows. I wanted to adore you and praise you and shower you with wedding gifts. What words of love can I now pronounce that don't taste of ashes in my mouth?"

I lay the pale, liquefying body of Ursus Tucher upon her tomb.

"Take him," I pray. "You have taken everything else."

"Don't waste your time, Felix." A voice comes quietly from the shadows. "Martyrs understand only two things: Love and Death."

I don't even turn around. The Dominican monk Arsinoë joins me at Katherine's coffin. With full eyes, she looks down on my patron's son. Gently, she wipes away the well water still clinging to his lashes.

"A saint's love is in Heaven, but her death is on Earth," says the Tongue. "When she loses touch with that death, Felix, she is no more use to men."

I don't have the strength to speak to this woman, brothers. She is even thinner than when I last saw her, and her sharp bruised camel-pad wrists drop limply to her sides. Once again, she wears the heavy feed bag of bones around her neck.

"Have you seen her yet?" she asks.

I shake my head.

"Would you like to?"

I have no answer to that question.

"The monks are so rushed, they did not securely refasten the lock when they showed me her relics," Arsinoë says. "I can open the tomb for us."

I look down upon Ursus's body, finally at rest. His febrile ulcers disappear in the red lamplight, creating the happy illusion of health. My boy must be moved, once again.

"Forgive me," I whisper, hugging his body close, breathing in its corruptibility. In the end, brothers, I am a weak man. I have to see.

I fold Ursus awkwardly in the corner while Arsinoë pushes back the heavy marble lid, incrementally exposing Katherine's oily parch-ment-colored bones. Scattered about them, brothers, on her mattress of vermilion silk, gold florins, rings, and rosaries all attest to the piety of centuries of pilgrims. So much of the saint has been carried away that her remains at Sinai comprise only one leg, her pelvis, four ribs, a forearm, her right hand, and that which Arsinoë slowly reveals, the orb we have lost everything to gain: Katherine's holy head.

The head's leathery brown skin is stretched taut over high cheek-bones, and its mouth curves in a tight smile. Both eyelids are gone, brothers; one, I know, was in the possession of the traveling Greek monk of my boyhood, lost, certainly, many years ago in Europe. The hard-won golden crown of martyrdom levitates above her hairless head, to remind us our riches are found in Heaven, not on Earth. This is the skull we have put a thousand faces on; that we have painted blushing on canvas and sternly amber on wood. This, broth-ers, is the face we have hacked into stone, stitched onto altar cloths. What do I see of my former bride in the blank structure beneath? What skin have I brought with me across the desert that makes her look like anything other than a monster? It does not matter. All other images of Katherine are forgotten. For once, brothers, I gaze into the face of Truth.

"It is so easy to take from here," Arsinoë whispers. "The monks are so distracted."

"Why haven't you, then?"

She shrugs, plants a kiss on Katherine's forehead. "Maybe I was waiting for you?"

I can play this game no longer, brothers.

"Tell me," I ask, almost beyond caring, "why have you and this saint destroyed my life?"

"We did not mean to involve you," she replies. "Katherine is tired. She wanted to come home."

"But not to the monastery," I say. "You wear her bones about your neck, but you make no move to add them to her casket."

"Not to the monastery," Arsinoë whispers.

"Where is home?" I ask.

"Oblivion." She says it so softly I can barely hear. "She is done with the world. She desires now only Heaven."

"She is done with the world, Arsinoë? Or are you?"

"What is the difference?" she asks.

I walk around the stone coffin until I am even with her.

"I can not let you do this." I take the poor, exhausted woman in my arms, wincing as the sharp bag of bones digs into my chest. "We have had enough death for one pilgrimage."

"But we have no choice, Friar," Arsinoë cries, and spins away. *"Death and Life are in the power of the Tongue."*

I do not see it coming, brothers, the coffin lid. I hear it slide like a heavy boat over rocks, but I do not realize what it means until it slams into my solar plexus. Wind. My spine crushed against the wall.

"Only when Katherine is gone can I be free," she sobs. "Her voice in my head is the only thing that pins me to this wretched body."

Helplessly, I watch Arsinoë stuff her feed bag full with Katherine's hand, her shin, ribs, a leg. Please, I pray, if you must take everything else, just leave that one relic. At least leave the world a face upon which to reimagine her. But my prayer falls unheard. Arsinoë reaches in and lifts it out with both hands, careful not to jar her golden crown: the precious skull of Katherine of Alexandria, Virgin Martyr.

"I waited so you might witness her desire to be taken," Arsinoë says. "She does not rise up to smite me. She does not struggle. See and know, Felix. It is Katherine's will that we disappear."

My arms are trapped; with my chest I try to push the marble lid away from my crushed ribs. I can't breathe.

"Kiss her before I go, Felix. I owe you that much."

I turn my head, but she follows me with it, pinning my cheek to the wall with the sweating head's flat cheek.

I dreamed a thousand nights of her kisses. I never wanted this.

Arsinoë rolls the skull until its gap-tooth smile is even with my mouth, then presses it hard against my lips. I am suffocating under olives and myrrh. Every stolen kiss from my novitiate visits me, tasting of goat's milk and growing boys, the same feeling of asphyxiation. I am falling into my own spine, O my brothers.

And then there is a set of thin, trembling lips against mine, and Arsinoë is kissing me like parchment. My streaming eyes meet her own, and she is crying too.

"Please," I beg. "I have lost everything."

"Now you begin to understand the martyr's life," she whispers.

Hands

I wake to cool hands under my robes, rudely pushing aside my testicles on their way to feeling up my armpits. One monk pushes the coffin lid aside; two more argue in Greek while they grope. If only I could draw a real breath, I would laugh at how painfully it tickles, or maybe I would scream at them to stop.

I wake a second time, and one of the monks is prodding me with his shoe, warily, as if I were a wounded wild badger on the side of the road, almost but not quite dead. I open my eyes and he shouts at me, then shouts at his companion, the monk who let me in, who shouts at me in Latin.

"What have you done with her?"

I close my eyes again.

The third time I wake, I am blind.

They have left me in total darkness, brothers, here on a cold stone floor, in a room that smells vaguely of mold and sandalwood. When I roll over, my ribs separate, and the most excruciating pain shoots across my back and into my neck. Once, as a boy, a horse kicked me in the chest, and I felt like this, as if any sudden movement would unsnarl this architecture of bones and leave me a collapsed white heap on the ground.

"Hello!" I call weakly, unable to get enough air in my lungs to yell. "Where am I?"

To my left, along the floor, I spy a faint line of midnight blue, barely a shade lighter than the interior pitch. Slowly, brothers, I roll onto my knees and painfully crawl to that line. Most definitely, a breeze circulates around it, and if I pat my way higher up, I begin to recognize splintery wood, two hinges, a cold metal ring. With all my might, I pull on this ring, brothers, but nothing happens. I am locked in.

"Let me out!" I pound the door with both fists, stretching my bad ribs even farther. Oh, God. I collapse to my knees and butt the door sharply with my head.

"Let me out!"

It all comes back, brothers: Arsinoë's theft. Her flight. My imprisonment. I vaguely remember two monks lifting me, the setting sun outside the church, and a small low door. They threw me in here like a shovelful of coal. But where is here?

I sense I am on a narrow path in an overly crowded room—creeping down an aisle of some kind—but this doesn't feel like a normal chapel. Gingerly, I stretch out my left hand to test the room's perimeters. I creep only a few feet before I come across what feels like a loosely mortared internal wall, carefully constructed from smooth eroded stone. I crawl farther along, patting my way to get its measure, when, suddenly, unexpectedly, a single round stone breaks off in my hand. The whole heavy wall teeters.

Quickly, brothers, I fumble for the cavity, but my hands are shaking so that I end up pushing the stone into a space already full. The top rows sway, a stone comes loose and strikes the floor hollowly, then bounces away. Oh, God, I recognize that sound. In my panic, I leap back, crashing into the rest of the wall, bringing it raining down on top of me. Hundreds of skulls, brothers, coconut hard and bony, bruise my back with their bulging brows and angled jaws. Centuries of preserved monk heads, from hundreds of exumed Saint Katherine graves, ricochet off the walls of the narrow ossuary like ecstatic berserkers, limbless grinning skulls, alive again and angry. I hunker against the avalanche.

But are these heads not you, brothers? Have you not faithfully followed me on all the meanderings of my pilgrimage, even into the charnel house? Is this slope-browed skull not you, Abbot Fuchs? It certainly feels like your bald pate. Like you, this head takes after the hairless prophet Elisha, who when climbing a mountain was mocked by bad children, crying, "Go up, thou bald head!" When the prophet heard them, he prayed God to curse them, and straightaway two bears came from the woods and devoured forty-two of those children.

I take up the skull and pitch it at the door. It bounces back to me.

No, pardon me, Abbot Fuchs. I am mistaken. You, brothers, are happy in your cells at home, as fully fleshed as I might keep you in my imagination. These heads must certainly be members of my *new* order; they are my kindred spirits, my companions and future. By accident, I have stumbled onto the ossuary where the Donestre store their wept-over heads. A monster might not mourn forever; eventually, he will require a new fool. What happens to all those bright-eyed, curious men who have come East to be devoured and mourned, genuinely regretted when the appetite is sated? Might not the monster, out of a fleeting kindness, think to stack them all companionately in a room at the foothills of Mount Truth? Might these puzzled heads not try to make some sense of their predicament? Surely, some foolish friar head among them would attempt to cheer them. "Brothers, let me give you several reasons why it is more desirable to be a head rather than a whole man," he would say.

"First: Philosophers, who might be trusted on such matters, say God formed the head into a sphere, to reflect the vault of Heaven; thus this shape is the only one capable of containing the Mysteries of the Universe. Be of good cheer! As heads only, we are better receptacles for Heaven, brothers.

"Second: It is better to be a head than a whole man, for in so being, we alone uphold the Word of Scripture. Behold: *God shall make thee the head and not the tail.*

"Third: While the shoulders might be dubbed in a knighting, and the feet washed in contrition, only the noble head, brothers, is anointed with oil on truly important occasions. Priests anoint the heads of babies at christenings; bishops anoint the heads of kings on crownings. Christ Himself chides His apostles, saying, Thou didst not anoint my head with oil, but this woman anoints my feet.

"Fourth and last: It is better to be a head than a whole man, brothers, because our bodies are what first brought us to this ruin. Had we been only heads before we met the monster, he would have had no desire to eat us. Moreover, had we been but heads, we would never have had cause to mourn, for no matter what selfish, hurtful pilgrimage we might have dreamed up, we would not have had bodies with which to fulfill them. Thus, harm might have befallen nothing but our own wretched imaginations."

How easy it would be to join this happy company, brothers. To feel my flesh melt away, my body loosen and drop off. I take up another skull, launch it at the door, and catch it when it comes back to me. Oblivion is crowded with friends. Can it not hold one more monk?

But I hear you whispering. Might you simply not have scaled Mount Venus, had you desired such an easy pilgrimage? Would you really fail Christendom, Felix, to fit your tired head into this pyramid of skulls?

Is it not more difficult to choose life over death in this wretched world; is faith not harder to maintain in the face of indifference?

I hurl a hundred skulls against the wall. I deny this brotherhood! I will not take its vows. There is a human woman in this desert who seeks her own Oblivion, and I know where she will find it. Let me out of here!

Frantically, I stumble to the other side of the room, tripping over the littered brothers. As I know most ossuaries are set up, skulls are kept along one wall and bodies on another. I feel my way along until I discover a large square of niches, stuffed full of femurs and tibia. I snatch a long hard shank bone and jump upon its end, feeling it splinter at an angle. I snatch up a skull and limp back to the door.

Fitting the broken bone to the door frame, I pound its round end with the skull. The first blow reduces me to tears, brothers. I feel the tissue around my fractured ribs tear, and the pain is so great I come near to collapse. Leaning against the wall for support, I hit the bone a second time, listening as the wood around the latch gives a bit. A third hammer and the lock comes away from the wood in a green cloud of dry rot. I look back at my abandoned brothers, a moonlit melon patch of skulls. I will not be just another wept-over head, this I swear to you.

Outside, the monastery complex is a maze of mud buildings and staircases impractically built in tiers up the foothill of the mountain. Ahead of me is Katherine's granite church and, behind that, a long row of double dormitories, built to house a hundred monks where now there sleep but eight. Between the church and dormitories, a solitary bush grows, my brothers, tangling over its red brick barricade. They say that no other bush of its species takes root anywhere in the whole of Sinai and that innocent children, before the age of consent, have been known to blow upon it, as if to snuff out a burning candle. This eternal bush has been a symbol of our faith since the Israelites first railed against God in the wilderness, begging to return to Egypt or be allowed to die, since Moses resolutely climbed this mountain to bring them down God's rule. From this bush the Israelites learned all that burns is not consumed, brothers. Sometimes faith is tempered in the flames and grows stronger in the ash.

Judging by the sky, I am north of where we arrived. We must hurry past the bush for now, for I know not how long I was held inside the ossuary while Arsinoë got away. The wall behind the dormitories has almost completely fallen, and I am honestly amazed the Arabs have not just walked right through. When the fortress was built, Emperor Justinian believed the desert nomads so naturally incapable of storming a wall that even mud could hold them back, and judging by this he was right. I peer over the tired fortification and discover that its stones have collapsed outward, forming a rubble hill down to the ground. It is agony to lift my arms, but I manage to hoist myself onto the wall and awkwardly scramble down.

"Felix, is that you? Oh, God, man, help me!"

I swing at the sound of terrified German. Flanked by two stern Saracen guards, the former Mameluke, Peter Ber, staggers up the path.

"That fucking Calinus. He turned me in."

I shrink back at the sight of him, brothers, afraid to return his salute. These Saracens are not wild Arabs but officials of the Sultan. Peter's clothes are torn as though he struggled to get away.

"Is Niccolo inside?" the apostate demands. "This is all his fault."

His two large-turbaned guards jerk him away and pull him roughly toward the torches of the Arab camp.

"Tell Niccolo I want to go home!" the Mameluke screams.

I will never again see Peter Ber, brothers, named for the Rock upon which our Church was founded, who lived for years as Abdullah, the Slave of Allah. Two men cannot exist inside the same body, no more than one man may serve two masters. I fear, brothers, this hybrid will forever war against himself, no matter where he lives or whom he worships, for in him I see the flower with which all of us who go abroad are seeded. I spoke before of what frightens pilgrims most upon their ships. At first I thought it was that narrow wall that held us from the Ocean, reminding us Death was too close by. Now I understand the honest fear of pilgrims is nothing so obvious as Death, my brothers. It is the terror that the walls within our very souls threaten always to collapse. We exchange so many pieces of ourselves in foreign lands for pieces of alien men that we, like this Mameluke, might easily become the true hybrids, a perfect admixture of East and West, with the conscience of neither country. I can only wish this Mameluke well. Saint Peter the Rock denied Christ three times and was still forgiven. Perhaps Peter the rapist and murderer will find his faith inside a Saracen jail.

Look not back, neither stay thou in all the country about; save thyself in the mountain, lest perchance thou be taken captive.

I misunderstood our Lord's message once before and let her get away. Peter Ber has now been taken captive; I, brothers, must save myself on the mountain.

The full moon finally rose over the patriarch's shoulder and sat behind his neck, of no use to me, there in the chasm where crannying winds knifed up to numb my hands and pry loose their grip on what handholds I could scratch out. My ribs came free of their moorings and floated around my spine, beyond pain, brothers, after hours of climbing, into another state of consciousness such as mystics discover after days of bare-kneed praying in frostbit churches in the wintertime. I pulled myself up by the roots of shrubs, grasping blindly desert thorn and scrub rose; their silver-blue leaves anchored me to the next level, where I might swing my naked leg up and over a cold outcrop of stone, and shiver there, afraid to climb higher because the wind had picked up and I could be blown down this rocky ledge, breaking off schists of red mountain as I fell. Below, a field of thistle sparks compassed the wild Arabs' camp, where John and Elphahallo and Conrad must have sat in a fireless circle, listening to the mastication of a hundred savage mouths, gorging themselves on fresh bread when we pilgrims had eaten nothing in days. Could they see me clinging like a tick to the throat of Sinai, deliriously frightened to skirt the jutting chin stubbled with loose rocks and nicked with caves that hung over my head? But I can speak no more of the nightmare climb up Mount Sinai, for to retell a story is to relive it, and, brothers, if I climbed this mountain a second time, I would surely die.

Now that I have attained the summit, pulling myself up by my fingertips, chinning over the final precipice onto the mercifully flat rockbed, I see my vision of moments ago was but one last prank of moonlight. I thought I saw a thousand doves waiting my approach, encouraging my labor with the oaring of their snowy wings. The peak of Mount Sinai, it comforted me to know, was not a fiery rock of retribution but a quivering cushion of wings, a New Testament mountain, alive with birds like angels dancing on the head of a pin. Now that I kneel among these doves, shuddering my eternal thanks to the God who helped me to the top, I see my birds are no more than flapping bits of Saracen linen, stuffed, as at Tucher's dream church, into every available crevice of the cliff. It seems the Saracens worship God here too.

I can look back, brothers, and almost trace the path that brought me broken to this place. Along a trail with no internal organization, I followed a hand, an ear, a tongue, and then a bag of jumbled bones to the one spot on earth where they all belong. Where else would she have possibly come, brothers, but here? I realized back in the ossuary that, deep down, we all desire to test each other's graves. Could the vessel Arsinoë bear to disappear without measuring herself one final time?

A hand, an ear, a tongue, a jumbled bag of bones; the desert has taught me we can rely on no guide to provide us a pattern but must fashion for ourselves what our saints should look like and hope we have the skill to shape them into something halfway human.

Arsinoë lies in the shallow indentation where the mountain gave way like wax, preserving the impression of Katherine's long-limbed body. She has strewn the martyr's bones over herself, with no thought to composition: Katherine's hand lies by Arsinoë's foot, her ear listens near Arsinoë's wrist; Katherine's pelvis, a sunken brown pie plate, Arsinoë wears for a scapular. How satisfying it would be, brothers, to take up these bones and become a Christian Deucalion, pitching them over my shoulder to create a whole new race of men— men so organically filled with martyrdom that they waste no time at all in dispatching each other and so end this wretched world. For a moment I can nowhere find Saint Katherine's skull, but then I notice a pregnant swell beneath Arsinoë's Dominican monk's robes.

"Felix," Arsinoë says, with her eyes shut against the wind, "I am still here."

"Shhh," I say, crawling to where Katherine's guardian angel sat five hundred years beside her head. "No one wants you to disappear."

And in that moment, brothers, I realize what I say is true. I forced myself up this murderous mountain for a woman, but it was not the miscellany of perfumed bones and flesh I climbed to save; it was this simple Tongue. The woman who had no self, simply by having been born one of my own kind, was suddenly as precious to me as twenty years of marriage.

Arsinoë runs her hands over her distended belly.

"I wouldn't mind having a daughter if she were born a relic," she says. "It is the only merciful way to bring a woman into this world, don't you think? With all her suffering already behind her."

The bitter wind lashes Mount Sinai, startling the cloth birds of peace. My hollow stomach fills with wind that shakes me from the inside out, a quivering, tooth-knocking mass of man, hunkered low against the cold. There is but one woman on this mountain, brothers, and she is of warm, living flesh: activity on the bone. I creep down beside her and fit my man's body into a woman's hollows. Stretched out in Katherine's crowded grave, we are warmed by that heat of two creatures who have sacrificed everything for the same cause.

"Arsinoë?" I ask, pressing her hand to my cheek. "If you wanted to hide forever, why did you come to the one place you knew I would look?"

"I am a fraud, Felix," the Tongue whispers, opening her eyes under the latticework of bones that divide us. "I said Katherine wanted to disappear, but that is not true. Deep down, I thought if I could make the world forget her, I might, one day, have a life."

"You can still have a life," I whisper.

"But I can never be a saint." She sighs, shutting out the world once more. "I am afraid to die."

So this is what we find waiting upon the pinnacle of Mount Truth, brothers; after a lifetime of scaling and falling back, after caring too fiercely and losing all hope, we simply find a waiting grave. Whether we chose to fill it with a hopeful martyr who fears to play her own tyrant or a monk who has gazed too long at Heaven is up to us. Mount Illusion gave us Love, Mount Truth gives us Death; we exist somewhere in the valley, brothers, trying on a hundred loves, imagining a thousand deaths. Arsinoë bears the fruit of both. The kindest thing I can do for her is induce her to labor.

With steady midwife's hands, I reach under her robes and grasp Saint Katherine's warm head, extracting it with as much pain as would accompany any virgin birth. Arsinoë shivers as if I have taken away a blanket but offers no resistance. Saint Katherine will be safe at last. I will see that her ear reaches Rhodes and her hand returns to Crete. I will place her blessed tongue back in its golden mouth on Cyprus. It will be a sad diaspora, brothers, returning all to normal, while I have been forever changed. I have no more bits of saint to follow, and anyway it is time for me to lead.

"Come away, Arsinoë." I stretch out my hand and help her back to life. Perhaps she might return to Hungary with John and begin to ease the emptiness of his sixty slaughtered nuns. Perhaps I might even escort her on to Ulm, to dwell among our sisters there. The world is an open place to her, if she will let herself be free. Carefully, she takes my hand, pulling herself up from the grave. Halfway out, she spots something over my shoulder, brothers, something over the mountain's edge, and hesitates in her resurrection.

"Oh!" Arsinoë whispers, stumbling against my chest. She holds out her hand as if to ward someone off or call him forward, I cannot tell which.

I turn, brothers, in both surprise and horror. How did he know we were here?

Now that we have found our saint, the hermit steps onto the mountain to provide us our legend.

He stands on the other side of the monk's wall, with one hand clutching the curved blade I last saw the Mameluke wearing and the other trailing a crimped length of jute rope: this conscienceless murderer of my patron, this translator of a happy child into vermin-poisoned, sun-rotted, putrid food for worms. How dare he show his face on this mountain? I will rip it from his head and throw it to the desert lions howling for his blood.

He hesitates not, when I charge at him, but brings the butt of his sword hard up into my ribs. Oh, God, the air, brothers. Who has stolen all the air?

"You are a very fortunate man, Friar Felix," Ser Niccolo shouts, himself still gasping for breath from the mountain's tortuous climb. He yanks hard on the rope in his hand, and a creature staggers up behind him, collared like a slave, looking more pained than may be explained by the rope or the mountain's tortuous climb. Its eyes are closed and it sways like a drunken man. Then I realize why. Half of its face has been caved in.

"Felix?" it begs.

"John?" Arsinoë screams.

"John." I crawl weakly toward this beaten creature who is my dearest friend. "Oh, God, John?"

Niccolo puts his foot out and kicks me back.

"When you came to me on Contarini's ship, Friar, you asked me about the Life I was translating." Niccolo maliciously yanks the rope around the Archdeacon's raw and bleeding neck. "You said, 'Tell me a little something about this obscure saint . . . tell me how she dies.' I couldn't say then, but remember I promised to dedicate that Life to you? I thought your friend might also like a part in her story.

"We are forty-eight short," Niccolo says to John and me, "but you can represent the Fifty Defeated Philosophers."

"You have retranslated the martyrdom of Saint Katherine?" I sneer from where I lie, suddenly comprehending his pathetic attempt to blackmail Heaven. "You think she will speak to you if you restage her martyrdom?"

"Is that what you think I'm doing, Friar?" Ser Niccolo laughs. "We could have just put on a little play in the village square, spun a girl on a wheel, and poured milk in her hair if that was all I wanted to do. This is scholarship."

Dragging the beaten John Lazinus behind him, Ser Niccolo walks to where his trembling sister stands stricken. Gently he touches her cheek.

"Tonight," he says, "We translate the Mind of God."

A Blank Saint

He fits each bone into its granite cast: the spine in its trough like a plumb line, the slender arms that once embraced the Christ child folded carefully across her piecemeal chest, the long-toed feet re-soled and touching at the heels. Like a sculptor adjusting his model, Niccolo lifts a hip to lend a more natural gait, and I see Katherine at the end of a long day, shifting her weight in anticipation of the Wheel. He understands the saint's body; it shows in how he gently cups the left hand under where a breast would be, offering up the heavy white mound for sacrifice; in how he anchors the spine for strength; in how far he separates the toes, so she will not appear tense and anxious to run away.

She is a marvel of humanity, brothers. Where Arsinoë covered herself in the chaos of Heaven, Niccolo insists on the order of Man. No stiff Byzantine relic princess for him; his Katherine could wear the marble skin of a Donatello saint and be comfortable, so fluid and yet so strong is she in form. Only her neck seems unnatural, for it, as yet, has no head attached.

Three starving, battered pilgrims were no match for the translator's knife, and he roughly bound us hand and foot with white Saracen prayer rags ripped from the mountain wall. Next to me, John kneels in a blooming garden of his own blood. Poppies, purple in the moonlight, blossom in the barren earth under the leak in his broken nose. On my other side, Saint Katherine's Tongue, the inscrutable Arsinoë, kneels next to her saint, gazing upon Katherine with wonderment, as if seeing for the first time the lineaments of life within her figure of perpetual Death.

The translator turns to us and holds up Katherine's head. He speaks like a university lecturer in front of a rapt audience, speaking purposefully and clearly that we might take notes.

"When a man wants to create," the translator says, "he has at his disposal only the barest tools: a rock, a nail, a mark upon a page. With them, he must construct thriving cities and history and works of great and lasting thought."

He pauses, taking a turn around his creation, his reconstructed saint.

"God, on the other hand," he explains, "works in living, breathing, human lives. He has superior tools, and, like a committed pamphleteer who risks wearing out his new printing press papering a town with tracts, God knows repetition, whatever the cost, will eventually bring the world to a higher understanding. So like an eternally reprinted page, each of God's martyrdoms, translated simply, spell: I am the Word. It may take many saints to make up that short sentence, for God's mother tongue is dense and deep as the sea. You might even think it is unfair—tens of thousands of Christian lives traded for those ten letters—but when deciphering the Mind of God, as Jerome, the master translator, said, 'Only fools would translate word for word.'"

The translator stands behind his sister, resting Katherine's skull idly upon her tonsured head.

"What do you want from her?" John growls through the blood in his mouth. Arsinoë, beneath the skull, stares fixedly ahead.

"Why do you love my sister so much?" The translator comes around to John curiously. "It has bothered me throughout our acquaintance. It seems you are the perfect priest for a border town; your passion is roused only by the weak."

"Leave him alone!" I cry. "He has been through enough."

"Are you much better, Felix?" Niccolo asks. "Yearning to bed Heaven but not willing to be consumed by it? In ancient times, Friar, the gods revealed themselves to their mortal lovers as pillars of fire. Not one among them escaped incineration."

"Those were pagan demons," I answer. "Our saints are not gods, they were common men and women."

"Would you like to know what she sounded like, Felix, when she was a common woman?"

In the icy moonlight, the translator brings Saint Katherine's head around to me. This leathern skull glows like a blue orb in his hands, willing to accept any face, any voice, that a man might put upon it.

"Look at her," he says, his voice cajoling. "Imagine her as you knew her in Ulm, as she hung in your library watching over your books. She could have been your neighbor, couldn't she? A blond, rosy burgher's daughter who had read a bit of Plato and taught herself geometry. When you hear her in your dreams, Katherine has a Swabian accent, doesn't she? Her voice is sweet but a little rough, like crushed almonds on the tongue, and in your dreams, Friar, she desires you as much as you desire her."

Despite myself, I begin to form a face. The open Katherine of our library, leaning against her wheel like a sunny milkmaid might rest against her pitchers.

"Don't listen to him, Felix," John says.

"Don't you want to know what she has to say?" Niccolo asks, marveling at her brown skull. "All I have to do is fit this head on *that* body." He nods over his shoulder at his reconstructed woman. "You cannot imagine what that will do to my sister."

Arsinoë, beside me, smiles to herself.

Niccolo kneels in front of his sister. "I want you to tell the friar how his wife feels about him," he says, and kisses her softly on the cheek.

Helplessly, I watch as the translator bends over Katherine's grave and completes the saint. As one struck by lightning, Arsinoë's body jolts and convulses, collapsing epileptically into itself. He has killed her. Beside me John moans in horror, struggling impotently against his bonds. But wait, brothers. The fallen woman moves. Cautiously, like a wild ass waking in the desert, she sniffs the cold night air.

"Melons. Worm. Sand," she says. "Bread. Bones. Blood."

She is disassembling me, reducing me to smell like she did Constantine the merchant when he revealed to her his dream of

drowning. I become aware of each stench the moment she names it, feel Ursus Tucher's body maggots still wriggling through my robes and the grit of sand trapped inside my shoes. This Tongue scents your own self-consciousness, brothers; the more aware you are of your own components, the easier it is to pry them apart.

"Look upon her," orders the translator.

She turns her silver eyes on me, her library eyes, her scholar's eyes, the eyes I have dreamed since I was fourteen years old. In them I see the perfect dispassion of pain, a dry, pure anguish, pulling me to where she lies upon her wheel. I cannot look away.

"Do you see it, Friar?" Niccolo returns to me, stares with me at his transformed sister. "Now do you understand what it does to a man to live with *that* and never understand what they are saying to each other? Don't you, too, want to make her talk?"

Dear God, brothers, I do. I do want.

"Give me the tongue, Felix," Niccolo says. "We can't make her talk without her tongue."

"Don't, Felix!" John pleads feebly. "Leave her alone."

Inside my money pouch, the bit of flesh stirs. Useless against Ursus Tucher's dying wounds, helpless in the face of his father's death; it corrupted our water, it allowed this man to steal our food. The tongue so badly wants to speak now, after a pointed stony silence when I needed it most. All the muscles of Arsinoë's exhausted face strain toward me.

"Your wife summoned you to this mountain, Felix, for a reason," the translator says. "Didn't you call it the Mountain of Truth?"

"Felix!" John falls into me. "Don't let him have it. He'll possess all of her then!"

"Don't you want to hear how much she loves you? Don't you want to hear the words from the Tongue's own mouth?"

Torn and aching, brothers, I look between the reconstructed woman in the grave and Arsinoë's selfless face. I want to feel my wife like fire on the mountain, how I want, brothers, to burn in her embrace; but not—I shall not know Heaven—if Its love means this Tongue must be consumed. The face I put upon the skull Niccolo holds out to me is Arsinoë's face, the delicate, pale creature looked

over too many times by too many seekers. I attach to Katherine's scalp the water-sleek hair of the suicide I rescued from the sea; I stretch across her cheeks the bruised, scabbed skin of a woman raped by the Mameluke; I give her the trembling chin of the Dominican monk who handed me the hollow Book of Wonders in our Lord's most Holy Sepulchre. For once this head shall wear a woman's face, instead of a woman suffocating inside a mask of Heaven.

"No," I announce. "I do not want to hear how much Katherine loves me."

"You are a fool, Friar." Niccolo reaches under my robe and snatches the money pouch from my neck. He pulls out the withered piece of tongue and flings it with all his might straight at the moon.

"Now you will never know."

With a cry, the translator yanks Arsinoë to her feet. The moment is gone. Katherine's eyes in Arsinoë's face, Arsinoë's face on Katherine's skull: both are gone. Arsinoë is once more a startled girl, and my scorpion tongue skitters down the mountain.

" 'Take thee a great book, a new book, write in it with the pen of a man taking away the spoils with great speed.' " Niccolo quotes Isaiah. "It is time for me to set you free."

Gracefully, Ser Niccolo severs his sister's bonds with his ludicrous sword. He unbinds her feet and releases her hands. Gently, he lifts her torn Dominican cassock from her shoulders, until the full length of Arsinoë stands naked before us. Moonlight shows a hundred scars hidden beneath her clothes, brothers, a lifetime's worth of hacking and cutting away of flesh without release from it. Beside me on the ground, John Lazinus begins to weep.

"I have a Life in my pocket," the translator tells her. "The vita I promised to dedicate to Friar Felix when I was finished. It is the Life of an unknown martyr who bravely faced her death and was translated by angels to a desolate mountain deep in the desert."

Arsinoë's flesh quivers in the cold. Her arms wrap around her chest, remembering the warmth of the grave with Katherine's relics embracing her. Wouldn't it be Heaven, she thinks, to be back there?

"I intend to take this Life back to civilization and hide it in the university library, where perhaps some clever young scholar, sometime near the next millennium, will stumble upon it and fall blindly in love with that saint. He will vow to seek her mountain, and lo, sister! What do you suppose he will find on that mountain's peak? That's right. The sweetly scented body of a young woman, preserved uncorrupted for five hundred years. And he will bless this vita as a treasure map, for it holds all the details of her Life, from her birth on Crete, through her years as a prophetess, to piteous death, provided by an eyewitness: a simple translator to whom Heaven refused to speak."

"Arsinoë, run!" John wheezes, from the ground. He has lost so much blood, brothers; it drains from every orifice.

"The only problem is," Niccolo says, ignoring the Archdeacon, "this saint doesn't have a name."

Arsinoë slowly drops her arms. I cannot bear to see it, brothers. From the valley between Love and Death, Arsinoë carefully picks her mountain. She has always known there was a grave waiting for her upon a peak, but in her mind the hills are superimposed. Death is the path to Love, and Love embraces Death. She sets out on her martyr's pilgrimage.

"How will you do it?" she asks.

"I will connect your pieces to Saint Katherine's; then, bone by bone, I will replace her." Her brother speaks gently, as if explaining the extraction of a tooth. "It will be an honest translation. Five hundred years from now, you will be discovered by your own lone hermit. You will live in Heaven, and I will have created a new saint."

I struggle desperately against my bonds. I cannot be hearing this. Man shall not compete with God for the manufacture of martyrs.

"I don't know." Arsinoë hangs her head.

"You can never be a saint through the front door." Niccolo reaches out to touch her cheek, and unexpectedly his eyes well with tears. "You are not a virgin anymore."

A sob escapes Saint Katherine's Tongue as she throws herself into her brother's arms. They embrace like children against a lightning storm, clinging desperately against Heaven's fury. What horrible thread of violence was woven through their fates, brothers, to lead them to this place? Arsinoë will take my bride's life in Heaven. Katherine will be obliterated, refound, five hundred years from now, in this violated, self-made martyr. Niccolo will play God a final time and carve his name across the heavens.

"Stop!" I cry. "You can't."

Carefully, the translator lays his violently shaking sister beside Saint Katherine's grave.

I cannot let this happen. I pull wildly against the bonds, twisting my wrists until they bleed, but they are tied too tight. Beside me, the sagging John Lazinus gives a final twitch against this evil, but he cannot even raise his head.

"You have Heaven inside you." Niccolo closes his naked sister's eyes. "Whole, you have been but a Tongue. In pieces, you will dwell with gods."

Niccolo lifts his Mameluke scimitar and traces a faint red line around her ankle.

John falls to the ground unconscious. Mercifully, he does not see the knife slice through, flaying skin. He doesn't hear the crack of bone breaking and the sick pulling away of tendons. As I watch, horrified, Niccolo fits his sister's severed foot onto Katherine's skeletal ankle, and places the saint's bones against Arsinoë's bleeding stump.

O God, if ever there were a time for wrath, let these bones rise up like a pack of wild dogs and tear this monster apart! Let them incinerate him in angry flame, preferring self-immolation to such utter sacrilege!

"*Stop!*" I scream.

I hurl my body at them, but Niccolo shoves me angrily back. Tears of pain flow down Arsinoë's cheeks, and she has bitten a hole through her lip to keep from crying out. Madly, the translator moves up his sister's leg, twisting her shin bone from her kneecap like a macabre Christmas drumstick. Arsinoë's back arches, her fists slam the ground, but still she won't cry out. He joins her human leg onto the skeleton's thigh bone, flexing it for mobility.

"*Katherine!*" I cry. "*Destroy them!*"

Niccolo raises his sword above her hip. Swings it down hard like a butcher.

"Oh, God!" she screams.

Abruptly, Niccolo drops his weapon. Puzzled, he stares down at his hands.

They are smoking, brothers.

Crisp hairs like squirming black ants race up his arms, the cuffs of his black tunic set ablaze. Wildly, he smacks the fires out, and in that moment butchered Arsinoë weakly crawls away.

"Come to me!" I cry.

A black blur runs past us in the night, and suddenly—O my brothers!—in a single pillar of fire, the entire mountain ignites. A thousand doves are set free to whir on wings of fire, diving at the translator, tearing at his face. White wings, burning red, tangle in his hair; flapping fire lands on Katherine's Tongue, scorching her bloody robes. The fire surrounds me, eating through my bonds, brothers; skips to John, burning him free. The Burning Bush. A sword of flame. God commands us off His mountain.

"Felix, *come on!*"

In the angry red light, I recognize my miracle, running through the thick blue haze of smoke, slashing with his torch in a fever of burning. Conrad, our barber, ignites the frantic Saracen prayer rags, setting loose the angry birds. Conrad, our miracle, swipes at the translator, who, heedless of the flames, lunges for Katherine's burning grave. Through the undulate heat, I see the thief reach into her trough and take for himself Saint Katherine's head.

"Arsinoë!" I lunge, free at last, for the dismembered almost-saint. She crawls toward me across the flaming grave, leaving behind her severed limbs like a useless sloughed skin. Her hair, Constantine's short man's hair, peels away from the scalp in black curling tendrils, Emelia Priuli's ruined face crosses hers like an aspect on its way to becoming some new being. Our miracle Conrad pulls me up and away—*Felix, we must leave this place!*—but I crawl back into the fire to pull her free.

A helmet of heat clamped across my face, I reach out to her, brothers, begging her to come away, but it is far too late. She pushes my hands aside, rapt in the joy of burning, trying on her new blue body of flame. A miser's layer of fat melts, what was once long ago, perhaps, a softness to her. A new layer of muscle snaps red, then white. That weight of flesh she carried with her for so long, brothers, falls away so that a new creature might emerge, a girl fortified by fire, a being wholly her own. She collapses gratefully into the heated embrace of Saint Katherine's bony arms, but now a cherished sister rather than a second self.

Then the Miracle is upon me again, slapping my face with the rage only a citizen of Botzen can muster against the fever. He pulls me to the ground, stomping my legs, beating my clothes, trying to put my fire out. A storm of fire ants eats the beard I have worn these many months, creeps into my hair to continue its greasy burning. We are all complicitous; no one may escape the wrath of Heaven.

We trade off dragging John Lazinus down the mountain. He fades in and out of consciousness, brothers, calling upon the name of his hometown in Hungary, calling for the burned Arsinoë. Conrad wants to stop and bandage us properly, but I push us on, brothers. The translator is somewhere down the mountain, sprinting through the night with Saint Katherine's head under his arm.

"John went up to the mountain to look for you," Conrad gasps, when at last we reach the foothills and stop to rest. "When he didn't come back, I got worried. More wild Arabs have come out of the desert, Felix. They heard the monastery lost its patron saint."

Dawn breaks when we have only one more rise to crest before the downhill broken-stone stretch to the monastery. The mountains are pomegranate red in the early light, slippery from the morning dew. The sun rises over the monastery to the East.

"Look!" Conrad points down to the valley below, just before the garden. A small, hobbling figure limps across the exposed boulder field.

"Watch John," I say, running down the mountain path as fast as my broken ribs and burned legs will carry me.

"*Niccolo!*" I scream. "*Niccolo!*"

The figure turns at the sound of my voice. Seeing me on the rise above him, he triumphantly holds up the head of Katherina Martyr. He is getting away, brothers, I cannot run fast enough.

I slip down the slope, banging my ribs grievously. I look up, but to my shock, Niccolo has barely stumbled a step closer to the monastery. He spins again to face me, and I see his utter lack of comprehension—and an arrow lodged in his left shoulder.

"Felix!" Conrad screams. *"Watch out!"*

I am certain in old age, when I look back upon this day, I will swear the wheel that slew that thief of Heaven came spinning from the sky. I will tell one of you how it revolved with the azure firmament, gourd green, clustered aubergine colors of the desert, and its spokes were made of bone. Another will see a wooden wheel, flung like a discus, catch the translator by the throat with its iron spikes. Still to one more, I will protest the orb of rising sun betrayed its orbit around the earth to slice that wicked translator into a thousand flaming pieces. And I would be telling each one of you the truth; for all the while it happened, brothers, I could not distinguish what made up that blurring streak of blue-red-yellow flesh that spun itself around his pinioned hub, pounding, screaming, releasing arrows. I caught a glint of metal, a chestnut hoof, a streak of flying hair. Blue hands I thought I saw, a flash of white barred teeth, but not until the exploded valley stilled and the sanguine dust began to settle could I distinguish the individual radiants on his torture wheel. A hundred panting, rage-spent Arabs reined in their stamping mounts.

I race to where the translator has fallen, push my way through frothing white donkey mouths, to step across the creek of blood running down this baked, poreless plain. Niccolo, affixed with a thousand arrows, is dead on his knees, bent double over my wife's stolen head. Weep, you envious creature. You are the death of all.

A familiar white-robed Saracen steps into the circle and forcefully pries Katherine's skull from Niccolo's perforated arms. Slowly, he walks toward me.

"Elphahallo," I gasp, conscious of the nomads' unreadable black eyes upon me. "Why?"

"The Bedouin love Saint Katherine too," he says. "She gives them bread."

Another Language

From somewhere East of this mountain, from deep in the lonely desert, the brothers of Saint Katherine's Monastery claim to hear bells toll every day. They say there exists a monastery in the wilderness filled with the holiest of men; but this monastery no man in modern times has ever been able to find. Still, every day the bells ring faint canonical hours, and still men set off in search of it. It happens, occasionally, that brethren disappear from Saint Katherine's, and it is believed that they have been translated to that hidden monastery in the desert to fill the places of those who die from time to time. I would like to think one of those kindly monks came and removed my patron's son for burial there. When we returned to Saint Katherine's tomb with her head, Ursus's body was gone, and no one knows what has become of it.

Today, I climb back up the mountain to separate out the heavenly from the human. Katherine's grave is a tangled mess, still hot to the touch, smudged black and oily. Our two natures have been fused in this exploded heart of mountain; the divine unites with the earthly or the earthly pollutes the divine—however you choose to see it. I will turn to my sad task of selection soon enough, but first, brothers, look with me a moment upon the World.

In daylight, from this vantage, a man can see for hundreds of miles around. Farther to the East lies the kingdom of Persia, once a glorious empire, now known primarily for the strange apples that grow there, in our language called *peach*. I have read those apples are poisonous in their own country, but in ours they are sweet; which seems to be the property of many apples. Beyond Persia, Arabia Felix, a barely known country, stretches wide with deserts, rich in veins of gold, and divers precious perfumes. The Saracens' holy city of Mecca lies in this land, to which men of the East make their own pilgrimages, the desire for earthly shoots of Heaven having been planted in mortals of every different faith. Many of the Bedouin who saved Saint Katherine are on their way to honor their prophet Mahomet there. These naked wild men, in their heathen tongues, invited us to join them and see for ourselves the truth of their Alcoran, revealed at Mahomet's floating tomb. Our savior Conrad has decided to go along with them, deeper into this puzzling land, and so learn more for himself of the World. John is too ill to go, recovering from his wounds slowly in the monastery's infirmary. My route is not meant to be farther East, with strangers, but homeward, in the company of my dearest friend.

Westward, then, I turn my eyes, to seek out the Red Sea and eventually our departure port of Alexandria. In my ignorance, I had imagined the Red Sea to truly be red, but it is a cool, inviting blue, brothers, and it is the first leg of my journey back to you. Up until today, our travels have carried us farther from home, but now comes the time to turn ourselves back, to set our faces toward our native land. I have lost everything I loved and cared about, brothers, but that one thing: home. It is many miles and many tribulations away, but it is God's single consolation, the gift He gives to fools. You may wander this entire earth to find your paradise, He says. But you will find it as you left it: in the quiet of your cloister, in your simple routine, among the ones who love you.

I reluctantly walk back to Katherine's crowded grave and set about my task. I, alone, was happy with Heaven as I found it, and yet here I am, upon this mountain, deciding which bones are holy and which are not. I sniff a foot. It smells like char. Where is the perfume of sanctity to guide me, brothers? To my nose, it all smells like ash.

When I was a boy, I learned the meaning of objects by accumulation. Here is an apple: It is round, it is red, it ripens in the autumn; if cut open it will reveal flesh, seeds, and juice. If I add round + red + autumn + flesh, seeds, and juice, I will understand this object: an apple.

Now that I am a man, I look at words with a more awakened eye. If I take the word *apple*, in Latin *malum*, and gaze inside it, as if putting my inner eye to one of those wet black seeds, I see its name comes from *mālum*, meaning distress and misfortune, woe, a misdeed. Now I understand the *origin* of apple, for knowing its core, as it were, I see by its very name its inseparability from Eve, who in offering it to Adam brought eternal woe and misfortune upon us all.

Might we not, then, understand a saint better by her parts than by her whole?

Katherine's name is melodious and familiar, centuries of women, good and bad, having borne it after her. When we cleave her name like the apple, however, we see Katherine comes from *catha*, meaning total, and *ruina*, ruin; hence *total ruin*. I once thought it was because she demolished the Devil's edifice through her eloquence, or perhaps because she defeated the Fifty Philosophers with her learning. Lifting up a hand that might be hers, or might be Arsinoë's, I see now how wrong I was. Katherine's name can only be read against my own, Felix, "The Happy One," her servant translator. We are only happy in ruin, brothers, for only then can we be sure we have nothing left to lose.

I choose my relics and rise to go home.

> *We grope for the wall like the blind,*
> *and we grope as if we had no eyes:*
> *we stumble at noon as in the night,*
> *we are in desolate places as dead men.*
> *We roar all like bears, and*
> *mourn sore like doves: We*
> *look for judgment, but there is none;*
> *for salvation, but it is far off from us.*

ISAIAH 59:10-11
DESERT OF THE SINAI
SUMMER 1483
F.F.F.

Author's Note

Friar Felix Fabri (1441–1502) seems to find a groupie in every generation. My own devotion owes everything to two English translators who preceded me, H. F. M. Prescott and Aubrey Stewart.

Dame Hilda Prescott's two works, *Friar Felix at Large* (Yale, 1950) and *Once to Sinai* (Macmillan, 1958), helped me organize Felix's own twelve-volume Latin work, *Evagatorium in Terrae Sanctae Arabiae et Egypti Peregrinationem*.

In the spirit of putting new flesh on old bones, I took Felix's pilgrimage and stretched my own concerns over it. This would in no ways have been possible without Aubrey Stewart, who translated the first half of Felix's journey into English (*The Wanderings of Felix Fabri*, Palestine Pilgrims' Text Society, 1896: Reprint, AMS Press, 1971). Whenever Felix speaks for himself in this novel—The Rules for Pilgrimage, Why the Eucharist May Not Be Celebrated on Shipboard, A Few Brief Descriptions of the Holy Land, to name the longest passages—I acted only as editor, and Felix spoke in Aubrey Stewart's words.

Aubrey Stewart was not alive in 1969, and I was only three years old, when the Roman Catholic Church annulled Friar Felix's spiritual marriage to Saint Katherine of Alexandria. Along with Saint Christopher, Saint Margaret, and many other immensely popular, colorful saints of the Middle Ages, Saint Katherine was removed from the Catholic canon. No one could prove she ever existed.

Acknowledgments

I have had more help in my life than one woman could expect, and I can only name a few people here. I'd like first to thank all the readers of the early drafts of this manuscript, a torture few can appreciate: my friends Bill Tipper, Jillian Medoff, Lindsey Tate, Katie Kerr, and Frances Jalet Miller, gifted writers and editors all, whose kind and stern criticisms were always invaluable. Most of all, I owe an enormous debt of gratitude to novelist George Dawes Green. He was my advocate long before I warranted it, and he has been a constant inspiration.

I cannot thank enough my colleagues at the Aaron Priest Literary Agency, for their support and understanding during my mysterious leaves of absence. Thank you, Aaron, Lisa, Lucy, Arleen, Barbara, and Paul, my other half, for being a true family to me. I am still offering burnt sacrifices on the altar of the god who first steered me to Molly Friedrich, my friend, agent, and role model for adult womanhood. Without her generosity and goodwill, this book would never have been conceived, written, or sold.

The staff at Atlantic Monthly Press has been another source of rejoicing; such happy, smart, committed people are rare these days in publishing. I want to thank Kenn, Elisabeth, Eric, my vigilant and wise copy editor, Janet Baker, and everyone else who has been so wonderful to me. Most of all, I want to thank my brilliant, hysterical editors, Carla Lalli and Morgan Entrekin. Thanks for putting my monk on your wonderfully sexy list!

Last, but not least, let me thank my mother, father, and sister for their tenacious support as I left the country and moved to the city. Without the love and unapologetically biased praise of my mom, Gerri Workman, I would be nothing in this life.

And again, thank you to Sean Redmond, to whom this book is dedicated. He read every word, far too many times. He tirelessly trotted to the library for me. He translated. He cooked. Oh, how he suffered! And I can never thank him enough.

ABOUT THE AUTHOR

Sheri Holman grew up in rural Virginia and now lives in Brooklyn, New York. This is her first novel.